PENGUIN BOOKS

THE WARNING BELL

Lynne Reid Banks, the daughter of a Scottish doctor and an Irish actress, was born in London and was evacuated to the Canadian prairies during the war. On her return to England she studied for the stage at RADA and then had several years' experience with repertory companies all over the country. The first play she wrote was produced by a number of rep companies and later performed on BBC television. She wrote and had published several other plays; one was put on in a London 'little theatre', and others have been performed on radio and television. She was one of the first two women reporters on British television. She worked for ITN for seven years – from its inception until 1962 – initially as a reporter and later as a scriptwriter. After leaving ITN she emigrated to Israel, where she married a sculptor. They lived on a kibbutz for nine years and have three sons. She now lives in Dorset and writes full-time.

Lynne Reid Banks's first novel, *The L-Shaped Room*, appeared in 1960, was made into a successful film and has been in print ever since. It was followed by *An End to Running* (1962), *Children at the Gate* (1968), the second and third books in *The L-Shaped Room* trilogy – *The Backward Shadow* (1970) and *Two is Lonely* (1974) – *Defy the Wilderness* (1981) and *Casualties* (1987), all published by Penguin.

Dark Quartet: The Story of the Brontës (1976) won the Yorkshire Arts Association Award in 1977 and was followed by its sequel, *Path to the Silent Country: Charlotte Brontë's Years of Fame*, in the same year. Both are now reissued by Penguin.

Lynne Reid Banks has also written a number of books for children and young adults. Her children's books include *The Adventures of King Midas*, *The Farthest-Away Mountain*, *Maura's Angel*, *The Indian in the Cupboard*, *Return of the Indian* and *The Fairy Rebel*. Her books for teenagers include *One More River*, *Sarah and After*, *My Darling Villain* and *The Writing on the Wall*. In addition, she has written two historical books about Israel, *Letters to My Israeli Sons* and *Torn Country*.

D1589343

Lynne Reid Banks

THE WARNING BELL

PENGUIN BOOKS

Penguin Books Ltd, 27 Wrights Lane, London W8 5TZ (Publishing and Editorial)
and Harmondsworth, Middlesex, England (Distribution and Warehouse)
Viking Penguin Inc., 40 West 23rd Street, New York, New York 10010, USA
Penguin Books Australia Ltd, Ringwood, Victoria, Australia
Penguin Books Canada Ltd, 2801 John Street, Markham, Ontario, Canada L3R 1B4
Penguin Books (NZ) Ltd, 182–190 Wairau Road, Auckland 10, New Zealand

First published by Hamish Hamilton 1984
Published in Penguin Books 1986
Reprinted 1987

Made and printed in Great Britain by
Richard Clay Ltd, Bungay, Suffolk
Typeset in Ehrhardt

In memory of Pat, my mother

Prologue

In a comfortably proportioned, but lately very empty-feeling, flat behind the Finchley Road lives a middle-aged woman called Maggie Langham.

Under her maiden name of Margaret Robertson, she was a moderately unsuccessful actress. Under her first-married name of Margaret Macrae, she was better known. When she visits the shops in Swiss Cottage, she is still occasionally recognised.

'Didn't you used to be on telly?'

'Years ago,'

'Yes ... A lot younger then, weren't you? When was it anyway?'

'In the sixties.'

'As what, exactly? Not acting, were you, as I remember – more sort of – ?'

'I was a television news reporter.'

'Oh! Was that before Angela Rippon then?'

'Long before.'

'Funny ... Always thought she was the first woman on the News.'

'No.'

'Can't remember anything you actually *did* ... What do you do now?'

'Oh ... nothing very much.'

And she has to restrain herself from adding, 'I'm a widow,' as if that, being a full-time occupation, excused her from having no other.

No other full-time work, but, despite the debilitation of grief, she dare not be idle. She does all sorts of jobs, paid and unpaid, though the second sort has scant appeal. It is psychologically as well as financially essential for her to earn her living.

And recently something extraordinary happened to her. More

1

to remind herself that she was still alive than out of any concrete hope, she'd obeyed a strange impulse and put herself back in *Spotlight*, the actors' directory – needless to say, not in the juvenile section, whence she'd vanished thirty years ago, but among the character women. And – incredibly – she got a part, a jolly, strident Yorkshirewoman in a Priestley revival at Colchester.

Her mother, now eighty-eight, travelled down from Edinburgh with her grandson Matthew (Maggie's son) and his new wife, Maggie's elder brother Ian and *his* wife and daughter – and her mother's companion, now, like Maggie, in her fifties, but as beautiful and startling as ever in her bright flowing robes and elegant turban headdress. Even Maggie's younger brother Steven flew over from Paris with his partner. They crowded the little theatre's front row. One would have thought it was a great West End début.

What it was, for Maggie, was a hard-won triumph over almost unendurable terror and even more formidable inertia. The gathering of the clan didn't exactly make the occasion less nerve-wracking. But when they crowded into her tiny dressing-room afterwards, going right over the top with armfuls of flowers and champagne, Maggie understood that they loved her and were proud of her come-back from the wilderness of bereavement and 'the years between'. In their eyes this far outweighed the fact that her performance had been – to be charitable – somewhere just on the right side of adequate.

When they'd all gone home and the two-week run had ended, dumping her back in Swiss Cottage, Maggie did some uncharacteristically rigorous stocktaking. The brouhaha about the play had not blinded her to the fact that she had made pretty much of a mess of her life, and that her present profound loneliness was only her due. Of course, it wasn't her fault that her adored husband had died comparatively young. On the other hand, it wasn't to her particular credit that she had had those wholly unexpected years of married happiness. Sheer luck, really . . . Luck to have met him: fabulous luck that he fell in love with her, against all the odds . . . Yet even this latecoming worldly portion she had gained at some cost.

Tanya hadn't come to the play. Maggie had not seen her for the length of her marriage. The only personal contact had been some white flowers, at the time of the funeral – a huge sheaf

2

of gladioli and lilac and roses, giant blooms that looked as if Tanya herself, with her genius for flowers, had grown them. No message beyond a card: 'To Maggie from Tanya'. Flowers for the living, not the dead ... It was balm, of a kind, to the old wound, but Maggie no longer deceived herself. Tanya was not going to reappear to help her through the lonely years.

Maggie had bought her marriage with Tanya's friendship.

Mary Robertson, Maggie's mother, once said, 'You know, Maggie, the vainest and most futile mental exercise in the world is tracing back some accident or blunder to its origins, and letting one's heart gnaw itself in regret that one didn't know what was going to result. *You* know: "If I hadn't gone there, met so-and-so, done this or not done that ..." One's whole life can turn on some tiny thing. It's not fair. There ought to be a bell, a warning bell, sounding at dangerous corners. But there never, never is.'

But Maggie, on reflection, decided that there very often is a warning bell. It may not go clang-clang with great noisy obviousness. But it rings in other ways. She could remember many turning-points in her own life which were marked by bells of a sort. Her innumerable blunders had not resulted from an absence of bells, but her wilfulness in ignoring them.

Sometimes she had rung the bell herself. Not Maggie so much as Margaret. For Maggie, like many of her generation, was effectively two women. She had always been aware that, although she felt like a Maggie, she had a definite Margaret sitting on her shoulder breathing down her neck, or to be more exact, crouching, stiff, watchful and censorious, inside her head. It was significant that her father was the only one in her family who persisted in calling her Margaret, for Margaret was his creation. Maggie was an extract, at first a sort of protoplasm drawn out of Margaret, quivering with insecurity, but gradually firming up, by infinitely slow accretions, into the real person, fully materialised, leaving Margaret in the role of powerful and resentful succubus.

3

PART ONE

Chapter One

Maggie's parents had married late. Her brother Ian was born when Mary Robertson was already thirty-four, and was given a strict upbringing, as befitted the eldest son of a rigorously Presbyterian father who expected him to follow his footsteps into the long-established family business, which was paper-making.

But this strictness, and the religion that backed it, happened to suit Ian. He was that type of child. He loved routine and order and tradition, and the biggish, rather gloomy stone house in Penicuik, outside Edinburgh, where he grew up. It was one of the largest houses in the little town, and that gave Ian honest satisfaction. It didn't occur to Maggie's older brother for many years that there was anything wrong in being satisfied with every aspect of himself and his life, so long as he fulfilled its rules as laid down by his father and his church.

If Mr and Mrs Robertson had stopped at Ian, their lives would have been quite untrammelled, and Mr Robertson would have died a proud and happy man. But in such families, a single son and heir, however satisfactory, is not enough. A back-up son and a daughter to fulfil the woman's role in the household are considered desirable. So, at the age of thirty-seven, Mrs Robertson dutifully gave birth to Margaret, and a year later, to Steven.

Mary Robertson loved all her children equally. But Maggie was a little more equal in her affections than the others. She would in any case, left to herself, have been more easy-going with her two youngest.

However, their father saw to it that the younger children received precisely the same raising as Ian, simply because he knew that was the correct way to bring up children, so that no softening or bending was possible. The trouble was that what

7

suits one child grates upon another; where Ian had fallen in with his father's fixed ideas because they suited his temperament, Maggie and Steven (whose family nickname was Stip) chafed and rebelled.

When Maggie announced her intention of going on the stage, in the second year after World War II when she was eighteen, her father, then approaching his sixties and locked in his puritan ethic like a neatly-carapaced beetle in an epoxy paperweight, was no less furious and appalled than his own father would have been, a generation earlier.

Maggie was not expected to entertain notions of a career for herself at all. Her brothers would attend to the family paper business; Maggie – Margaret – was expected to stay at home and help her mother and look forward to being the comfort and prop of her parents in their old age. Unless, of course, she should happen to marry; but that was not really on the programme.

Not because she had no looks. All the women in her family were 'comely', with the same dark, strong, curly hair, bright blue eyes and apple cheeks, not to mention sturdy, wide-hipped, high-breasted figures – made, one would say, for child-bearing, though a number of them never got a chance to prove it.

If you live in a small provincial Scottish town, keeping to a rigid schedule of early rising and early retirement with the intervening periods constantly filled with hard and useful work; if you are brought up on the Christian ethic which lays heavy stress on the second commandment; if your parents treat modern institutions such as dating, dancing, cinema-going and social drinking with the gravest suspicion, they cannot be accused of throwing you on to the marriage market.

Probably it was these dour facts of her life, rather than an innate need to express her histrionic gifts, which caused Maggie's reaction to the first theatrical performance she ever saw. Oh, she had seen a few films and amateur shows during the war years – Mr Robertson could hardly have stood out against every modern diversion. But the full-blown professional production of *Oklahoma* which she was taken to at the King's Theatre, Edinburgh, on her eighteenth birthday was a revelation to her.

8

It was not her parents who took her, but her English teacher. This remarkable woman, whose name was Fiona Dalzell, was to have an enormous influence on Maggie's life. A childless widow, she was all too familiar with the situation of girls like Maggie. She herself was the product of just such a family. She had wrenched herself away in her teens to elope with one of her own teachers; but he died. And as her family refused to forgive her (he was a married man) she had been obliged to make her own way, using the modest education she had had as a basis for further study, and finishing up as an extremely gifted if slightly eccentric and decidedly under-qualified teacher at Maggie's local high school.

She took a fancy to Maggie and decided to interfere in her life. And she was astute in her meddling. The first step was *Oklahoma*. When Maggie asked her, years later, 'But why a musical?' she replied, 'It seemed to me that what you needed was a splash of real colour.'

And this was true. Looking back, Maggie felt that, prior to that night, she had seen everything in black and white – or rather, the sepia tones of the photographs in the heavily-bound family album which lived in a huge, ornate mahogany sideboard in the Robertsons' dining room. This Victorian monstrosity typified the furnishings of the house; its light-drinking blackness seemed to suck up even sunshine (when it managed to penetrate the thick velour drapes and tight-meshed lace curtains).

Every room contained some minion of that sideboard to do a similar office. All were dedicated to darkening light and deadening colour – the bedheads with their twisted pillars, the tables with their bulbous legs and rack-like stretchers, the immovable black piano which Maggie, in childhood, had supposed knew none but hymn tunes. (This was not as silly as it sounds. It was a pianola, and its rolls were all hymns. No one ever really played it.) Then there was her father's vast rolltop desk, its innumerable partitions stuffed with all the incomprehensibilia of his boring business life at the paper-mill, and the bureau-bookcase in the living room, with its glazed doors, arched like cathedral windows, behind which lay dusty volumes, reverently spoken of but never read, for the doors were locked, the key long mislaid and never really searched for.

Even the children's bedrooms were repositories for the less imposing items inherited from spinster aunts and grandparents

9

over the past hundred years. Maggie's carpet was a deep, ponderous crimson, its pattern doused by the unbrushable residual dust of the years. Her bedspread was a mere membrane of faded dun on which she was forbidden even to sit, for it had no body left to withstand creases. Nothing in that household was ever discarded until it fell to bits, and in those days (postwar austerity helped a natural inclination to parsimony) nothing ever did, so nothing was ever new, or modern, or frivolous, or fragile except through wear – nor was anything ever bought simply for fun.

It must have been due to this that Maggie can actually get nostalgic for that dreadful style of decor which came in just after the war and was known derisively as 'Contemp'. At a recent exhibition commemorating the Festival of Britain, Maggie made a beeline for the reconstructed 'room of the period' and stood, gazing enraptured at its speckled wallpaper, flimsy cubist-patterned curtains, bits of gimcrack, asymmetrical furniture, yellow figured lampshade and loud rag rugs. 'Oh, look!' she breathed to a perfect stranger who was standing next to her gazing at the 'room' in horror. 'Isn't it fun? How I would have adored a room just like that when I was eighteen!'

Did Mrs Dalzell, sitting beside her protegée in the red-plush stalls on that fateful anniversary, realise that she had done more than translate the monochrome of Maggie's life into devastating technicolour? As the brave brown men of the chorus tossed their bonneted girls into the air, as 'the amazing potency of cheap music' laid its hold on Maggie's hymn-pickled vitals, stopping her breath, injecting spurts of adrenalin into her system – did her companion know that she might as well have punched her fist through the sacred skin of the Robertson family unit and dragged Maggie bodily out, as if bringing her to birth, at the age of eighteen, by some violent form of Caesarian section?

The music was not amplified to deafening point as it would be these days, but it was loud enough. It filled Maggie's head, and her heart, to bursting. She wouldn't have been to blame, this time, for failing to hear the warning bell; she wouldn't have heard one that night if it had rung as loud as the ones that deafened Quasimodo.

For the next fortnight, Maggie's mind tossed deliciously upon the high crests of turbulent dreams. She secretly bought the sheet music of *Oklahoma* and learnt the songs, picking them out

10

on the old black buttoned-up-spinster piano when no one was at home. Next came the need to share her revelation. She cornered her younger brother and confederate Stip, and after pestering him for a week, finally bribed him into coming with her on a totally illicit outing to see the show again.

Stip, whose own bent at sixteen lay in a soulful literary direction, couldn't understand what had got into the girl. To defy their parents and risk an almighty row to go to some idiotic American musical made little sense to him. But Maggie promised him ten shillings if he would come, to be increased to fifteen if he was prepared to take his oath afterwards that he hadn't enjoyed it.

They laid down a network of elaborate falsehoods to cover their tracks, and also to screw the excitement of the adventure up to a higher pitch. They said they were going into Edinburgh to visit cousins they had recently met at a wedding, to play tennis and then attend some suitably sombre church-based meeting. Their parents swallowed this tale whole; it was dear brother Ian, at twenty-three just as straight-laced as any parent and twice as dangerous, who smelt a rat, checked with the cousins – and shopped them.

They arrived home at 11.30 p.m. in the highest possible spirits. Stip had refused to accept more than five shillings in the end, and spent that on huge quantities of fish and chips and large draughts of bottled cider after the show.

They stood stock-still on the path leading up to the black, fanlighted front door, hand in hand like guilty children. Every light downstairs was blazing, an unheard-of extravagance, which instantly alerted them that the game was up.

'They'll murder us,' said Stip hollowly. 'We'll be hung, drawn and quartered.'

'I don't care,' said Maggie loudly. 'I don't care one damn.'

This was not only the cider speaking. It was *Oklahoma*. It was, in particular, a song which lyrically enquires why a woman who is healthy and strong should blubber like a baby when her man goes away. This absolute refusal in advance to have one's heart broken appeared to Maggie then as the most forthright statement of women's rights imaginable, and applied, in its way, to daughters vis-à-vis fathers as much as to girls vis-à-vis men. As she marched up the steps, the lyrics were spurring her on: she too would snap her fingers to show she didn't care, wash

11

her neck, brush her hair, and start all over again. It was time to stand up for herself, to tell them what, during that last exhilarating chorus, she had irrevocably decided: to sit no longer tamely in that light-denying house, but to go away and learn to be an actress, so that she could do for others what had been done for her that night.

Unfortunately she muffed it. She picked a bad moment, when her parents were furious anyway; divided her slender forces by attacking the smug-faced Ian for betraying them; showed her temper too much to her father who wasn't accustomed to it, and lacked the perspicacity to realise that she might, just might have had an ally of sorts in her mother if she had only gone another way to work.

The outcome was a total and irreversible ban on the whole absurd and unRobertsonian notion. And that was where Mr Robertson made his fatal mistake.

Maggie, left to herself, might have rushed out of the house and into the night on the spot. But Margaret, her alter-ego, laid the hand of caution and good counsel (and cowardice) on her, as indeed did Stip when he crept into her room much later to help dry her furious tears of humiliation.

'They spoilt it! They spoil everything! And we just knuckle under and allow ourselves to be bullied and controlled, as if we had no minds or lives of our own!'

'Shhhh . . .'

'I won't shush!' retorted Maggie, but Margaret, who didn't want to be bellowed at any more, saw to it that she did. 'And as for Ian,' she hissed, 'I'm finished with him for the rest of my life! Just because he was in the army, he treats us like babies.'

'He always did.'

'He's a traitor. Traitors deserve to be shot.'

'It was only a wee row,' said Stip uneasily. 'We did ask for it.'

'What did we do that was so awful? And when I said I wanted to be away to London to study for the theatre, you'd have thought I'd said for the *streets*!'

'*Maggie* – !'

'*You* didn't give me much support, I noticed, you that was in it as much as I was.'

'You were shouting so loud I didn't get a chance.'

12

They were silent for a moment, listening to the silent house, testing in their minds and memories its ineffable pressure on them – the prison walls of dependence, of habit. Maggie reached for Stip's hand in the darkness. 'I'm sorry, Stip. I got you into it. But you did enjoy it – the show – didn't you?'

'I did. I wouldn't have missed it for worlds.'

She hummed 'Out of my Dreams' softly, with her forehead against his shoulder. At seventeen he was underdeveloped, tall but still narrow, no muscle yet; he was worried about it, refusing to expose himself in a swimming costume and self-conscious even at home, perhaps due to the hulking (relatively) proximity of Ian. Once he'd shyly asked Maggie, 'D'you think I'll ever be a man, I mean have a proper kind of body that slopes out from my waist, or will I be straight up and down for ever?' It was a variation on the question they had all – even Maggie – made a great joke of, when he was a little boy and asked, 'When I grow up, will I be a man or a lady?' Now Maggie, leaning on him, felt his slightness, his insubstantial, reedlike quality, and wished herself that he were more solid.

'I'll not stand it,' she whispered. 'I'll do as I said I would. I'm going.'

'How can you? You can't,' he said flatly.

She pulled away from him. 'You'll see if I don't! I'll show him. I'll show him!'

13

Chapter Two

Maggie's punishment for deceiving her parents and leading Steven astray was to stay at home for two weeks and do extra chores. The only person allowed to visit her was her teacher, Mrs Dalzell – the Robertsons could see nothing inimical in that. Little did they know.

'Are you serious about this, Maggie? It's not just a childish whim?'

Maggie, rather wishing Mrs Dalzell had offered her a stack of bibles to swear upon, reassured her with an air of such utter earnestness that her teacher was instantly convinced. She thought a moment and then said, 'Well, I'll need some proof of it before I'm prepared to stick my neck out, as the saying goes.'

'What proof?'

'It's not for me to tell you that. If you're set on a stage career, you've a lot of preparatory work to do. What have you seen?' she asked rhetorically. 'What have you read? What have you learnt? Nothing at all, except the bit of Shaw and Shakespeare I've brushed you up against. Now let's see how serious you are. Come to me in July, when you finish school, and we'll see.'

'But I've got to study for highers.'

'You'll find time for what you want to find time for,' she said firmly.

For the next few months, Maggie put *Oklahoma* behind her. She read nothing but plays in such spare time as she had, and on Sundays, when her father insisted she take a break from studying, she would sit by the parlour fire apparently reading, but actually memorizing. She mastered Nina in *The Seagull*, Amanda in *Private Lives*, Varya in *The Cherry Orchard*, all the

14

long speeches from *St Joan* and a good chunk of Juliet. Alone in her room at night she would lock the door and rehearse. Her room was no longer a drab or depressing place. It became as multi-coloured and multi-faceted as a diamond, throwing sparks of future fulfilment in all directions.

At the end of July, she made a proper appointment with Mrs Dalzell at her flat. Nothing less formal, somehow, would have suited the importance of the occasion – though what, in practical terms, could be gained by winning Mrs Dalzell's support, she had no tangible idea. But Maggie had great faith in her. For six years she had watched her getting her own way in contests major and minor with the school bureaucracy. Where other teachers had shrugged away their dream-projects, defeated by regulations or budgets, Mrs Dalzell would flatter, wheedle and cajole, or alternatively attack head-on. Sometimes she would invade the sanctums of governors or principals. At other times she would get whole classes to work after school, fund-raising, costume-making, copy-typing, scene-painting. And eventually, *her* plays would get staged, her class magazines produced, her favourite festival presentations visited. Once, when she needed a set of books which was denied her, she pinched them wholesale from the library of a public school she was visiting with a group of poor-relation state-school teachers. She carried them away, twenty slim cloth-bound volumes, in her hold-all, used them for a whole term, had them beautifully cleaned up and fresh brown jackets put on them by the class in one of her extra-mural sessions, and returned them, pulling a fainting fit to get the librarian out of the room while she put them back on their shelf.

It was because of such memories that Maggie did her audition before the elderly, pink-faced, white-haired Mrs Dalzell with as high a degree of nervous tension as if her teacher had been the representative of a London management.

She began by handing her a list of books read, plays studied, parts learnt. She had written to the Royal Academy of Dramatic Art to get their current entrance audition set-pieces, and had learned all of them. Mrs Dalzell sat at one end of her narrow, cramped living-room, erect and watchful, every inch the part herself, making notes and saying. 'Thank you, next piece please.' Maggie suffered appropriately. She dried up once, fluffed once, and made one false start. 'Never mind, begin

15

again,' came the cool voice out of the neat silhouette against the small french window.

At the end Maggie sat down, breathless and shaky. Mrs Dalzell looked at her though her rimless 'specs'.

'Well!' she said. 'You've talent. You've a whole lot to learn of course – a great lot. Your breathing's all wrong, you've a faulty 's' and you don't know what to do with your hands, but that's what drama school is for. And that, my girl, is where you are going.'

Maggie gazed at her. Her heart, which had begun to beat normally after her small ordeal, picked up speed again. Unless she entirely misread the signs, what she faced now was going to be a great deal more than she had bargained for.

'Daddy will never agree.'

'I'd scarcely expect him to. We'll have to see about it. Maggie, are you set enough on this course to be willing to deceive him?'

'Yes,' she said before terror could stop her mouth.

'To lie to him over a long period, and to get money out of him by false pretences?'

Oh no, she had not misread the signs! – unless to interpret them too mildly. Margaret would have stopped dead right there, but Maggie blurted out 'Yes!'

'You've no money of your own, I take it? Pity. So we'll have to convince him the fees are for something else. Now, let's see. What is it he wishes you to learn?'

'Domestic science,' she said, with a faint bleat of her voice.

'Ah! He would do. Well now, the first thing we have to do is to get you a place at the RADA. Competition is high and you've left it late for this year's intake, but we'll see what we can arrange.'

What she arranged, in the first instance, was an 'educational' trip to London to coincide with a last-minute audition, which Maggie passed – quite a coup in those days of returning veterans on government grants, not to speak of the usual swarms of beautiful, talented and ferociously determined girls from all over the world. Then came the really difficult bit.

'Why, but of course the dear girl must be away down to *London* to study, Mr Robertson! What can you have against that? Such a well-raised girl can come to no harm if it's all suitably arranged, as it will be, I promise you. I shall personally attend to all the details – you can safely leave everything to me

16

No, indeed! She can *not* as well study domestic science in Scotland, for you know such few institutions as we have here are over-subscribed, and the one I am thinking of in London is far superior. I'm sure you want the best for Margaret and for your money, do you not? Well then, it's all settled! As to her living arrangements, I have close relatives – Scots, of course, and members of our own faith – who let out lodgings to respectable girls. You need not trouble yourself at all on that score.'

The traumas of Mrs Dalzell's youth had made of her something more than a rebel perpetually on the lookout for fresh causes. She had become a fanatic in the cause of women's liberation before it acquired its capital letters and the flaws and follies which attend all crusades. For her it was not a matter of joining a movement already initiated, but of acting out of unique, personal and organic conviction. Compulsion would probably be a better word – she was not entirely right in the head. Did the warning bell ring for her as she said all this, or at any time while she steadfastly carried out her plans to change Maggie's destiny? Even if it did, it's doubtful whether she could, or would, have acted differently.

Maggie confided her plans in no one but Stip.

'Mrs D's got Daddy absolutely mesmerised. Of course he's known her for donkey's years, but I don't see how she got a year's allowance out of him in one lump, fees and all!'

'Well,' he said thoughtfully, 'she's saving him a lot of bother, promising to see after you and visit you in London and all that. You know how he hates travelling.'

'Hates the expense of it, you mean! I can see that as an excuse not to come home every time there's a bit of a holiday.'

Stip stared out of the window over the rooftops to the far, blur-edged hills. 'You'll be off then,' he said in a muffled voice.

'I hope you'll be after me soon enough!' she said robustly.

'After you?' His tone was dreary.

'Of course! You're not going to stay here all your life!' Maggie was thinking with a pang that for the past months they had talked only about her plans, her dreams – his had been pushed aside. 'It's a pity you weren't the oldest, so you could be first off the nest, but never mind! I'll be trail-blazer. I'll make the contacts for you. I'll be bound to meet some writers. And in

17

the meantime, keep writing! I mean, your own writing, your plays and stories –'

'With no one to read them to?' There was naked reproach in his face now.

She ignored it because it was unbearable. 'Maybe one day I'll act in a play of yours. Just think, Stip, it'll come to the Festival, and we'll send Daddy anonymous complimentary tickets – the curtain will go up, and there I'll be –'

He turned away, and she saw jokes and old dream-games were no use. She was abandoning him to the dark house and the mahogany sideboard and to Ian-the-traitor, to their father's increasingly compelling references to the Advantages of Starting at the Bottom in the mill whilst possessing the Qualifications to Reach the Top. She gripped him, turned him, fixed her blue eyes upon his, which were exactly on her level, and said, 'You've got to resist him, Stip! I have.'

Stip was looking at her as if he had never seen her before.

'Are you *really* going to do it, Maggie?'

'Of course I am!'

'I can't believe in it, somehow. It's like – like levitating. People say it happens but my reason says no.'

'What do you mean?'

'Listen. You're going to London and to the Radar or whatever you call it, and Dad's going to pay, thinking it's something else.' Maggie suppressed a shiver. 'But when you're studying, there are things that the college sends home. Reports, bills – I don't know. The Radar will be sending those to your home, won't they?'

'No, because Mrs Dalzell is my sponsor and they'll come to her. Dad won't see them.'

'And won't he expect to see ones from the college you're supposed to be going to, the domestic science place?'

Maggie giggled, and hugged herself with wicked glee. It was all a delicious game to her. The warning bell was simply an accompaniment to the dance of her spirit.

'No! Listen. Mrs Dalzell has a friend who works in the other place, the one Dad thinks I'm going to. She's the deputy head there, and Mrs D. often visits her in her office when she's in London. So she's going to pinch some report forms and bill forms and so on, and fill them out for me herself every term. Isn't she wonderful?'

18

Steven stared at her a long time.

'I don't know if she's wonderful,' he said. 'I think she's mad. What's it her business? And what when Dad finds out in the end? He'll kill her, and you too.'

But Maggie was incapable of looking so far ahead.

'By that time I'll be an actress. There'll be nothing he can do about it.'

'Don't do it, Maggie.'

'What do you mean? I must.'

'Not this way. You'll be sorry.'

'Sorry? No, I won't. I'm never going to be sorry for anything I do. I've been made to feel sorry all my life not just for every little mistake, but for all the things I wanted to have and to do. Dad's always said they were the wrong things. He's never let me, never given way to me, never given me anything I longed for. You remember him that night, shouting and raging because we'd played a little trick to get an innocent little pleasure. He'd never let me act, Stip. Never, no matter how I begged. He wants me to stay at home forever doing housework, and I can't.'

'What about Mum? How will she feel?'

This was Maggie's Achilles' heel. She relished the whole plan so far as her father was concerned. Her mother was something else. Yet her parents formed an indivisible unit. Never to Maggie's knowledge had her mother stood out against her father's wishes to the end. She was well-tarred with the Robertson brush and thus merited no individual consideration. That was, at any rate, how Maggie reckoned at the time.

19

Chapter Three

Mrs Dalzell's perjury of her soul had only extended to the nature of Maggie's course of training. Regarding the lodgings, she had not uttered a deceitful word.

When Maggie first entered the house in Bloomsbury owned by the M'Crimmond sisters, Mrs D's first cousins, her heart sank at the meticulous accuracy of the description her father had been given. She had thought such houses existed only in the environs of Edinburgh; she was now to learn their ubiquitousness. Stone steps up to a black-painted, brass-embellished front door. A sonorous chime on the brass-rimmed button bell. A ghost-face pressed to the engraved glass panel, then the door opened on a dark passage which might have been the one at home – only close inspection disproved it. The Robertson's inner doors were dark green; these were brown, like the dadoes, but there was an almost identical carpet runner, patterned to camouflage mud, the same red-and-blue glass round the window on the half-landing where the M'Crimmond sisters had stood a thick pillar, graceless as a fat woman's leg, bearing a lugubrious majolica pot . . . The smell was different, too. The smell here was of very old Jack Russell terrier.

The M'Crimmond sisters themselves were twins, equally old-fashioned in their outer and under garments; the former featured tweed skirts, peter-pan collars and hand-knitted cardigans, and the latter, evidently, rigorous corsets. Their faces were kind and curious, but Maggie, peering at them in the dim light from the fan-glass and panels in the door, instinctively knew how quickly those gentle, welcoming lineaments could do a downturn into the tight ones of disapproval if she put so much as one toe across the border between acceptable and unacceptable behaviour.

After the mandatory cup of tea she was shown to her room,

20

the Jack Russell waddling ahead. It was no worse and no better than her room at home, except for one incredible aberration, at the sight of which her heart lifted. The counterpane was new, and furthermore it was chenille, a fabric which could safely be sat on, lain on, left in a heap or wrapped round cold knees and ankles. Its colour was what her mother called 'shocking pink', completely out of keeping with its surroundings, a fact the elder Miss M'Crimmond felt called on to apologise for. 'It was a gift,' she said, casting down her eyes as if the colour made it somehow indecent.

'I love it,' said Maggie, with a fervour which surprised even her.

A letter had come for her that morning from Mrs Dalzell.

'Well, Maggie!' it began bracingly. 'So you're on your way! You're probably feeling a little odd, so this is just to remind you that I will see you soon. I come to Town as often as I can to visit theatres and exhibitions, some of which I hope we may attend together. But even without me, you must go to plays at every opportunity. The gallery seats are very cheap. It is reported to be an excellent season. I've told my cousins that whatever other prohibitions they may see fit to impose while you are under their roof, you must not be restricted in your theatre-going.

'I have no worries about your working hard or not being what used to be called "a good girl," if only because you know how far I have "stuck my neck out" for you. Have you read much modern American drama? You should. It has a vitality and originality which our own contemporary plays notably lack. There is one about New York detectives. One of them lets a young miscreant off on his own responsibility, and his last word to him is: "Don't make a monkey out of me". A word to the wise, Maggie. I, too, would not fancy myself in the role of monkey.'

Mrs Dalzell was to write a good many bracing and admonitory little notes to Maggie in the course of the next two years. These notes, and her old teacher's occasional visits, 'added unto her' something important, something sustaining, if only because she might otherwise have felt sorely the lack of someone who knew

21

her flawed situation and to whom she could fully unburden herself. Yet, oddly, she seldom did so.

The reason simply was that she had never been so happy in her life as she was during the following two years. Maggie, that is. Margaret was the trouble. She was continually barking her emotional shins against the iron impediment of her conscience.

Mrs Dalzell, whose own conscience had been bent into a fairly flexible instrument since her elopement (which had caused her mother a heart attack and forced her younger sister to take her place as home drudge), nevertheless respected the worth of the organ and advised Maggie to pay heed to it – but within limits. 'If your conscience gets out of hand,' she once said, after one of Margaret's rare outbursts of guilt, 'it can do as much damage as any of the passions. Nobody who starts life in any kind of bondage can ever win their freedom without hurting someone.'

Life in the M'Crimmond mausoleum was a bit trying at times, for they took their responsibilities seriously; but Maggie was too busy working at what she loved to want to kick over the traces. True, they frowned if she came in late, tutted when she skipped breakfast and would not allow men past the front door even at four in the afternoon; but this last was not important. Maggie only had fellow-students, not men friends, in those two years. The fact of being where she was, doing what she was doing, used up all the daring and rebellion she possessed. As for her sex drives, any time they roused themselves in Maggie, Margaret hit them smartly on the head.

Mrs Dalzell came to see her at least once a term. They became as close as two women can who are forty years apart in age. 'Mrs D' did not want intimacy anyway; she never pried, and such confidences as she made to Maggie about her own past life were part of brief, unirksome homilies or anecdotes illustrating some point relevant to Maggie, such as the utter impossibility of living a fulfilled life in one's parents' image. She was never boring, and her knowledge and love of the theatre proved an endless spring, from which Maggie filled and refilled her own little bucket.

Theatre became her world, learning about it the whole business of her life. Sometimes, as the months flew by, she reflected on the contrast between what her parents imagined she was learning, and what she really was. In her father's

22

underdeveloped imagination were probably vague pictures of his domesticated child intent upon hand-smocking and hospital corners, breaking eggs for soufflés with one hand and chopping onions to a mush with her eyes shut. What if he knew that instead she was mastering such esoteric skills as running the length of a room and jumping into a man's arms, reciting 'Mary Had a Little Lamb' as if she had just brought the good news from Ghent to Aix, sitting perfectly still for fifteen minutes, acting out the alphabet?

Sometimes when she was in ballet or singing classes, throwing her body and voice into their refining and controlling exercises, Maggie would imagine that her father was watching, powerless, outraged, as the dead might watch the living, and it made her strive the harder for perfection. She learnt to throw a whisper for thirty yards; to time to a split second the striking of a match; to fall downstairs bonelessly; to hold a pause till the instant before the first cough. She learnt to improvise an entire scene at a moment's notice with only a cadenza on a battered upright for inspiration; to memorise Shavian speeches overnight; to smack someone in the face without touching them; to bring her tongue to a point; to expand her throat and command her diaphragm, and withal to hold her breath for seventy-three seconds, the second-longest in the class.

She also learnt to act.

Every term she took part in two plays – or rather, she took a part of a part, for there were always too many girls. She thus tasted the flavours of a dozen wildly assorted contemporary and classical roles. And in her final year, she was rewarded with a whole act of the soubrette in a musical comedy and, in the Public Show, a scene of the mother in *Death of a Salesman*.

This was regarded by her fellow students as a howling joke. Hitherto her rather bucolic good looks had led to a relentless diet of ingenues or juveniles. But to everyone's astonishment she won the prize for the best character actress, which got her name into *The Times*.

When she was shown this, her triumph fled before a tide of ice. Though her family took *The Scotsman* as a matter of course, enough copies of its London rival were circulating in the neighbourhood for it to be virtually certain that her parents would have their attention drawn to the item. For a week she lived in

23

torment, till Mrs Dalzell arrived in the M'Crimmonds' front parlour, all but dancing with glee at her latest ploy.

'My dear, I took it to them!' she gurgled. 'Yes! I did! I carried it to your father and said, had he seen his daughter's name in the paper? He blenched. But when he read it for himself, his colour soon returned. He never dreamt it might be *his* Margaret Robertson. I didn't even have to lie. I haven't told one lie yet, by the way – not a lie-direct, as Shakespeare has it. My goodness, though, Maggie, what a stroke of luck you didn't win the Bancroft Gold Medal! Then your picture would have been published, and that would have torn it!'

Maggie, assailed suddenly by a profoundly sick sensation, said, 'It will have to be – torn – soon, anyway. Won't it?' And the long-suppressed horror of what lay ahead burst upon her. She broke into tears.

Mrs Dalzell hurried to sit beside her. 'Now then, what's this? A prize-winning actress, crying real tears? You must never do that on stage, you know, you'll ruin your make-up!'

'But what am I to do? I want to stay in London and get a job, or what's it all been for? I can't just trail home and start housekeeping. I've got to tell them the truth now, and how, *how* am I going to do it?'

Mrs Dalzell sat quite quietly until Maggie was calmer. Then she said, 'Now, my dear, listen to me. In a few months you'll be of age. You must face it out! After all, you've done nothing to be ashamed of –'

Maggie, ravaged with the imminence of the impossible, stared at her.

'Nothing to be ashamed of!' she gasped. 'I've practically stolen hundreds of pounds from my father. I've lied to him – you may have avoided it, technically, but I've told dozens of lies, scores! Every holiday at home has been a performance. Oh, I've had a wonderful two years. I've learned. I've made friends. I know exactly what I want from my life, but – it's all been built on . . .' She stopped because 'wickedness' was such a melodramatic word and she could think of no other.

'Would you have been able to have all that, any other way?'

'No –'

'Did you try the straight way? Did you ask him?'

'Yes, once, but –'

'Had you a right to your own life, do you think?'

24

Silence.

'Margaret, weren't you in *The Barretts of Wimpole Street* last term?'

'But Daddy isn't Mr Barrett!'

'Only because this is 1949 and not 1849. Take it from me, dear, you did the only possible thing – except abandon your hopes.'

Maggie was silent.

'Now if you'll take my advice, you'll give yourself a week to think things through and rehearse what you're going to say to your parents. I'd planned a fortnight in town, but I'll cut it short if you like and come up with you and we'll do it together.'

Maggie quickly refused this offer. 'No! Of course not. This is for me to do.' And then – two years too late – the thought came. 'What will he do – to *you*, when he knows?'

'What can he do? I'm independent. But you're not, Maggie. And you must be. You'll need to get yourself a job as soon as possible, if not acting straight away then something else.'

'I've already started writing to managements. The prize should help.'

'I wouldn't count on that.'

'And Mrs Dalzell, might I – could I leave here now? I feel I want to live on my own. Your cousins have been very kind, but –'

'I've told you. You're of age. If you can keep yourself, all your decisions from now on are in your own hands.'

All the normal fears of those leaving drama school for the soul-devouring world of show business were summer dapples compared to the black shadow that hung over Maggie. She realised she had simply been shoving the guilt up ahead of her in an ever-increasing lump, like a heedless dung-beetle, until now it was ominously poised to roll backward, right over her. Facing her father and putting herself in the path of his righteous retribution seemed only marginally less terrifying than being squashed by her own unfightable shame at the cost, in her father's money and her own integrity, of what she had so deeply and improvidently enjoyed.

None of Mrs Dalzell's words had helped. In fact, a judgement against her benefactor and fellow-conspirator was creeping

25

across Maggie's mind, a shadow upon shadows. Was this woman, on whom she had relied for so long, into whose hands she had put her life and to whose cheerful pragmatic morality she had entrusted her own – was she not responsible for this awful crisis in which Maggie found herself?

So far she had confided in no one but Stip. He was useless to her now, being four hundred miles away and in any case deep in exams. So she took another confidante, out of sheer inability to bear her burden alone. She chose her closest friend at the Academy, a girl called Tanya Zandler.

Tanya had had a good deal more life-experience than the other girls at RADA, and was also older by several years. At twenty-three she had found herself cast by her classmates as a sort of surrogate mother-figure. She had the build for it, being tall and statuesque, with a well-cut, rather patrician face and long hair which was infinitely adaptable to the matronly or heroic roles she usually played. The only dangerous corner in her friendship with Maggie occurred when the casting was announced for the Public Show. Tanya had been quite convinced she would play the mother in *Death of a Salesman*. Wasn't she the class character-woman as of right? And when the prizes were awarded, Maggie's joy had been clouded by fear that her friendship with Tanya might be over. Mature, wise and generous though she was, Tanya was an actress first and last, with an actress's all-excluding and unreasoning ambition. But fortunately Tanya was able, given a week or so, to rise above this blow, and when Maggie's need drove her to telephone her friend and beg a session of soul-baring, Tanya swiftly agreed.

Tanya had had an English father and a Czechoslovakian mother, both of whom had vanished in the fires of Hitler's Europe. Tanya had a British passport, and this saved her life, for the British Foreign Office does not indicate maternal ethnic origins in its documents. The Germans occupying Lyons, where Tanya was studying, were cautious regarding British subjects, presumably because the British held a number of German citizens who had been caught in the United Kingdom when war struck; so a camp was set up for them. Not a concentration camp of the kind where her non-aryan mother and the man who would not renounce her were being starved and eventually gassed, but an internment camp. She very seldom spoke of what

26

she experienced there, rightly balancing her four years of fears and privations against what might have befallen her.

In 1945, when the camp was liberated, Tanya was shipped to England more or less willy-nilly with the others. She was taken up by some of her father's relatives, who sent her to RADA and provided her with as much of a home background as she was ready to accept. All hope for her parents had been abandoned. Taking her mother's name (or part of it) as a memorial, Tanya faced front, and marched.

She arrived at the M'Crimmonds' one summer evening, ringing the brass button bell that little bit longer and louder than most callers; the *brrrrring*! shooting through the house ahead of her was like an announcement heralding the arrival of someone who knew herself to be marked out for a special destiny. It was like a shout of 'Here I am! Come quick!' which sent Maggie dashing down the worn-carpeted stairs to greet her.

Tanya sat on the now rather washed-out chenille counterpane, chain-smoking in her enviably insouciant fashion, quite silent as she listened except for the little squidge as she stubbed out each cigarette. She watched Maggie at first, her dark eyes unblinking, but after a certain point in the story she stopped watching and stared at the wall so that her bold straight-nosed profile was all Maggie could see.

She was a girl of swift, remorseless judgement – this Maggie knew, having, during the past two years, been occasionally on the receiving end of some of her more trenchant criticisms. Half-way through her recital, Maggie was wishing she'd never started. Tanya would be sure to disapprove – how could she not? – and would not hesitate to say so unequivocally. Maggie felt that if that happened, in her present state she would not be able to stand it.

But in the end, all Tanya said, in her still slightly accented voice, was: 'H'm. Well. Judge not that ye be not judged! My God though, my hair is standing up a bit I must say. I've always thought you such a goody-shoes, refusing to go into pubs and kissing on stage with your behind sticking out . . . Still, I could a tale, or even two, unfold of my own which would straighten the curl in your hair, too, so I'd better just give you the advice you are looking for and then shut up.'

27

A desire for a foretaste of punishment drove Maggie to ask for it.

'You think I'm awful.'

'Awfully reckless, and scarcely what you could call honest, but also incredibly brave. I think I would be shocked if I were not so *surprised*. To be truthful, Maggie, I didn't think you had it in you to be so *spunky*.'

Maggie, tense as she was, could not restrain a giggle. Tanya looked stricken. 'Oh God! What have I said wrong? Is it wrong, "spunky"? I *know* I've heard it!'

'Where?'

'Or maybe read?'

'Do you read old comics?'

'No. Boys' adventure books,' she confessed. 'I love them.'

'Read them but don't copy the dialogue.'

Tanya grinned at her. She had a wide, red, mobile mouth but imperfectly aligned teeth, so she was more apt to grin than smile. She put out her hand and Maggie, sitting on an upright desk-chair for the purpose of confession, jumped up and went to sit on the bed with Tanya, who held her hand and gave her the advice she had asked for.

It was that Maggie should try to get a job-offer *before* going back up to Scotland to face the music. That would not only give her essential confidence, it might mollify her father.

'Because the first thing you must try to do is to pay back the money, of course,' said Tanya. 'It may be the money, more than the deceits, that will gall him the most.'

Then they talked it over more and the room grew dim and the glow of Tanya's cigarette-end came and went. They savoured the special intimacy – for which there is no substitute – of woman-friendship. After a couple of hours they went out and drifted through the streets of London, arm in arm, talking. They ended up in the spaghetti joint near RADA, starving, and, in Maggie's case, much happier than she had the slightest right to be.

Getting a job-offer in the week Maggie had allowed herself sounded impossible, but the prize did help, after all. London managers and agents might behave as if they'd never heard of the Public Show, but a small, well-reputed company in Wales

28

to whom she had written a not very hopeful letter wrote back and offered her a season of weekly rep by the sea for the summer. She was to start rehearsals in a week, during which time she was expected to provide herself with clothes and make-up for the season ('All the plays scheduled are modern. We can't afford costume hire, so bring every rag you've got') and begin to memorise the part of Pat in *Flare Path*, a French's acting edition of which was – most thrillingly, for it was as good as a contract – enclosed.

At this point Maggie was forced to realise that winning the prize had given her ideas above her station. Since listening to Tanya, she had revised the scenario Mrs Dalzell had advised her to rehearse, to include the announcement to her parents of some glamorous job with the BBC or a number one tour, or at the very least, some notable provincial company such as Coventry or Birmingham ... Since at least eight out of ten of the people she'd written to had still to reply (she was inexperienced enough to suppose that most of them would) she might have spurned the Wales offer, had it not included the play book.

Reading it – imagining herself in it, a leading part all to herself – she grew irresistably excited. A seaside town, where people would get to know you, where the company was small and everyone got a fair share of good parts, where she might be playing character one week, juve the next, SM-ing the week after, learning, learning all the time ... the fun, the sheer fun and challenge of it! She would have to buy some clothes, borrow others ... If *only* her mother had been on her side! She had loads of clothes, and they were the same size ... It was now that a little irritation, an imp to fight a big black devil of guilt, crept into her thoughts about her parents. How could it be that they stood in the way of this first small but indicative triumph? Her first job! She needed them, to know, to be glad for and proud of her, to *help* ...

She put *Flare Path* aside long enough to write a joyous letter of acceptance to the Welsh company. Then she picked it up again. She lay on the pink chenille (soon she would say goodbye to it, and this house, for ever) and sank herself into the part and the play. In the back of her head a voice was saying, 'This is me, this is my life, they have no right to stand in my way or deplete me with fear ...' And quite abruptly, she put *Flare Path* down

29

again, left the room, went straight downstairs and put through a person-to-person call to her mother.

'Mummy?' Her voice was high with defiance. 'It's Maggie.'

'I thought it must be,' said her mother drily. 'Nobody else phones from London reversing the charges. When can we expect you home?'

'I'm not coming home yet.'

'Indeed, are you not? And why is that?'

'Because I've got a job.'

'A job! Doing what?'

'Acting.'

'Acting,' repeated her mother, without a question-mark.

'Mummy, I've got something to confess to you.' She had used this formula in childhood. Now as then, she felt frozen as she said it.

'What is it?'

'I've deceived you and Dad for two years. I've been going to drama school – the Royal Academy,' she added with pathetic bravado, as if the royal charter made it all less heinous. From there she heard herself babbling on, trying to explain, suddenly knowing that this was the wrong, the coward's way to do it, over the phone instead of face to face, but as with so much else, it was too late now.

In the end she stopped talking in mid-sentence and a long, long pause ensued. The hairs of her flesh stood erect.

'Where is your job?' her mother asked at last.

Maggie felt as if she'd turned over two pages at once. Something was seriously missing from this conversation.

'It's in Tenby,' she whispered. 'South Wales.'

'Is it a good job? Are they to pay you properly?'

'Mummy, have you understood what I've just told you?'

'I understand your words. I haven't yet comprehended them. I haven't yet come to grips with them. I know you said them and that, unlike everything else I've heard from you for two years, they are true. Reproaches and tears may come later, but they won't change what's past. I must try to arm myself with some practical details in case your father asks practical questions.'

'You don't have to tell him, Mummy! I will.'

'When?'

30

'Well . . . my job starts next week, I don't want to come home before it starts . . .'

'. . . if ever! And I am supposed at this stage to join you in your conspiracy, to invent something to explain your non-appearance? I'll not entertain it, Maggie.'

Maggie was silent, crushed. She was weeping.

'What I will and must do is tell him for you if you don't come to tell him yourself. I cannot keep such a secret from him, now that I know – for sure.'

The 'for sure' passed Maggie by at the time. She was to remember it later.

'No, Mummy! You don't have to do that – don't do it –'

But the connection was broken. Whether Mrs Robertson, too upset to say more, had hung up, or whether they'd been cut off, Maggie didn't know. She lacked both the resolution and the shillings to ring back – somehow she knew she could never telephone home reversing the charges again.

That night Margaret and Maggie lay in their joint bed, in their joint head, and fought it out for the first time. It's a poor look-out for any woman if her first profoundly honest look at herself doesn't come till she is twenty. Maggie's, when it came, was like Faust's into the pit. She had the classic disadvantage of a strict religious upbringing: those unavoidable occasional glimpses of her true nature compared so irreconcilably with the model she had been conditioned to believe was attainable.

Reviewing her deeds in the light of her mother's reaction, she felt her beetle-strength fail: the dungball of guilt rolled slowly back and crushed her. Her father might be joyless, oppressive, rigid; as his mahogany furniture absorbed light and would not reflect it back again, so he and his religion drained life of its fun and spontaneity. But what was that compared to being a liar and a thief? She had used her father, and fraudu-lently converted his money. Bad enough. But there was a deeper pit of her own iniquity to peer into. For now she was leaving it to her mother to tell him the truth, while she, cravenly, fled to her world of pleasure and make-believe, the tinsel world of play-acting.

It was not Maggie-as-actress that would make it impossible for her father to endure her perfidy, she realised. It was the

31

awful spectacle of his own ruthlessness carried to the level of a fine art in his daughter.

Her long anger against him was avenged – played out. She was left with what he had bequeathed her through blood and nurture – the morality which lies, like bedrock, under all that the devious mind of the runaway can lay on top of it, waiting to prevent descent past a certain point ... a point which Margaret, and, with grudging reluctance, even Maggie, knew by the end of that night she had reached.

Next morning she got up early, and, leaving the house before the M'Crimmond sisters were up, went off to catch the businessmen's train to Edinburgh.

Chapter Four

Five hours on the train, half an hour on the bus, all filled to bursting by her overheated imagination with ever more harrowing apprehensions, were not enough to prepare Maggie for what she had to face at the end of it.

Exhausted from the journey and the preceding all-but-sleepless night, she dragged herself up the steps to the black front door and rang the bell. It was Ian who opened it. One look was enough to show her that he knew what she had done, and furthermore, considered that nothing more iniquitous lay within the bounds of human frailty.

Yet there was something in his look of disgusted astonishment at the sight of her which gave her back a little of her fighting spirit. First, because she did not regard him as worthy to judge her, and second, because he was obviously dumbfounded to see her there at all, proving that, in respect of her courage at least, he'd underrated her.

In any case, far worse for her than anything Ian might conceivably have to say to her was the realisation that *his* knowing meant that her mother had blown the gaff. Why? Perhaps she had shown her distress and Maggie's father had 'got it out of her'. In any case, to some extent Maggie's gesture in coming was vitiated. The deed was done, the first shock absorbed – the worst perhaps over. Maggie suffered a sense of failure and anti-climax.

The first thing, however, was to go at once into the offensive with Ian, as the best means of defence against the outrage in his eyes.

'Yes, I'm home,' she said.

Ian simply glared at her.

'Where's Daddy?'

'Well may you ask!' he burst out. 'He's taken to his bed.'

33

Her heart stopped, as he had meant it to; he paused, but then went on, 'It's his ulcer playing up. Small thanks to you it's not a heart attack.'

She pushed past him into the house. Ian was close behind her, like a bloodhound.

'I can't get over it, the brazen cheek of you, walking in here like this! I personally thought you'd never dare come home again.'

Maggie's overwrought nerves twanged, but she kept her voice down. 'Shut up, Ian, it's nothing to do with you. Where's Stip?'

'At college, of course. And while we're on that subject, one word of advice.' He pulled her none too gently into the front parlour and shut the heavy door. 'If, as I strongly suspect, Steven knew all the time what you were up to, tell him to keep his mouth shut. Not for his own sake, for Dad's. If Dad knew there were *two* rotten eggs in the nest, it'd be the death of him.'

Maggie stared at him. Behind the facade of defiance, tears were coming. Act, she ordered herself, act! Don't give him the satisfaction of seeing he can hurt you.

'Will you kindly go up and tell Daddy I'm here?'

'What do you take me for, your messenger boy? He'll not see you anyway, I'm sure of that!'

'I've come four hundred miles to see him and I'm not leaving until I do.'

Ian stared at her for a moment. Then he turned on his heel and left her.

She stood motionless, feeling very sick. He came back. 'You're to go up,' he said shortly.

Her mother met her at the top of the stairs. She looked distraught; her usual tidiness was blurred at the edges. She made no attempt to kiss Maggie.

'Mummy . . . I wish you'd waited! How did he take it?'

Her mother looked at her dumbly.

'Is he really ill?' asked Maggie, her throat dry.

'That's the least of it – a minor business reverse can bring on worse than this. He stayed home because he can't face people. He's convinced the whole town knew you duped him.'

'Nobody knew! How could they?'

Her mother gave her a strange sideways look. For a moment a crazy thought crossed Maggie's mind, an answer to the nagging question of why her mother had not seemed more *surprised* by

34

her announcement last night on the phone. Why she had not demanded more detailed explanations. But that was absurd – unthinkable. For if her mother had even begun to guess, that would have been collusion.

'If you've made up your mind to take what's coming to you,' she was saying, 'get away in. It won't improve with keeping.'

Her father was not in bed. He was sitting on the edge of it, his bowed head in profile against the massive mahogany bedhead, wearing a dark dressing-gown. His shoulders were stooped. He had a look of defeat which simultaneously relieved her fear and increased her guilt. But the look was deceptive.

He turned slowly to face her. In his eyes she read the reproach due to a child who has fallen into some irretrievable disgrace.

'Have you anything to say to me? Anything at all to make me feel less ashamed of you?'

Maggie opened her mouth to deliver the speech of mingled contrition and self-justification she had prepared. But nothing came out – not a word. An old, old wound was breaking open again, old, bad blood welling up . . . Eighteen years of repressed resentment can't be wiped away, after all, by two years of purloined freedom and fulfilment. The rest of her life ahead was calling her, and she knew suddenly that if she knuckled under now – even to the extent of admitting she had wronged him – it would be inconsistent and impossible to fight her way back.

At last she said gauchely, 'I had to do what I did. I have to be an actress, I have to live my own life, and you'd never have let me. If you're determined to feel ashamed, feel ashamed that you drove me to deceive you.'

Her father rose to his feet. She saw such sudden menace in his stance that she had to hold herself from cringing.

'You dare to turn it all back on me, do you? I might have expected it. I gave you a chance in my thoughts. I decided, if you came to me humbly, if you seemed truly sorry –'

Margaret choked out: 'I'll pay back every –'

'Aye,' he shouted, 'you will! But not as you think. It's not money I want from you. It was into other hands I entrusted that, and it's from them I shall require repayment.' A livid line round his thin mouth made Maggie shudder for Mrs Dalzell, although she had said she was safe. 'What I want from you, my

35

girl, is evidence that you recognise the sheer badness of what you've done, the slippery chute you've set your feet on. Oh, yes, I know – you'll soon be of age, and you've a job, of sorts. For a derisory sum you're prepared to disport yourself before a lot of idle lascivious beer-swilling Welsh troglodytes –' (Maggie, despite the sheer paralysing awfulness of the scene, could scarcely help smiling at this description of Tenby audiences). 'But if you think either of those facts spells independence, financial *or emotional*, the next year or so will teach you otherwise! You imagine you've broken away from your background, but I know you. You'll need your home and your family before you're much older. You'll need a shoulder to cry on and a pocket to dip into, and probably a roof and a bed into the bargain. Well, don't think you can come crawling back here when you're jobless and homeless – or worse. I know what actors are. When next your mother comes to me with that look of anguish on her face that twists my heart to breaking, no doubt it will be to tell me that you've followed your bent of depravity to its ultimate – ' Suddenly his face darkened with an uprush of blood so that he looked as if he might have a seizure. 'Margaret! I warn you! If you laugh at my words, I shall not be answerable!'

Maggie had not known that her smile, which was more than half hysterical, was getting the better of her rigid face-muscles. But when she saw his hand upraised she instinctively cringed, and in this position she quite unwittingly laid balm to his fury. The choleric purple subsided from his face and his arm relaxed.

But she knew, then, what he had in him, and in the sudden answering wave of her own anger, she had further proof of how alike they were in their worst aspects, and thought frantically: 'I must guard myself! I must change my nature somehow, not to be like this, like him!' Because it was not Mr Bennett she saw, so much as Capulet, Juliet's father, who cries out in his rage at her disobedience: 'Hang, beg, starve, die in the streets!' This was not mere rigidity or misguided religious principle. It was the despotic cruelty that demands the right to mould his children or reject them.

I was right, she thought fiercely. Remorse – humility – those were only the outward signs of the total capitulation he wanted. One sign of recantation, and she would never get back on her own feet.

36

She straightened up, trembling all over, and faced him as well as she could for her sudden deep fear of him.

'I'll not give way to you! Mind that. You'll beg for me to come back before I'll crawl as you said! I've got to live my own way. Maybe I *am* wicked, but not the way you think. It's not in disobedience or wanting to lead a bad life, it's that I can be as ruthless and single-minded as you! If I'm bad it's your badness, I get it all from you!'

He did hit her then. Her defiance broke the remains of his control and he slapped her face. Then her mother rushed into the room and got between them, and after a few inarticulate words to her father, half of reproach and half of a sort of muffled pity, she dragged Maggie away.

'She's to get out of my house! Out! Out of my house!' she could hear her father shouting almost insanely as her mother hurried her to her old room.

'You'll have to go, at least for tonight,' her mother muttered, hastily cramming things back into the small suitcase Maggie had brought and which her mother had begun to unpack. 'You can go to Aunty Helen's, she knows all about it. I won't say she condones what you've done, but she's my sister, and she'll put you up if I ask her.'

Still with her mood of hysterical defiance upon her, Maggie protested: 'Nobody has to go against their consciences for me – I'll go back to London!'

'You will do as you're told for once. You don't want to lose your family altogether, do you? We'll see if he feels differently in the morning.' Standing before her with the case in her hand, her mother looked at her directly. 'Maggie, could you not say you're sorry?'

'I wanted to. I meant to. I am sorry in a way. But not after this! Not after he hit me –' Against her strongest intentions, she lost hold of herself and began to cry.

Her mother didn't move to comfort her, but her voice softened. 'I won't ask it of you tonight. He'd not accept it anyhow. Maybe tomorrow. No, now don't say you won't. Maybe you will. Maybe he'll see it differently . . . If not tomorrow, sometime. I couldn't lose you, Maggie.'

Through her own emotional storm, Maggie felt her mother tremble, heard her voice break. She looked up, quickly, incredulously. She was crying, too. Her mother, crying! Unwillingly

37

she remembered the only part of her father's speech of accusation that had not made her want to shout at him or laugh in his face: '... that look of anguish on her face that twists my heart to breaking ...'

'I can say it to you!' she burst out. 'I'm sorry! I'm so sorry –'

Her mother speedily pulled herself together, getting one of her small linen handkerchiefs from the pocket of her long cardigan. She had always dodged any hint of sentimentality, however truly felt.

'Not now. We'll talk some other time. Now be off with you to Helen's.'

Maggie's Aunt Helen was a spinster, and she looked it. As a child, Maggie had not liked to visit her – loving and playful though she invariably was – because she looked like a dry old version of her mother. Later she was able to separate the two in her mind, and became fond of Helen for her own sake. She no longer begged her mother after each visit, 'You'll never, never let yourself get like Aunty, will you?' Perhaps because, in some odd way, her mother already had.

Helen was at the door to meet her, and welcomed her in, wordlessly but not without a kind of furtive warmth. Her habitual kiss on the cheek was firmer than usual and her faded eyes had a faint but unmistakable gleam. Just plain curiosity, thought Maggie wearily, or probably an unfightable enthusiasm for anything that broke the monotony of her solitary existence. She had always relished a bit of family scandal.

She gave Maggie an omelette and some tinned fruit, saying: 'You'll not be wanting anything heavy after all that upset.' Maggie's mother had evidently telephoned a bulletin, in some sisterly code, while Maggie was walking the three blocks to Helen's little house. While Maggie ate, or rather picked, Helen sat across the table, her hands folded under her chin, those unusually eager eyes fixed on her. She looked like an elderly child, confronted by a thrilling example of adult transgression.

Those eyes, though not overtly reproachful, made Maggie in her present conscience-flayed state very uncomfortable.

'Do you think I'm awful, Aunty?' she asked at last, laying down her fork.

'Eat your supper, dear. What does it matter what Helen

38

thinks?' She often spoke of herself objectively, as if she lived outside her own head.

'It does matter,' said Maggie, and, to her own surprise, this was true.

'Well, I'll tell you one thing about it. It was marry or burn.'

'Pardon, Aunty?'

'As St Paul said. It's better to marry than burn. He meant if you can't resist the temptation of the flesh, you'd better marry, which of course he disapproved of because he thought we should all live like the saints in heaven. You've not been a saint, Maggie, but if you'd not taken your chance – stolen it, perhaps I should say – you'd have burnt with longing all your life. And that's something I know a good deal about.' She got up to put the kettle on.

'Then you –'

'Oh no, I'd not be able to say I approve. Stealing's very wrong, and stealing from your own father is wronger still. But that's not to say I condemn you.' She turned at the old fashioned stove and looked down at Maggie. She was a tall woman, and for a moment Maggie wondered why everyone called her 'poor Helen' – she looked quite formidable. 'If I'd known at your age what I know now,' she said, 'I might have done anything – anything at all – to avoid the life I've had. Fifteen years I looked after Father, after poor Mother passed away. One shouldn't speak ill of the dead, but I'm going to. He was a selfish, curmudgeonly, demanding, ungrateful old man and he drained me as dry as you see me now. If I had known that with his death my life's story, I mean the part with *plot*, would come to an end, I think duty and goodness and all the rest of it would have been frail cobwebs to stand in my way during those terrible years. Into a home he'd have been put, and away I'd have been with scarce a backward look.' She turned back to the stove, picked up the kettle which had been shrilling an accompaniment to her confession, and prosaically made the tea.

Maggie got up early the next morning, before Helen was awake. She folded her bedclothes and emptied the hot-water bottle, which Helen had crept up to slip tenderly between the sheets the night before, and to lay against Maggie's shock-chilled feet. She didn't eat breakfast or even make herself a cup of tea – one of those small quixotries rather typical of her, the pointless nicety of feeling she didn't deserve her kind aunt's

39

hospitality. She scribbled a note of loving thanks, and, carrying her case, quietly left the house.

She had to walk past her own ex-home to reach the bus-stop. As she passed it she slowed down and looked, convinced it was for the last time, at the solid blackstone frontage, the swaybacked stone steps, the prim lace curtains in the windows ... She suddenly remembered hearing her mother once, arguing with Aunt Helen: 'I *hate* the things, shutting the world out! What have we got to hide?' And Helen, astonished: 'But you're right on the main road! Prying eyes ... Besides, the sun would fade the carpets.' 'Let it,' Mrs Robertson had retorted. But the lace curtains were still there ...

Maggie was half-way down the next block. She looked at her watch. She had seven minutes to spare, no more, if she wanted to make the train. Dropping her suitcase over a low wall, she ran back, and round to the back door.

A glance through the small window by the drainpipe – yes – she was there, in her dressing-gown, filling the morning kettle. Maggie's shadow fell on her mother's face. She looked up, startled, and Maggie saw – really saw her for the first time in years, if not ever. Nearly sixty and looking every hour of it, and, more than age, sadness, anxiety, and the stifling of all her secret personal dreams. Like Helen, she must have had some. What had they been?

Maggie felt a rush of love for her mother, pure love. She was later to reflect, sitting crying on the train, that she had never *felt* love before, physical, sharp as a migraine.

Her mother hurried to the back door, unbolted it and let her in. With no time to do anything but act spontaneously, Maggie flung her arms round her mother's neck and hugged her as she hadn't done since she was too little to have learnt that her mother subtly avoided physical contacts ... Yet now she felt, after the first startled second, arms going round her.

'I wasn't going to come – then I ran back – I had to see you –'

'Couldn't you stay a little?' her mother implored.

Maggie took one glimpse at the prospect of seeing her father again, now, and a long shiver shook her.

'I can't, Mummy. I simply am not able.'

Her mother held her in silence, without reproach.

'What's wrong with me?' Maggie burst out suddenly. 'Maybe I *am* bad, as Daddy said –'

'Bad? Nonsense! Of course you're not!' said her mother robustly. And Maggie saw tears come, and hugged her again to hide them. Suddenly she heard her mother whispering love-words, such as she hadn't heard from her since she was a tiny girl: 'Never mind, sweetheart, never mind! You're a good girl and your mummy loves you, don't ever doubt it.'

Maggie felt her control, not cracking so much as simply dissolving in some painful acid-bath of feeling. Was this her mother, cuddling and consoling her as if she were a baby? Do people change so radically under stress, or – unbearable thought! – had she been like this all the time, buried somehow under encrustations of deadening restraint? Had the lace curtains, the mahogany, and most of all her husband's expectations and demands, done to her mother the very thing Maggie had been terrified they would do to her?

For a moment, mother and daughter stared at each other, holding on with eyes and hands, on the verge of a breakthrough to the empathy which the years and the rigid rules of their lives had bricked up, but which was still – each sensed it – viable, waiting to be developed into a real, adult relationship.

But it was too late. Maggie would miss her bus, her train – her life.

'Mummy – I'm going, I've got to – *please* –'

She didn't know what she pleaded for, but her mother knew.

'You're doing right. You've done wrong, but you're doing the right thing now. Go on. Leave him to me.'

'I love you. I love you.'

She kissed her with passion and started out. Her mother's voice stopped her at the back door.

'Think of me when you're acting. Share it with me. Will you do that?'

Maggie had no time to interpret this remark, or her astonishment at it. 'I will,' she promised, and ran.

Chapter Five

Wales was marvellous, every bit as marvellous as Maggie had expected, if not more. The best part of this marvellousness was that Maggie felt justified. The company was small; it was a bit tatty; it didn't lead anywhere; and since she played all sorts, she was not always at her best. But she learned, and she enjoyed, and that meant she was able to forget about her father much of the time, and during the rest (Sundays, mainly, having her once-a-week lie-in, no rehearsals and no lines to learn till a quick brush-up after supper) she could tell herself that it had been worth it, that she would be a fine actress one day and make him proud/sorry, and also that she would pay him back every penny. She gave considerable thought to how this was to be done. Out of a salary of four pounds a week plus free digs it was hard to do anything very helpful about her repayment fund at the moment, but her intentions were good. All in all it was quite impossible to imagine herself ever crawling back for shelter and succour, as her father had promised her she would.

She wrote a number of letters on these divinely idle Sundays, mainly sitting on the beach. Regularly to her mother, full of detail and company gossip; a couple, hopefully, to Stip (what did he think of her since the row?) which he didn't answer; and long girl-chat ones to Tanya, who had been walking-on at the Vic all summer 'in wrinkled tights and a tabard that fatally reveals my big bum. Luckily the pay is so little that I cannot help but diet.'

She did not write to Mrs Dalzell. Mrs Dalzell was lurking somewhere behind the dung-ball of guilt; this, though off her chest due to working, stayed poised, near enough at hand to cast its shadow over her when the emotional light was at a certain angle.

The season ended with the end of summer, and Maggie

returned to London, buoyed up with confidence and raring to go (anywhere but to Edinburgh). The first port of call was the M'Crimmonds', to see if there was any post. She anticipated plenty, in reply to all those job-letters enclosing glossy photos with 'Please return to . . .' on their backs. Some managements at least must have had the decency to do that much! Well, three of them had, two with compliments slips and one with a polite letter of regret. That meant approximately thirty-seven costly little glossies lost forever.

Of other mail, there was only one: the long-awaited letter from Stip.

It contained no overt reproaches, which was generous, considering what the atmosphere at home must have been like (her mother had hinted that her father had by no means 'got over it'). Stip rather sheepishly related that he was, after all, going into the family business – 'at least for a while, till my plans mature . . . It really wouldn't have done, to cross Dad just now, *all things considered.*' Maggie, reading this, had the grace to blush. 'The stories came back from *Argosy*, and from *Story* , but I can't really expect to start selling right away. I'm rewriting them . . . . I'm saving money. I've given up smoking and I hardly ever go out. Dreary as the mill is, and obnoxious as it is to be working under Ian, there's some satisfaction in a weekly pay-packet, though I sometimes wish Dad were more of a nepotist – he gives me less money than everyone else, not more, and more rockets too, if I make mistakes . . . By the way! What happened to all those "contacts" you promised to make for me?'

Totally forgotten. That's what happened to them. Another clod flung at the dung-ball, but its little bulge hardly showed up on that massive sphere.

Maggie said what she fondly believed was a last farewell to 'Miss Brenda' and 'Miss Roberta,' fondled the wiry deaf ears of the Jack Russell (who gave her hand a valedictory nip) and was off – to share what Tanya called her three-room dosshouse in the Goldhawk Road. Tanya's season, too, had ended and the two of them settled down to their first experience of joblessness together.

This first patch was not too bad. The best thing about it was its brevity. Two of the lads who had been in Tenby started up their own company in Ilfracombe, Devon, and invited Maggie

43

to join them for 'a winter of discontent, subsidised, for their own unfathomable reasons, by the local council' The list of plays to be presented was uninspiring, and the two self-appointed managers apologised for it, adding: 'One has to sink pretty low to attract even tourists in this benighted region, so think what we have to stoop to when it's only the residents!' The one speck of gold in the dross of thrillers and farces was Noel Coward's *Blithe Spirit*, in which Maggie was astonished to find she'd been cast as the ghost – 'the other juve, darling, is even less ethereal-looking than you.' She'd rather have had a go at Madame Arcati, but who was she to fuss? At least it was a job, which was more than Tanya had.

Tanya was very good about it, in a slightly two-edged way. 'Even if I was offered, I wouldn't go,' she said. 'I am going to stick out for a good company. After the Vic, I couldn't bear tat.' And speaking of tat (which Maggie wished she hadn't), Tanya lent her half a dozen marvellous character outfits which she had recently inherited from a defunct landlady.

Maggie was packing these into her trunk (picked up cheap at the lower end of Portobello Road) one dingy late September morning. Tanya's dosshouse flat was three floors up; the bell was the sort that has to be turned like a key and emits a harsh, rusty gargel. So Maggie knew nothing of her visitor until someone shouted up the stairwell to her. She went out on to the linoleum-covered landing and leant over the bannisters. Down below, standing erect by the hideous hall-stand, clad in her same old caped tweed coat and brightly feathered hat, was Mrs Dalzell.

Something went *ping* in Maggie's head at the sight of that familiar figure, foreshortened by height but unmistakable and unchanged. Her first craven impulse was to run and hide. But it was useless. In any case, a contrary impulse was already bearing her swiftly down the stairs toward that Pears'-soap-scented embrace. *How could I not have written, all this time?* She had no answer to give herself.

'Mrs Dalzell, how marvellous to see you! Where have you come from? How did you find me?' she babbled, aware that of course she should have let her know where she was, not leave her to find out from her cousins. Mrs Dalzell was smiling as Maggie led her up the narrow stairs, still rattling on, but she

44

said little, and Maggie began to have a distinctly uneasy feeling which had nothing directly to do with her own sense of shame.

She settled her visitor down in front of the gas-fire, and, still chatting, went through into the kitchenette and put on a kettle. She was half-way through a rather high-pitched monologue about Tenby when she suddenly stopped to think.

She put her head round the dividing door.

'Mrs Dalzell, isn't it term-time?'

'It is,' said Mrs Dalzell, nodding her firm, single nod.

'Then what are you doing in London in mid-week?'

Mrs Dalzell, who had been leaning forward to warm her hands at the fire, sat back and turned, meeting Maggie's eye for the first time.

'I've had the sack,' she said, 'and a bag to put it in, as they say.'

Maggie stood stock still with the coffee-jar clutched in both hands.

'The sack? You?' she said numbly.

'Yes.'

Maggie stepped back to where she couldn't be seen. She set the jar down and gazed at it. This was, on the face of it, terrible news. And there was something – some instinct told her with piercing certainty – even more terrible behind it.

'How did it happen?' she muttered at last.

'Come in here, where I can see you.'

Reluctantly, Maggie obeyed, and sat down at her side.

'Well!' Mrs Dalzell began brightly. 'I was invited to retire early. I declined. They insisted. Nothing I could acknowledge as an adequate reason was given. But there was a reason, of course.'

Of course. 'What?' asked Maggie with a dry mouth.

Mrs Dalzell shrugged, and the shrug turned into a little shiver. 'I can't be sure. There were . . . forces at work. Behind the scenes, so to speak.'

After a pause Maggie licked her lips and obliged herself to ask, 'Do you mean that someone – ?'

'It may not have been just one person. I've not gone through my career at that school without ruffling a few feathers. And the tide was running against me in any case. You know I'm not a qualified teacher. Ever since the war, there's been a movement to replace teachers like me with young people with degrees.

45

Many of them of course know nothing whatsoever about teaching, but they have their qualifications. The likes of me are just – untidiness in the new bureaucratic pattern.'

'Perhaps it was just that.'

'Perhaps.'

'But you don't think so,' said Maggie slowly.

'I think there was more to it than that.'

Maggie stood up and withdrew to the kitchenette. There she stood perfectly still, staring at the chipped tiles behind the two-ring gas-stove. Her father was not on the school board of governors, but he knew several men who were.

And all the time this shabby little Machiavellian plot was being enacted, she, Maggie, hadn't written. She had been shoving Mrs Dalzell out of her thoughts, not sharing anything with her or reaching out to her. She made the coffee with fumbling hands and carried it on a tin tray into the tiny bed-sitter.

They sat together before the gas-fire, scorching their shins at it and warming their hands on the slippery mugs. At last Maggie said, 'What can I say? I don't know what to say.'

'Don't blame yourself in any way, Margaret. We can't know for certain.'

'I know for certain.'

'You never told me how he took it.'

'He was angry. Very, very angry.'

'Ah well. Perhaps I deserve it at his hands. Perhaps it's only just.'

At last Maggie choked it out. 'I'm so sorry not to have written.'

'Yes, it would have been nice to hear how you were going on. But I know what it's like in those weekly reps – so little free time. Rehearsing one week, playing the next, learning the part for the week to follow –'

Maggie gladly slipped into forward gear. 'And getting costumes together. Honestly, after a few weeks finding clothes is more of a problem than learning lines –'

'And no doubt you took your turn stage-managing?' Maggie nodded eagerly. *This, yes. Let's talk all about this. Please.* 'And tell me, did you paint your own scenery, find your own props?'

'We had a scenic artist, but he got drunk a lot and had a girl in the town. One awful Monday – we were opening that night

46

with a five-hander – we were dress-rehearsing and painting the set all at once. The minute you'd made an exit, you had to throw on an overall, pick up a stencil and paintbrush and paint on a few more fleurs-de-lys ...' Her voice trailed away, although Mrs Dalzell was gazing at her, apparently all attention. There was a dreadful anguish to be sensed behind the polite, interested expression which made it impossible for Maggie to go on. 'What are you going to do?' she asked instead.

The anguish vanished as if a window, accidentally left open, had been firmly shut.

'Me? Oh, I don't know! Yes I do. Of course I shall look for a new job. Because I must teach, you know, the way you must act. There's nothing in our area at home, so I thought I'd try my luck in the south, though I fear they're even more obsessed here with "bits of paper" ... At my age it couldn't be easy in any case ...'

'They did give you a testimonial?'

'They could scarcely refuse that, after all these years. But it was not what you'd call a rave notice.' She took a letter out of her commodious handbag and showed it to Maggie, who read: 'To whom it may concern: Mrs Fiona Dalzell has been a teacher at this school for the past twenty-nine years and has proved herself quite satisfactory.' 'My God,' said Maggie quietly. She had a sudden feeling almost of desperation, part rage and part helplessness. Her hands made a convulsive move, as if to crush the letter, but Mrs Dalzell hastily snatched it back.

'Here, give it to me! It's an unspeakable insult, to be sure, but it's a whole lot better than nothing.' She put it away again, and touched Maggie's shoulder. 'Oh come along now, my dear, cheer up! Things aren't so bad. I've a wee pension, after all, and I have not even started to look for a job yet. Speaking of jobs, do I detect signs that you have another one?' She indicated the half-packed trunk, rising like a table-top mountain from a surf of clothes, wigs, shoes and tissue paper.

'Yes,' said Maggie dully. 'A season in north Devon.'

'At this time of year? Heaven help you.' She got up and peered into the depths of the trunk. And suddenly she began to laugh. 'Good gracious, what on earth is this extraordinary device?'

She dived her arm in and lifted a padded garment fashioned

47

of pyjama flannel, shaped like an open-ended barrel with long tapes like braces looped to it.

'That? It's my middle-aged spread,' said Maggie. 'For when I play large character ladies.'

Mrs Dalzell was briskly shedding her coat, which she had retained against the chill. Now she hung the flannel barrel on herself with the tapes over her shoulders. Next, she dived again into the trunk, emerging with one of Tanya's bequest dresses which she slipped over her enlarged form. Maggie, watched her in astonishment over the back of the sofa, found she couldn't even raise a smile at the abruptly comfortable, matronly figure.

'Did you make this yourself?' asked Mrs Dalzell, parading in front of the long mirror. 'Well done! I'm delighted you're not too vain to spoil your looks in the interests of realism.'

'I love playing character. Give me a good landlady with curlers, a big bust, carpet slippers and falling-down lisle stockings –'

Suddenly Mrs Dalzell interrupted. 'Do you know what? I think we should celebrate your new job. Something modest but fun. A meal out! What do you say?'

'I'd love to! But –'

'It's settled, then. I'm staying at my cousins', of course, so you can phone me there. I shall be out job-hunting during the day but home most evenings. Make it soon. I must go.'

At the door she turned and gave Maggie's shoulders a little shake, as if to shake away the sad thoughts she had visited on her. She smiled into her eyes as if nothing on earth were amiss.

'Dress up nicely,' she said. 'Remember! An actress is never off duty.'

But when it came to it, Maggie discovered that she did not want to be alone with Mrs Dalzell for this essentially private celebration. It was not that she feared Mrs D would bring up the matter of her victimisation at the stealthy and vengeful hands of Mr Robertson, or do anything else to remind Maggie of the deplorable straits into which her life had fallen on Maggie's account. It was simply that the proximity of her old teacher made her deeply unhappy and uncomfortable, just when she wanted to be otherwise. So without consulting Mrs D, she invited Tanya to go with them.

48

The venue was Lyons' Corner House in Coventry Street, where the three of them had some very thin steak and very thin chips washed down with a glass of red wine (also on the thin side) for five shillings a head including a roll and butter.

The two girls talked without cease, and often simultaneously. Mrs Dalzell did not appear to mind. She was not depressingly silent; her eyes moved interestedly from one eager young face to the other, and she ate with a good appetite.

Afterwards they all strolled along to Leicester Square, still talking shop. They stopped outside the lighted window of Frizell's Theatrical Chemist and yearned over the displays of greasepaint like children outside a toy-shop.

'I wonder which numbers one'd use for a ghost,' mused Maggie. 'Probably not sticks at all,' said Tanya. 'You'll have to do your hands and arms, and part of your chest if you wear a low dress. They could probably make up a special wet-white.'

'What about your hair?' asked Mrs Dalzell.

'Well, I won't be given a wig, our company is too hard up even to hire a moustache.'

'You might make one yourself from cotton wool,' Mrs Dalzell suggested.

Maggie and Tanya shrieked.

'Cotton wool! It's not the black-and-white minstrels!'

'Or amateur night on the pier – not quite!'

Mrs Dalzell looked abashed. Maggie had never seen her look abashed before. The expression sat strangely on her face, which had always radiated an undefeatable confidence. In fact, in the lunar glow of the neon, she seemed altogether to have shrunk in some odd way. Maggie, who had been too full of herself all evening to pay Mrs Dalzell much attention, suddenly felt a belated pang of something more than sympathy – a sort of protectiveness.

'Of course I haven't forgotten the marvellous effect you got with cotton wool wigs in your production of *The Relapse* at school – ' she began. But Tanya, owing nothing to Mrs Dalzell, was not listening.

'The best thing would probably be to set your own hair smoothly and then smear Meltonian White shoe-cleaner all over it.'

'Shoe-white on my *hair*! It might make it all fall out –'

49

'You would do your bow at the end, and – plonk into the floats –'

The two girls laughed hilariously, and Mrs Dalzell joined in. Then they oought ice-cream in the Square and strolled around 'theatre mile' licking their cones and looking longingly at front-of-house displays. Maggie had an urge to put her arm through Mrs Dalzell's but she felt embarrassed about what might seem an unwarranted familiarity, so she put it through Tanya's instead.

They parted, two and one, at Leicester Square tube.

Afterwards, Maggie tried obsessively to remember exactly how they had said goodbye, but she couldn't. Something quite commonplace about how much fun it had been (had Mrs Dalzell said that, or was it herself or Tanya?) and that they must keep in touch. One thing Maggie was absolutely sure of later was that during the whole course of the evening she had not once asked Mrs Dalzell anything about her own quest for a job, nor made any real effort to draw her into the conversation. And at the end, they parted on a high, shrieky, theatrical note – a superficial, silly note, a note of self-absorbed and impervious youngness.

Chapter Six

Maggie set off for Devon shortly afterwards. She had meant to 'phone Mrs Dalzell before she left, to say goodbye, but she kept getting side-tracked. She did fully intend to write to her and sent off, quite soon after her arrival, a postcard showing Ilfracombe beach on the sort of sun-soaked day that evidently does come once a year, even to that storm-ridden coast, for the special benefit of postcard photographers – the scene certainly bore little resemblance to the rain- and wind-swept vista that met Maggie's eyes every morning when she donned pac-a-mac and gum-boots to trudge from her digs to the little seaside theatre.

Precious few were making that pilgrimage, aside from the actors; in fact, the inhabitants of the town appeared to have gone to ground for the winter, except for a few hardy shop-keepers and fishermen. Most of the rest were over seventy anyway, to judge by the audiences. On week-nights these consisted of a handful of faithful old ladies, several in wheel-chairs; they sat under their rugs, often clutching hot-water bottles, with their felt hats jammed well down over their neat white perms. Their enthusiastic hand-claps as the curtain fell could be individually distinguished. At weekends the numbers were marginally more encouraging. One Saturday in early November, when the company was playing a new play called *The Young in Heart* which had a strong sentimental appeal, one of the young managers rushed round the dressing-rooms with the incredible news that there were forty-five people out front, four of them clearly under thirty.

Added to the small houses and the dismal weather were their confined and introverted 'private' lives in a small, cramped lodging house. This was being kept open specially for them by a landlady more accustomed to summer visitors, who behaved

51

as if the actors had to be beadily watched for outbreaks of depravity. All this told sorely on their nerves. Quarrels and bitching became endemic; but it was not till December, when Dudley, one of the managers, imported his girl-friend to play leads, that the real trouble started.

Until then, the good parts had been shared round, as at Tenby. (Ah! Lovely sunny theatre-minded tourist-filled Tenby, just across the whitecapped grey estuary! Maggie thought back to it as to paradise lost.) But now the other three women in the company were relegated to secondary roles, and lost no time in making clear their resentment. Maggie was that bit more vociferous on the subject than others, earning herself an unenviable appointment as spokesman. This was to prove her undoing.

Knock, knock on the door of the small room backstage used by the two managers as an office-cum-dressing room. Scuffle. Thump.

'Come in? Oh. Hello, Maggie, it's you.'

'Sorry if I interrupted anything.'

'No, no. Just hearing Avril her lines, wasn't I, love?'

Avril was sprawled in unblushing disarray on what the disgruntled ladies of the company had taken to calling the already-cast-couch, though it was actually an antediluvian ottoman with its padding hanging out. Avril had quite a bit hanging out too.

'What can I do for you?' asked Dudley.

'May I talk to you alone?'

'No secrets from Avril, have I, love?'

'No,' said Avril firmly.

'Well!' began Maggie, unconsciously adopting Mrs Dalzell's opener and tone. 'I was invited to join this company on the basis of fair shares for all. Now Avril's getting all the plums. And the rest of us are fed up.'

The young man's face, alight a moment before with vacuous postcoital benignity, froze into fixed lines of dismay. Avril sat up, put her feet on the floor and drew her dressing-gown around her as if preparing to ward off a physical attack.

'Who's fed up?'

'All of us. The whole company's upset about it. Even the men don't like seeing one person playing leads week after week whether she's suitable for the parts or not.'

52

Avril rose slowly and menacingly and fixed her eyes on her champion, whose jaw had just dropped.

After one or two audible swallows he said, 'Who says she's not suitable? Do you imagine you could have played her part this week better than she does?'

'Oh no. She's type-cast in bitchy roles,' said Maggie, finding she got a delightful frisson from Avril's gasp of fury. 'But,' she went on, in top gear now, 'she made a dog's dinner of "Marion" the week before. She's hopeless at older women. You only gave it to her because it's the best part in the play. She wouldn't even grey up for it, for fear someone might think she's really forty.'

Avril closed in and grasped her lover's shoulder in a convulsion of rage. This seemed to impart some gumption because he sprang belatedly to his feet.

'How dare you talk about her like that!'

'How dare you let your sex-life mess up the company!'

Flummoxed, Dudley glanced for inspiration at Avril, who jerked her head sharply at the door.

'Er – yes. You'd better go,' he said rather unconvincingly.

'Go? What's that supposed to mean?' asked Maggie.

Avril smiled her pussy-cat smile at Maggie and purred, 'It means, permanently.'

There was a stunned silence. Maggie hadn't bargained for that. Neither, probably, had Dudley, who looked aghast.

'Are you firing me?' she asked finally.

Avril nodded pleasantly. 'From Saturday. We'll pay your fare back to London, won't we, love? Oh,' she added as Maggie stood motionless, 'and thank you for your criticism about greying up. It may interest you to know that I've run out of silver dust. Besides, lots of women of forty aren't grey at all.'

Maggie, feeling the numbness of shock already wearing off, turned at bay. 'She'd murdered her husband with a panga knife and been ten years in a Malayan prison,' she snarled. 'If you don't think she'd be grey after that you're stupid as well as vain. And who needs silver dust? *I* use talc!'

And she made a splendid exit. But all the bravado collapsed two minutes later. Going on that night to an audience of eleven and chirruping through her part, which was a foil to Avril's, took all the professionalism she had so far managed to acquire. The support of the rest of the company, though needless to say

53

it didn't run to mass walk-outs or anything of that sort, did something to help her through the rest of the week. But there was nothing and nobody to help her pack her things and get on the train on Sunday morning, and she cried a good part of the way back to London.

Who could she turn to, when she got there, to support her through her first professional crisis? Not her mother, unexpectedly supportive though she had been about her career. Not Stip. Tanya was in rep in Sheffield – a real rep, Maggie reflected bitterly, not just a doomed winter migration without roots or traditions or funding or audiences. She herself should have done as Tanya had: wait, instead of grabbing the first thing that offered, for something sound, something which could further her career. The more she thought about what she was leaving, the more appalled she felt at its seediness, its lack of any real professional foundation. She was ashamed, now, of having been part of it, but that didn't make her less ashamed of having been summarily kicked out of it.

There was only one person she could think of who might be able to comfort her – only one person, as her train drew into Paddington, whom she wanted to see.

There was no reply from the familiar number in Bloomsbury. After a short debate with herself, she bought a Mars bar – the most filling thing on earth for the money – and then took a bus. The sound of the phone ringing and ringing had made her feel even more desolate. She would go round there. She had nowhere else to go, anyway – the doss-house in Goldhawk Road had been sublet for the winter and she had to have a room. She even, as the bus swished through the slushy remains of a hail-storm, began to feel quite nostalgic about her dim little room at the M'Crimmonds' with its metered gas-fire to which she had returned night after night from RADA.

As she walked round Russell Square, feeling the cold cutting into her bones, Mrs Dalzell's cheerful, dynamic image marched beside her along the icy street. Maggie's chagrined spirits lifted. It wouldn't be bad, staying in that house if Mrs Dalzell was there. They could eat together and have lots of good talks. Maggie would unload her tale of injustice bravely opposed. Reviewing for the twentieth time her scene with Avril, Maggie began to relish in anticipation the prospect of re-enacting it; Mrs D was always a perfect audience for a good meaty anecdote.

54

Maggie mounted the steps and rang the bell. It echoed through the house. For a few moments it seemed there was no one at home. But the M'Crimmonds on their rare excursions were always back in time for tea, and soon she heard steps. The door opened, and there was Miss Brenda, the smaller and frailer of the twins.

'Hallo, Miss Brenda! It's me, Margaret.' (She had weak sight, Maggie recalled.)

The pinched face broke into a wan smile. 'Och, hallo, dear! Fancy seeing you. Come along in, you look half frozen.'

Maggie stepped into the gloomy hall. Nothing had changed. Even the Jack Russell, which for three years to her certain knowledge had been on the verge of a natural demise, was waddling down the dark corridor to greet her, snuffling asthmatically and giving off his smell of bad teeth. Maggie bent to give his rough side a pat, surprised to find she was glad to see him, glad of the feeling of continuity. She would have been glad to see a decaying stuffed pike if it had looked pleased to see her.

'And how have you been?' Miss Brenda was asking. 'You'll take tea with us? Sister's just brewing.'

'Thank you, but what I really came for was to see your cousin. Is she in?'

Miss Brenda peered short-sightedly at her. 'Cousin? You don't mean Fiona? Surely you've heard – !'

Crouched beside the dog, Maggie's hand paused on his side. She looked up as one might at a Damoclean sword.

'She's passed over this two months or more.'

Maggie stood up slowly. The sword was on its way down.

'It happened at the beginning of November. We're only just getting over it. Why, look at you! You'd better come through and sit a wee, you look very pealy-wally!'

Pealy-wally indeed. And more so when she heard what had happened. Mrs Dalzell, it seemed, had spent September and October trying to get work. She had written many letters and gone to a number of interviews in and out of London, but none of them came to anything. And she became, in Miss Brenda's words, 'very quiet – very put-down.' And then one day she didn't come home, and that night a policeman came to the door and told the sisters that their cousin had been run over and had died on the way to hospital.

Maggie had had quite enough by then and would have been

55

glad to be spared further details, but by this time Miss Roberta, the more voluble sister, had brought tea in, and took up the tale.

'At the inquest, the driver of the lorry said she was standing at the curb, looking straight at him, so he never thought to slow down. And just as he reached her, she stepped out in front of him . . . Sister and I understood then that she'd done it deliberately, though the coroner passed it off as accidental death. We were very, very distressed, as you may imagine. Ending her life in that way – it was not like her, not like her at all, not as we used to know her when we were girls. She was never one to give in, was she, Brenda? But we all have our moments of weakness, the strongest of us perhaps more than the rest, for those are the ones not used to defeat, who may not know how to manage it.'

Maggie turned her face into the worn plush wing of the chair and wept bitter tears. They were not only for Mrs Dalzell and her lonely, forlorn and desperately courageous end, but for herself. For if Fiona Dalzell, who stole library books and defied governors and risked perdition to set Maggie's life on its course, could throw herself under a lorry's wheels after a mere two months out of work, then who was safe from the ultimate exigencies of despair?

Besides, Maggie could not keep Margaret quiet about that one sun-sodden postcard with its scribbled message:

'No houses – ghastly weather – landlady's a witch – but I'm happy.'

Chapter Seven

There followed one of the most traumatic periods of Maggie's life – nine months of living alone in London, out of work and steeped in guilt and sorrow.

At first, she tried to regard it (Margaret's idea, of course) as a punishment, so deserved as to be almost desired, for her part in Mrs Dalzell's suicide. Now she was sharing her ordeal: the cup of idleness and unwantedness was passed on to her to drink, if not to the dregs – at the worst Maggie could not conceive of not wanting to live – at least deeply enough to expiate her sin of selfishness and letterlessness. Part of the punishment, and not the least part, was the fact that a lot of the offices that her job-hunting obliged her to visit regularly were in or around Leicester Square. She could never go there without physical pangs.

Altogether apart from that aspect, being out of work proved to be one of the side-chambers of purgatory. To begin with, she was constantly aware that within her lived some imprisoned entity, as real and tangible as a baby in the womb, struggling to get out. This she could not call her talent, because as long as she wasn't acting (and the longer, the more so) she couldn't be sure that she had any. The only thing she could be certain of was that the *desire* to act was there, all the time, every waking moment, no matter whether she was lying in bed late because she lacked a motive to get up to another day of defeats and disappointments, or whether she was active, marching in and out of agents' offices, or writing to managements, or hanging around the Salisbury or the Buckstone Club or the snackbar at the Arts, hoping for the rumour of a rumour of casting, or just bemoaning her lot with fellow-sufferers. Or, indeed, doing what she knew she ought to be doing in order (as Mrs Dalzell had used to say) to 'deserve success', not to mention keep sane:

57

learning parts, practising vocal and physical exercises, doing trial make-ups or sitting in the theatre, watching others in the throes of that joy of joys which was denied to her.

This last was a refinement of torment. Occasionally Maggie had to sit and watch one of her former classmates playing a part she believed she could have played better. However, this was rare, since on the London stage at that period sub-standard performances were few. More often the acting was so good that Maggie was humbled, dismayed. How, she would muse, dared she aspire to this shrine of professional perfection? The answer was, she didn't, not yet. She craved only the equivalent of what she had had in Tenby, in Ilfracombe. The shortcomings of these companies became blurred in memory as the months passed; she remembered only the essence, which was that the struggler-within had been free. Sitting in the gods, Friday after Friday as winter budded into spring and spring opened into summer, she suffered a raw and bitter envy, which had nevertheless at its core a fiery molten kernel of pure bliss. Because after all, if she couldn't enjoy theatre, even from the wrong side of the footlights, even sunk in general misery, then what was all her suffering about?

Idleness became the very quintessence of her existence. After the first sustained and hopeful burst of job-hunting had spent itself, it took more and more willpower, greater and greater expenditures of energy, to overcome the inertia which was seizing hold of her, in order to do anything at all.

If such a procedure did not sicken any normally vital and life-affirming personality, then the most attractive course would have been to lie in bed all day in the dark, getting up only to eat, answer the phone and go to the lavatory. Maggie tried that, once or twice at her nadir. But it proved self-defeating. An idle mind breeds dreams – taunting dreams of letters or phone calls bringing good news, which she well knew would transform her instantly from this flaccid, hopeless, tousled wreck into a being alive with purpose, excitement and confidence.

Like anyone in pain, she sought alleviations and distractions. But what is there, she asked herself, if there isn't *that*? Friendships? An ambivalent comfort at best. People outside the business have no inkling of what one is feeling; those inside are either in work and thus intolerable to be with, or, like oneself, insects struggling in the mud, reflecting back an image

58

of worklessness which one dreads to look at. In all their varied moods of depression or anger, or even hope, they are faithful mirrors of one's own conditions.

Diversions of the sort people are supposed to resort to in bad times – drink, sex, books – counted for nothing. Maggie resorted to none except, occasionally and futilely, the last, because she knew she must emerge from any surrogate occupation into the same barren, pointless aridity: the unstructured days, the shapeless evenings, the dreaded mornings when there was nothing for it but to discipline herself to get dressed (and dressed properly – 'An actress is never off duty') to face, yet again, those outer offices ... 'Keep in touch dear, something may come in ...' Those words came to seem so cruel. Maggie found herself almost hoping that some power-wielder, some day, would drop the pacifying smile, turn on her and snarl: 'For you, ducky? Nothing, not today or ever. Forget it. Get lost. Drop dead.'

But even idleness was not the worst.

The worst was fear, fear that it would never end. She knew there was no reason why it ever should. She would sit alone in the evenings, with only five bars of the gas-fire lit to save pennies, and brood upon the ultimate horror that lay at the end of the tunnel if no phone call or letter ever came. The horror of having to give up, leave the business – emerge from the rich, warm world of theatre, her only natural element as she then profoundly believed, into a grey, formless vacuum.

'Keep at it!' Mrs Dalzell had once written. 'Keep acting. Act into your mirror, act in your bath, act in your sleep.' But she should have known better. What would she have felt if Maggie had turned round, last September, and said, 'Teach in your bath, teach into your mirror?' Can one teach without an audience? Perhaps, but only in the same way that one can rehearse, and on the same condition – that tomorrow, others will be there to see.

Maggie was so deeply miserable as the months dragged on that only the sheer necessities of life kept her going. She learned now (and this hooked the tapeworm of bitterness deeper into her gut) that her father had been right. She was not independent except when she was happy and fulfilled. Frustrated, lonely and

59

hopeless, she longed for home, for the undemanding safety and comfort of it, for her mother and brother at least, and the gentle easily-fulfilled regime she had so staunchly marched away from. A dozen times she nearly capitulated. Had the scene in her parents' bedroom been open to the slightest reinterpretation, had it left even a narrow crack through which she could have crawled back without her own wilful rebel pride blocking her way, she would have found herself on the train to Edinburgh without knowing how she got there. Only the most rigorous and conscious restraint prevented it from happening, the more so since her mother and Stip in their letters eroded her determination by begging and imploring her to give up and come home. Ironically it was her father, his past words and his present austere silence, which kept her in London and on the battlefront.

Miss Brenda and Miss Roberta were kind to her in their buttoned-up, respectable way. They let her pay for her room and board partly in kind, by helping with the housework or taking the dog for walks when their rheumatism kept them at home. For the rest, she did what others did: late-night dishwashing and waitressing, manning a stand at the Ideal Home Exhibition in March, baby-sitting – anything that paid and yet allowed time during office hours for job hunting.

And then, during the summer holidays, a friend who worked at the Players' Theatre – not on stage but at the sandwich bar – arranged for Maggie to stand in for her while she went on holiday.

That was almost fun. The show, *Late Joys*, was delightful, the customers were characters, the 'artistes' friendly and sympathetic. She was allowed a free drink and a sandwich in the evenings and was usually stood a few more. After the show it was her additional duty to put records on the panatrope for dancing, and sometimes men asked her to dance, though she hadn't much heart for it. But it passed the evening and earned her a bob or two.

The mere proximity of a stage had an invigorating effect, and from time to time she felt almost happy in the purlieus of the theatre itself. She would cheer herself on the long walk home to Bloomsbury by singing the songs from the current show. It was quite safe, in the early fifties, to walk the night streets of the West End alone. Occasionally a man would approach her,

60

but, seeing his mistake, would usually say 'sorry dear'. 'That's all right,' she would say, and walk on singing softly: 'Oh, father, dear father, come home to us now, for the clock in the steeple strikes one – BOING!'

The walk home was, of course, to save the fare. All these odd bits of employment barely served to feed and clothe her. Apart from half-a-crown for her seat in the gods once a week there were no luxuries whatever. And nothing put aside for the repayment fund.

As September put the first nip into the air, Maggie wincingly turned to face the unfaceable – the long winter, alone, without work, with the bogey-man of ultimate defeat leering down the tunnel at her from what looked to be none too great a distance. But the influx of friends back into town after summer seasons brought distractions which mingled pleasure with pain. London seemed a ferment of actors urgently striving to place themselves for the winter season, and Maggie was revitalised by their hope, which she was free to share – having not had a job in the summer did not necessarily put her behind those who had, in the race to get a job for the winter.

Pantomimes were being cast, and tours. Gossip reported and speculated on forthcoming films, reps new and old, and West End productions in prospect. Surely, thought Maggie, she would get something now – there seemed to be no end of work in the offing. She almost ran from office to office. She wrote new letters, sent out new photos, to practically every management, agency and casting office in Britain. To pay for the photos she had to borrow money, and at this critical moment Tanya reappeared.

Tanya had kept in touch with Maggie, undismayed by her gloomy or non-existent replies. She had thrived at Sheffield and risen to playing second leads; not for her the job queues and the angst, for she was merely enjoying her first 'play-out' break for months, before returning for the winter season of lovely plays and two-week rehearsal periods. She was also in funds, and cheerfully lent money to Maggie for her photos. Maggie repaid her by asking the M'Crimmonds if her friend could share her room for a couple of weeks.

The twins conferred, then consented. 'As long as she's a dog-lover,' they said. 'Oh, she is!' lied Maggie earnestly. Tanya had acquired an almost pathological hatred of dogs, big dogs

61

anyway, in the camp, which had been patrolled by Alsatians. But the Jack Russell could by now scarcely move off his cushion, let alone patrol anything, even the railings outside – he had to be tenderly carried to a lamp-post – so Maggie felt the lie was justified.

Tanya arrived one rainy afternoon and stood on the threshold of Maggie's room, looking round in some dismay.

'God, Maggie! How do you stand the gloom?'

'I'm used to it.'

'Couldn't you jazz it up a bit with a coat of paint or some flowers?'

'You're kidding. I can't afford a bunch of dandelions. No, now Tanya, come back – !'

But Tanya had rushed out of the house, returning ten minutes later with two huge bunches of yellow and white pom-pom chrysanthemums, one for the M'Crimmonds, who fell about with excitement so that Maggie cursed her parsimonious Scots self for never having thought of it, and one for their now shared bedroom. The big glowing blooms were startlingly effective, seeming almost to shed their own light.

'You shouldn't!' said Maggie, nonetheless. 'You can't afford –'

'There is for everyone something that they can always afford, until they are actually starving. With you it's theatre seats. With me it's flowers.'

'You mean, if you only had half-a-crown, you'd buy flowers with it and not a seat in the gods?'

'Depends what was on,' Tanya temporised. 'What *is* on? We must see things together. I'll pay,' she said quickly, 'look what I'm saving on somewhere to live.'

Maggie's heart lifted at the thought of extra playgoing. 'Well, there's a good production of *The Merchant*,' she began – and at once, as if the title had flicked a switch, they were back at RADA.

'Remember Dickie – ? How he clowned around as Gratiano and corpsed us all? And how mad Hugh Miller got?'

"Typical transatlantic lack of reverence!" thundered Tanya, in imitation of the professional producer of their student production.

Maggie, with an American accent, proclaimed: "In future, I will fear no other thing, so *safe* as keeping *sore* Nerissa's 'ring'!"

62

"Richard, if you cannot take Shakespeare with a little more seriousness, I shall fling you out of the cast!"

"Aw, please, Mr Miller, sir, don't do it, sir! It would be too *humillerating*!—

They collapsed on the pink chenille, muzzling their shrieks with their hands.

'And what about that mad Greek who did *Antigone* with us?' Maggie spluttered. 'Remember?'

Tanya abruptly stopped laughing and looked at her. 'Yes, indeed.'

'Wasted half our rehearsal time forcing us to relive our most traumatic emotional experiences.'

'And got more and more exasperated because no one had had any.'

'Except you.'

'And Dickie sent him up rotten by pretending to break down and sob about his mother taking his rocking-horse away when he was four.'

'He fell for it, too. No sense of humour, these Greeks. You know, you could have had a chunk of Antigone if you'd wanted it.'

'I wanted it,' said Tanya.

'If you'd told him about the camp, and your parents –'

'That would have earned me the whole part,' Tanya said. She stood up, heaved her case on to the bed to begin unpacking.

'So why didn't you tell? Couldn't you bear to?'

'I'll tell you why. Because his motive in asking us to spill our guts for him was false. He didn't do it to find out if we had the emotional depth to handle Greek tragedy. He did it to confirm his prejudice against the British. The fact that seventeen-year-olds in post-war England hadn't usually had many traumas was proof to him that you were all repressed and shallow and emotionally retarded –'

'Which we were –'

'Don't talk nonsense,' said Tanya with sudden sharpness. 'If you had ever seen traumatised adolescents, crippled by emotions experienced far too early in their lives, you would realise that your state was normal and desirable and only what every right-thinking mature person would want to see. That little black satyr wasn't really exasperated as you all stammered out your tales of Mummy getting cross because you wouldn't eat

63

powdered egg or your little trials as evacuees or whatever. He was revelling in his smug convictions of Levantine superiority. Didn't you notice how he mocked, all through the rehearsals, saying outright that us girls were all sexually repressed and the boys were "not men", whatever he meant by that? I suppose he meant they didn't measure their manhood by the number of young girls they had seduced, like him –'

'I remember he made us all play a kissing game at a party, and French-kissed us all –'

Tanya snorted. 'Greek-kissed more like, dirty little man!'

'You do have it in for him,' remarked Maggie, her curiosity, like her sense of humour, stirring from its long torpor. 'What's the difference?' she added. Her own sexual experience, despite a few rep flirtations, hadn't effectively advanced since she had been startled by the strange sensation of the saturnine little Greek's tongue piercing her prim, purse-lipped defences.

'Greek kissing includes what you used to call organ-grinding.'

Maggie burst into a shriek of laughter. She had once unwarily remarked that one of the boys at a party (he was Icelandic, and very heavy-breathing around women) danced like an organ-grinder, meaning that he whirled her arm like a handle. Of course she never lived it down.

'Maggie, are you still a virgin?' asked Tanya suddenly.

'Yes,' she replied, with none of the ambivalent feelings a twenty-two-year-old might have now about such an admission. 'Why?'

'*Why?* Because I – aren't you?'

Tanya gave her an amused, wry look. 'No. Not by a good bit.'

'Oh!'

'Are you shocked?'

'Of course not. Just interested. Who was it?'

'Who were they, do you mean?'

'Crumbs. How many?'

'Three.'

'Goodness.'

'Does that seem a lot to you? I'm twenty-six.'

'When did you – you know –'

'Start? When I was sixteen.'

'In that camp?'

'No. It was before the war, when I was a student in France.

64

God, no, not in the camp! Those English women, my fellow-inmates that the Germans put in charge of us, watched us young ones like hawks. They were far worse than the guards, who, poor devils, were only interested in keeping their heads down in case their superiors sent them to the Russian front. They were as keen on staying put as we were. It was those WVS types who bossed us around unmercifully and weren't above telling on us to the Germans if we showed the slightest signs of getting out of hand ... Running around with the male inmates would practically have got us shot. No. I lived a life of active celibacy for four years in that place, and after having had a lover already, I am telling you, it wasn't so easy. You hang on to your virtue, Maggie, as long as you can.'

'Go on about you. Your Frenchman was one. Who were the other two?'

Tanya was silent for a long time, putting her things into drawers, and finally she said in rather a casual tone, 'I have a very sweet fellow in Sheffield now.'

'An actor?'

'No. He's a lecturer at the University. He is divine. But alas, married.'

'Oh, Tanya.'

'Yes, you are right, it is "Oh Tanya". But what can I do? I love him, she said simply,' she said, not simply at all.

'Really love him?'

'Yes. His name is Joel. Isn't that a beautiful, unusual name? And he is a beautiful person, just to be touched by him dissolves all the rest of the world.' Maggie stared at her, startled and envious. Tanya gave her a quick, wry look, and added prosaically, 'There is no future in it so don't tell anyone.'

'But you've missed somebody out. Who was the second one?'

Tanya started to chuckle. 'Can't you guess? Damned little opportunist! He saw I was starving for it so he gave me a Greek kiss, all the way down.'

Maggie gaped at her. 'Heavens! I never *dreamt* – you really were ahead of us!'

Tanya sat down on the bed and looked affectionately at Maggie. 'Maggie, don't take this as a criticism, but you know you are very naive. I was not the only one. The girls in our class were going down before his classical Greek sex-appeal, and his taunts, like victims of some epidemic.' Maggie was

65

silent. Now she was shocked, shocked and confused, and somehow, obscurely, belittled. Not that anything would have persuaded her to sleep with the little Greek director – she could imagine nothing more horrid – but that she should have been so childish, so unworldly as not to be in on what was going on ... To what extent was she even now a victim of her parents' constricting upbringing, being shut off from what everyone else could see, comprehend and accept? She remembered how, in both the Tenby and the Ilfracombe companies, she had been the butt of jibes and teasing because she was, as Tanya said, so unsophisticated that often she would fail to grasp innuendo or would come out with something (like the organ-grinder business) apparently quite extraordinary in its naivety. She felt now, not so much that Tanya was 'ahead' of her, as that she was somehow left behind, held back by powerful strings still attached at their farther ends to the house in Penicuik.

'Do you think there's something wrong with me?' she asked.

'Wrong with you? What do you mean?'

'Being a virgin, and – and naive, and all that.'

Tanya lit a cigarette, and blew out smoke. 'Life is long, Maggie. Feelings are what count. You are only wasting yourself, and wasting time, if you are not *feeling* anything. It is not always pleasant or improving to have a lover, still less to understand every smutty joke you hear. There's a right time for everything. Your time hasn't come yet, and that's all.'

That evening Maggie took Tanya with her to the Players. Tanya bought herself a seat and sat through the show with a glass of beer at her elbow, helping Maggie to serve sandwiches in the intermission. And when the compère announced at the end that the audience might stay, and dance, and eat, and drink till midnight and very welcome too, Tanya sat with her by the panotrope and chose records and they talked on and on.

Maggie confided in Tanya her worst fear.

'What if I never get work again?'

'You will.'

'How can you know?'

'It's a matter of holding out. Think of our class at RADA. Five have dropped out already – got married, gone abroad, got

66

other jobs – and more and more of them will. If you can hold out, and keep trying, you are bound to get work eventually.'

Maggie well realised the total fallaciousness of this, but Tanya said it with such assurance that she allowed herself to imbibe from it a little hope, however false.

'It's terrible, though – waiting.'

'Yes. Waiting is always terrible. To wait hopelessly is worse than never arriving.'

'*Clever* –'

'There's a chap there noticing you.'

'Where?'

'On the stage.'

Maggie looked up from the records she was sorting. Among the few dancers was a tall, good-looking, red-haired man, staring at her over his partner's shoulder. When she met his eyes he smiled straight at her and she gave him a rather muted smile back.

'Choose the next record for yourself, because he will ask you to dance,' Tanya advised. 'After that he will offer you a drink, and eventually he will take you home in a quite nice car, probably a Rover. Or a Vauxhall. Such fellows always drive one or the other. So now I'll go home while there is still a tube, because I make a poor third man. Look what happened to him in the film.'

'Don't be silly –'

But Tanya, as usual, was not being silly, because what she predicted came about, except that the quite nice car was a beat-up Morris Oxford. However, on the way to Bloomsbury the red-headed young man announced that he was planning to buy himself a new car, probably a Vauxhall Velox.

Chapter Eight

When Maggie first met Bruce Macrae, he was twenty-three, a big, booming, handsome, over-confident, going-places young Scot preparing to be a city oil-slicker. His red hair was brushed into a quiff in front and darkened with Brylcream (which, despite a superficial belief to the contrary, was by no means exclusively a working-class emollient). Six feet of height, broad shoulders, good clothes and large allowance from his father. He made an excellent impression, and no bells rang.

In any case Maggie was ripe for the picking. She had only just begun to realise, partly through Tanya and partly through inner stirrings which were no less strong for having been so long suppressed, that she had been starved all her life of something essential to her – the kind of affection which shows itself in ways all but unknown in her family. Except, perhaps, Stip . . .

Once, just once, Stip had come down to see her during that miserable out-of-work period. He had sat in the M'Crimmonds' front parlour, brooding into the fire, his knobbly boy's hand toying with the ears of the Jack Russell. They had run out of conversation alarmingly quickly and were just sitting there, balancing their teacups, testing the distance that was growing up between them. And suddenly Maggie couldn't bear it. She put her cup on the floor, jumped up and ran to hug and kiss him. And although he had looked amazed, he was not abashed.

'That's grand,' he said, 'like in "Jenny Kiss'd Me". No, now don't go running off again, sit beside me.' And he'd caught hold of her and made her sit on the arm of his chair and had actually let her fiddle with his hair and tease him, and then they had really begun to talk. Their renewed, now adult, physical closeness made it possible.

It was nevertheless a painful conversation because it became clear at once that Stip had given up his dream of becoming a writer and knuckled under, but one thing that soothed the pain was that Maggie found she loved him just the same and didn't judge him as she might have done once; she knew that whatever happened he would never be like conformist, priggish Ian, but would always be Stip, her darling brother.

At the station they had hugged and kissed again, and as the train was pulling out Stip had suddenly begun to whistle, 'Oh what a beautiful morning'. It was then, watching with stone-dry eyes and sinking heart the withdrawal of the train carrying Stip back to his self-chosen sentence in the family paper-mill, that Maggie fully accepted that *any* emotion, even piercing sorrow and loss, is healthier than banked-down feelings, and that this tangible love she felt for Stip with all its pain of empathy was just a token of what she would one day feel for a lover.

It was from then on that she began to be aware of the starvation symptoms. A desire to touch even people she hardly knew – to ruffle heads passed finding a seat in the cinema, to rub the backs of necks in buses, to take the arms of strangers crossing the street, to hold out a hand to people coming through doors – and to kiss everybody. Everybody. At meeting, at parting, and in between. Of course she knew she mustn't, and she didn't, but she longed to, and worried about her longing. So it was not surprising that she fell into the arms of the first attractive warm-blooded man who made a serious pass.

He made it on the night they went out to celebrate the fact that her long exile from happiness was over. She had a job.

Of course no one really wants to understudy, but after nine months out of work, who refuses? A beautiful theatre in the heart of the West End, steeped in tradition, a lovely play spangled with august names, and a very good little part, should she ever get to play it. And it was work, paid work! The stalled career-train was off its dismal siding and back on the main track, getting up steam ... The bogey-man and his tunnel had vanished as if they had never been. She was euphoric, feet clear off the ground, and Bruce was just the boy to spot her vulnerable state and turn it to his advantage.

He laid on a glamorous evening with all the trimmings: soft lights, sweet music, good food. Dancing. Waiters wafting. Fingers touching in the candlelight. Elaborate eye-play. Sweet words and sweeter silences. And quite a lot to drink.

69

Then home in a taxi afterwards.

A taxi, to Maggie, was, and still is, a highly erotic vehicle. Isolated in a little glass house, sealed off from a driver who knew how to keep his eyes on the road, they glided through the lamp-lit night (proper, pale gold lamps – none of your sulphurous horrors that reduce skin tones and your favourite dress to the colour of a dead toad's underbelly). The motion was in itself arousing, but even more so was the sensation that she was neither here nor there, but part of some sensual continuum which no one, from here or from there, had any jurisdiction over nor right to expect her to resist.

As Maggie sat, bolt upright, her hands tense in her lap and her whole body simmering with awareness of Bruce beside her, she felt stirrings, interior volcanic seethings and swellings, like slow-bursting lava bubbles. And when he took her hand and kissed the back of it, then kissed it again on the palm, and then touched the hard trembling point of his tongue between each pair of fingers, her long-banked-down sensuality erupted in rapids of fire.

When they arrived at the M'Crimmonds' he handed her out of the taxi, not knowing that without his help she could scarcely have moved. Words from a recent novel of what in those days was considered the more explicit kind were raging through her head: *clean, fiery lust*. Could lust be clean? Till now the word had always been inextricably associated with moral squalour.

With buzzy-tipped fingers she unlocked the front door. The M'Crimmond sisters no longer kept their ears open for her solitary return, nor did the dog rouse them with his senile yapping at her step – or even, it now appeared, the step of a male intruder on the stairs. Tanya had long ago returned to Sheffield. There was no one to stand at the doorway of her room brandishing a blazing sword.

As soon as the door had closed behind them, Bruce picked her up manfully and deposited her on the pink chenille, where, having divested himself (as the Players Compère was wont to say) of his upper and outer garments, he shortly joined her. She had never lain on a bed with a man before. That, and some kisses (the Scots kind were much like the Greek, she found, but nicer because she was helping) would have sufficed her for that night; in those days it was received opinion that softly softly catchee the slippery monkey of sexual bliss. But Bruce was born

70

before his time – 'having it off' was his style, long before that expression was thought of.

As long as Bruce proceeded slowly and seemed in control, Maggie, and even Margaret, went along gladly. It was only when his carefully acquired technique lapsed and he began to pull and pant and grapple, that Margaret reasserted herself and began to resist.

It had never occurred to her that anyone of her 'own sort' would not stop when a woman said 'Stop'. She did not know that a man may find it impossible to stop, or find himself so unwilling to that he will call it impossible. Bruce was well roused and rather drunk and he had spent a week's salary on her; he had no intention of stopping. Her increasingly panicky struggles to free herself and regain control of the situation only goaded him on. At the very end, at the point when, had he been a stranger, had the past evening not been as happy and exciting as it was, Maggie would have screamed and scratched, she suddenly went limp and let him have her – not because she any longer wanted him but because some deep female honesty informed her that having come this far, to disgrace or mark him would be a humiliation and a shame on her, worse than submitting. So she submitted.

Afterwards, of course, he was full of remorse – genuine enough, though it showed itself in the form of reproaches.

'You should have told me.'

'You knew.'

'I swear I didn't!'

'Why should you think I wasn't?'

He had no answer for that. They sat in silence. He gave her an occasional under-the-lashes glance to see how she was taking it. He was relieved that she was not crying, but in fact she was well beyond tears, and for the moment quite numb.

At last some feeling trickled through, mainly of anger.

'Why didn't you stop, anyway, when I asked you to?'

'I didn't think you meant it,' he said sullenly. 'Lots of women like to be – well, overpowered. I thought it was a sort of game.'

'You couldn't have thought that,' she said blankly after a long moment.

He stood up and began to pace about. She watched him,

71

trying to recover some of the feelings she had had about him before, to see at least his physical attractiveness, even though, she supposed, she would never like or trust him again. She was looking for justification of what she had allowed to happen – encouraged to happen.

'Well, I'm sorry anyhow,' he burst out at last. 'I am, I'm extremely sorry. And if you think I'll chuck you now or anything like that, you're wrong about me. I want to go on seeing you.'

'How very decent of you!' she said shrilly. 'Is there no limit to your chivalry?' His big handsome face under the tousled hair turned a dull red. She thought he looked horrible – not a civilised young man any longer, but like some uncouth country lout caught tumbling a girl under a hedge. This sudden revulsion from him shocked her almost more than what had happened.

She told him to go away and leave her alone, and he went out looking crushed, but then kept her in a panic for twenty minutes by standing outside her door, beseeching her in a low voice to let him in again, 'just for a minute'... Luckily the M'Crimmond sisters were sound sleepers (and the Jack Russell deaf). By ignoring him she eventually got rid of him, and only then was she free to go to the bathroom and finally crawl into the crumpled, and now suggestive, bed. She was physically sore, mentally disgusted and spiritually profoundly lonely. She wanted someone to comfort her, but she couldn't even imagine who. Stip would be shocked; she could lose his respect. Her mother – ? Never in this world, not about this. Tanya might have been the right person, but she was, at this moment, probably in bed with her adulterous lecturer. In desperation, Maggie let her trapped thoughts throw themselves, as impulses travel from the brain toward a severed limb, against her old leaning-post, Mrs Dalzell.

And now, for the very first time, Maggie found herself living imaginatively through that hideous death. The frank, disarming look into the lorry driver's face as he drove toward her, the mind behind that look giving the impossible order: *Wait till he's almost here, give him no time to stop – poor wee man, he must have nothing to reproach himself with* – then the bold, unhesitating, perfectly timed step off the curb. The ghastly shock, hurling her backwards, the sound as she hit the road. A last coherent

72

thought? God forbid. No last moment of clarity inside the broken body. Maggie, weeping, spared herself that.

But the tears, which seemed to be all for the dead, aided the living. By morning she felt a bit better. The inevitable guilt had started, but she had been prepared for that. Even in the beginning, when Bruce's love-making had seemed 'right', she had not hoped, with her puritan conditioning, to escape guilt-free; but she had meant to fight it by offsetting it against the joy and pleasure of love. Now she felt – what? Defiled? Sullied? Too ridiculously old-fashioned and melodramatic, but it was something like that; so the guilt was far more difficult to fight. Mrs Dalzell had once told her that an unbridled conscience can do as much damage as any of the passions. Maggie, mindful of this, determined to do her best, because she was simply not prepared to have her whole view of love, men and sex ruined by one incident, however upsetting.

Maggie was deep in understudy rehearsals by this time, managing to be almost perfectly happy during her hours at the theatre; this positiveness gradually crept, like a healing tide, over the area of trauma and washed the inflammation out of it to some extent. To advance this healing process, she decided, two weeks after the incident in her bedroom, to spend a Sunday with Tanya in Sheffield.

Tanya met her at the station and, after a typical digs lunch with two amusing fellow members of the company, they went out for a walk in the rain to look at the theatre.

Till then the talk had all been shop, but Tanya's intuition was an acute instrument. As she closed the front door behind her, she instantly said, 'What is up? Or should I say, what has recently been up, and who put it there?'

Even Margaret was constrained to smile at this, and Maggie giggled outright. 'How did you know?'

'You have the look of one who no longer doesn't know what it is all about. Welcome to the club.'

'Thanks very much. If my initiation ceremony was anything to go by, I'd rather be blackballed.'

Tanya gave her an appreciative look. 'You are beginning to be far too articulate and even witty for our profession. That is the sort of line we actors expect to have written for us. So tell.'

Heads well down, arms linked but hands in gabardine pockets, they walked into the wind-driven rain and Maggie told.

73

'So now do you loathe him?'

'I don't know.'

'Could you possibly like him again?'

'I want to. It would make it all seem less awful.'

'So give him another chance.'

Maggie stopped dead, swinging Tanya almost on to her face. 'Another *chance* – !'

'To be the gentleman you obviously want him to be. Let him take the bad taste out of it with a few nice evenings.'

'How do I know they would be nice? Am I supposed to ask for more trouble?'

'It's up to you to keep out of dangerous situations. If he gets sulky about that, you can drop him. He can't rape you in a restaurant or a theatre.'

They walked on. Maggie was silent, approaching this new concept. Had she been raped by Bruce? She remembered the sharpness of the pain, the show of blood on the pink chenille. She remembered the humiliated, soiled feeling. Margaret, left to herself, would have fought this as her mother fought cockroaches – with a scrubbing brush and Jeyes Fluid; but Maggie took a more tolerant view. She recognised that she *had* wanted sex, been ready for it, and although God knows she had had something gentler and more – well, gradual in mind, her main objective now must be to feel better, to get over it. Maybe Tanya's advice, disturbingly worded, was nonetheless sound.

After all, for the past fortnight Bruce had been turning up day after day at the stage door, wanting to take her home, or out to dinner – wanting to make it up, with her and to her. Each time she saw him standing there by the stage doorkeeper's window, something in her felt relieved, if only because his hangdog stance and eager, apologetic expression showed that he, too, knew that something had happened which required therapy. He was ashamed, which meant he was not unprincipled after all, only uncontrolled. She felt inclined to forgive him.

Besides, Tanya advised it. Tanya the wise, the intuitive, the well-versed, advised her to give Bruce another chance. Maggie was not to know that Tanya was herself destined to blunder from mistake to mistake. None of her wisdom or experience kept *her* from falling for the wrong men. Maggie met one of them that very day – Joel, the adulterous lecturer.

He was standing outside the locked glass doors of the

74

building, sheltering under the marquee. Maggie's first impressions of him were vague; she was not paying him close attention. But she registered lean height, soft floppy hair, glasses on a typical academic's face. When Tanya introduced them and Maggie shook his hand she noticed it was warm for such a chilly day, and that his forehead bulged intelligently. 'A bit like the Mekon in *Dan Dare*,' she teased Tanya later. Tanya was not amused. Her sense of humour, which had proved itself equal to a great deal in her life so far, stopped short of jokes about Joel.

'In my eyes he is perfect,' she was to say tersely. 'If you see any flaws, spare me your myopic misobservations.'

All this occurred later, after the three of them had had a rather uncomfortable tea together in one of the few places in Sheffield which offered such a thing on a Sunday – the station hotel.

The tea-service was heavy, scratched metal and the cups thick white china bearing the hotel's crest in navy blue. The tea was bright orange and none of them exactly fancied Kunzl cakes, especially yesterday's, but only Maggie noticed any of this, or the gloomy, silent lounge in which they sat at a small table. Though Tanya and Joel tried to include Maggie in their conversation, they failed. They were discussing Joel's prospects of a Chair at the University – a perfectly unprivate topic; but their tones were so passionately intimate, so somehow melifluous with love, that they might have been opera singers, rehearsing some tragic recitative in a public place where they didn't want to be overheard.

Maggie, watching them, was smitten with irrational envy. Of course she was romanticising stupidly; she should have stopped to think how hopeless it is for a woman to be in love with a married man who does not intend to leave his wife. It seemed to her that Tanya's love was mature and rather splendid, far above her own inept coupling on the pink chenille . . . Covertly watching Joel's warm hand creep forward under the table, yearning towards Tanya's knee, Maggie felt something else – an unexpected, but very strong and sharp, prickle of desire. It was as if she felt those fingers touching her own knee. For a split second, before a startled Margaret took control and stifled the thought, they started to slide upwards toward that acutely vulnerable line where her nylon stocking stopped . . . Bruce's

75

hand had paused there, fumbling with the maddening suspenders, bringing Margaret out of her trance. What if a man like this, a *gentle* man, but with magic in his hands, had been on the pink chenille with her instead of . . .?

But this would not do. Rigorously, Maggie helped Margaret by deflecting the lust back to Bruce. 'I must,' she thought, 'I must make it right with him, or it will cripple me and I'll never be able to love anyone properly, even a worldly other-worldly man like Tanya's.'

By the time Joel had taken leave of them (he didn't, of course, kiss Tanya – illicit affairs were much more circumscribed and discreet in those days – but held her upstage elbow and gazed at her for so long that Maggie had to cough to remind them it was time for her train) she had made up her mind. She had time for only a short conversation with Tanya on the platform – 'Isn't he beautiful?' – 'Very clever-looking, like the Mekon,' etcetera as already related – and then, as she got aboard the London train, Maggie said, 'I'm going to take your advice.'

Tanya, who had a grey, pinched look as if she'd just been woken at 3 a.m. with bad news, said, 'Good, although I fear I shall be in need of some myself if I stay in this damned town much longer.'

She never spoke a truer word. But by the time her need had become desperate, Maggie was even further from her side than Tanya had been in Maggie's hour of need.

Bruce, reinstated within strict if undefined limits, was restraint its very self.

He would meet her outside the theatre after Maggie's principal had made her last entrance, at which time she was free to leave. Then he would either take her for dinner somewhere pleasant, or drive her straight home. He had recently moved into a new flat, and when, her wall of mistrust already breached, she agreed to go there to inspect it one morning (not at night, of course) he behaved with such meticulous propriety that she found herself wondering whether perhaps he didn't find her attractive any more.

When three weeks had passed in this staid fashion, with no physical contact whatever, the tension began building up again.

76

The volcano started to emit hissings and bubblings and little premonitory jets of steam.

Isn't he being good, thought Maggie. Almost too much? Maybe he didn't enjoy it either and doesn't want to risk a repetition. She wondered if it would be very imprudent to give him a twinkle of the old amber light – naturally not the green – just to see. More and more, Maggie found that she was counting on his presence in her life, if only to compensate for the revived shortcomings of her career. Understudying had begun to pall.

For the first couple of weeks after opening night, it was thrill enough to hurry through the stage door every evening, to be greeted with impartial courtesy by the door-keeper, to glance at the notice-board and exchange a few words with any of the company's lesser lights who happened to be around at stage-level. But then – up the endless flights of stone steps to her dressing-room under the eaves, there to sit out her mandatory three hours, reading, mending, doing cross-words, listening to the play on the Tannoy ...

Within a week, Maggie knew the entire play by heart and could have gone on for any of the cast. She yearned to do so. She would sit in her distant eyrie mouthing the lines as the actors spoke them far below, interspersing them with the under-study's prayer: 'Please God, let her break a leg!' But her prin-cipal was a robust girl with a ruddy complexion and sturdy, unbrittle limbs like her own, who irked her by saying brightly each time they met: 'Sorry! – still alive!'

Understudy rehearsals continued, but only once a week. They were high-spots – she stood on the hallowed stage and spoke her lines – but it was a low sort of high-spot, after all. Most of her fellow understudies were 'professionals'. They 'walked' their parts at rehearsals and smiled indulgently at Maggie for really acting hers.

'Don't throw yourself about, ducky,' advised one old pro. 'Save it for "the night" – and pray it never comes.'

'Have you ever played?'

'Oh, a night here and there. Had to do a whole week once – ghastly. Played havoc with my tum, I got through it on Bismuth. I was so relieved when she came back, I gave her a lovely box of liqueur choccies.'

A new bogey began to leer down a new tunnel. What if

77

she, Maggie, were to get like this? Everyone said you mustn't understudy more than once or no one ever considered casting you in a real part. The thought of spending months and years in a 'dead' dressing-room, one without costume, make-up, or ultimate purpose, soon came to seem little less horrendous than spending it at home hoping for and striving to secure a proper job.

Such is an actor's natural ingratitude. Thus Maggie began to look more and more towards Bruce for distraction and comfort.

Alone in her bedroom, she took stock. The pink chenille had lost its suggestiveness and become its dear, common old self again. Maggie began to view the whole thing differently. Bruce was proving himself such a master of self-control that Maggie even began to wonder who had seduced whom. Her determination to resist his advances at all costs was proving so dauntingly unnecessary that a distinct sense of disappointment was intruding on her guilt. Cautiously, tentatively, the amber light blinked on – low wattage, but on.

Then, with its usual impeccable timing, fate presented each of them with a startling piece of information, which radically altered everything.

Maggie's wouldn't have startled anyone less naive than herself. As for Bruce's, that was more in the nature of an exciting surprise than a ghastly shock: his firm was offering him a long posting in Nigeria, with a sizeable rise in salary and status, and free accommodation for 'self and wife (if any)'.

And it so happened that Bruce, big bad Bruce, for all his steam-roller tactics and bluff overconfidence, was scared witless by the challenges and changes that lay ahead of him. He needed someone, and looking at Maggie, he noticed – not the amber light so much, though that registered, but a well-brought-up, capable girl whom he was quite attracted to, who would adorn his little colonial bungalow for him better than most and keep him out of trouble with – well, whatever kind of women chaps like him tended to get into trouble with if they were imprudent enough to go to Africa without a wife.

So he proposed. Lots of camping about, in case she should snub him, whereupon he could have passed it all off as a gag. It was hardly the kind of proposal one dreams of, but Maggie hadn't a snub left in her by that time. The spectacle of Bruce

78

on one knee crying 'Ma bonnie Maggie – ma Scots bluebell – be mine!' triggered off two almost instantaneous reactions.

The first issued from her true self and was the correct one: pure contempt, a desire to tell him precisely where to put his frivolous and undignified proposal and the entire African continent with it, if room were found. It was this first and honest response, instantly stifled with the second, which made it so difficult later to cope with Tanya's reaction, and later still with the inevitable results of her not having heeded that, either.

But looking into Bruce's bland, fatuous, but undeniably handsome face, seeing in his eyes and in his blush that the proposal was for real and that in his way he was as insecure and terrified as she was, Maggie saw her father loom before her again, his expression one of naked triumph. She had fulfilled his prophecy. The ultimate degradation was upon her. The only possible escape route lay in marriage and flight – and Bruce was offering her both.

She heard herself accept him. Felt herself being embraced and kissed for the first time since that fatal night. Sensed the recoil in some deep inner place which she could neither reach nor control. Told herself – loud and clear, while his lips and hands were still on her – 'You can't do it!' Answered herself: 'I must! Besides, I love him in a way. I do love him. I must love him.' Even while her loins were shrinking in that most fundamental denial.

That same night, at the theatre, the girl she was understudying failed to say, 'Sorry! – still alive!' In fact she looked decidedly wan. Half-way through the show there was a knock on the door of Maggie's attic dressing-room and in she came.

'Listen, darling. Something ghastly's happened. I've got a bun in the oven.' Maggie stared at her. 'I'm going to have to leave the show, anyway in a couple of months and a lot sooner if I don't stop feeling so rotten. I had to dope myself to the eyeballs to go on tonight. Just thought I'd warn you. Don't start jumping about till I've gone, will you? I feel so absolutely suicidal about it . . .'

Far from jumping about, Maggie burst into tears on the spot. It was the first time she'd cried since she found out about her own bun. During the previous week she'd been so numb with shock that the relief of tears had been beyond reach.

The other girl was naturally bewildered. 'What's this? Tears of bliss?'

Maggie put her face down on the place where her make-up would have been, had the dressing-room been a live one. 'I'm going to be married!' she sobbed despairingly.

Tanya, when she heard about the engagement, didn't improve Maggie's mood by rushing down to London to try to talk her out of it.

'I never said *marry* him! God in heaven, Maggie, he's not for you! For life, darling? You are mad! And Africa? What about your career? What about your *self*?'

Maggie, who had had time to recover a little, returned a wry smile and retorted, 'I love him, she said simply.'

Tanya stopped cold and looked at her. She, Tanya, had lost weight. She had also finally cut her beautiful long chestnut hair very short. She had written that it was better for wigs, but Maggie suspected Joel. When rendezvous are too curtailed to allow for the taking-down and pinning-up again of long hair, a man may prefer something he can run his fingers through. The short crop destroyed Tanya's premature matronly look at a stroke, making her seem younger than her age if anything, and very vulnerable. At the same time she could still look fierce, almost vulpine.

'I don't believe you love him.' she said harshly. 'You haven't the look.'

'And you have, I suppose!' said Maggie sharply, knowing that she did.

'Yes. I wouldn't wish it on you, what I have to go with it, but at least I do love. And you don't.'

The old cruel anger spurted up in Maggie's throat, as always when she was made to feel shallow, feeble, inferior.

'Well, it's none of your business, actually!'

'Don't say that. It is my business. Friends are just as important as lovers and as a rule, last longer. So now listen to me. You wait until you are sweltering in one hundred degrees of wet heat with no theatre worth the name for miles and miles and that big gingery highland bull jumping on top of you every night!' She took Maggie's limp hands and squeezed them strongly, compelling her with her eyes. 'If you were really in it,

80

Maggie, in the love-pit like I am, I wouldn't say a thing because then it's hopeless, one can't help oneself then. But you are *free*! You can give him the busman's sign and go off and work and make love with different men and make choices for years yet until you finally fall in the pit. Don't marry this one, Maggie! Don't go to sodding Africa. Stay here, and be an actress!'

Maggie struggled with herself, with her anger. Because now it was settled, and once something is settled, the battle lost or won, it takes immense courage and energy to re-open it again. She had decided not to tell Tanya, or anyone, about the prime reason for her decision; but when Tanya said, 'You are free,' she changed her mind.

'I'm not free,' she said at last.

'Oh, sweet Jesus,' responded Tanya. She sat down. After a long time she could restrain herself no longer and burst out, 'Get rid of it, Maggie!'

'*What?*' cried Maggie, aghast.

'Come on, you are not that naive! Don't tell me you haven't thought of it.'

'No! I couldn't!'

Tanya looked at her. The tension, the persuasion, went out of her, and she slumped. 'I believe you. But you will be sorry.'

'Could *you* do it? Joel's –'

'I am not so stupid to let it happen!' Tanya was suddenly shouting. 'And that would anyway not be in the least the same!' She had a wild, almost crazy look and her English had gone funny. Maggie understood at once that it was all she longed for, a child from Joel; yet at the same time she felt Tanya's words as a blow, calling her stupid, putting her down, and she felt trapped, not so much at that moment by her situation as by her own shortcomings which had landed her in it. And the hate always lurking for those who showed her herself in a poor light lashed out of her before she could muzzle it:

'I may be stupid, and naive, and perhaps I don't even know about real love, but at least I'm not stealing somebody else's husband.'

Tanya turned white to the lips, stood up, picked up her coat and bag and left Maggie alone. And that was the last they were to see of each other for many years.

81

PART TWO

Chapter Nine

It might be supposed that Bruce would be a bit put out by Maggie's announcement, three weeks after their hasty wedding and two after their arrival in Port Harcourt, Nigeria, that she was two and a half months gone. Expressions such as 'You trapped me into it' or 'I had a right to know' had been haunting Maggie's fevered expectations. But oddly enough, he didn't seem to mind, and adjusted to rather too-imminent fatherhood very quickly. One advantage of a phlegmatic temperament – you don't cry over spilt sperm. Of course, it helped that they were far from the Presbyterian Ayn Folk, and that none of the members of the WC (as Maggie soon came to call the white community among whom they lived) knew the date of the marriage.

'Would you have married me if you'd known beforehand?' Maggie asked once.

'Of course I would!' Bruce answered heartily. 'What do you take me for? Anyway I couldn't have managed in this heathen wilderness without you.'

But this turned out to be untrue. Bruce took to Africa. His new surroundings, and his job, supervising the establishment of this important new African oil source, accorded splendidly with his secret image of himself. The very primitiveness of their situation – the brand-new concrete house in a clearing, the stifling air, the tropical lushness and noisy wildlife, the highly restricted facilities – especially, perhaps, the masses of black faces everywhere and the strange language and stranger culture of the Ibos – all excited him. In fact, they, together with his work, soon absorbed him so totally that even if he had not brought Maggie with him he would probably have managed perfectly well. That, at least, was how it seemed to Maggie, cast

85

adrift on this ancient continent without the slightest preconception or preparation.

Looking back, it would seem as if she took one look at the whole set-up and fell almost at once into a lethargic, dim-witted trance. From the moment she stepped out of the plane she felt somehow stunned, as if the top part of her consciousness had been sliced off with one of the machetes that the natives used to clear the jungle around their encampment. She felt cut back, pruned of her alertness, her resilience, the life-affirming quality which had sustained her since childhood.

Part of this was the numbing effects of fear, though she didn't acknowledge it as such. She had been prepared to find the black people hostile and sinister, but they proved quite otherwise. Her little posse of servants – steward, houseboy, cook and gardener – welcomed her with broad, artless smiles, and thereafter went about their tasks if not with any great zeal or efficiency, at least without any indication of sullenness or ulterior design. So it was not them she feared. Nor was it the surrounding bush, for all its inimical denizens, its ear-piercing nightsong and its exhalations of primordiality which hung tangibly in the wet, heavy air. All this she could have accepted, and perhaps even learnt to love, as others apparently did, for there were women here, widows of colonial civil servants, who had come back alone to serve the new oil-based community in the modest role of governesses and teachers. No; the thing she feared deep down, the thing which had such a devastating effect on her own will, was that she was being sundered from herself. It seemed as if Africa were a different planet where she breathed rarer air and ate less nourishing food and spoke a deficient language, and thus barely subsisted, barely kept alive.

Most of this degutting effect was the result of her decision to marry a man she didn't love. But she could not face that yet, and so blamed Africa.

Bruce, supposing that her pregnancy combined with the rainy season, which was upon them, were responsible for her filleted manner, encouraged her to lie in bed as long as she felt like it, and be waited on. The novelty of this lasted some time, and was exacerbated by the white community wives. These gave the impression of latching, like leeches, to anyone new who offered the prospect of a little temporary stimulation. Dripping, mud-spattered and twittering like sparrows, they would scurry

86

indoors out of the persistent rain, all alike in their vapidity and limitedness ... If Maggie had hoped to find friends here of a calibre to replace Tanya (the breach with whom was still raw and rankling) she was disabused inside the first few days.

There was one woman, and only one, who at all took her fancy, and she could, presumably, never be an intimate friend, being thirty years older than Maggie. Beyond some indefinable and (initially) superficial affinity, they had almost nothing in common. Her name was Joan Hillman and she was one of the civil service widows.

'Halla-o!' she boomed, marching in toward the end of the first week. She was an instant relief after all the twittering and scurrying. Big and broad-shouldered, with the leathery look white women get after years of punishing equatorial heat, she plonked herself down on the edge of the daybed where Maggie had her feet up in the living-room. 'Feeling under the weather?' she asked, after introducing herself. 'Ruddy rain getting you down?'

'Yes, it's wearing,' said Maggie, and anyone who had known her in England would have been shocked at the lack of vitality in her voice, the languidness of her movements. 'Would you like something to drink?'

'One always would at this hour. No, don't move, just give a shout for your boy.' Seeing Maggie's fleeting grimace, she grinned knowingly. 'You'll have to get used to it – shouting for the boy, I mean, not just the rain.' She peered at Maggie narrowly from under a somewhat eccentric hat from which she had just removed a dripping piece of waterproofing. It was an old solar topee; a large crownless straw brim was pressed down over the top. 'No servants at home, probably? Eh? Used to doing things for yourself? Like me. Well ... we had a cook-general in Wiltshire, fairly useless, worse than the fella I've got here now if possible – both quite feckless. This one churns out the same four recipes in remorseless rotation and pinches more than his share of my supplies ... By the way, may I give you a tip? Never expect them to serve meals made of left-overs. No matter what you send back uneaten from one meal, forget it. It all goes out at once, to the relatives in the hutches.'

Maggie did not need to ask what the hutches were. Everyone in the WC seemed to have his or her own name for the wooden and tin huts built a garden's length away from the house, where

87

the servants lived. Bruce called them the kennels. Maggie didn't call them anything and tried not to think about them or about the squalor that must characterise the life inside them. Joan seemed to guess what she felt, because she immediately said, 'And that's another thing. Don't start wasting pity on the Ibos. They're damned lucky to be here and they know it. *Queueing* up at the work-manager's office, day after day, hoping to get jobs with the likes of us.' She paused to light the first of the innumerable cigarettes she was to smoke in Maggie's presence. 'Their tribal life's breaking up, you see. They've more or less begun to accept it, and they want "in" on the only advantage they can see to *our* arrival, which one can sum up as better grub, and possessions. Imagine living on a diet of yams and watching your children dying of attritional diseases for generations and then you start getting your teeth into some good meat and fruit and chocolate; suddenly you're getting paid in actual money and can go to market and buy yourself all sorts of miraculous things like bicycles. Damn it, you're not going to risk losing your job and having to push off back to the bush with your tail between your little black legs, now are you? So you won't have any real trouble, apart from perks and a bit of very natural laziness. What's your boy's name?'

'William.'

'WILLIAM!' she roared. Maggie jumped. William, unused to commanding contralto bellows, came running. He wore the blue uniform shirt with big collar and open neck and long shorts that all the servants wore.

'What Madam want?' he asked, rolling his eyes to indicate he'd been given a fright.

'Tea, please,' said Maggie.

'And biscuits – lots of biscuits!' boomed Joan. The moment William had gone, she continued: 'If you want to feel bad about the blacks, blame the missionaries. Are you religious?' she asked in her direct way. Margaret hesitated, but Maggie shook her head. 'Good. Most of them here are, you know, in a silly, unthinking way. I chucked all that nonsense long ago, when I saw what Christianity has done to these poor people. It's a most fearful responsibility, breaking up traditions and a whole way of life which fitted their bit of the biosphere like a glove. Mark you, I'm not saying nothing was wrong with it. They had and still have some pretty hair-raising customs. But at least arrogant

88

interference and the ultimate destructions of an entire social structure weren't among *their* little foibles ... They leave that to us civilised folk.' She puffed, and seemed to watch Maggie, who simply lay looking back at her. 'Look my dear, you mustn't mind me doing a bit of interfering, but you shouldn't lie around too much unless you're really ill. You know the old song, "Old Rocking-Chair's Got Me?" Well, here it's a matter of old daybed getting you. You must try to be active, as active as you're allowed to be, anyhow.'

'How do you manage?' asked Maggie, wondering who it was this woman vaguely reminded her of.

'Me? Oh, I teach.'

Of course. Fiona Dalzell. Maggie at once sat up, as if it were Mrs Dalzell's eyes reproving her limpness.

'White or black children?'

'Both. The black ones belong to the Nigerians working for the Company. Any bits of education the others get comes exclusively from the Mission. They don't do a bad job, only they make all the letters spell Jesus Christ, in a manner of speaking ... Ah, here's tea! Well done William, that was quick.' She laid hands on the teapot, but then drew back. 'Here, Joan old girl, what are you doing? Taking charge again! Sorry, my dear. Your job, come along, up you get and do the honours.'

Overcoming inertia (had old daybed already begun to get her?) Maggie obeyed. She and Joan asked and answered questions about each other's past. Joan was impressed to learn that Maggie was an actress.

'What an asset that training would be if you turned to teaching!'

'What's the connection?'

'My dear ...! To be a good teacher one has to be able to act, sing, preach ... and if possible tap-dance, juggle, eat fire and swallow swords. Anything to keep the little varmints entertained. That's the basis of teaching, you know, keeping them amused, and hence on your side. They'll forgive you a lot if they're laughing while you push the boring facts into 'em. Maybe I could persuade you to come along sometime and give me a hand.'

Maggie vaguely said of course she would. But she didn't. The same terrible disease of idleness, contracted against her will and nature while jobless in London, now broke out again

89

She used her pregnancy as an excuse, and indeed her genuine tiredness and lethargy much of the time may have had a physical basis. The climate didn't suit her; the humid heat had a really crushing affect on her system. But the other side of it was that her domestic situation took the guts out of her.

Bruce's passion for his work and for the country and, in fact, for everything about this new life, made her feel relegated to the position of a mere facet of it all, rather a small and lustreless one at that. He seemed to love her as a part of his Nigerian experience, rather than as the most vital person in his world. Only this might have reconciled her to the heat, the narrowness of the society, the subtle unease she felt at being waited on by pidgin-speaking black people still more than half immersed in a culture so alien to her own that she realised without even having to think about it that no more than a skin-deep relationship could ever exist between her and them.

In the months of waiting for her baby to be born, she consoled herself with the hope that when it was, the deepening sense of uselessness, disorientation and – this was the worst – diminution as a person, would be done away with. Other women of the WC had evidently found motherhood a complete justification for their existence; yet, except for Joan (who had married young and whose children had both grown up) she saw nothing in any of them, or in their lives, which she could respect enough to want to emulate; and the consolation of hope turned to apprehension. What if motherhood, instead of ratifying her dwindling sense of her self, simply sank her further into the vapidity and drive-less langour that she observed in the women around her, and which she realised she was well on the way to sharing?

As she grew heavier and lazier, her guilt awoke to join the other forces that were bowing down her spirit. Yet whenever Joan tried to do her some real, active good, Maggie backed away.

'When are you coming down to give us a talk about theatre?'

'I can't come like this.'

'My dear, they won't even notice. Most of them are taught at home that ladies get fat tummies if they pick their noses. Come along, you haven't been out of the house for a week, have you? Not since Molly Harrington's bridge do.'

'Wasn't that deadly . . .'

90

'If people aren't *doing* anything interesting, their level of conversation is bound to be lamentable. Where did you learn to play bridge?'

'It was one of the few things my brothers and I were allowed to do on Sundays.'

'Where are they now?'

'My brothers? In Scotland. They're both in my father's paper business.'

'Bet you miss them!'

'Well . . . Only the younger one. And my mother. I miss her a lot.'

'Couldn't she come out to be with you when you pop?'

'I . . . I don't think she'll be able to.'

Naturally Maggie had no intention of telling her family the exact date of the birth. She would send them a cable two months late. That was the plan, and Bruce had agreed to it.

When he first learnt that he had a son, Bruce's overwhelming self-satisfaction deprived him of his wits. He rushed out of the hospital into the streets of Lagos, sought out the post office and began firing off cables in all directions. Thus Matt's life began as the focal-point of the first really devastating row between his parents.

'What do you mean, you *forgot*?' Maggie stormed at him from her hospital bed. 'Forgot that it's only seven months since the wedding? Forgot what kind of parents I have? Forgot everything I told you about my father?'

'Shhh! Well, what if I did? What does it really matter? We married in plenty of time. It's not as if he'd been born in the vestry.'

Maggie felt herself powerless and betrayed and close to hysteria. 'You – you idiot!' she shouted. 'You smug bloody half-wit! Why didn't you wait? Why didn't you ask me?' She sank back in bed panting and white-faced, imagining her father's grim satisfaction masked as holy horror, her mother's simple shock, Ian's sense of outraged propriety, Stip caught in the middle. . .

But Bruce had consciously shed a lot of his very similar background in the freedom of this new place. 'Oh, rubbish!' he said, with bluff incomprehension of Maggie's anguish of mind.

91

'It's all rot, really. It's all ended well. That's what counts. If the old people can't see it like that, it's as well they're a few thousand miles off, that's all I've got to say.'

It was not all Maggie had to say, but she had exhausted herself with her first outburst and now fell silent. She lay with her head turned away from Bruce, staring at the little white box on wheels which contained her baby. It had not been a very easy birth and her stitches were biting. This peculiarly sharp and localised pain reminded her of Matt's beginnings in a way she had so far managed to avoid.

'Dinna be fashed,' Bruce said jocularly. 'Look at all the flowers I brought you.'

'I hate mimosa,' said Maggie sullenly. 'All the damned pollen makes me sneeze.' She didn't want him to come round to the other side of the bed and see her tears.

He kissed the side of her head and left, taking the flowers with him. Maggie hoped she'd seen the last of them, but the nurse soon bustled in with them in two ugly vases. She was an English nurse, and she said with coy reproachfulness: 'Weren't very nice to poor hubby, were we? Never mind, I told him it's nobody's fault, just a touch of the old post-natals. Soon as we start suckling, all that bad temper will melt away.'

It proved less simple.

When Matt lay in her arms, she trembled with an indefinable anxiety. He was beautiful, with his faint silky auburn thatch pulsating over the soft spot, the pink mark of the 'stork's beak' still smudged between his eyes giving him a scowly look, and his tiny fists not much bigger than new bracken shoots on the moors at home. He looked to her like a little baby-shaped lump of some infinitely malleable substance, so impressionable she hardly dared to hold him close or press him with her fingers. Putting him to her breast on the second day, she experienced such a painful clutch at the heart that she felt a sudden panic. She called a passing nurse.

'My chest hurts – I can hardly breathe!'

Looking back years later on this vital turning-point, Maggie was to wonder what would have been changed if that black nurse had rung the warning bell by smiling and saying, 'That's your mother-love, lady. It comes in with the milk. You'll have to bear that for a long time.' Instead, she whisked Matt away, snatching the nipple from his eager gums, and Maggie heard

92

him break into a wail – a sound which, from the first time she ever heard it just after he was born, never failed to pierce her like the thrust of a sword. The nurse put him into his box-bed and left him to scream while she sounded Maggie's heart, felt her pulse and forehead and generally fussed about her.

'I call the doctor,' she pronounced at length. 'You sit quiet. Don't move now!'

'I'm all right. I'm better – it was probably nothing –'

But she was gone. Maggie half-lay against her pillows, her eyes fixed to the box from which Matt's cries issued piercingly. Her instincts urged her to get out of bed and go and fetch him, hold, comfort and nourish him. But something – some deadly conformity, some built-in obedience to rules dating back to her own pre-childhood, kept her there, stiff-muscled and motionless, staring at the box, whose contents she could not see but could sense deep within her, moulded from the timbre and volume of his shrieks. They were cries of outrage, even of torment. Yet she sat for minutes on end, listening and doing nothing, till the crying stopped. It was the sudden silence that galvanised her.

She almost leapt out of bed, and had Matt in her arms before she felt the blood begin to flow. There was some pain, but it was nothing compared to the agony of hearing him cry. When the nurse brought the doctor, Maggie was weeping aloud.

The doctor was taken back by the state she was in, and when he discovered she was suffering a mild haemorrhage he was also alarmed. The nurse got her back into bed and they both tried to prise Matt out of her arms, but she held him so tightly and cried so much that eventually they left him at one end, while they dealt with the other. She tried to feed him, but it didn't work. He wouldn't suck at first, and when they had both calmed down a bit and he tried, nothing much came. He threshed about and shouted with frustration and hunger. The nurse, bewildered, tried to help. She was new to her work. In her native environment she had probably never encountered the phenomenon of a mother unable, through neurosis or agitation, to produce milk for her baby. All she knew to do was to keep pressing the nipple into his mouth, but he was wailing so much he didn't notice it. Slowly Maggie grew desperate.

'Why doesn't he suck? Why does he go on crying?'

The nurse looked at the doctor. He nodded. The black girl

93

put her arms round Matt, and this time Maggie relinquished him. He was carried out of the room. She could hear him all the way down the corridor.

She lay back exhausted, tears rolling down the sides of her face.

'That was all my fault,' she whispered as the doctor administered a sedative injection.

'Nonsense. Now don't you worry. Nurse will give him a feed.'

'But why am I in such a state?'

'You've just given birth. It happens to a lot of women. Don't worry. He won't go hungry. You can try again tomorrow.'

But by that time Matt had had the fat, fruitful rubber teat in his mouth. Maggie's barely-ripened little spike could not but seem an unrewarding proposition after that.

So breast-feeding was abandoned and Matt took to the bottle.

Physically it suited him. When Maggie took him home, Bruce, as his contribution to his son's welfare, took to weighing him every morning, and noting the added ounces with a gloating glee which irritated Maggie secretly. It never seemed to occur to Bruce that while the bottle might feed Matt's flesh, it was doing nothing for his bond with his mother. It never crossed his mind that there was anything pathetic in the fact that she opened her blouse when she fed him, to imitate as closely as possible the true conditions of nursing.

He saw that she was depressed, though, and jumped to the first solution that came into his head: she must be tired, and therefore in need of more rest, more help. One afternoon Maggie awoke from her nap to find a strange black girl in the bedroom with her. She was sitting by the shuttered window, silhouetted against the venetian-striped brilliance outside; Matt's crib was next to her, and her hand was on his back as he lay there, rubbing, rocking him gently.

Maggie sat up with a jolt.

'Who are you?'

The girl turned her face placidly to Maggie.

'Master say, I work for you, help with baby. He say, I present for you.'

Her flawless white smile gleamed in the half light.

'I didn't say I needed a nursemaid! He shouldn't –'

The smile fled. The tone of voice radically altered to one of dread. 'You no want? You tell master you no want Tolly?'

94

'Is Tolly your name?'

'You call Tolly. Please Madam, not tell Master you no want! I work hard, I learn quick. Please.'

Maggie remembered what Joan had said, how the Ibos wanted to work for the whites, what the alternatives were. Did that explain the desperate tone, the rolling eyes, the clasped, beseeching hands?

'Where are your people?'

'No got people.'

'No tribe?'

'Tribe no want. Send Tolly away.'

'Why?'

The girl hung her head. There was a long silence. Matt began to whimper. The girl glanced at him, and Maggie saw the reflection of the strips of sunlight on her wet cheeks.

'Well . . . I don't really need you, Tolly. But we'll see. You can stay for the moment.' She heard the quick intake of breath, the sudden, relieved slackening of shoulders. She felt a little sick. It was terrible to have such power over people! She wished the girl would vanish. She was an unwanted burden that Bruce had unwittingly laid on Maggie, the burden of needing to employ her usefully, worry about her sleeping out in one of the hutches, wonder what inscrutable 'crime' she had committed to bring about her ostracism from her family, and no doubt eventually to learn about it and have to care . . . At this moment it was a simple matter of deciding whether to ask Tolly to bring Matt to her for his feed, or whether to risk hurting her feelings by getting up and fetching him herself. The immemorial 'servant problem', which so far she had managed to avoid by leaving Bruce and the black steward to cope, was upon her, and she saw herself forcibly drawn into the muddle and stress of petty problems the other wives interminably discussed . . . Oh God! To be back in England, where such things simply had no place in your life because you did everything for yourself! – where the air didn't press you down, and the light was gentle, not this vicious brilliance which forced you to shut it out, so you couldn't see properly, adding to your half-aliveness, your frightening sense of separation from the real world. . .

She sighed heavily. Still not enough air entered her lungs, somehow. 'Bring me the baby, Tolly, please.'

The girl all but sprang to her feet, her face shining now with

95

happiness as well as the forgotten tears. She bent over the crib, lifted Matt expertly and carried him to Maggie's bedside. As she stood there, waiting for Maggie to settle herself, Matt turned his face instinctively toward the girl's full breasts under the uniform dress, and nuzzled her experimentally. Maggie noticed a very curious thing. A dark round stain abruptly spread out from the nipple whose generous outline Maggie could make out under the blue cotton cloth.

'Tolly, have you got a baby of your own?' she asked sharply.

The girl's eyes again began to roll. She trembled. Swiftly she put Matt into Maggie's arms and walked, stiff-legged, from the room.

'Tolly –'

'I bring bottle for Madam. Master tell what to do,' she said in a choked voice, without turning.

Chapter Ten

When Joan called later that day, to bring birthing gifts, Maggie consulted her about the Tolly mystery.

'It's no mystery at all, my dear, I can guess exactly what's behind it. That poor little girl of yours has had twins. Twins are taboo, and her tribe has followed its age-old custom by shutting them up in earthen pots and hiding them in the bush. Yes, well, I told you. It wasn't all sweetness and light till the missionaries hove in view. Oh don't look so stricken, it can't be helped. Usually the mother gets over it quickly enough, but occasionally, when she's young and it's her first birth, she might follow the babies into the bush and try to nurture them, although she knows quite well she can't go back afterwards. Of course the poor little things die anyway and then she's got nowhere to go and before the whites came, she'd have died too. As it is, your Dolly or whatever her name is, made her way to our village and queued up with the others for work, and was lucky enough to draw you. You'll have to keep her, my dear, at least for a while. She's been through a bad time and probably needs feeding up... Oh dear! Now you're upset. I shouldn't have told you.'

Maggie cried helplessly on Joan's shoulder for a while and then borrowed her handkerchief. 'How her poor breasts must hurt!' she gasped out at last.

'Now there's a sensible thought! I'll get her some drying-up pills from the dispensary.'

'Why didn't the mission fathers who've been teaching her English stop her people from killing her babies?'

'They try to, but often they're not quick enough to catch them. It's one of the things they're finding it hardest to deal with because even if they stop them abandoning the twins, they

97

can't force them to accept them. That means the mission has to adopt them, and they're just not geared for it.'

'But what future has she got? Won't she ever marry again?'

'Probably not, if the blacks around here get wind of the fact that she's "done born double piccens", as they put it. Even after years, working with us, they won't go anywhere near even white twins if they can help it. You must look after her as best you can and let time take care of it.'

Before the drying-up pills arrived, nature had somehow taken its course, and Tolly had become Matt's wet-nurse.

Bruce was very uneasy about it. Something basic got in the way of his accepting it as something natural. Maggie had to fight. It was the first time she had ever had to fight Bruce on an issue, and she was, while the bout lasted, pleased to find herself roused to something like her old self.

'Do you think her milk will turn him black, or what?'

'It's not that sort of thing, don't be absurd! It's just that ... well, I've talked to a couple of the chaps. They say it's simply not done. Black nursemaids, *that's* okay, but wet-nursing ... Well, I mean, the whole concept's somehow out of date.'

'Mother's milk is the healthiest thing he can drink. Everyone knows that. In this climate, where there's such a risk of infection anyway –'

'I know, but somehow ... Aren't you – I mean, don't you miss feeding him, holding him and all that?'

Maggie did not want to discuss this. 'He must have what's best for him, never mind me. I can cuddle him at other times. You gave her to me,' she burst out. 'You – landed me with her! This way at least she's got a vital function in our lives. Otherwise she'd just be in the way.'

She did not mention the real, true reason why she was relieved to think of Matt in Tolly's arms, at Tolly's black satin breast. Aspects of her feelings went so deep she scarcely took them out to look at them until they were long past. Tolly was her direct link with Africa, and with the deep primitive instincts which Europeans overlay with 'civilisation' and so lose touch with. She had got very close to this primordial self while actually giving birth. She had become an animal, but an animal which, because of some cruel distortion of nature, could not function

98

properly. She had longed to crouch on all fours to deliver, but she had had to lie on her back with her legs in the air, helpless as an inverted tortoise; later the baby had been taken from her and for a whole day she hadn't been allowed to see him. . . Now she was having to behave toward her baby in ways that seemed to cut her off from the natural animal instincts which were struggling to guide her. When she watched how Tolly treated Matt, she felt some of the stress of her personal alienation from her instincts, eased.

She could not carry Matt everywhere next to her skin or let him sleep in her bed, as she yearned to do. She could not do it because she was imbued, programmed by the civilised, unnatural mores of the white world. But she never stopped Tolly from lifting Matt at the first whimper and carrying him about with her, retiring to some corner to feed him whenever he nuzzled. She politely ignored the advice experienced white mothers gave her about how Matt would be spoilt, how she must stick to a schedule, 'get him trained . . .' When Bruce, still eagle-eyed for deviations from what was 'done', objected, Maggie simply said, 'I can't bear to hear him cry. It tears me inside.' 'All babies cry,' he said bluffly. 'Good for their lungs.' 'The black babies hardly ever cry.' 'Oh well! They're so uncomplicated, like little animals.' 'That's just what Matt is!' Maggie exclaimed. 'I want him to be a happy, uncomplicated little animal.' Though in all other things she fell in with Bruce's blueprint for her life, in this, despite all his arguments, she went her own way.

Her resistance started early. During the daily weighing sessions, Bruce began smugly and roguishly calling Matt 'our little love child'. It was, Maggie felt sure, to demonstrate his freedom from guilt about Matt's conception. Perhaps because she sensed this, Maggie's instantaneous reaction to his misnomer was a mental correction: *Our little rape child, you mean*! She never said it, but thinking it did her harm.

Her guilt at not doing everything for Matt herself did not lessen; but whenever she thought *rape child* she was stung by a fierce gladness that he was so often in other arms. And when he was in her arms, in her care, she trimmed her mind like a sail, spilling out every thought or impulse that might damage him. It made for a stiffness which was also unnatural. But she persisted in it, feeling she owed him this effort, that she must

99

be perfect towards him – as perfect as her stilted, overcivilized conditioning allowed her to be – and her deficiencies must be made up by the simple, robust, loving black girl, who knew more by instinct than all the silly books which Maggie kept reading long after she'd given up hope of learning anything from them.

'What Madam read?' Tolly once asked, looking over her shoulder at a picture of a woman hanging a mobile above a child's cot.

'A book,' Maggie answered ironically, 'that tells white ladies how to bring up their babies.'

Tolly gave her that look of mild curiosity she sometimes wore for white people's more eccentric behaviour. She reached down her long fingers and turned over the pages, looking at more pictures – pictures of substitutes for what she, left to herself with Matt or with her own dead children, would have provided without thought. Jiggling prams for continual body motion; cuddly toys and blankets for warm, scented flesh; a dummy for an ever-ready nipple... She gave a sudden laugh, and flicked the book shut, moving off without comment. And indeed, thought Maggie, shrinking with a sudden sense of inadequacy, none was necessary.

Occasionally she even thought: 'He'd be happier all his life if I gave him up – if I just gave him to Tolly.' When she caught herself following this strange line of thought, Maggie felt guiltier than ever. Who could imagine a mother, in her fortunate circumstances, playing with the notion of giving her baby away? Yet it was truly not to rid her life of him, for he was the most precious thing left in it, but rather to save Matt from herself.

Her work had once been inestimably precious, and she felt, perpetually in the background, the pressure of her treason in having given it up at the first true test. And she was aware even more constantly that Bruce should be precious to her, and that he wasn't.

As time passed and her marriage relationship failed to develop, remaining stunted and lifeless like some stillborn creature pickled in a jar, she began to see Bruce, see herself-and-Bruce, with appalling clarity. She saw his motive for marrying her, hers for marrying him; saw that neither had anything at all to do with the kind of relationship that she needed to make her grow.

100

She got a lot of the sort of 'spoiling' that a certain type of man imagines will keep his little woman contented. She got sex with predictable regularity and in the most uncomplicated fashion. But it all gave her nothing that she could believe was particular to herself.

Anyone would do, she thought (and there was all too much thinking-time, motherhood had not changed that). Anyone reasonably nice-looking who would consent to this life, who didn't rebel or disgrace him or stand out too awkwardly; anyone who would let him make love to her every Tuesday and Saturday, and listen uncomplainingly to his boring talk about derricks and pipelines and world markets, and pour tea for his boring colleagues' vapid wives, anyone who would not step out from between the narrow, narrow white men's guidelines nor hanker (at least out loud) for a fulfilling life of her very own. . .

And the irony was, she filled the bill. Because she had Matt. Because, for Matt's sake, she had let herself marry Bruce. Because she'd made her bed and must lie on it (as Ian with his relentless addiction to moralistic clichés might have said). Because, when you added it up, her childhood conditioning proved stronger than all her efforts, and Mrs Dalzell's efforts, and Tanya's efforts, to free her to make her own rules.

She used to take Matt to the local airport sometimes, ostensibly to let him watch the planes taking off, but since these outings began before he knew that a plane wasn't a bird it was obvious even to her that it was for herself that she went. Standing in the draining heat, watching the turbo-props heaving themselves into the air, she remembered a film about a woman trapped by life on a lonely prairie farm somewhere in North America, standing in the doorway of her barn watching the trains stream past, uttering their cries of challenge: 'Come away! Come awaaaaaay!' The pre-jet engines of the planes snarled out the same message, instilled the same sense of futility and despair.

Why didn't she rebel? Why didn't she? There was no answer, except that Africa, marriage and motherhood had laid hands on her, inducing a great waking sleep. The seasons came and went like slow rhythmic beatings of a tropical pulse, pushing the endless hot stream of days through Maggie's system like a drug that never wore off.

101

Chapter Eleven

They were entitled to a month's leave a year, and for that first eleven months, behind and on all sides of her other concerns, Maggie dreamt of it and longed for it. But when the time actually approached when she could go, she found she didn't want to. She was terrified to look at London and see what she had forfeited. She was far more terrified of Scotland.

The ill-advised birthday cables had elicited a stunned and censorious silence lasting for several months. Then had come the first letter. From Stip, of course. He said nothing about the cables, about the local reaction to them, or about his own part in the subsequent boycott. It began glibly, 'Sorry I haven't written for a while – terrible rush at the mill – several key-people left or died and Ian and Dad were forced to promote me ...' Frantically scanning the four close-written pages in his still childish writing for some acknowledgement of Matt's existence, she finally found, at the foot of the fourth page, 'How's the sprog? Send me a photo.' Was there the ghost of a line under the 'me', indicating the need for secrecy? Yes. She mailed answer and photo to the mill, hoping some neutral minion would do the postal sorting.

Next had come a note from her mother, written, Maggie supposed, furtively. She didn't mention Matt at all. She merely inquired, three or four times in barely-differentiated phrases, after Maggie's health and well-being. 'Take care of yourself. Don't overdo. Too much sun is so bad for delicate constitutions.' Such a description was laughably inapposite – Maggie had always been as strong as a horse. This was the nearest her mother could come to mentioning her grandchild ... Maggie wondered if her father had been standing at her shoulder as she wrote, like any Victorian husband... Things must have been quite terrible when that accursed cable came, and how

102

Maggie blamed herself now for not having warned her. The situation was evidently still fraught. No one mentioned a reunion.

So when Bruce casually suggested that they give home-leave a miss till Matt was older, Maggie made no objection. 'We'll take him next year,' Bruce said. 'The "scandal", ha ha, will have died down by then.' She knew full well that this was just an excuse; the reason *he* didn't want to go home was that he was perfectly happy where he was. Besides, there was the possibility of promotion for a man diligent enough to forego his full leave until the wells were properly established.

So they had a fortnight on the coast and settled down again in their rut. None of the WC thought this in any way odd, with a four-month-old baby. But when, the following year, they decided to go south to the Cape instead of north to the British Isles, then there were some raised eyebrows.

'Don't you want to show off Matt to your family?' asked Joan, who, as Matt's godmother, felt she had the right to ask. 'You haven't had a row with them or anything, have you?'

'Not exactly.'

'Don't your parents like Bruce, is that it?'

'They don't know him.'

'Oh! Oh well . . . I sometimes think it's no bad thing when the in-laws are too far away to interfere. One reason why I adored Africa from the outset was because it didn't contain any of mine!'

So that year they visited South Africa, leaving Matt with Tolly. At sixteen months Matt was convinced he had two mothers, of whom the black one was not the least important. Maggie had grown accustomed to this emotional dispensation; when he was with her he made it clear that he loved her just as much as Tolly. But when she returned from her holdiay (which she had not enjoyed, despite – or perhaps because of – having visited every theatre in Capetown, some of them twice), she found Matt treating her as if she were an intruder. She swore she would never repeat the experiment.

'From now on, where we go, he goes,' she said to Bruce, and to redress the balance took Matt to sleep in their room. This put a temporary stop to the Tuesday and Saturday ritual – Bruce had inhibitions about sex in Matt's presence – but for her that was not the worst of the arrangement.

103

Matt soon remembered who she was, and Tolly rather reluctantly stopped monopolising him. Matt grew, and talked, and called Tolly 'Tolly' and Maggie 'Mummy' as was right and proper. But it was still Tolly he cried for when he was hurt or in one of his sad moods; and when, at Bruce's insistence, he was moved back into his own room, and some time afterwards was not to be found there when Maggie drifted in early one rainy morning to look at him, it was to Tolly's hutch that she unhesitatingly ran.

She didn't go in. She never had gone in, afraid of the contrast, about which (Joan had made it abundantly clear) there was nothing she could possibly do because 'that was the way things were'. But she knocked gently while the rain made a bead-curtain hanging straight down all round the rim of Bruce's big umbrella.

'He here, Madam,' came Tolly's voice instantly from within. Her face appeared in the wood-framed door jamb, shining, her hair, short as a boy's, shining too, with its dressing of pungent oil. 'He came to visit me in the night. Bad dream.'

'Why didn't you bring him back?'

'I no come in house at night, Madam. And it rain so bad. I think better bring him back in morning.'

Maggie felt a pain in her heart, but there was neither anger nor jealousy in it, only a profound regret.

'Is he asleep now?'

'Yes, Madam. I bring him across when rain stop.'

'Thank you, Tolly.'

She walked back across the lawn, squelching; the tough roots of the kikuyu grass kept her from sinking far in, but the gardener wouldn't be pleased . . . She wondered if he was watching her now, from his hutch, if any of the servants could view her splashing retreat from their domain with her mac pulled on over her nightgown and the cold rubber boots over bare feet. . . Lucky they couldn't see her face, anyway. They hated you to cry in front of them. It distressed them more than it would have done white servants, somehow; they seemed to think it must be their fault. And it wasn't Tolly's fault, of course it wasn't, that Matt would run through a tropical downpour to get to her in the wooden shack where, even at two years old, he knew he shouldn't go, instead of into the next room to his mother. . .

She decided she must have him to herself for a while. So

104

when it was time for their next leave, home to Scotland they went.

At least, Maggie and Matt did. Bruce, big bold shameless Bruce, cried off. *He* went to Paris. On a spree, Maggie vaguely supposed, and wondered why she didn't mind more about that than about the fact that he had, cheerily and quite determinedly, refused to come with her and lend her moral support.

'It'll be all right, you'll see! And if they pull any faces, dump Matt on your mother and take off for London. See your old theatre chums, have some fun – I'm going to. I've earned it. So have you,' he said robustly.

His suggestion about 'dumping' Matt was so patently silly that she didn't even argue. Their meeting-grounds, conversationally speaking, were getting narrower all the time anyway; they just didn't seem to be on the same wave-length about anything.

Tolly didn't expect to be taken. At the same time she didn't relish being left behind. Matt didn't relish it either, and there was a scene at the garden gate when Matt clung around Tolly's neck and Tolly cried and didn't do much about pulling him off. Maggie had to do it, and rather roughly too in the end because Matt simply knotted his hands somehow and had to be forcibly unknotted or they'd have missed the plane.

The flight was ghastly. Matt started screaming from the noise of take-off and the ear pressure, and when Maggie unbelted him and took him on her knee, the stewardess insisted he should be put back to comply with regulations. Maggie was unwontedly furious and shouted at her, and Matt, unused to hearing her shout, stopped crying in astonishment for a moment and then burst into even more high-pitched shrieks. Though they subsided eventually he kept up a continuous whining and whimpering; it was only for an hour while he slept that Maggie had any peace in which to compose her soul for the ordeal to come – the ordeal-by-Robertson.

One good thing – she could feel the change of air coming over her as the plane flew north. Perhaps it was psychological, but as they passed over the shining Alps she was certain she could feel a rush of cool, well-oxygenated, invigorating air flowing around her. She sat up straight, soothed Matt with a steady hand (it had begun to shake with nerves earlier) and her brain, long padded in African cotton-wool, seemed to free itself and begin its reversion to a pre-African tempo and clarity.

105

Was it babyish to care that the family disapproved of her? To be nervous of facing them out? Obviously their attitude was ludicrously out of date, antedeluvian in fact. For all *they* knew of the circumstances, she and Bruce had simply followed in the footsteps of ten million couples before them. *They* were not to know that in this case, it had all been as wrong as it could be. But whose business was it? She'd left England, averting all gossip, and if Bruce hadn't gone mad with those damned premature cables no one would have been the wiser.

But her rationalisation availed her nothing. All that counted was her father being able to crow, and her mother, minding. What if her mother fixed her eyes upon her and said, 'As long as you're happy,' meaning: 'Was it worth it?'

She looked down at Matt, sleeping now, slumped against her side. Beautiful, ever-evolving, enchanting creature, she'd got *him* out of it, anyway – part of him. The part that wasn't Tolly's, the part that wasn't, inalienably, unreachably, already his very own. Once she had thought that if you bore a child, it was automatically yours, that some part-physical, part-mystical bond united it to you for always. She'd assumed that the love generated by birth could only be broken by some cataclysm or deliberate act. But she, of all people, should have known better. Mother and child love, like any other kind, had to be earned, then maintained; it could be shared, or transferred, or terminated, or superceded. In a word, having a child was no answer to loneliness, in fact by demanding so much, raising such high expectations – *costing* so much that one had a built-in expectation of being repaid – a child could produce the most poignant disappointment and loneliness of all.

She had not thought such thoughts in three years.

She changed planes in London and tasted the air properly. Her whole inner being was abruptly reflated. She lifted Matt effortlessly on to her hip and strode briskly through the long passageways, bowling her hand-luggage ahead of her on its trolley. She breathed deeply. It was just like waking up from a long torrid dream. She thought of the life she had left, only hours before. All she could distinctly remember about it was the mildew on Bruce's tennis racquet, and the fact that she had neglected to remind the servants to hang his damp suits out after the rains ... She gave a laugh which Matt innocently echoed. 'Smell that air!' she exclaimed aloud, ebulliently, nuzzling his neck. No cloying scents or dank vapours to clog it on its surging way into her lungs. . . Oh, what did it *matter* what her father said, or her mother thought? She would handle it. She would even make Ian laugh! That would be her holiday task.

The flight to Scotland was lovely. She ate, Matt ate — scones and real English tea . . . 'Look, Matt! Chivers strawberry jam.' 'Is it cold?' 'Not *shivers*, pumpkin! Oh, you are sweet! Wait till they all see you, they won't be able to help loving you . . .' She *would* go to London, she thought suddenly. For a weekend. Why not? She'd seek out Tanya, and other old friends; they'd go to three shows on a single Saturday — two-thirty matinee, five-thirty matinee, and another at eight-thirty (taxis in between!) and then, satiated, home again on the early train, Sunday. Why not? Her mother wouldn't mind, not once she'd seen Matt . . .

She almost danced down the gangway and through the concourse at Edinburgh. Stip's face seemed to leap from the crowd.

'STIP! Stip – !'

'Hallo, Mags.' His mouth formed the words without an exclamation mark. She stopped cold for a moment, then pushed forward ruthlessly to reach him. Something was wrong. Perhaps just with him? Perhaps the dreariness of his life, the stifling of his dream, had wearied him to the point where there *were* no exclamation marks?

'Stip – don't just stand there – give me a hug!'

He hugged her, then met her eyes.

'Oh, *what*?' she whispered in shocked dismay.

'It's Dad.'

'Oh God! Is he dead?'

'I have to take you straight to the hospital.'

She stood stunned, her mind racing hither and yon.

'I can't! What about Matt? Oh, look – look at him – do say something – ' She held Matt up, her one achievement. Stip put his hand on the red head. He looked only for a second, then switched back to her.

'He's dying, Maggie,' he said softly.

Maggie felt, for a moment, nothing but the ultimate exasperation. 'Wouldn't he just!' burst from her before she could stop it.

107

'*Maggie*!' The old Stip. So good. So easily shocked.

'Sorry. *Sorry* Oh God. Oh, *hell*! What shall we do?'

'We're to drop the boy at Aunt Helen's on the way.'

All the way to Helen's in Stip's car, with Matt alert and bewildered on her knee, she was thinking furiously: *Trust Dad. Trust him to ruin even this.* And behind the anger, a paralysing fear of his death, of the final closing of the ledger with all the debts still unpaid.

Helen was waiting. She had the front door open as they came up the path, and at once took Matt into her arms, crying: 'Oh, look what a bonny wee boy!' She kissed Maggie. 'You poor little thing, what a shock you've had! It only came on him a while ago – last week . . .'

'Auntie, cuddle him, he's going to cry when I leave –'

'Och, he won't cry, will you, laddie? I've got his supper ready –'

'Come on, Maggie!' Stip urged. 'Mum's waiting.'

'Auntie, he's wet his pants, I'm sorry, there was no time –'

'Get along now, I'll manage.'

They left all the cases. Stip had to drag Maggie away, still calling instructions over her shoulder. More driving, this time with a cold, wet knee. No tears. Anxiety about Matt diminished as distance grew between them. Numb, dumb anticipation. A death-bed . . . Stip talked. The old familiar ulcer, that everyone, including its host, had got used to living with, had ruptured. They'd rushed him to hospital, operated at once – but it was no use. A widespread malignancy. Nothing to do but sew him up and wait.

'How long?'

'No one knows. That's the bad thing. Not long, though.'

'Is it hurting?'

'They're keeping him pretty well doped. I'm more worried about Mum than Dad. Dad's soon going to be out of it. Mum's got to go on, without – her reason for living. I don't know how she'll cope.'

'She'll have you, and Ian.'

'Ian doesn't live at home now, he's got his own flat.'

'Oh yes, you told me –' Stip had written. Funny how little she registered home news. Even the theatre-crits her mother cut out for her, and the occasional draft of a short story Stip

108

was struggling with, stung her painfully. She would usually put them aside half-read.

'And,' added Stip, 'he's going to get married.'

'Whoever's going to marry Ian?'

'You don't know her. Her name's Lilian. Very buttoned-up "missish" sort of girl, just his style.'

The car drew up against the black bulk of the hospital. Stip came round to help her out, and she needed his hand. She hadn't washed or gone to the lavatory or had so much as a cup of tea since the plane; she'd been travelling for many hours and she suddenly realised how deadly tired she was. He held her arm closely and led her through the building to the private room where their father lay.

She had known her mother would be there, but she hadn't even thought of Ian. He was standing by the bed, his lean, unlaughing face three distinct years older, his hands behind his back straining his shoulders and stiffening his elbows. His hair had gone thin. It was almost uncanny how he didn't look at her as they came in, as if he had gone blind and deaf – he had even stifled the human reflex to turn as the door opened.

But Mrs Robertson jumped up instantly and stumbled into Maggie's arms. It wasn't till they'd held each other for a long time and Maggie almost forced her to stand back so that she could look at her, that she saw – not three years, but nearer ten had been added since the day they had kissed goodbye at the wedding. Guilt once again smote Maggie, like a flat blow in the face with a paddle.

'Mummy –'

'Oh, darling – where *have* you been?'

The reproach was undisguised. She remembered an incident in early childhood, when she had been punished and run away to hide in the cellar behind the apple-boxes ... The relief at being found. *Oh, there you are, you bad girl – you bad, bad girl, I've been so lonely!* Not worried, not frightened, not angry. Lonely.

Her father looked so unfamiliar when she reached his bedside that she felt nothing, or almost nothing. She had not expected to, but for a different reason. She had thought she would have to make a conscious effort to withhold her sympathy from him. She had not forgiven him for Mrs Dalzell, and she knew he had not forgiven her her perfidy and theft. At first sight, she

109

thought it was too late anyway. His face was tenantless; the drip that was relentlessly feeding his body seemed as pointless as milk deliveries to an empty house. Her mother motioned her to sit in the chair that Ian (judging by its warmth) had risen from just before they entered. Ian was now standing with his back to her at the window, hands still clasped above his buttocks, uncompromising disapproval in every line. Stip stood at the foot of the bed, his hands holding the white-painted rail, and their mother sat opposite her. She was not looking at her husband but at Maggie, drinking her in hungrily through her eyes.

'How are you, darling?' she asked in a whisper, though there seemed no danger of disturbing the deeply-unconscious figure lying between them.

'Mummy, this is awful – it's a terrible shock –'

'I wanted to cable you, to warn you. Ian thought best to just let you come.'

Maggie's eyes flicked to him. An act of kindness, or of subtle cruelty?

'If I'd known, I would have left Matt behind.'

Her mother's eyes swerved away.

'Where . . . is he at Helen's?' she asked.

'Yes, and I dare not leave him there long. He'll scream the place down, he's not used to strangers.' She wriggled in her hard chair. The doom-laden atmosphere, which she felt incapable of entering emotionally, felt like a suit of armour worn back to front. She could not wait to get out of it. What she had said about leaving Matt behind was true, but since he was here, he provided, she cravenly realised, the perfect excuse. Otherwise she would be expected to sit here for hours and days on end, spending her whole leave – her time of revival, of recreation – imprisoned in this white cell at the side of a dying father for whom she had no feelings left except a little scorpion of guilt, still rustling around the empty shell that had once held her proper, daughterly feelings.

Stip drove her back to Helen's. As they drove, Maggie strained forward in her seat, the pull of Matt's angry misery dragging at her physically. But the feeling turned out to have been entirely subjective. Helen greeted them gleefully.

'I managed fine!' she said. 'He ate his dinner and fell asleep straight away. Och, he's a lamb, Maggie, a perfect little lamb!'

110

'How did you manage about changing him? Did you find the nappies?'

'In all that luggage? I didn't even look. I used one of my best damask napkins,' she said, with all the pride of a brilliant innovator. Then, misunderstanding Maggie's dropped jaw, she added quickly, 'They're very soft, I'm sure it won't rub him.'

With Matt evidently in such good hands Maggie had no excuse not to return directly to the hospital, but Stip took pity on her.

'Get to your bed now, Mags, you must be played out. I'll come and fetch you in the morning.'

She saw him to the door. She wanted to talk to him, but suddenly she felt so exhausted there were no words. She simply leant against him and hid her face. He put his arms round her. He smelt different, and he was broader, stronger than she remembered – he had always been so slight, like the proverbial reed that might break. 'You're an oak-tree now,' she murmured.

He gave a little chuckle and patted her.

'How's your life, Stip?'

He was silent and his hand was still.

'You've been away a long, long time, Maggie. Maybe we can talk about our lives when we've dealt with Dad's death.'

'Do you love him? Will you miss him?'

He shook himself and let her go. 'I don't like such questions. I don't look into myself much. I just try to "walk in quiet through the days" ... that's why I hate dramas. They break that – concentration I try to keep, on the path just ahead of my feet. Do you understand what I'm blethering about?'

'Yes. And it's just as bad a way to live as mine.'

'How's your way?'

'Remember my skimming dreams? Feet just above the ground, no effort, no resistance, once you've taken that deep breath and levitated yourself ... It's like that. And it's bad. I felt my feet touch ground when the plane landed. It was the first time for an eternity, Stip.' *Since Matt was born.* That was real enough.

'Are you not happy in Africa, then?' He sounded afraid of her answer.

She stared at the light from the street-lamp which penetrated the coloured panels, set in lead, in Helen's front door.

111

'No. What I have isn't happiness. It's not real enough,' she said at last. 'Don't tell Mummy, will you?'

Stip heaved a very deep sigh. 'Oh God,' he said hollowly. 'We *are* a pair of failures, aren't we?'

He opened the door and walked down the path without saying goodbye. Maggie felt mortally alone suddenly. She crawled up to bed, and for once there was nothing to prevent her taking Matt in beside her. He cuddled close like a big warm bed-toy. She dropped asleep, consoled by love, not thinking of her father at all.

Chapter Twelve

The next few days were frightful. The frightfulness was not so much caused by sorrow and morbid apprehension – that would have been easier to bear because of the feeling of 'rightness' which would have accompanied it. The reason they were frightful for Maggie was because of how little real dread she felt about her father's death. Because, a lot of the time, she felt empty of all but guilt.

Hour upon hour she had to spend sitting by the bedside contemplating that corpse-like figure, aware of her mother's anguish and totally unable to share in it. 'I don't care about him,' she kept thinking. 'I don't honour him.' The biblical phrase, oddly, tormented her conscience more than the other.

But something else tormented her far worse. The money.

How could it be that, throughout the soporific years in Africa as Bruce's appendage and Matt's mother, she had been able to push aside the urgency of this debt? It became, as the never-ending days crept past, a token of the whole inexplicable syndrome of her escape from every aspect of reality and of herself: her career (which had been her fundamental motivation until the night of Matt's conception), her sense of responsibility for herself, her talent – even her mistakes. Bruce had entered her; and as he broke her open and planted her with his seed, so he breached her walls of selfhood. He had taken her over, and, mysteriously – she couldn't fathom it, sitting here in her home-place, breathing her native air – she had gone limp, as she had allowed herself to go limp that night on the pink chenille, let him have her, then let him bear her away to a form of personal oblivion. The fact that she must now sit beside her dying father, and be unable to say to him, even in her thoughts, 'I've paid my debt to you. I worked for it and saved it and denied myself things and it is paid,' seemed to her the main device on the tarnished banner of her situation.

She dreaded his regaining consciousness. She sat with her eyes fixed on his closed, sunken ones, willing them not to open. She could not face him. Yet she knew the awfulness of her wish. Her mother, sitting opposite, holding the cold, vein-strung hand and gazing at the dwindling face, must be willing the opposite – that the eyes would open just once more, and the voice speak a few words to her that she could carry with her on the relentless long march of the rest of her life.

To resolve this unbearable dichotomy, Maggie's newly-activated brain, revitalised by proximity to the source of guilt, began clicking, like a machine left well-oiled and ready but needing to be run in. Bruce had given her a generous allowance to spend on her leave. Enough to go to London if she liked, to stay in a hotel . . . Of course, it was not her own money, not her *own* money. Nothing you hadn't earned by your own work could ever be your own. But still, it was hers to spend, hers to forego . . . Yes, she would do it, it was better than nothing; it would end part of the discomfort. It was nowhere near enough, but it was something.

'Mummy.'

'Yes, dear.' (They were whispering – why?)

'I've got some of the money.'

Her mother looked at her blankly. 'What money?'

'The money I . . . stole from Dad.'

The look became darkling, unreadable. 'Is it not a bit late to be bothering with that?'

'I couldn't before. I've not been earning.'

'No. It's a great pity.'

'What is?'

Her mother looked surprised. 'Why, that you didn't go on with your career. The money . . .' She shrugged.

'Did he ever mention it?'

'Neither it, nor you.'

Somehow, despite everything, these words struck her heart cold. 'Never?' All these *years* . . .

'I would tell him news. Read him letters. But he didn't respond.'

'But he listened. He knew about Matt.'

'He knew. He was waiting.'

114

'Waiting?'

'I thought so. That was my impression.'

'For what?'

'I thought you would know that. I wasn't in the room that last time.'

Maggie said no more. She was too startled. All traces of boredom vanished as she sat thinking, reliving. Oh yes, she knew what he had been waiting for. Now she suffered – not 'properly' from love and sorrow – but from the old guilt, more clearly rationalised. A strange thought came to her in its midst: If I had to be so wicked, why couldn't I have had a less sensitive conscience? Or, being cursed with one, why couldn't I be a better human being with less to feel guilty about?

Staring at her father's dying face hour by hour had a hypnotic effect. She knew it was overdoing it; she was punishing herself almost consciously, as one does for a guilt that it is too late or impossible to assuage in any way that will do the wronged person any good. But nevertheless, she saw her father as someone who had slaved all his life and off whose sweat she had scraped her chance. Not the least of the guilt was having failed to make use of that chance, to have stolen, and then thrown the stolen treasure away.

She contemplated never going back to Africa. Staying here. Trying to get back to work. But there was Matt. Matt tugged her back from this idea like a leg-iron. She hardly thought of Bruce; Bruce melted out of her calculations. But to Matt she returned every night. Matt was utterly, ineluctably real.

Mr Robertson died a week after Maggie's return to Scotland, without regaining consciousness.

Mrs Robertson's collective noun for relatives was 'a descent of vultures'. They never came to happy occasions like weddings – they were not invited. But funerals are come-all-ye occasions which exclude no one.

The phone at home rang at intervals for three days and nights. 'It's yer Auntie Fiona from Fife – can ye no' come to meet a body at the station?' 'It's yer second cousin Donald – not the Robertson Donald, the Reid Donald. Tell yer mother I'm the eldest of her step-cousin Fanny. We've come down for

115

the funeral from Inverness and we've nowhere to stay, can ye find a corner for us for a couple of nights . . .?'

Maggie, Stip and Ian had, perforce, to work side by side, even Ian had to do his share – there were not enough women to make beds, do shopping, slice the funeral baked meats (very thin) on to ritual dishes.

Lilian, Ian's fiancée, came to help. She was a tall, thin-lipped, almost but not quite elegant girl (she missed through being too rangy and not dressing well enough to hide it) with very short hair like a man and a maddening reluctance not to wear the glasses she desperately needed so that she kept fumbling and bumping into things. Maggie, watching her put the salmon sandwiches on the same dish with the beef ones, reflected that if Tanya or someone she loved had had this foolish vanity she might have found it endearing. But Lilian was going to marry Ian. And Ian was making her life a misery.

Once, in a brief intermission in the frenzied preparations, he came upon her – caught her, rather – coming out of the lavatory with the local paper turned back to the entertainment page.

He spoke to her for the first time, apart from essential domestic exchanges. 'Why not do the crossword while you're about it, or read the comic-strips? That would just about sum you up, with your trumpery concerns! Perhaps you'd prefer to scamper off to a play or a cinema tomorrow instead of attending our father's funeral? You're certainly dressed for some kind of frivolous outing,' he added, indicating her perfectly ordinary summer dress.

'Do you expect me to dress in black?'

'It would be more fitting,' he retorted. He himself wore a black arm-band which presumably Lilian had stitched to the sleeve of his sombre grey worsted suit. Lilian had worn the same navy-blue dress, unadorned, for the three days Maggie had known her.

'Mum isn't.'

'Our mother's mourning is in her heart,' Ian actually said.

Such sententiousness put Maggie past all patience.

'You pompous ass!' she burst out. 'Do you think you've got a monopoly on grief because you wear yours literally on your sleeve?'

He regarded her with narrowed eyes. 'Of course, you never had a very strict regard for the truth,' he said slowly. 'But surely

116

even you would find it hard to look anyone in the eye and say you *feel* anything very much about the fact that our father is lying down there in his coffin.'

She flushed, gripping the paper in a spasm that made it crackle revealingly.

'My feelings are my business,' she said.

'Very small business, then.' She started to turn away angrily, but he caught her arm. They were standing alone on the upstairs landing. It was rather dark; but she could see his eyes, the bright points of piercing light in them, and smell his breath. It bore a trace of whiskey.

'I'd rather be pompous than be what you are,' he said with deliberate provocation.

'And what am I, according to you?'

'An immoral woman,' he said. 'Without principle or a sense of purpose. You go where every wind blows. I'm sorry for a certain someone, for I don't think you're fit to be a mother.'

Maggie stared at him, winded.

'How dare you say that – ' she gasped.

His fingers still biting her arm, he said, 'I know what you and Steven think of me. I know you've always despised me. I know my own faults, but despite them I know I'm more of a man than he is, and I'll be a better parent when the time comes than you. I'm honest, and I accept my responsibilities. And I don't let myself hanker after what I can't pay for myself. Nor do I lash out at people as you lashed out at Father, throwing his little weaknesses in his face so that he never got over it – when you were unrepayably in debt to him.'

After a terrible, paralysed moment, Maggie tore herself away. Like a hurt child, she rushed straight to her mother.

She was in the bedroom she had shared with her husband for thirty-five years, sitting on the double bed sorting her husband's clothes. She looked up, white-faced, as Maggie burst in. Maggie stopped short, realising with deep embarrassment that she was interrupting something as private as parental love-making. She started to back out again, but her mother said, 'Come along in, Maggie, what's the matter? More "vultures" in the offing?'

Maggie went and joined her on the bed. Around them were piles of dark suits – each suit divided into its three components: here the trousers folded into squares, here the waistcoats, here the jackets, turned inside out except for the sleeves – all dark.

117

Dark brown, dark blue, dark grey. Black. Some with fine pinstripes which emphasised rather than relieved the sombreness. On the floor beside the huge old-fashioned open wardrobe lay a row of shoes, only four pairs, good quality, very old, scrupulously maintained and still on trees. What would happen to them now?

'Why are you doing this now, Mummy? Why aren't you resting?'

'This is a kind of resting,' she said. She laid another jacket on the pile, its worn shiny lining reflecting the dim light. Both curtains were drawn.

'Must you sit in the dark?'

'My eyes ache,' she said. 'I can do this in the dark, anyway. I know every fold of all these garments by heart. He hadn't bought anything new for years. I used to give him sweaters and shirts at Christmastime, but I couldn't give him suits, he had to be measured for those. He didn't treat himself to a new suit for about – oh, it must be five years.'

'Was he – so hard up?'

'Well, things had begun to pick up. After the big mill closed, we got a lot of their business. Ian's done wonders, you know. But we had our own private austerity.' Maggie said nothing. She was looking at her mother's dress. Even in the dark she recognised it as the one she had been wearing that last day, at the wedding – mauve crêpe, with a pattern of drab-olive leaves. She had rushed into the room with the rhetorical question on her lips: 'It wasn't all my fault, was it?' Now she feared the answer, or the evasion, too greatly to ask it. Tears rolled. Her mother, for once misunderstanding her, took her in her arms almost gratefully.

'There, there, darling. You see, you did love him really! These things are so painful. Don't make it worse for yourself!'

In the very midst of being comforted, Maggie froze and withdrew herself. She took refuge in extreme practicality. Blowing her nose, she said, 'Mummy, what's going to happen now? Are you going to be all right financially? I've got some money, as I told you. And I can get more –'

'Oh, no, dear,' her mother said instantly.

'Why not?'

'I don't want to hurt your feelings, but I really couldn't take your husband's money. I don't know him.'

118

There was a silence. Maggie empathised so perfectly with this reaction that it was useless to argue.

'Besides,' Mrs Robertson went on, 'it's unnecessary. The business will run on much as usual. Ian and his staff will see to that.' Maggie noted that Stip was not mentioned. Was he then such an inconsiderable factor in the ongoings of the firm? It shamed her somehow that Ian was the rock to whom her mother now clung, not herself or Stip.

'But Ian's going to be married.'

'What has that to do with it?'

Maggie didn't know exactly what had made her say it. In her subconscious, marriage equalled desertion of her mother. But Ian was not going to Africa. Ian would be living nearby. Lilian, purblind and bony and uptight and with whatever other faults she might prove to have, was already down in the Robertson kitchen in an apron boiling tongues. She was not removing Ian from the clan, she was joining it. She would be more of a comfort and a help to Maggie's widowed mother than Maggie would.

'I wish I didn't have to go back!' she burst out. She had not known till that moment that it would not matter to her, deep down, if she never saw Bruce again. She had everything here that counted. That other world, that steamy, disorientating, debilitating other life, yawned like a pit.

'Maggie, you mustn't say that on my account. You've your own life to lead.'

Maggie stared at her.

'It's not only for you,' she said at last, her tongue clumsy with unspeakable thoughts.

Her mother's face changed. She seized Maggie's hand in a fierce grip. 'Oh, my dear! Don't say all my loneliness has been for nothing! Don't tell me you're not happy!'

And she meant, Maggie saw, precisely that – that if Maggie were not happy, she was to spare her mother knowing it. So she hugged her, and lied, and said of course she was happy, that Bruce gave her all she wanted and was never unkind to her and was every bit as nice as ever she could have hoped. And so the dangerous corner was passed and they began to talk about Matt.

Mrs Robertson had not been able to stand out against Matt's charms, and even if she had, Helen's besotted enthusiasm

119

would have won her over. Helen had been almost as loth to be relieved of him as Tolly, when the time came for Maggie and Matt to move back into the family home; she had insisted on coming with them in Stip's car, holding Matt possessively on her knee; and when they arrived, it was she who had borne him into the house, crying out his praises so loudly and continuously that even Ian had not been able to avoid looking at Matt, though he had drawn the line at touching him.

But Mrs Robertson had him thrust into her arms before she knew what was happening.

'Ah, here's your Granny, then! What a lucky Granny! Look at him, Mary, only look at his darling face, isn't he just the spit of Maggie when she was that age?' He was perfectly unlike Maggie at any age and in every particular, but the discussion that followed on this contentious topic between the two sisters tided over the awkward moment, and throughout it Matt sat beaming in Mrs Robertson's arms and doing himself no harm at all by saying 'Gran-gran-gran – ' and patting her face. Helen had probably conditioned him to the belief that all grey-haired wrinkle-faced humans were benign to the point of slavishness, and here was another of them, soon reinforcing the lesson by jogging him up and down and letting him play with her necklace. Nobody, and certainly not Matt, noticed Ian stalking furiously from the room.

And since then, Matt had been the nucleus of the only bright area in the sombre old funeral-shadowed house. All the vulture-relatives, even the dreariest and vinegariest, softened a degree or two at the sight of his bright red hair and pearly-toothed grin. Even dreaded Auntie Flora from Fife was spotted giving him a sweetie when she thought no one was looking. Only Ian held out.

Over and over again, Helen said, 'If ever you want someone to leave him with, just you ask Aunt Helen. *Great*-aunt Helen! I'll be only too pleased. Only too delighted!'

And even in her state of shock and mourning, this roused Maggie's mother at last to remark tartly to Maggie: 'He's got a grandmother, you know. I should hope I'll get first refusal.'

But Maggie said, 'Of course, Mummy, but I don't see why I should ever need anyone to look after him. After all . . .' To herself only, she continued, '. . . I'll be stuck out there for years yet.'

My loneliness has all been for nothing ... A week after the funeral, Maggie carried those words, poker-worked into her memory, back to Africa with her. She knew she would keep thinking about them, long after she had stopped thinking about her father, or Ian, or anything either of them had said *deliberately* to wound her. She could not escape from the bed she had made. It now seemed to be mainly for her mother's sake that she must make it possible to lie in it less defeatedly.

Chapter Thirteen

The first effective thing she did on her return to Port Harcourt was to get in touch with Joan Hillman. Some residual pockets of Scottish air in her lungs not only impelled her to do this, but gave her such impetus that instead of tamely telephoning Joan at home, she bearded her in her professional lair, at the school.

It was a long, low building, architecturally related to all the other buildings erected by the oil company for the use of their employees. It accommodated some hundred children aged from five to eleven, about two-thirds of them white. The classes were small, the discipline firm, the headmistress English and the curriculum likewise, with strong emphasis on the three 'r's, plus geography and history. British history, of course. Once, early on, Joan had tried to introduce a bit of Nigerian history. The head, Mrs Hatchard, 'had her in' with a vengeance. 'Surely their own culture and history have some relevance?' Joan had asked. Mrs Hatchard's reply might have stood for the credo of the school. 'We are not here, Mrs Hillman, to break our heads or theirs with concepts of relevance. We are here to follow the English syllabus. The future of this country is in our hands. *That* is all the "relevance" we need take into account.'

The school was well-shuttered and fanned though still unbearably hot. But there was a pleasing air of orderly calm as Maggie walked about, peering through the glass panels in the doors in search of Joan. Black heads and white were bent intently over conventional desks while teachers stood before sturdy, well-chalked blackboards. Apart from the heat, and the chiaroscuro element, it all smacked of Maggie's own schooldays. This was reassuring.

She found Joan dictatorially dictating to some fifteen ten-

122

year-olds. When she caught sight of Maggie through the panel, she stopped short and goggled comically

She came at once to the door and shut it behind her.

'My dear! Welcome back! What brings you to our little indoctrination centre? Nothing wrong, I hope?'

'Well, you did say I ought to come and give you a hand.'

'Did I not!' She looked at Maggie more closely. 'Has something happened? In Scotland? What's given you that sudden do-or-die expression?'

'Nothing! I just felt I had to make a move quickly, before I –'

'Before old daybed renewed its clutch,' supplied Joan briskly. 'Quite! Very wise. All right, in you come, and let's put you through your paces.'

And without more ado, she held open the door.

Maggie could see five black and ten white faces gazing at her expectantly. Her audience! She quailed. But it was too late, as she had wanted it to be – for this inevitability, she had made herself come without warning or preparation.

'Stand up, class!' boomed Joan. 'We have a visitor.'

Maggie took a deep breath and walked in. Her heart pounded, her mouth was dry and her palms itched. She recognised the sensation instantly. It was stage-fright. But it was all right. She knew her lines.

'Good morning!' she said sunnily. 'My name's Mrs Macrae. I'm going to tell you all about acting.'

It was arranged that Maggie should come to the school as an auxiliary drama teacher three mornings a week. Unaccountably, the formidable Mrs Hatchard took a fancy to her.

'Normally all our teachers are graduates,' she said. 'But then, you are a graduate, in your *field*, aren't you, my dear? You'll have no trouble, I'm sure. Just keep them busy. We don't expect a production of *Hamlet* at term's end, you know! Lots of pretend games, acting out little songs and stories from their reading books, that sort of thing. You'll find the Africans a trifle slower to memorise than ours, I dare say, but you can make allowances . . .'

'Patronising silly old trout!' Joan rumbled later.

Maggie found the whole enterprise fascinating. Drama and

acting were very much to the children's taste and they threw themselves joyfully into everything she gave them to do. After a term of getting to know them, she decided to push beyond the 'pretend games' and try something more challenging.

She searched through books of playlets she found in what passed for the school library, but they were all as dated and bloodless as the Girls' Own Annual 1933 which also had its place there. There were, of course, no blacks in the casts which were anyway far too small. She needed plays with a bit of meat in them, a bit of – well . . . 'Relevance!' cried Joan. One evening Maggie sat down in her kitchen and wrote a play of her own.

'What Madam write?' Tolly could not read and showed no signs of wanting to learn, but the whole business of writing intrigued her.

'It's a play, Tolly, a story, all told in talking. About the Prince of Kula.'

Tolly's eyes grew wide.

'Kula Prince like I know?'

'Yes, of course. It's your story, that you tell Matty.'

She was basing her play on an old Ibo legend about a tribal prince and princess and their star-crossed love, which comes in its tragic and grisly climax when the princess's father eats the prince. It happened to be three-year-old Matt's favourite story. Bruce, overhearing it in Tolly's version, had been appalled.

'Cannibalism – honestly, Maggie, should you not apply a bit of maternal censorship? He might think the blacks will eat him!'

'He loves that part best. Tolly gobbles him up.'

It was Joan who had thought of looking the legend up in a book of Nigerian folklore, and, finding it 'authentic' (another of her favourite words) had slyly suggested they use it for the play. Maggie was dubious, as well she might have been.

'What will Mrs Hatchard say?'

'Who cares?'

'Don't we?'

'Not I! I'm fed up, anyway. I'm thinking of leaving the company school and starting up a little dame-school, the dame being me.'

'Who'd go?'

'Thanks a lot!'

'No, seriously. Look before you leap. Who's left? Or would you poach pupils from Mrs Hatchard?'

'I'm not committing myself at this stage. I'm confident I'd find some piccens to teach, black, white or khaki.'

'Could I join you, if I get the sack?'

'Need you ask? Come on, girl, where's your gumption? Give the kids something to get their teeth into! It gives me a pain, watching them being moulded into little artificial Englishmen.'

The eleven-year-olds from the top class fell in love with the play at first reading. Black and white alike hurled themselves into it, almost fighting for the leading parts. After consultation with the children, Maggie cast the black ones as the Kulas who came to avenge their prince, while the whites were the cannibal King Onyo, his daughter and their retinue. They were to have their skins doctored with a mixture of cold-cream and cocoa.

'You ought to let the king at least keep his white face,' said Joan sardonically. 'Taking bites out of black princes is highly symbolic of the way we exploit them.'

Mrs Hatchard was delighted to hear that there would be – if not *Hamlet* – at least a play of sorts to set before the parents at the end of term. She was always seeking to enhance the school's prestige. In fact, she was so busy rehearsing her choir and drilling squads of juvenile athletes to augment the entertainment that she had no time to vet the play until the dress rehearsal.

'Now we're for it,' whispered Joan on that chaotic occasion. Her leathery face was creased into a schoolboy grin, and the 'fag' that she permitted herself extra-curricularly jiggled on her nether lip in response to a silent interior chuckle.

Maggie was in no such jocund mood. She was scared. It was all very well for Joan . . . Mrs Hatchard doubled as the wife of Bruce's superior in the company.

But providence, in the shape of a timely telephone call, took a hand. The Head's possible wrath was postponed, and the show went on.

And what a show! Of course, Joan shared the honours. The sets and props, costumes and music which embellished the production and clearly inspired the child actors were the results of her ineluctable bombastic pressure upon the arts and crafts

125

department and her own servants, from whom all but basic household chores had been withdrawn to enable them to hammer, paint and sew to the experts' instructions.

But the play itself, and the production, were really Maggie's. Her special talent for the theatre had brought it to birth. The throne in its straw-walled 'palace', the dug-outs on the 'river-bank', the splendid befeathered robes, replicas of tribal body ornaments and the throbbing and bleating of the school orchestra playing their native instruments for once, were the embellishments. The main meal was of Maggie's providing; and as the electric waves of excitement generated by the play swept the audience the main triumph was Maggie's.

It was not unmingled with terror.

Through a peephole in the jungle-painted wing she watched Mrs Hatchard's face. Amid her audience of company-official parents she very quickly came to the realisation that they were being shown an uncensored rendition of a full-blooded Ibo legend. When the princess rushed into the throne room, found her mutilated prince at the foot of the steps and cried, 'As I feared! My Father has eaten his flesh!' a thrill (whether of horror or delight) ran visibly across the audience, and Mrs Hatchard, pale as a wraith, half rose from her chair. Inhibition alone restrained her, Joan remarked later with relish, from stopping the show then and there.

But no such restraint was in evidence when she 'had Maggie in' the next morning.

She sent a message to Maggie's house to summon her at eight o'clock in the morning. Hollow-stomached but still with the sweet smell of success in her nostrils, Maggie put on her large picture hat and walked through the drenching heat to the school.

Mrs Hatchard had had eighteen hours to prepare her scene and she was word-perfect. She had dressed and hairdressed the part – all strong rigid lines and good, English taste. She was wearing her dark glasses with the gilt rims, severe and inscrutable.

'You know, Mrs Macrae, why I have called you in.'

'Well,' said Maggie with a diffident smile, 'there was such a crush last night after the show, you didn't have a chance to tell me what you thought of the play.'

'I was extremely shocked by it.'

126

'Oh?'

'And so, I may say, were many others.'

'One didn't notice it from backstage. When an audience is shocked, they don't usually applaud and cheer like that.'

'The more – how shall I put it? – naive elements may have responded over-vociferously. Several of the others made a point of approaching me afterwards. To complain, Mrs Macrae, and before you ask, they were not all *our* people. Several of the Nigerians were very offended. They don't care to be reminded of their tribal past, which is by no means remote. It was in the poorest taste and I hardly knew how to apologise.' She coughed and drew herself, if possible, a little straighter, a mannerism she had when about to pontificate. 'We are here to impart, and, where they exist in the bud, to reinforce, Western values and culture. Could you not have chosen to dramatise one of our splendid classics to enlighten and uplift the children?'

'What a good idea,' said Maggie warmly. 'One of the Greek myths, perhaps.'

'Precisely.'

'What about Cronus?'

'Who?' asked Mrs Hatchard unwarily.

'Cronus,' said Maggie blandly. 'You remember, the one who ate his children.' The stern face around the sunglasses altered. 'Not King Onyo's bite or two, all the lot, "with the bones and the beak".'

She paused to give the headmistress an opening here but she was speechless. Maggie softened. 'I'm sorry, Mrs Hatchard, but our splendid classical myths, as you call them, are just as full of horrors and taboos as any of the local ones. I must say I thought it all went marvellously. The children really rose to the occasion. Honestly, now – weren't you proud of them? I was. Your choir was lovely, too,' she added generously.

Mrs Hatchard stared at her dumbly. This was definitely not in her script. Maggie pursued her offensive boldly.

'Of course if you see it differently, you might want me to stop teaching here.'

Her intended crisp dismissal thus pre-empted, Mrs Hatchard stammered, 'Do – er . . . do you wish to leave?'

'Me? Certainly not! I love it. But of course it's for you to decide. If you feel I've blundered, I suppose you'll have to let me go. Bit of a pity . . . I had a marvellous idea for the

127

Christmas show.' She folded her hands on her knee demurely and gazed wide-eyed at the black blanks of Mrs Hatchard's sunglasses.

Maggie's teaching career continued. Joan was overjoyed, as well as hugely impressed by what amounted to the rout of Mrs Hatchard, who in the end had almost begged Maggie to stay on.

'And you're the winner in more ways than one! You've struck a blow for colonial wives against the daybed and the bridge party. Who was that Victorian feminist who said, "A woman who works is by that alone better than one who does not"? I couldn't agree more! Though there are some who won't forgive you for it. You're letting the side down, making them feel perhaps there's more to life than the wretched little gossipy tea-parties you and I are too busy to go to.'

One Sunday there was a pre-lunch cocktail affair which Maggie had felt obliged, by Bruce and by the fact that her turn was well overdue, to give. All Bruce's immediate circle of colleagues and their wives had to be invited.

If these had seemed shallow and boring at first, they seemed far more so now that they had been thoroughly chewed over till they were tasteless, like inferior chewing-gum; the trouble was, Maggie was not in a position to spit them out. There was no real escape.

The company this particular day was abuzz with a really exciting titbit. A new female worker from America had arrived to augment the local Anglican mission. Her name, appropriately enough, was Angela, and it appeared she was a far cry from the WC's received ideas of a missionary, being young, blonde, and pretty to the point of downright seductiveness, according to several of the men who had seen her.

The women were inclined to be disapproving (due, perhaps, to some natural wifely anxieties) but the men loudly welcomed the newcomer and made a lot of heavy jokes about the salutary effect her advent was likely to have on the Company members' religious observances. Bruce's somewhat lubricious contribution was that the male members of the mission would obviously get first go and that oil company staff would have to wait in line after Sunday service.

128

This was poorly received by the women, who nevertheless settled down happily to a bitch-in about the newcomer which got sorely on Maggie's nerves.

Turning to Joan, who was hovering on the fringes gloomily downing her habitual pint of iced beer, Maggie muttered, 'Can't you stop them? Poor girl! We haven't even set eyes on her and already her character's in shreds.' Joan, however, was low-spirited from boredom. 'Can't be bothered,' she said shortly. 'They're your guests. You stop 'em.'

So Maggie elbowed Margaret aside for once.

'Tell me,' she asked innocently, into a lull while William refilled glasses, 'has this Angela actually been caught in bed with any of our husbands yet?' Joan snorted into her beer froth; otherwise the lull was startlingly prolonged. 'Because if not,' Maggie continued, 'I wonder if we're not overestimating their attractions. After all, if she sees herself as a bride of Christ, what on earth have *we* got to worry about?'

After they'd all gone home Joan gave Maggie one of her great exuberant hugs.

'Top marks! First class!' she exclaimed delightedly. Bruce, on the other hand, accorded her neither hugs nor praise, but stalked off without a word – he considered she had broken the rules. Neither he nor Maggie could have dreamt what a radical change the much maligned Angela was to have on their lives.

129

Chapter Fourteen

Maggie had not realised the degree of Bruce's attachment to the African continent. So far as she was aware, the Company's writ would run just so long as they saw fit to keep Bruce in the tropics, and this did not generally exceed four or five years, due to the unwholesome climate. So she looked forward, almost without thought, to a return to Britain within the next year or so.

The fourth year (which Maggie took to be their last) Bruce once again sent her home alone with Matt. He was not going to Paris this time; he said he had business in South Africa and she accepted this unquestioningly. She was aching to get home.

Her mother and Aunt Helen were delighted to see Matt, and all but tore him in two between them. They had planned something special for Maggie's holiday which they revealed to her as excitedly as two little girls with a secret surprise. It was a month – her whole time at home – in the Hebrides, on one of the lovelier islands where Helen had an old friend who ran a private hotel. They were not to know how Maggie's heart sank at the prospect; all she had longed for was to stay in the purlieus of Edinburgh and attend the Festival – she had timed her leave exactly to coincide with it; but looking into the two elderly, eager faces, she knew she must forego her heart's desire for yet another year.

And, lying awake at nights on the island, listening to the night-birds and smelling the sea, she found comfort in the thought that it would have been a species of torture to sit in theatres 'on the wrong side of the footlights' as Tanya used to say, perhaps watching old friends and fellow students whose careers were burgeoning, and feeling her mother's vicarious disappointment in her ... No. Better this way. Better the innocent unsullied fun of the beaches, watching Matt jumping

130

and sliding down the dunes with shrieks of glee, collecting shells, looking for 'creatures' as he called every living thing with legs; persuading her two 'old ladies' (as they called themselves) into the stretchy bathing suits she had made them buy and which they'd sworn they would never, never wear, and revelling in the sight of them splashing and playing – with Matt and with each other – in the shallows, and even lying in the unpeopled sand to sunbathe their pale city skins and ageing bones, before strolling back to the hotel for wonderful Scottish food. Matt ate scones and bacon and roast lamb and even porridge until great-aunt and granny swore they could see him growing before their eyes. They doted on him and he rewarded them with gifts of shells, and popping seaweed and ropy seaweed and lacy seaweed, and hermit crabs which Helen carried about with her on the beach, talking to them. For ever after, Maggie was to call a certain kind of nonsense-conversation 'hermit-crab talk', in memory of this holiday. Matt, young as he was at the time, never forgot it either. Africa was as if it had never been, and so was everything else; it was just Maggie, her mother, her aunt, and the boy they all loved. Maggie even forgot about not being a good mother. There was no reminder of it, because Matt, being perfectly happy, was perfectly good.

The only times Maggie really thought about her husband was when she noticed Matt picking up a faint Scots accent. 'That'll please Bruce,' she thought.

Saying goodbye to Helen and her mother for another whole year, after such an intimate, happy time as they'd had together, was particularly hard. Little did Maggie guess how soon she'd be seeing them again. Nor did she have a clue what awaited her in Nigeria – what Bruce had been up to in her absence.

The night after her return, he laid on a special, intimate little dinner at home. He had something very exciting to tell her.

Maggie could scarcely believe her ears. According to Bruce's plans, they were never going back to live in the British Isles. He loved Africa too much ever to leave it. He had arranged for the Company to post him to South Africa after his tour in Nigeria, and to this end had bought them a beautiful bungalow in Capetown, and had given orders for its decoration and furnishing, which was going on at this very moment. Within a few

131

months they would move there, into that 'beautiful country' with its 'superb climate'. She would live a life of ease and plenty, looked after by even more servants than they had here; Matt would, of course, in due course be shipped back to Scotland to prep school, but meanwhile would go to school down there and have a wonderful, privileged life.

'There's a gorgeous garden,' Bruce enthused, 'nothing really needs doing to that – you should see the fruit trees, the date palms – oranges, lemons, grapefruit, straight off your own trees – and a far better social life than you've had here! Theatres and things, too, of course. You'll go crazy for it.'

And at last he stopped enthusing, leaned back in his chair, a picture of self-satisfaction, and waited.

Maggie thought she might well go crazy right now. She was so angry she could find no suitable expression of her feelings. She wanted to upend the table into his lap, to hurl things at him, to shout, 'How dare you! How dare you! How dare you!' at the top of her lungs. Margaret, on the other hand, simply wanted to stand up, drop her napkin on the chair, and walk out into the night without a single word.

If Maggie did not act out her feelings at once, Margaret usually won, or at least the compromise struck favoured Margaret's way. Eventually it was Margaret who said with apparent control, 'Do tell me, Bruce. Am I a partner in this enterprise – our marriage, I mean – or just some kind of adjunct?'

Bruce looked very taken aback. After a moment he leant across the table and put his big hand over hers.

'Oh come on, darling! Of course you're a partner! I just wanted to surprise you about the house. I took all your little fads and fancies into account in choosing and decorating it. I did it with you in mind every minute. It was all for you. Every bit of it.'

Maggie thought she might scream. But she held herself in rigidly.

'Well,' she said when she could speak reasonably calmly, 'thank you for giving me a peep at the programme. It's very interesting. But I have to tell you that I don't appreciate *faits accomplis*. I don't like little surprises which affect my entire life. I like to make my own decisions. I see I have some to make very shortly. When I've made them, I'll let you know.'

The 'celebration' dinner ended in frozen silence. Bruce

132

made one or two attempts to thaw her, but she was wholly unresponsive. They did not, that evening, perform the customary ritual of going in to Matt's room to look at him together, normally one of the few moments of real communion in their day. Maggie silently took some sheets out of the linen drawer and arranged herself on the daybed. Bruce, hangdog, though whether from guilt or simple disappointment she couldn't say, went to the connubial bed alone and without protest.

Quarrels between lovers are full of passion, and seldom end without a period of bitter sulking brought on by deep hurt. Maggie was not hurt, only very angry, and she did not sulk. If she didn't speak much either for the next few weeks it was not because she wanted to 'show' Bruce, or hurt him back; it was because she was thinking, as she had said she would, about his plans for her and how best to extricate herself and Matt from them without depriving Matt of his father. She went back to the double bed the second night because she saw no reason to make a gesture of it; besides, she couldn't sleep properly on the daybed. Bruce made overtures every night for a week and every night was rebuffed. Finally he said plaintively, 'How long are you going to keep this up? I'll be a nervous wreck.'

'Oh all right, then,' she said, 'go on.'

After a few minutes he said, 'Not like this. I can't.'

'Good for you, that's something in your favour,' she said acidly, and rolled over and went to sleep without a qualm. It was the first time he had noticed or let himself be aware that she was, from the point of view of pleasure, a non-participant. It was the first time he had ever said 'I can't' because *she* couldn't. She felt no remorse at having shown him the real state of the game for once. She'd always acted her way through it before, for his sake. Now the anger got between her and her usual adequate performance.

No solution to her other problem occurred to her, and she was still brooding over it several weeks later when William brought her in a telegram with her lunchtray.

'Aunt Helen is seriously ill. If you want to see her again you had better come. Ian.'

133

Maggie registered the style before the content. Trust Ian not to resort to the demeaning slickness of telegramese – he'd rather pay more. Then, with a belated pang, harsh as a blow, came a mental picture of Helen tucking a hot water bottle into her bed, followed by a series of others involving Matt . . . Bruce came home to find her tear-stained and packing.

'You don't need to go home for her, surely!' was his thrifty reaction. 'Good grief, you've only just come back! If I rushed to the bedside every time one of my aunties conked out –'

'She's the only proper aunt I've got and I love her,' said Maggie.

'You're not taking Matt!'

Maggie hesitated. The trouble was, she didn't know whether Helen was in a state to recognise anyone, whether seeing Matt would be a comfort to her. Matt had just started nursery school. It had not been easy to get him settled. To hike him out now would mean ructions later.

'No,' she agreed reluctantly at last. 'I'll leave him with you and Tolly.'

Tolly, who was handing her things from the wardrobe, beamed from ear to ear at this news. She had not liked to ask.

'Tolly take good care!' she cried, wringing her hands in a way she had when she was especially happy.

Bruce took time off work to take Maggie to the airport. This was uncharacteristic, but then he had been behaving with quite unusual punctilliousness of late, rather as he had after their encounter on the pink chenille, and for the same sort of reasons, she supposed. She had not thought about it much, having learnt better in the intervening years than to be so cheaply won over. The house in the Cape had not been mentioned since the fatal dinner party, but it was still there between them, the pain of its unilateral purchase as sore and humiliating to her as had once been the pain of his invasion of her body.

Still, she allowed him to kiss her at the barrier.

'Take your time,' he said. 'We'll manage fine. I'll write.' He looked at her, bit his lip and kissed her unresponding cheek again. 'Don't go on being angry,' he said.

'I'm not angry,' Maggie replied. Actually, it was Margaret. Margaret had been very much to the fore these past weeks, all on her buttoned-up dignity where Maggie would have blown up. It was Margaret who stood there letting him kiss her without

134

jerking away. Only deep inside was Maggie, whimpering, 'I'm saying goodbye to my husband and I can't feel anything except pain that I don't care.'

But she cared about leaving Matt behind. She rejoiced at the strong pangs, and promised lavish presents to quell his tears. In Scotland, she thought suddenly as the plane took off, the residual padding would slip from her heart, leaving its naked skin unprotected. There she might be able to apprehend what she felt for Matt, especially if he were absent. For surely mother-love should have more of anguish in it; be more than a placid contentment underlaid by a stifled unease.

Chapter Fifteen

Again it was Stip who met her at the airport. He was about twenty-five now, but he looked more. His open, snubby face was open and snubby no longer, but somehow closed and rather pinched; his skin had lost the ruddiness she remembered and taken on an office pallor emphasised by strange maroonish circles under his eyes. Even his tuft (she had noticed this last time) no longer sprouted but was trained to lie flat and unobtrusive. There was a sense in which the whole of him looked trained to lie flat and unobtrusive. This was surely Ian's doing. Ian was the boss since their father died.

Impulsively she put her hand on Stip's knee as they drove through the city in his sober little black Morris. She remembered his dream – how, when he was a successful writer, he would wear flamboyant, dashing clothes ('No three-piece suits – never!') and drive a 'high-powered low red car'. She felt suddenly angry, for him and towards him.

'How is she?'

'Bad.'

'What is it?'

'Renal failure.' He glanced at her. 'Kidneys. One gone and one on its way.'

'Can she talk? Does she know people?'

'I wouldn't have let Ian send for you if she couldn't recognise anyone.'

The rain was teeming down. Maggie watched the windscreen wipers dealing with it. She wanted to revel in its grey coolness but she felt too sad about Helen to enjoy anything. She had left her hand on Stip's knee but so far he had not acknowledged it. She gave him a squeeze and he glanced at her again and then back to the wet road.

'And how goes it with you?' he asked.

136

'All right,' she said. 'I still hate the climate. It's good to see grey stone and green grass and the kind of rain you wouldn't mind walking through.' Suddenly she remembered walking toward the theatre in Sheffield that Sunday long ago, her arm linked with Tanya's and their hands stuffed in their raincoat pockets . . .

'Stip,' Maggie said tentatively, 'could we . . . could we drive past the theatre?'

'The King's? But we've passed it. Why? Did you want to mark the location of our juvenile escapade?' He whistled a few bars of the title song of *Oklahoma*, but petered out as if embarrassed. Maggie hadn't, somehow, liked him calling it 'our juvenile escapade.' The years had, for her, increased rather than diminished its importance.

'No, I just wanted to see – any theatre would do. What about the Lyceum?'

'It's a bit out of our way. Are you that keen?'

He looked her in the face and changed his mind.

'Oh, okay. If you don't hang about.'

'You thought I'd be over it,' she said discoveringly.

'Your stage phase? I suppose I did. One grows out of these things. My writing phase is long since past.'

She said nothing. She hardly heard, she was straining so eagerly ahead to catch the first glimpse of the theatre. Perhaps it would be 'dark'. That would be awful. She longed to see it alive, with a title on the marquee and photos in the front-of-house frames, get a glimpse of an open box-office, perhaps a queue, to show that it was all still real, still going on, even though it was lost to her . . .

And now she saw it ahead through the evening gloom. Would Stip draw up for her, or only – grudgingly – slow down? It was important to her, a sign that this sense of alienation from him was only superficial. Her hand, still on his knee, clutched it, a convulsive signal. He stopped the car.

For several minutes she sat still, her eyes roving hungrily. The theatre was not 'dark'. Suddenly she saw something almost too amazing to credit.

'Wait!' she begged urgently, because Stip was slipping the car into gear. She flung open the door.

'Mags, we ought to –'

'Just one minute!'

137

She jumped out, running across the pavement to the shelter of the marquee as the rain soaked her hair. She stood gaping at one of the photos. Stip called through the car window, 'Someone you know?'

'Yes – ' she breathed. It was incredible. Swiftly she looked at her watch. Yes, Tanya was in there somewhere, making up perhaps – the performance began in under twenty minutes. 'Stip – I *must* – ' she began, turning to him in almost a frenzy of eagerness. But then she saw his face, and her conscience clouted her roughly. How could she be standing here, pushing all else aside? How could seeing Tanya, being in a theatre again, be more important to her than rushing to see Helen and console her mother? In Stip's eyes she saw the wrongness of her priorities.

With a wrench which shamed her by the effort it cost, she turned her back on the theatre and got into the car. As it pulled away, she felt as if she were tied to the building. Irresistibly she looked back over her shoulder. As they turned a corner and the theatre was lost to sight, she could still see Tanya's photo in her mind's eye – a portrait with that nimbus of light round her head, smiling straight at her, her mouth slightly open as if calling ... Maggie sat round, facing through the weeping windscreen, thinking, appalled: Will I feel this pang of loss when darling Helen dies?

Helen was fully conscious, and chattering, chattering like a starling – her eyes and hands restless, her mind gradually lapsing into confusion but her voice going shrilly on and on, as if, now that she had all the company she wanted and was for once the centre of attention, she was getting all the words out that she had stored up in half a lifetime of living alone.

She talked to them all, by turns and *en bloc*, but it was Maggie's hand she held. Helen's little hand was so dry Maggie half expected to find her own covered with powdery dust each time she had to withdraw it. She did this only when Helen drifted into sleep, at which time her flow of words dried up, only to bubble up again, perhaps as some of the watchers were creeping away, and her hand would begin groping for Maggie's like a blind person's.

' ... I kept doing that thing, you know, with the Bible ... I *loved* that game, I used to play it for hours ... But there are so many verses you can't find any message in, no matter how

138

hard you try. And sometimes I'd cheat. There were friendly places my Bible fell open at, if I tilted it a certain way, verses I loved, that cheered me up. Like, "Blessed is he who expecteth nothing for he shall not be disappointed". Not that I stuck to it. Every time the postman came or the phone bell rang, I always expected. But it was always throwaways and election notices or the man to read the meter. Oops! – hold tight, Maggie! Hold me tight, dear, I'm sliding . . .' The tension would run through the room like ground-lighting. Was she 'going'? But no. After a few moments the innerly-striving old body would relax and she would say, 'That's better, I'm back. Well now, what was I saying . . .?'

Maggie refused to leave her, even at night, and the hospital staff, seeing the use of her and also out of kindness, fixed up a camp-bed in the ward (a private one – Ian had, quite unexpectedly, insisted on that) so that Maggie could be with Helen all night. Stip would relieve her sometimes during the days but Maggie, briefly at home or eating at some nearby café, was never easy. The doctors said it couldn't be long now.

Towards the end Helen got very lively and rather naughty. It happened when most of the family, including Ian's wife Lilian, were in the room.

'I love phone calls, you know, even those funny ones I sometimes get. I think it's because I'm listed as "MacFee, Helen", so they know I'm a female living alone. At first, I thought they were talking double-dutch! I simply didn't know what it all meant. Then those same words began to crop up in modern novels and I found out their meaning. After *that*, I learnt to manage those naughty, naughty callers quite well. Only a little while ago one young man phoned me and said . . .' She paused, and blushed really rather prettily, so that Maggie wanted to kiss her. 'Well! Do you know I can't bring myself to use those words in the family. But he said he wanted to put his *something* into my *something else*. So *I* said, quick as a flash – they expect you to gibber or burst into tears you know, that's why they do it, to shock you, but I refused to be shocked. Wouldn't give the naughty creature the satisfaction. I said, "Well, young man, your offer is appreciated but as my something-else has been lying about untenanted (yes, I did!) for sixty-five years now, I really think you would do better to put your *something* elsewhere!" She paused for effect. Then came the tag-line,

139

beautifully delivered in a tone of innocent pride: 'I used the right words to *him*, of course.'

Lilian stood there breathing noisily through her nose. Maggie caught her mother's eye. Her mother was staring at Helen as if seeing her anew. Later, she was to say, through bitter tears of grief such as she hadn't shed – at least not publicly – even for her husband, 'Helen was always such fun when we were young, she loved to make people sit up – oh, the little parties! She used to do the most wicked imitations of our elders, she had us in stitches, no one could ever make me laugh as Helen could! What a waste, what a terrible, terrible waste!' Only then did she reveal that Helen had been engaged to a boy who was killed at Ypres. And the reason no one had ever mentioned it before was because she was also engaged to another one who was killed at Verdun, and a third, who vanished without trace on the Somme. It had caused a shocking scandal because all the mourning parents had come to the house to commiserate with Helen as the affianced of their dead sons, all within a few months of each other. 'Any one of them would have done. Any one of them would have saved her. Oh, damn their hideous wars! Damn their hideous wars!' It was the first time Maggie had ever heard her mother swear.

The night Helen's slide had grown too steep for her to pull herself back up by Maggie's hand, Maggie slept at home in her old bed and had a tangled dream – tangled almost literally in the worn twists of the dun-coloured counterpane which, for once, she had neglected to fold before falling into bed. She dreamt Helen was sliding down to the front door at the M'Crimmonds toward a dark shadow beyond the coloured glass panels. She herself was at the top by the majolica pot calling, 'Come back, Auntie darling, it's curtain-up in a minute!' Then she dreamt other dreams, with Tanya mixed up in them. In one, there was a man standing outside a theatre with the rain beating down, staring at Tanya's photo. She drifted nearer and he turned, and it was Joel. He said, 'She's perfect in my eyes. Look, she's got a halo.' Maggie said seriously, 'Oh no, that's Landseer of Leicester Square, he does it with back lighting.' He reached his hand towards her without touching her and said, 'I hate Leicester Square, don't you?' And Maggie felt suddenly very warm toward him and said, 'Yes.' The prickle of desire was there and turned into a bright white bubble which

140

swelled and burst blissfully. Then Tanya came out of her photo and said, 'Whose fault is that? Look out, his fingers are magic.' And Maggie awoke with a strange sense of disloyalty.

The Vultures descended again relentlessly, and since they had all seen each other relatively recently they took even more liberties than before. They pottered in and out of the kitchen to make themselves cups of tea at all hours. Some of them hardly seemed to know whose funeral it was. Auntie Flora from Fife remarked, 'Helen . . . She was the little dark one with the squint, wasn't she?' Mrs Robertson actually barked at her, 'No, she was not! I would have thought you could keep track of your own cousins even though you never bothered to send them so much as a Christmas card!' This uncharacteristic outburst had a most beneficial effect. Flora had never been spoken to like that in her life (she said), took umbrage, together with her two infinitely stuffy elderly sons, and went home. Ian was very fussed, but 'Good riddance!' said Mrs Robertson, put more tongues on to boil, and then went back up to her room to cry some more.

Maggie worked side by side with Lilian and tried to find something in common with her but couldn't. Lilian had been a high-grade secretary with 'a great deal of responsibility' but had stopped work on her marriage and very clearly disapproved of women who didn't. This made it impossible to talk to her about teaching. Since Lilian had clearly imbibed from Ian his feelings about Matt as a bastard-by-conception, she couldn't talk about him, either. In fact Lilian appeared to find any kind of conversation in the shadow of a funeral faintly improper, unless it dealt with practical concerns, or with the dead. And as Helen had gone out of life on a scandalous note, Lilian's response to any loving comments about *her* was purse-lipped silence, or, pressed (for she made Maggie angry), with the remark, 'Yes, a very lively old lady. I wonder that she could not have employed all that mental energy to do something useful.' Maggie had always secretly felt that Helen had wasted her life, but had never blamed her for it; still, she found it hard to refute this priggish accusation. She had been won over to Joan's creed, that all able-bodied women should work and that those who did 'were, by that alone, better than those who didn't'.

If the Vultures had come for pickings, they were disappointed. Helen had left whatever she had – her house, essentially – to

141

Ian, Maggie and Stip equally, plus all her books to Maggie. There were an astonishing number of these, including some which bore unmistakable traces of having been borrowed, over many years, from various libraries. Ian, of course, insisted on these being returned, and was furious to learn that Boots had stopped its library facility and would not take theirs back.

'You've no right to these, you know,' he said to Maggie as she sorted through them on her knees in Helen's parlour while Ian took an inventory of the furniture. 'They were not rightfully hers to leave. You ought to give them to charity.' But Maggie without a word packed them all into a box, sealed it with broad strips of brown sticky tape and labelled them with her name and the legend: 'To Await My Return. Do Not Open.' Then she obliged Ian to help her transport them to the attic of their own house.

Helen's house went on the market, and was bought at once. It fetched £3,500. Not much, split three ways; but Maggie sent a little message of gratitude across the Great Divide. It was the first lump of money of her own she had ever had and it gave her a wonderful feeling. Brooking no refusal, she put the whole of the sum she still owed her father plus interest into her mother's bank account. The gesture gave her immense relief, because her mother needed it. As Stip had said, he and Ian 'saw her right', but that was not the same as independence; her mother had hinted several times at the irksomeness of having to 'ask' every time she needed some little extra. Now at least she had something of her own.

Maggie and Stip went out for walks when they could get away, and sat in the little park they had played in as children. It was autumn and all the shrubs and bushes were at their best; the air had a pale fragile coldness like golden glass, especially in the early mornings before the taint of chimney-smoke took the sharp edge off things and gave an acrid bite to breathing. There was no Clean Air Bill yet; the 'turning' bushes had soot on them and Maggie's white slips needed washing every night if she'd been out, to rid them of their grey borders. But Maggie and Stip were used to it; it didn't spoil their pleasure in the old localities or in each other, or in getting away from the house and its cross-currents for half a stolen hour now and then.

'With your thousand you could leave the firm, strike out on

142

your own,' Maggie said as they sat trying to lure sparrows to their hands with crumbs.

Stip was adding to the gathering smoke. He smoked a lot now. He stared across the grass for a while and suddenly burst out, 'I wish she'd not left me a penny!'

'Why on earth do you wish that?'

'Och, Maggie, how can you understand? If it had come sooner, I might have – but then again, I might not. Dreams are dreams. Help in realising them isn't so welcome when you've long given them up.'

'Is it really too late, Stip? You're only young. There's time –'

'For what? To go down to London, to live in my garret, to write . . .?' He gave a short, harsh laugh. 'Look at me. Look at my haircut, my waistcoat, my neatly-polished shoes – he's very hot on shoes, is Ian. Look at my blasted *socks*, for the Lord's sake . . .!' He hiked up his neatly creased trouserlegs and displayed socks with 'clocks' down the sides. She tried to laugh but she knew what he meant. 'Besides,' he added, with a trace of reproof, 'someone's got to live at home with Mum.' He was silent, frowning. 'You know what, Mags? I don't think Mum would mind so much you not being around, if you were still acting. She often talks about "your career" the way . . . Well. I imagine she'll use the same tone, now, when she talks about Aunty Helen.' Maggie went cold, as if his words had rung a knell. 'But,' he went on, 'living in indolence in the tropics with just the one child she hardly ever sees and a husband she doesn't know, well, I think it's fair enough if she resents that a bit. I won't pretend I'm entirely free of resentment myself.'

Maggie stared unseeingly at a sparrow, hopping toward her limp hand, its head cocked. She was still as a statue, her spirit absent; but it returned with a painful jolt when Stip went on hesitantly, 'I know you think I've been weak-kneed and taken the line of least resistance, but there's more than one kind of weakness. You didn't exactly chase your dream either, not when comfort and safety beckoned.'

'I was going to have a baby.'

Stip actually blushed.

'Yes, old Ian worked that out in a flash, of course. I remember thinking I must have been dim-witted or abnormally naive not to have realised it till he told me. Still, Mags, that – that's not something that can just *happen*, like falling downstairs, is it?

143

You must have willed it, some way or other. Maybe, like me, you were afraid of failing, subconsciously looking for a way out.'

So this time it was her younger brother's words which were etched in her brain when she returned to Nigeria.

She never got to the theatre to see Tanya. She phoned, once, but Tanya was on stage. It was only afterwards Maggie let herself wonder why she'd phoned at 8 p.m. instead of at seven. And why she hadn't left her name.

Chapter Sixteen

'Well? How was it?' Bruce asked when she had cleared customs. He was loading luggage into the car. She had bought a fairy-cycle for Matt, with stabiliser wheels; she thought Bruce would say something about this – either that it was the wrong thing or the right thing – but he didn't remark on it at all, humping it into the boot like another suitcase. His kiss seemed more perfunctory than usual, and his answers to her questions – fired at him the moment she had arrived – were the briefest possible.

'Very, very sad and upsetting.' She had cabled him when Helen died.

'Naturally. I told you not to go.'

'Oh, but I'm glad I went! It would have been awful, not to have gone.'

'See anyone you liked better than yourself?' He always asked this, even if she'd only been shopping.

'I nearly saw an old friend of mine. She was playing in Edinburgh. But in the end, I didn't have time.'

'You should have stayed longer. There was no hurry. You know everything runs like clockwork here without you.'

Stung, she asked, 'Didn't Matt miss me at all?'

'Not noticeably. He's got Tolly, after all.'

She felt an authentic stab of jealousy through the African padding which was already threatening to creep round her, like the jacket on her mother's boiler, holding out cold but vital feelings.

'Why didn't you bring him to meet me?' she asked with unwonted sharpness.

'He was playing. He didn't want to come.'

She turned in the car to look at him. Was he hurting her on purpose, to get back at her for her behaviour about the house in Capetown? His bland, blunt profile gave nothing away.

'Did you tell him where you were going? I mean, so that he realised it was to meet me?'

He shrugged. 'You know how he is when he's absorbed.'

Not the lie direct, then, but a lie by implication, and Maggie reacted with astonishment. Was she being punished? But it was unlike Bruce to punish her, and certainly not so subtly. Well! Maggie thought. We'll see soon enough what's at the back of this. But the pain of thinking, even for a second, that Matt had not wanted to come lingered, even after she'd dismissed the idea as ridiculous. The aeroplanes would have fetched him, even without her!

Sure enough, when they got into the bungalow and Matt saw her, he flung himself on her with such unstinted enthusiasm that the residual ache was assuaged.

'Why didn't you come with Daddy to meet me?' she asked when she had surfaced. He was sitting astride her hips, his arms round her neck, his damp little face pressed to hers.

'He didn't tell me.'

'Of course I did, old boy!' said Bruce forcefully. 'You never listen to your poor old Dad.'

He went through into the bedroom, carrying suitcases. Mother and son looked into each other's eyes.

'He didn't tell me,' Matt repeated earnestly.

Maggie believed him. She felt relieved, and at the same time most uneasy. She couldn't recall Bruce ever lying to her before. How like him to begin with one so inept! Tolly came through from the kitchen, all one big body-smile. How beautiful she would look in the new red dress Maggie had brought her! She came to Maggie for a kiss, and Matt put an arm round both their necks, making a human bridge between them.

'Come and see your present!'

They went out to the car, parked beyond the front lawn. Matt, on his feet now, pulled her in a curve so that the whirling spray dappled them as they crossed the grass – his favourite joke. The boot was open, the bike exposed.

'Oh!' cried Tolly, wringing her hands. 'Lucky Matty!'

Matt just gazed. Then he began to dance about. 'Get it out!'

'Daddy will, he's just coming.' And he was. Quickly, Maggie asked Tolly, 'Did my husband tell Matt he was going to the airport?'

146

'Master not be here all day,' Tolly said. Which wouldn't have been so very odd except that it was Sunday.

Basically Bruce had no duplicity in his nature, and had to adopt it to meet his situation, wearing it like an ill-fitting suit of clothes belonging to a much lither and more sinuous man. His natural artlessness bulged through the fabric of lies at every seam.

A wife with a sharper – that is, more loving – eye, would have spotted at once where the danger lay. Almost as soon as she got back she met the girl, striding on long American legs through Port Harcourt market, shopping for vegetables. Maggie happened to be with Bruce on the same errand, and she even noticed his sudden flush and the stumble in his voice, but attributed it to some remark of her own. The girl saw Bruce and waved cheerily, and Maggie noticed her (who could help it? She was just as pretty as they'd said) and remarked, 'That must be the Zuleika Dobson of the mission.' Bruce gave her a puzzled glance. 'Her name's Angela Milston.' 'Do you know her?' 'We're acquainted.' 'Oh ho!' said Maggie in one of those meaninglessly roguish ripostes. And she smiled in a friendly fashion at the girl (after all, everyone was being so spiteful behind her back) and passed on without giving her another thought.

From this time on, Bruce's behaviour caused Maggie a great deal of bewilderment. He treated her with consideration and courtesy, much more than before. He brought her a regular weekly present, usually flowers (which she didn't need or like – she felt smothered by the extravagant scents of tropical flowers and longed for the cool subtle fragrances of daffodils). He took a studied interest in her teaching, and invariably attended any shows she put on with the children, though she could tell he was bored and rather embarrassed. He inflicted his colleagues and their wives on her much less than he had once done, and when they did have to entertain he would help her as much as possible with the arrangements, even to making the coffee for the guests after William had gone off duty. Maggie never even noticed that he had taken to percolating coffee the American way. She really was quite dead to feminine intuition, but no

147

doubt that useful faculty does not function fully where love is absent.

Joan did try to warn her. She skirted round it several times, as Maggie was to realise in retrospect, but hesitated to come right out with it. Her way was to talk a lot more than ever before about her own husband – her 'ould-fella' as she affectionately and wryly called him.

'He was always very good to me, in his way, my ould-fella,' she said once in what was apparently a mood of reminiscence. 'But you know what men are. He had the faults of his gender.'

'What, for instance?' Maggie asked idly. Joan's ould-fella had been dead and gone these ten years. Maggie was marking exercise books and not listening very carefully.

'Oh, my dear! Need I specify? Who knows what he'd have been like if we'd stayed in a temperate climate? This damned wet heat has a staggering effect on some people, you know, not only the men! Well, you've been out her long enough to know *that*.'

'Mmm,' murmured Maggie. Scandals did not exactly abound among the WC but an occasional bit of hanky-panky went on which one got wind of. Maggie wondered remotely what Joan was bringing it up for; gossip usually filled her with scorn.

'Had a spot of bother with a black girl once,' Joan suddenly said.

Maggie looked up.

'Yep. Wouldn't have credited it if he hadn't admitted it. Poor old Jimbo! Didn't seem to know what had hit him.' She puffed away on her 'fag', staring at the low ceiling where a small pink lizard was resting upside down.

'Your husband had an affair with an Ibo?'

'One of the servants. Besotted. Potty about her. Couldn't help himself, he said, and I could see it was true ... Love, that kind anyway, is a sort of madness, or perhaps a sort of drunkenness. Jimbo didn't approve of too much drink, though he liked his evening glass, of course. But he got blind drunk on that girl. I think myself it was her sticking-out seat. I was always very flat behind – carried all my charms before me, so to speak.' She patted her large and still shapely bosom ruminatively. 'I read something about it later. Something to do with the angle, I believe.' She coughed. 'Of course I didn't know a damn thing about such matters in those days. Positively

148

Victorian, me! Shut your eyes and think of Wiltshire. I literally used to do that. Poor old Jimbo, who can blame him? Not me.'

'Not even at the time?' asked Maggie, chin on palm, exercise books quite forgotten.

'Ah! Well . . . At the time I was young and intolerant. At the *time*, I made a most fearful scene. You wouldn't believe it of me, would you? I actually belaboured him about the head with a pillow.' Maggie lowered her eyes. 'Till it burst.'

Maggie tried not to laugh, without success, and Joan, after a moment of bridling, irresistibly joined in.

'Sorry,' spluttered Maggie. 'The mental picture –'

'Yes, yes, yes, I can see the funny side now, feathers every-where . . . Just like Jimbo to wait till we were in bed and I was trying to snuggle up, to tell me earnestly all about this girl . . . 'Course I had her off the roster first thing the next morning. Almost the first thing. Seem to recall I made her clear all the feathers up first, seemed only fair somehow . . .'

Maggie laughed till she hiccupped. They both got quite helpless. Wiping her eyes and blowing her nose, Maggie finally asked, 'Why on earth are you telling me all this?'

'Seemed to me an . . . apposite cautionary tale,' she said.

Maggie sobered in an instant.

'What do you mean?'

'Well . . . Just wondered if you might be having a bit of the same sort of trouble with *your* ould-fella.'

Maggie stared.

'Bruce? Joan, are you crazy? You're not thinking he's got an eye on Tolly?'

Joan looked very shocked and hastened to say that of course she had no such notion. 'Good Lord, no! Bruce wouldn't look twice in that direction. Good Lord! Trust me to give you the wrong idea! No, not Tolly.'

'You've heard something.'

'No. Not a word. I swear,' Joan said. 'It's . . . just a feeling, plus a few observations.'

Maggie opened her mouth to demand a name. But just at that moment Bruce, who'd been out at a meeting, was heard coming home. Maggie gave Joan a look which said, 'Later!' But afterwards when she thought about it she made an almost deliberate decision that she didn't want to know, not who, not even whether. She never went back to the strange, quite

149

uncharacteristic conversation. And Joan, like a doctor with a terminal patient, seeing she didn't want to know, didn't press it, but let matters take their course.

That year when it was time for their leave, Maggie's subconscious had been at work. Some deep alarm made her suggest to Bruce that they take their leave together, and if nowhere else would attract him, then to Capetown to the new house.

When he seemed reluctant, Maggie's suppressed disquiet burst out in the form of anger.

'Why? Why don't you want to go? You seemed so crazy about that place when you first bought it, longing to show it to me –'

'And you, flatly refusing to take any interest in it –'

'Well, I've changed my mind. If it's really ours, I want to see it.'

'Not now,' he temporised. His manner was definitely odd. He seemed nervous, furtive – even rather aggressive. 'You've never shown the slightest desire to see it. You'd never even talk about it. Not a single question –'

'I wasn't ready. And you hurt me by buying it without consulting me. But now I've got used to the idea.'

'How typical. Now when it's too late!'

'How do you mean – too late?'

He hesitated as if trapped. 'I've – I've sold it.'

'Sold it!'

'Well, nearly. It's being sold.' He took one look at her face, and turned his head away. 'I – I thought you didn't want it.'

Angry as she had been when he had told her about buying it, she was, however irrationally, even more infuriated now.

'Am I never to be told or asked about anything! What the hell is going on? You behave as if I were a mental defective, simply not here at all!'

'I feel as if you weren't here, most of the time,' he retorted.

It was the first time for many months that his studied politeness had been ruptured by a little real feeling. But the row, which might even have done some good, did not develop, because Bruce reined himself in instantly. The servants were still about. Later, the pair went as usual to kiss Matt and by this shared ritual reminded themselves that they were, technically, husband

150

and wife. Maggie suddenly asked, as they got into bed, 'Bruce, what's going on?'

'What do you mean?'

'Something's wrong. There's a lot you're simply not telling me.'

There was a silence. They lay side by side.

'I should have told you about selling the house. I'm sorry. I was hurt too, you know. It was just like a smack in the face to me when you reacted the way you did about it.'

'Was it – a nice house?'

'I thought so,' he said with a shrug in his voice.

'Is it really too late?' she asked.

The question when she put it meant no more than, 'Is it too late to stop the sale?' but the minute it was out, she heard in it all sorts of echoes. He heard them too, or so she thought later, replaying in her head the way he had said, with unwonted hollow-sounding soberness, 'Yes, I'm afraid I think it is.'

And at that Maggie was so frightened that, for the very first time in their whole marriage, she tried to bridge the physical gulf that had opened between them. She tentatively laid her hand on his thigh, copying, out of her basic ignorance, the gesture (abandoned for many months now) by which he had invariably used to open what passed for his love-play. For a moment she felt an answering tremor through his thickly-muscled leg but it stopped with a little jolt, and then he turned away as if he had not noticed anything, and she was left – as he had sometimes been – with her hand in mid-air. Though she had not desired him, his rebuff stung and dismayed her. She had always taken it for granted that he was keeping aloof for her sake.

Still she did not understand, though she could no longer avoid suspicion. But instead of opening her eyes, she turned them away, busying herself in her work and Matt. Only occasionally in the strange months that followed did she allow herself to *look* at Bruce, even in the simplest physical sense. He no longer suggested a paradigm of complacent masculine fitness. His skin became sallow and drawn and his eyes were shadowed. She asked him once or twice if he were ill or needed a tonic, but when he brushed off her enquiries and pushed himself harder than ever at work (thus, at any rate, he accounted for his frequent absences) she assumed that he was

151

succumbing to the punishing effects of the climate, the reason why however successful a man may be, his company or government does not allow him to stay in the tropics for more than a few years. These years were nearly up for Maggie and Bruce; but when Maggie occasionally asked Bruce what plans he had made he became evasive.

'You didn't care for my first plan. Let's hear one from you.'

'Well, why can't we go home, and you can work for the London office?'

He shuddered.

'The horror of London! Those grey skies, those grey streets . . . I think about it as a cold, filthy prison.'

'Well, what then?'

He shrugged and offered nothing. It was very disquieting, as if he foresaw no future beyond the next few months or weeks.

The blow fell suddenly. Maggie had been away for a weekend in Lagos to shop, and when she came back, Tolly met her on the front doorsteps and told her, 'Master done gone.' Just like that.

It was quite as shocking as a death, more so in a way because people can't help dying but they can help leaving. They leave because they don't want to stay, and that, even to an unloving but dutiful wife, can be a terrible affront as well as a loss far more profound and crippling than ever she might have expected.

Tolly told her how Bruce had come into Matt's room at about 6 a.m. and stood by his bed and looked at him sleeping for a long time. Tolly said he was crying, but she must have been wrong because Maggie had never seen Bruce cry, and privately thought he probably never had, at least since he was Matt's age himself. He turned round at last and said, 'Goodbye, Tolly. Take care of my wee boy, won't you? I know you will.' And without looking her in the eye he pressed quite a lot of money into her hands (all of which Tolly gave straight to Maggie) and hurried outside to where his car, piled with suitcases, was waiting. Puzzled, she stood watching at the window. She reported that he sat in it for a long time before he started it up and drove away.

There was a note: 'I'm sorry, but it never was a real marriage, we just lived together. If you had ever loved me the way I love

152

Angie I would have known about it. I can't miss out on this chance for real living and real *feeling*. I am going to live an entirely different kind of life and I'm longing for it. I thought I wanted to stay in Africa but that was before I knew what wanting meant. The worst is Matt. I feel terrible about leaving him but there it is. I will not try to excuse it. I just can't help myself. But you will not be short of money, certainly not at first. I'm going to set up a trust for him to go to my old school, Glencora, in the Highlands.' (The ominousness of this struck Maggie only much later). 'I only ask one thing, that you don't try to turn him against me. I have tried to treat you both as well as I could, till now anyway. Whatever you feel about me I deserve for leaving you, but *please* let Matt keep some good memories of me. I will give you a divorce as soon as you want one and I hope you find someone you can love the way I love Angie. Then perhaps you'll be able to forgive me.' He signed it simply 'B'.

Maggie looked up from this to see what appeared to be a great black wave rolling relentlessly towards her. She stared at it, petrified, and when it reached her she fainted for the first time in her life. When she came around, Joan was sitting beside her; the company doctor was holding her wrist and Tolly was whimpering and rocking her body rhythmically like an old Jew at prayer.

'Right,' said Joan the instant Maggie opened her eyes. 'You've hit bottom. Now up you come.' Maggie had heard her use that tone to recalcitrant children at the school, but without any tears lurking in her steely blue eyes. The doctor was muttering about rest and shock but Joan would have none of that. 'Sit up. That's it. Feel woozy still? Head between your knees, that's the girl . . . Just give Tolly the prescription, doctor, that'll be fine. I'll deal with the rest.'

When they were alone, Joan gave Maggie a whisky, then stood her up firmly and marched her up and down the room, talking all the time.

'Bastard!' she said. 'I saw this coming. Should have told you. I did try – none of my business, I thought. What a ghastly shock for you. I blame myself, though nothing could have stopped it –'

'Please Joan, let me sit down! – Did everybody know?'

153

'Oh come on, what do you care? I shouldn't think so. Doesn't matter, anyway. What matters is what you're going to do now.'

Maggie saw a shadow of the wave looming and kept it off with tears. 'I want to go to bed!' she sobbed piteously. '*Please*, Joan! I want to sleep –'

Joan looked at her narrowly.

'All right. I'll tuck you up for a couple of hours. But then I'll be back. And don't forget tomorrow's Monday, you're due at school.'

She meant all this for the best, of course, but it didn't work. The wounded can't be ordered on to their feet before they've had any time to heal. When the couple of hours were up and the doorbell pealed, Maggie summoned Tolly and told her not to let Joan in. She would no more have welcomed her invigorating presence at the moment than a cold douche. She took two of the pills the doctor had left, curled up foetally in her dark bedroom and took to unconsciousness.

Later she was to upbraid herself for the almost feudal state of dependence she had fallen into. How could she have allowed the man-prop to have become so important that when it was, entirely predictably and even deservedly, yanked away, she collapsed?

All possible encouragement was given to her to have a breakdown. Tolly seemed to expect nothing less than that she turn her face to the wall and die. The doctor came daily with bleak looks and enough sleeping pills to end it all with even less delay. The WC contributed a series of telephone calls and unannounced courtesy/curiosity visits which, through her closed door and her drowsiness, Maggie could hear the servants dealing with; the awful prospect of having to deal with them in person would have been quite enough to keep her immured for weeks.

It was Matt, of course, who saved her. Matt was in a sorry state. His father vanished, his mother taken to her bed, and Tolly, his remaining pillar, in a state of emotional retreat . . . But mercifully this was not her normal condition and she returned. On doctor's orders she resolutely kept Matt away from Maggie for nearly a week, and then, her instincts triumphing over imbecilic modern medical advice, she carried him one morning into the bedroom and stood at the bedside quite silently until Maggie's eyes opened.

154

What Maggie saw was Matt giving an anguished imitation of an orphaned orang-utan – a leggy little orange-topped creature clinging silently to Tolly with all his limbs, staring at his mother with huge, pain-filled eyes. The effect was much the same as that of his elemental cries as a newborn baby. Instant contact was made with some primordial source of strength within Maggie, who threw herself out of bed, perhaps symbolically knocking the sleeping pills to the floor where most of them scattered under the bed. She took him in her arms, kissed his face all over and said, 'I'm better, darling. Look! I'm fine! Now I'm going to shower and get dressed and you and Tolly and I are going to the sea.' How, without a car, she didn't know, but in that moment she had the strength to walk all the way there with Matt on her back if need be. The fact that Joan turned up in the nick of time to take them was no surprise to Maggie.

Chapter Seventeen

'You're really going, then.'

Joan stood in the doorway of Maggie's bedroom, looking round at the chaos of trunks and suitcases, open doors and drawers and heaps of clothes. Some of them were Bruce's. There was a special crate to receive these; they were going to the mission, though it was hard to imagine an Ibo in any of them.

Maggie glanced at Joan, and then looked again, harder. The light was, as always, shuttered to dimness; but Joan looked very much as if she were about to burst into tears.

'Joan . . .'

'What?' she barked.

'Don't mind that much! Please. I have to go.'

'Why?'

'What do you mean, why? What alternative have I?'

'Oh, you've got an alternative! You could stop here. Well, why not? You've got a job. I know it doesn't pay much, but I could work on Mrs Hatchard to give you a full-time job on full-time pay. As for somewhere to live, what's wrong with my place? Two can live as cheaply as one.'

'It's three. Plus Tolly.'

'Yes, I've been thinking about poor Tolly. How are you going to feel about leaving *her*? How's she going to feel? How's Matt going to feel?'

These terrible questions did not need to be vocalised to make them vitally real and pressing to Maggie.

'I can't help it,' she said shortly.

'Turning the child's life on its head – dragging him back to that bitter bloody cold climate, that awful gloom – Scotland! Went there once. Just once. Personally I'd rather be dead.'

'Joan. *Shut* up, please, and put those things into that crate.'

156

There was a period of silence. They worked back to back. Then Joan renewed the attack.

'Presumably you've told Tolly.'

'Not directly, but she's not half-witted.'

'On the contrary . . . she's very bright. You've been immensely fortunate to have her.'

'I *know* that, Joan.'

'And now you're throwing her on to the scrap-heap. *And* William.'

Maggie threw a pile of cotton pants on to the bed with a childish gesture of rage, and turned on her.

'Joan, I am not throwing anyone on the scrap-heap! How many times have you told me that it's the Ibos who are lucky, that one mustn't worry too much about them, and that where the Company is concerned, they go with the house and the job? William will be perfectly all right with whoever takes over Bruce's job.'

'I know something you don't know. He's a bachelor.'

'Who is?'

'The new man. You know what that means. No job for Tolly.'

Maggie's heart sank, but she kept up her defensive.

'What are you saying then, that I ought to take her to bloody, gloomy, cold Scotland with me?'

'No. That you should stay here, and teach, and – and keep me company. How the devil am I going to manage with nobody to talk to except those dreadful little female toe-rags of the WC?' She plonked herself on to the edge of the bed and lit a cigarette with hands that, large and capable as they were, were visibly trembling.

Maggie sat beside her and put her arm round her shoulders. After a long time she said quietly, 'Joan, I do love you, and in a way I wish I could stay, but I can't.'

Joan blew out a long thin stream of smoke and stood up. 'I know that pefectly well. Just wanted you to know you'll be damned well missed, and not just by me. The children are heartbroken . . . All right, all right! Not another word. Now, where does this lot have to go?'

Once resigned, Joan shouldered much of the technical and logistical burden of Maggie's departure. She supervised the

157

packing and shipping of such bits of furniture and other impedimenta as Maggie thought she might have some use for at home (though some of her local market-cullings were going to look distinctly odd in the old house). She saw to it that the things Maggie didn't want to take were equitably distributed among the servants. Her dry, invigorating presence served the dual purpose of keeping Maggie's own doubts and fits of depression at bay, and shielding her from the intrusions of the WC, who were nosing round in search of titbits.

Tolly's behaviour was distressing, a constant, nagging worry. She had reacted to Bruce's decampment rather quietly, giving no sign of judging him, though she could see what damage he had done to the two people – Matt and Maggie – who mattered to her most. It was only when it became clear that Maggie was leaving too, and taking Matt with her, that Maggie got an indication of the fires of emotion banked down in that small black body – the fires which had driven Tolly, in her early womanhood, to follow her doomed and banished babies into the inhospitable forest.

She said nothing. But her behaviour spoke in howls. For several days she followed Maggie about like her shadow, literally on her heels all the time, answering questions in monosyllables, her eyes, with their yellow whites showing all round the irises, fixed upon her burningly. Matt was going to school by now, but when he came home Tolly seized him and bore him away to the kitchen. Several times Maggie caught her luring him across to her hutch. Against Joan's advice, she decided to ignore this breaking of white taboos.

Then one morning Tolly did not cross the lawn to work. Maggie sent William to enquire. He came back shrugging. Maggie went herself, then.

'Tolly?' she called through the closed hutch door.

She came at once, and stood staring at Maggie. Her eyes were not rolling now, but half-closed, remote, enigmatic as the eyes of an Ibo straight out of the bush. It was as if the six years of sharing Matt had never happened. Even on that very first day, when Tolly, fresh from her ordeal in the forest, had leant over her with Matt in her arms, she had not looked as much of a stranger. Maggie had come to reason with her, to comfort her, but now she only said:

'Come to the house.'

158

She turned and walked away. She knew Tolly would follow, and so she did; but when she got there, she wouldn't work. She walked straight into the kitchen, but when Maggie went in there later to see how she was, she found her sitting on the floor in the corner with her face on her knees, doing nothing.

Maggie stood before her.

'Tolly, it's no use. I have to bear the master going away, and you have to bear this.'

Tolly did not answer or move.

'Get up and come and help me now.'

The girl obeyed slowly. Obedience was second nature to her – she could not withstand a direct order. She helped all day in a silence which was not so much sullen as withdrawn – she moved like a robot responding to remote controls. When Matt came home from school, Tolly disappeared. Matt hunted every- where for her, even in her hutch. Failing to find her, he sank into a silence of his own, baffled and alarmed. At bedtime he asked, with that pathetic, apprehensive, wincing quality that so many of his questions had had since Bruce left: 'She hasn't gone away too, has she?'

'Matt, it's we who are going to leave her, and it's hard for her.'

His eyes opened wide and so did his mouth. He knew about going to Scotland, but not about this.

'But we're not leaving Tolly *behind*!' he exclaimed, incredulously.

'We have to. This is her country. She wouldn't like Scotland.'

'Why not, if we do?'

'She'd be cold there,' said Maggie, for lack of something better.

'Colder than us?'

'Yes, because she's not used to it.'

'Nor am I used to it.'

She tried to joke with him. 'No, but you're a Scot. You've got thick skin to keep out the cold, like a polar bear.'

'A polar bear's furry.'

'You'll be furry too. I'm going to buy you a sheepskin coat.'

'Couldn't you buy one for Tolly?'

Baa baa black sheep, have you any wool . . .? Maggie put her face down on Matt's tummy to hide her sudden tears. As once before, she could feel Tolly's pain in her own breast. She'd lost

159

so much, and now – another child, and not a newborn one but one she had lavished love and nurture on for six years ... It was too cruel! For a moment, Maggie thought, 'No. I can't do it to her. We'll stay, I'll find a way to stay! How happy she'd be, how quickly that pain would melt – ' The burden of power was pressing her down like a pile of stones. No one should ever have such power over other people's happiness.

She summoned Joan, who came after school. It was winter; the days were short. They sat together in what Joan called 'the shrill of the night' and drank some of Bruce's whisky.

'You were right. Leaving Tolly seems nearly impossible. What am I do to do about her?'

Joan smoked steadily and thought.

'I wonder,' she said at last.

'What?'

'She's so *good* with Matt. She seems to have a real gift with children. I was just wondering if I could take her on at the school. Train her to assist the kindergarten teacher.'

Maggie sat straight. 'But Mrs Hatchard –'

'Yup,' said Joan sardonically. 'A formidable obstacle, no doubt. But you know, you and I between us have already dug over the ground in that department. She's not the rigorous white supremacist she was a few years ago. Things are changing ... None too soon. Anyway, she's leaving.'

'Leaving?'

'Nobody stays long here, you know. You're one of our oldest habituées now. She'll be going home soon enough, and ... Well, there have been approaches.'

'What do you mean? To *you*? Joan! Really? To be Head?'

'I may not get it, but I have one advantage – I'm here for life, I'd never up-stakes again now. I'm a bit long in the tooth for it, but I won't hide from you the fact that I wouldn't give them time to change their minds if they did ask me. And *if* they did, I'd bring in a few black teachers. Through the back door at first. This might well be the answer for Tolly.'

'But when would it happen? I'm going in two weeks.'

'Not before then! But she can come and live with me. We'll find her something to do.'

'She'd have to learn to read.'

'Won't hurt her.'

160

'It would be marvellous ... A tremendous weight off my mind. If she'd only go along with it –'

'What choice has she, poor little thing?'

They lapsed into companionable silence. Joan smoked and sipped her drink. The night shrilled piercingly, stopped suddenly – like a premonition; there was a few seconds' perfect stillness, and then the heavens opened and rain deluged down. Maggie went to the window to watch it. It always fascinated her, those torrents of water coming down so thickly you could hardly breathe if you were out in it. She wondered where Bruce was, what he was doing, whether he thought of her and Matt, felt guilty ... She fiercely hoped he felt awful, as bad as she had about her father, but she doubted it. Bruce's conscience was not such a finely-tuned instrument as hers. She thought of her mother, from whom a happy letter had just come ('Bless you, darling, now I have something to look forward to again!') Of Stip's relief ... She was in debt – heavily in debt to her family. As with bankruptcy, she must clear herself of this debt before setting herself up in any new enterprise ... But she didn't fool herself it was going to be much fun. Without Tolly, she could foresee terrible difficulties with Matt ...

Suddenly her steward, an elderly Ibo called Assaf, came bursting in, nearly scaring the wits out of her because the servants never entered at night except in an emergency.

'Madam! You come! Your girl Tolly, she done hurting herself!'

Joan was out first. She simply leapt at the door. Maggie found space amid the horrors crowding her brain to marvel at the older woman's fleetness of reaction and movement. She herself almost caught the screen-door in her face as she ran after the steward and Joan, round the outside of the house – already wet to the skin – and down toward the hutches.

There was a crowd of Ibos bent over Tolly, who was lying on the lawn outside her hutch. They made way for the white women. There was very little light, but what there was glanced off the wet black skins and stretched white-rimmed eyes. Assaf had a torch and he shone it down through the white shafts of rain upon Tolly. Maggie was afraid to look. If Tolly had attempted suicide it could not be by any easy, bloodless way, for she had none – no convenient gas-ovens or sleeping pills for the likes of her. Joan was on her knees beside the girl, with her ear

161

to her chest. Maggie, dry-throated with terror, forced herself to look. There was no sign of blood that she could see, but she couldn't see much.

'Is she alive?' Oh God, how would she tell Matt?

'Yes. I can't actually see what's wrong with her. William – are you there? Good man. Help me carry her to the house. Assaf, run and phone Dr Simmonds. Quickly! Maybe she's eaten something . . .'

Tolly had eaten something. The doctor pumped out her stomach with the pump he used, discreetly, on the occasional white woman who took an overdose. It was hard to commit suicide with Dr Simmonds around; he had once worked in a London hospital and was an expert. Soon enough Tolly was conscious and lying in Maggie's bed looking grey-skinned and bewildered, but at least recognisable as the Tolly who was part of her life

Joan wanted to stay, but Maggie said she could manage. She saw everybody off the premises, and then made herself and Tolly some tea and sat down to her vigil. Tolly was very weak and couldn't talk. She slept fitfully till nearly morning. When she woke then, she was better. She turned her head on the white pillow and looked at Maggie, who said the only thing possible.

'Do you want me to take you with us to Scotland?'

'I want you stay here.'

'Tolly, I have a mother and brothers and no husband. I must go where my family is.'

She shouldn't have said that. Tolly turned her face away. Maggie, who was holding her hand, squeezed it. Tolly said in a hollow voice, 'I not got no person.'

'Mrs Hillman says she'll take you. You'll learn to be a teacher.'

'White people not let Ibo girl teach their piccens.'

'There are black piccens at the school as well, Tolly, you know that. Mrs Hillman thinks there should be black teachers, too.'

Through the slight hand which had so often soothed Matt, caressed and cleaned and comforted him, Maggie felt a shiver run.

'Ibos not let me teach their piccens, too,' she whispered.

'Nonsense, Tolly! Why ever not?'

162

'They know I done born double piccens.'

It was the very first time she had ever spoken of it.

'Lots of women have twins, Tolly. White people think it's a blessing.'

Tolly stared into her eyes silently. Maggie thought, all these years she's carried this – this sense of her own uncleanness, of being cursed.

'If they would let you, Tolly – would you like it?'

Slowly the black head nodded.

'I'll talk to Mrs Hillman. Now try to sleep.'

The hand clinging so tensely to Maggie's fractionally relaxed. After a little while, she slept.

Maggie detached herself and went to wake Matt. She closed her bedroom door but of course he had to find his way in there while she was getting his breakfast. He came running.

'Mummy, what's Tolly doing in your bed?' he asked, half scandalised and half delighted at the novelty.

'She's not feeling well so I thought I'd look after her.'

'I'll look after her!'

'You'll go to school.'

But nobody had to look after Tolly as it happened, because by the time Maggie returned from taking Matt to school, her bed was made with clean sheets and Tolly was washing dishes as if nothing had happened.

The actual parting, when it came, was practically painless – at least for Matt. Tolly saw to that. Instead of clinging to him or letting him cling to her, as on previous occasions, Tolly did a very clever thing. She collected together a number of small objects – small carved animals, a set of miniature earthenware bowls, an ebony totem-figure, some strips of bright-coloured cloth stapled together, as well as some items of food, a picture-puzzle cut from a magazine, and a little creature made from a scrap of fur and some wire. All these were jumbled together in one of the little local baskets, wrapped in a blouse of Tolly's which Matt knew well. (It even smelt of her. Maggie found this out when she saw Matt, a long time later, with his face buried in it.)

While Matt was examining this miscellany, Tolly quietly retreated. Maggie watched her back away, her eyes fixed on

Matt. She never looked at Maggie, and by the time Maggie had put Matt into the taxi the black girl had vanished into the deep shadow of the porch. There were no goodbyes. By the time Matt had woken up to the fact that they were on their way, the airfield, the plane and all the thrills of the journey were in sight. It was Maggie, and not Matt, who, once they were airborne, turned her face to the window and wept.

PART THREE

Chapter Eighteen

So Maggie came home.

If her tail was between her legs, she tried not to show it. Once again, in a new context, her training as an actress came to her help. She walked tall: often, crossing a room under the eyes of Ian and Lilian, she would imagine she had books on her head, or consciously emulate the African women's beautiful proud carriage as she had enviously observed it in Nigeria. She spoke clearly, remembering a joke her diction teacher at RADA had told his students to induce them to 'project', about a speaker's notes, found after a meeting, which bore the pencilled self-injunction: 'Weak arguments, raise your voice.' She met everyone's eyes boldly and tried, with her straight looks, to communicate the inner ebullience of the old *Oklahoma* song about 'never looking back to sigh over the romance behind me' – a sort of to-hell-with-it, survivor's mien.

But these were all, at best, superficial signs. What she really had to work hard on was the thoughts and moods that underlay them. For inside the brazen Maggie was a suddenly faint and huddled Margaret, ashamed, deserted, insecure, facing trials she had recklessly forced herself to face but now found terrifyingly beyond her known strength. It was Maggie, insouciant, selfish and defiant, who was pushed 'up front' to face the music of coming home to cope with motherhood, daughterhood and sisterhood. And divorcehood.

No Robertson had ever been divorced before. This was partly, no doubt, because many of the poor things had never been married, but it was an undeniable statistic of the clan, which like Bruce's regimental banners had been held aloft with an unthinking pride, even the bloodstains of personal suffering within all those unbroken marriages being held as an enhancement.

167

'However unhappy we might have been,' Auntie Flora of Fife had once remarked (and was often quoted), 'we stuck it out. A vow is a vow to a Robertson!'

And now here came Maggie to shatter the tradition, to tear down the banner and trample on it.

Even her mother couldn't conceal her shock.

'Does it have to be a divorce, Maggie? Could it not be just a separation?'

'It's not my choice, Mummy. *He* left *me*.'

This was another dreadful thing. Nobody, in their hearts, could credit that a man would run away from a blameless wife, if only because it was not a thing any *Robertson* had ever done. If the Robertson women took their vows seriously, the Robertson men – to do them justice – were not ones to duck their responsibilities either. To leave a wife would have been disgraceful enough. To abandon a son was unthinkable.

So there was the underlying suspicion, of which Maggie was made constantly aware, that she must have 'done something'. Ian came closest to voicing his suspicion, not openly but in a series of irritating hints.

The contrast between Maggie's brothers was now more marked than ever. Their paths had not taken them far from each other geographically or professionally; but in character they were now poles apart, and their attitudes to Maggie illustrated this. Stip led the welcome-home Maggie received. He was seen at his very best, from her point of view, for the first month after her return. Full of vigour and enthusiasm, he had done all he could to smooth her path, including invaluable practical things. He had arranged a place at the local school for Matt and prepared a beautiful nursery for him in Ian's old room, embellished with all the old toys, long relegated to the attic – a rocking horse, old-fashioned wooden jigsaws, and best of all, Ian's well-preserved Hornby trains. He had contacted those of their old friends who were still around, to greet her with phone calls, visits and parties.

All this bustle and sense of wantedness eased both Maggie and Matt over the first shock of change. It endeared Stip to Matt, which was a great comfort to Maggie, who had been quite as worried about how Matt would manage without a man in his life as how she herself would.

Nor would Stip allow anyone to put Maggie down. He

168

hovered near her at all gatherings, ready to stamp on any discomforting remarks or awkward questions. He particularly stood up to Ian, and this made Maggie proud of him, for she suspected – rightly – that Ian was the dominant one in every other situation. (That Ian had to dominate Stip at work to make up for being dominated by Lilian at home was also a suspicion very soon confirmed by observation.)

Maggie had a plan, which she put into operation as soon as the first settling-in was over. It was to use the remains of Helen's legacy to redecorate the house.

She had expected to have a free hand, and to share this exciting enterprise with no one but her mother. But she had reckoned without Stip, who, it soon appeared, had no intention of being left out of an undertaking so much to his liking.

At first Maggie found this irksome.

'I thought you were in such a hurry to move out,' she said, when he brought home his third or fourth consignment of wallpaper books and carpet samples, colour charts and swatches of chintz and velvet and brocade.

'Am I getting on your nerves?' he asked cheerfully.

'I just like to know what's going on.'

'Well, what I thought was that I'd stay on a bit, and help with the redecorations. I'm quite handy in my modest way, only I've never had a real chance to practise. You've no idea how expensive it is to get the so-called experts in, nowadays. Let's have a try at doing it ourselves.'

'What, all the painting and papering, you mean?' asked Maggie, appalled and intrigued.

'Why not? I did Matt's nursery by myself. It'll save a fortune. I'm even prepared to have a go at laying the carpets, if you'll make the curtains.'

Mrs Robertson found the prospect of a pair of rank amateur decorators messing about in her house daunting, to say the least, but when she'd had a couple of estimates which nearly made her hair stand on end, and Stip had dashed off a comparative costing, she yielded with good grace. This was well before middle-class do-it-yourself really set in, and Ian and Lilian condemned the project as not only wildly impractical but faintly scandalous; manual work was for menials and that was the bottom line of their objections. But by the time they got wind

169

of it, Stip and Maggie were already up ladders in their dungarees, and refused to come down.

It was just as well that they liked the position, because they had to maintain it for many months. They made endless blunders to begin with; many a job had to be done twice or even three times before Mrs Robertson would agree to pass it. She helped on the sidelines, setting the standards and learning all the terms ('That strip will have to come down again, Steven – it's not random-match, you know!'). And it was she who made most of the curtains in the end, because her ageing Singer treadle defied Maggie's infuriated attempts to master it.

Besides, Maggie was into stripping. She began with a fire surround which had been chocolate brown for as long as anyone could remember, but which, with the layers of paint scraped off, proved to be beautiful dove-white marble. Maggie had it dismantled, took it out into the back garden piecemeal and worked on it with a vicious mixture of her own invention of which the main ingredients were pure caustic soda and wallpaper paste. She used the hose a good deal, burned through three pairs of overalls and five of rubber gloves and killed a whole row of her mother's pansies with the run-off; but when she'd finished, the fireplace was a thing of beauty and a joy forever. Reassembled in the drawing-room (*hors de combat* for weeks) against Stips's magnolia wallpaper it gave Maggie such immense, almost sensual satisfaction that she at once began on the hall panelling.

For this she invested in half a dozen scrapers of eccentric shape to dig into the crevices of the moulding, as well as an array of wire brushes and other implements. She even invested, to her mother's horror, in a blow-lamp. Here, too, there were blunders; the golden pine panelling, a hundred years old, revealed by her efforts, bore in burns and gouges the proof of its first-ever stripper's inexperience; but the overall effect when sanded and polished with beeswax was both aesthetically and psychologically profoundly satisfying.

At least Maggie and Stip thought so. Mrs Robertson was dubious – 'a nice coat of white gloss' was murmured about – but when she saw Maggie's look of outrage, she resigned herself. And she did get her own way about several other features of the house. She, like the others, learnt that the skilled

170

piper can call his own tune. She chose the curtain material because she refused to use her sewing-machine on any other.

Stip was as good as his word about the paperhanging and carpet-laying. And his taste astonished both his mother and sister. When Edinburgh's shops failed to provide designs or shades which pleased him, he took money from their 'float' (all accounts were strictly kept – Mrs Robertson insisted on that) and took the train to London, whence he returned after three entrancing days with an assortment that left the women speechless. 'I don't know!' Mrs Robertson kept saying, fingering the new synthetic velvets in shades of mushroom and eau-de-Nil, the wallpaper samples with their silky eggshell finish from which infant fingermarks could be wiped. 'I just do not know at all!'

'Well, I do,' said Stip firmly, 'and I've placed orders for this, this, and this. They'll arrive on Friday, so let's clear the decks in the bedrooms and alert the upholsterer to collect the dining-room chairs and the sofa.'

Mrs Robertson looked dazed. But she was willing to try anything. Both Stip and Maggie were very proud of her, and, increasingly, fond and proud of each other.

'You're getting really good!' exclaimed Maggie, some time later, watching Stip bearing lightly-pasted wallpaper, folded over on itself, swiftly up the ladder and affixing it to the twelve feet of the stairwell without wrinkle or tear. 'You'll be able to do up your own place, when you get it.'

'Don't think I hadn't thought of that,' said Stip. 'Why do you think I'm making all my mistakes here?'

Matt was settling down all right. He liked his school; he liked the town with its modern shops; he loved his room with its gas-fire and fender you could sit on, and the big, exciting toy-cupboard. He liked all the bustle of having a family, though the ritual Sunday lunches bored him. He sensed Ian's innate disapproval and he cordially hated Lilian. But he wrote every week to Tolly and slept with her blouse to his face and the little wire-and-fur creatures on his bedside table. And he talked all the time about going back to Africa. No gentle off-putting remarks of Maggie's shook him in his conviction that all this, pleasant as it was, could conceivably be anything more than an interlude.

171

For Maggie, things were not so easy. She had always recognised that she didn't know the half of motherhood, the good side or the bad side; she had always been cushioned against its sharper realities and had felt guilty that she was not fulfilling the pattern of parenthood that she had been conditioned to believe was the only right one. Now this guilt, at least, was removed. Matt was all Maggie's. She was responsible for everything about him, from seeing that he brushed his teeth and moved his bowels to keeping him fed, clothed and entertained. If she could see that he was getting in the way, or getting tired and fractious, she had to drop everything and take him out, or alternatively, get strict with him. She soon realised how very little practice she had had in being strict.

One Sunday the whole family was sitting round the lunch-table. Lilian was being more unbuttoned than usual. She was beginning to see, through the rough-and-tumble of the redecorations, how efficient Stip was getting, and how much money he was saving by this novel do-it-yourself approach.

'You'll make some lucky girl a wonderful, handy husband,' she remarked waggishly as she helped herself to more peas.

Stip crossed his eyes behind Lilian's back as she leant forward. Matt saw this and burst out laughing. Lilian looked round sharply and Ian raised his eyebrows. Matt began to act up, snorting and giggling, trying to involve Stip in an eye-conspiracy against his uncle and aunt.

Maggie could usually be fairly patient with Matt when it was only her Mother or Stip; but when his behaviour gave Ian and Lilian an opportunity to exchange looks, as they were now doing, she became unwontedly furious.

'*Matt*,' she said, in her special tone of warning. But instead of responding he slithered down in his chair, almost disappearing under the table. He must have been sitting on a corner of the cloth; everything began to slide dangerously. Mrs Robertson gave a little cry and grabbed the cloth, but too late – Matt's plate crashed to the carpet.

'Matt! Look what you've done! Stop it and sit up properly!' exclaimed Maggie, hot with shame, hiking him upright. He was boneless. He hung his head like a badly-made Guy Fawkes, uttering idiotic sounds. Ian rose with dignity and left the room, evidently finding the whole scene intolerable. Lilian sat still,

172

watching with a sort of detached curiosity. She seemed to be deriving some inner pleasure from Maggie's struggles.

Stip stood up, lifted Matt bodily from his chair and carried him out of the room, feebly kicking and hiccupping. There was a pause. Maggie was too sunk in embarrassment and anger to speak, but she picked up the fallen plate which luckily was still in one piece, and the knife and fork. Then Ian made a studied re-entry.

'Well, well, well,' he said, swept his napkin across his knee with a speaking gesture, and went on with his lunch.

'Poor wee boy,' said Mrs Robertson. 'It's not his fault.'

Maggie knew what *that* meant. It meant, 'He needs a father's hand.' But Ian interpreted the remark according to his own ideas.

'Of course it's not the boy's fault,' he remarked tartly.

'I suppose you mean it's mine,' said Maggie.

'If the cap fits,' said Ian maddeningly.

'Ian, don't,' said Mrs Robertson.

'In what way is it my fault? Not that he did anything so terrible.'

'You should try harder to civilise him.'

'To *what*?'

Ian laid down his knife and fork.

'Children are born in a state of nature,' he said loftily. 'They have to be civilised by their parents, otherwise they're nothing but intolerable little savages.'

If Stip had been there, Maggie wouldn't have felt the need to defend herself – his simple presence had come to have this beneficent, relaxing effect. Now, stupidly, she felt she had to give battle, and on Ian's own ground – a fatal error, always.

'You saw me doing my best –'

'I saw you shake his arm and say "Stop it". But you didn't *mean* it. When you say "no" to a child, he's got to know you mean it.'

'How the bloody hell am I supposed to convince him that I mean it? By beating him up?'

Ian and Lilian exchanged looks. Ian said with infinite and lofty calm, 'All right, Maggie. Let's leave it. I suppose all things considered, it's not your fault that you can't handle basic situations.'

173

Maggie saw bright red. She picked up her glass of water and threw its contents in his face.

Lilian got splashed and jumped up and backwards, knocking her heavy chair over. Ian also jumped up with an inarticulate shout, brushing the cold water out of his eyes. The water-stains spread on the white Irish cloth. Mrs Robertson, at whom Maggie cast an instinctive, frightened glance, sat perfectly still, her hands clenched in her lap, her eyes behind her glasses tightly shut. Maggie wanted to die, she was so profoundly in the wrong and so conscious of it.

'Are you mad?' Ian shouted. Her aim had been excellent, her glass full, and he was thoroughly soaked.

'If I'm not I soon will be, with you around! Try bringing up a child yourself and see if you're so good at "basic situations" before you start on me!'

'I'm happy to tell you,' Ian said, very quietly though his narrow face was dark with outrage, 'that your nasty little crack about our childlessness falls upon stony ground. Lilian and I have decided to adopt a child. I was going to tell you all after lunch. We expect to hear quite soon that we have a child of our own, and then we shall see whose theories of child-rearing are right, and whether self-control and a good example don't produce better results than random fits of anger interspersed with spoiling! I think we'll go home, Mother, if you'll excuse us. I couldn't eat any more and I'm really too angry to paper over cracks.'

Mrs Robertson didn't move or look up. Maggie didn't follow Ian's and Lilian's depature with her eyes or her mind; she sat at the devastated lunch table staring at her mother until they heard the front door shut and Mrs Robertson's eyes opened. Maggie waited as if for sentence.

'Maggie dear,' said her mother. 'Just use the napkins to put under the cloth so the water won't mark the polish, will you? Where have Steven and Matt got to? I'll just go and bring in the apple pudding. It's Matt's favourite. Do you think I ought to whip the cream or serve it as it is?'

'Whipped,' muttered Maggie, shaking suddenly. 'Shall I – ?'

Mrs Robertson laid an unexpectedly firm hand on her shoulder. 'No, dear. You sit still and rest. One needs to, after an upset, or it takes all day to get over it.'

She went out. Maggie stood up and began carefully bunching

174

up the linen napkins and inserting them under the wet cloth. Abruptly, her mother returned. Maggie, nerves on edge, swung round guiltily.

Mrs Robertson stood in the doorway.

'You *can* handle basic situations,' she said firmly. 'Ian had no right to say that.' Then she went again, calling: 'Steven! Matt! Pudding!'

Maggie stifled the onrush of sudden tears with a sopping napkin.

Chapter Nineteen

It took many months – nearly a year, in fact – for Maggie to realise why it was that she did not feel a great deal better in the redecorated house than she had when she first came home

The improvement in her surroundings was startling and undeniable. By the simple device of substituting pale colours for dark, the whole aspect had changed. The great gilt-framed mirrors which had previously only emphasised the gloom, now expanded the vistas of the square high-ceilinged Victorian rooms; the finer points of period – the panelling and the mouldings, the picture rails, turned bannisters and fireplaces – had been brought out. Stip had an instinctive feeling for such things. He had spent hours at a neck-ricking angle up ladders, chipping the deadening layers of smoked whitewash off the central roses, revealing delightful bacchanalian designs ... And his colour sense proved impeccable.

Everyone who came into the house reacted more or less gratifyingly. Ian always narrowed his eyes against what he called 'the glare'; Lilian surreptitiously twitched the new curtains in an abortive effort to make them do the office of the lace ones which had been ceremonially burnt in the back garden, with Stip, Maggie and Matt dancing round the pyre and Mrs Robertson handing out libations. Maggie's and Stip's contemporaries performed stranger antics, rolling about on the pale velvety carpets and demanding extra-mural showers in the new bathroom. In short, the whole enterprise was justly regarded by its perpetrators as a success.

And Stip, his apprenticeship complete, took a last satisfied look around at his handiwork, packed his things with his mother's help, and decamped to his own little house, new-bought and all but derelict.

'My God, Stip! Are you sure you can handle it?' Maggie had

gasped on first seeing it. 'I can't wait,' said Stip with that new air of self-confidence he had begun to display, and that was the last they saw of him for some time.

Thus Mrs Robertson, Maggie and Matt had the reborn family house to themselves, and Maggie began to savour the reality of her life-change for the first time. While the house had been upside down and she had been working on it, there had been neither routine nor time in which to reflect on what her new situation was going to be like. It was only now that she began to realise, not just what Bruce had done in leaving her, but what he had done by taking her to Africa.

Africa had wormed its way into her blood like bilharzia. The effect was nothing less than the distortion of all her visual and sensual perceptions. Once upon a time, these light, bright rooms would have wholly charmed and satisfied her. But it came too late. At eighteen she had yearned for 'contemp'. In her early twenties, struggling with the foreignness of Nigeria, she would have adored this. Now, she felt that all this pallor, this restraint, this essentially northern-hemisphere good taste was no longer a reflection of her present self. She had been seduced away from its essentially moderate pleasures. Needing the bite of strong, rich colours and rough textures, she found herself surrounded by a bland diet of pastel shades, quiet designs; when her hands reached out for tactile stimulus, the fabrics were all smooth, the wood polished, the carpets soft, the walls slippery. Nothing resisted. There was no friction, no salutary sudden shocks.

Sometimes she would sit amid the pale beauty of Stip's drawingroom, all magnolia and ash green, and imagine Tolly. Blue-black Tolly, dazzling the eye. Maggie looked at her mother's flower arrangements (daffodils, pink roses, lilac, apple blossom) and remembered the hibiscus and jacaranda, the bougainvillaea in all its splendid vulgarity, and wondered what her mother would say if she were able to effect a sudden complete substitution. What an effect it would make, what an impact!

But it wouldn't do. She proved it one day by bringing down her African souvenirs from her bedroom and scattering them about – an ebony statuette with metal neck-rings and down-pointing breasts, an oval shield carved in dark wood hung on a regency-striped wall, a big brazen dish glinting luridly, a

177

brilliant body-wrap with geometrical designs – blood-red, purple, acid green, mustard yellow and a harsh, equatorial blue – draped over the old piano.

The effect was stunning – in the pejorative sense. Even Maggie could see that. The two styles fought for supremacy; the more primitive won, almost at a blow, and stood crudely dominant against a background suddenly washed-out and defeated. Maggie felt disloyal to it. She hurriedly collected up all her alien trophies and bore them back to her room, before her mother could see and be shocked by the contrast they made with her pretty, tasteful interior.

But on Maggie the imprint had been made. She kept seeing the things where she had momentarily, treacherously, arranged them. She kept seeing Tolly moving through the house, not at all like a ghost but as if she were really there, bringing Africa and Maggie's past – her failed but married past – with her.

And on a practical level, Maggie often longed for her. When Matt behaved in some incomprehensible fashion or went into one of his moods, Maggie wondered why on earth it had seemed so impossible to bring Tolly here. Sometimes she dreamed of sending for her, dreams almost as compelling as (she knew) Matt's of returning to Tolly . . .

From the outset – from Matt's birth – Maggie had had her deep secret doubts about her abilities as a mother. Her dependence on Tolly, of which she had always been guiltily aware, Ian's caustic remarks, and her own inner conviction that her bent lay elsewhere, had undermined her confidence.

Her mother – in whose conventional view, motherhood was every woman's birthright, mothering ability as natural a talent as conceiving – was baffled by Maggie's outbursts of self-laceration when she felt she had mishandled a 'basic situation'.

'Darling, you shouldn't upset yourself over every little thing! Goodness, if I'd eaten away at myself every time I'd been cross with one of you, there'd have been nothing left of me by the time I'd raised you.'

'But why did I have to smack him? He didn't mean to break the bloody thing, it was an accident!'

'You'd told him not to play with it, and he did, and he broke it, and you smacked him. That's *all right*, Maggie, it's within the limits of what you must allow yourself.'

178

'I didn't smack him for disobeying me, I smacked him because of the noise, the mess, because I lost my temper –'

'Better than hitting him in cold blood. Now go up and cuddle him and read him a story, and I'll make chips for supper.'

Mrs Robertson became a skilled make-it-up-er; she saw that as her main role. However, there was another side to her. Maggie found her not only a kind and loving companion and helper with Matt, but, in subtle ways, a spur and even a goad.

One evening, about a year after Maggie's return home, her mother seemed unusually thoughtful.

'What's on your mind, Mummy?' Maggie asked. She herself was restless and nervy as she was so often. Matt was in bed and she should have been able to relax after a taxing day with him, but she couldn't. She felt like talking.

'It's really none of my business.'

'Is it to do with Matt?' Maggie asked quickly.

'In a way. It's more to do with you.'

Maggie curtailed her prowlings round the room and sat down in one of the big mushroom-covered armchairs.

'Go on.'

'Have you thought at all what you're going to do with yourself?'

Maggie felt an uncomfortable little shock inside her head.

'I'm going to live here with you, and bring up Matt as well as I can.'

'Hm.'

'What's that supposed to imply?'

'Is that really going to be enough?'

Maggie said nothing.

'Are you happy with the local school for Matt?'

'For the moment.'

'He'll be eight soon.'

'He's only just turned seven.'

'When Ian was eight, we packed him off to boarding school.'

'Yes, and look at him!'

'You misjudge Ian. I know his faults, but there is a great deal of good in him.'

'Let's just say I wouldn't want Matt to grow up like him.'

'Matt is an entirely different type.'

'I really wouldn't feel right about sending any child of that age away from home, Mummy. Anyway, what would be the

179

advantage of it? Perhaps you think he'd be better off away from me?'

Her mother laid down her work and looked at her over her glasses. 'Maggie, stop it. You are not to get an inferiority complex about yourself as a mother. If there is one quality above all others that a woman needs to be a good mother, it's self-confidence.'

'I thought it was patience.'

'A poor second, I assure you. Patient women can be cabbages, or rather, doormats. A child needs something to strive with, something which resists and stands firm and even hits back. "Patience" is too flabby a quality to come first.'

'All right, so say I have no self-confidence. As well as not much patience. Would that indicate that he should go to boarding school?'

Mrs Robertson worked in silence for a while. Maggie grew restless again.

'I'm much more concerned with you than Matt. I believe a child needs a fulfilled, satisfied mother. I see very little possibility of your being either if you go on the way you are at present.'

This was drawing uncomfortably close to the secret Bluebeard's chamber in Maggie's mind, where lurked the fear that, if Matt were somehow off her hands, her undoubted subresponsibility for her mother would not alone be sufficient to keep her from running away to London to pursue her own life – her own career.

'Didn't you tell me,' her mother went on, 'that Bruce has set money aside and wants Matt to go to his old school?'

'I'm not bound to do what Bruce wants!'

'Certainly you're not. But if what he wants happens to coincide with what's best for you and the wee boy . . .?'

'What do *you* think is best for us?'

Mrs Robertson crocheted in silence while Maggie watched her with a strange sense of being on a brink.

'I would like,' her mother said at last without looking up, 'to see you on a stage, just once, before my sight totally gives out.'

Then she looked up and their eyes met. The blue of the older woman's was worn pale with discouragements and lack of fulfilment, while the blue of Maggie's was still vividly dark and full of fight. Something flashed between them which united

180

them in a complicity of needs and desires which could once have made them comrades-in-arms against the repressions of their lives; for a painful second, Maggie was angry with her mother, because now it might well be too late – she was spurring a horse securely tied to a post.

'I've no right to advise you,' Mrs Robertson said. 'I made a mess of my own life, though I've had my satisfactions. But I often wonder if I wouldn't have had more to give to you children, and even, oddly enough, to your father, if I'd taken more for myself. That's the only thought I can offer you.'

Maggie thought it over during the next few days. She tasted and tested her restlessness, fearing it like some fledgling wild thing within her which would, when full-grown, rend her, and through her, Matt . . . The little town with its parades of shops, its mills, its pubs and garages and bus stops and community hall, without even a railway station any more to give an illusion of being on a main line to anywhere, proceeded on its bland way, offering no challenge, no satisfaction. It was a backwater, without even the exotic novelty and disquieting foreignness of Africa . . . Its denizens began to seem close kin to the WC. Maggie knew she couldn't stand it for ever, not for Matt, not for her mother, not out of a conviction of duty or indebtedness – not to prove to Ian that she was good mother-material. Not even to prove it to herself.

She went to consult Stip.

His house was on the outskirts of town. He was intensely happy, doing it up after work and at weekends. Maggie was astonished by what he had done already. There was no safe Homes-and-Gardens effect here. The hallway and stairs were clad in a napped paper, which drew the hand like fur, in a brilliant burnt orange. The double-ended living-room was to have one black wall. 'A *black wall*!' shrieked Maggie. 'Horrors! Why?' 'Because it will look sensational with my new abstracts on it,' said Stip, unmoved.

His bedroom seemed to be all mirrors, 'How decadent!' said Margaret, and Maggie added, ' – delicious! How can you afford this fin-de-siècle-brothel look, on your salary?'

'Helen's legacy, plus savings – Mum would hardly take a penny while I was at home. Besides, all the mirrors are junk-shop gleanings. You'd be amazed the beautiful things people don't want.'

181

Maggie looked somewhat doubtfully at the gilded light-brackets. 'It's a bit precious, Stip.'

There was a pause. She looked at him quickly.

'This house,' said Stip, 'is going to be *me*. As much as I can possibly afford to make it. So if you say anything negative about it, kindly remember, you will hurt my feelings.'

'I'm mad about most of it.'

'Good.'

They went down to the kitchen which was still in complete chaos. There was only an oil stove to make coffee on.

'You haven't been to Sunday lunch for weeks,' Maggie mentioned.

'I see enough of Ian at work. Any Sunday he can't come, let me know and I'll be round. How's Matt?'

'He misses you.'

'Bring him here one day after school. He can lend a hand with the painting.'

Coffee mugs in hand, they wandered round the derelict garden and Stip enthusiastically told her exactly what he planned for this area of his property. It appeared he had ambitions as a landscape gardener as well. Maggie was amazed. He seemed to have taken on a new lease of life. In the spring breeze, his tuft of hair stood up tentatively, as if raising itself to peep out of its firmly combed-down rut to see if life was perhaps worth taking an interest in again. Strolling out here with Stip, Maggie felt all her restive urgings to be off, her deep fears about herself and even her anger with Bruce, which still simmered only just beneath the surface, not vanishing but at least falling into perspective.

Into this deceptive calm water, she casually dropped her boulder.

'D'you think I should send Matt away to school and try to go back on the stage?'

It took a moment for the ripple to reach Stip. Then he stopped abruptly and stared at her.

'You wouldn't,' he said at last. 'You wouldn't leave her again. You've only been back a few months.'

'It's a year, Stip. She's okay. It was her idea actually.'

Stip bent down and dragged an elm seedling out viciously. The basic empathy between them made her aware of his thoughts.

182

'*You* wouldn't have to go back there, you know.'

He turned on her. 'Oh! Indeed? What makes you so sure? What if you'd be away on tour or something, and she was ill or had a fall? She's just at the age when they fall and break their bones, and if they're living alone they can just lie there for *days* –'

Now it was Maggie who stared. He looked quite wild, and his voice was pitching up shrilly, as it had when he was a child. He heard it and silenced himself sharply. When he spoke again his voice sounded simply curt.

'Sorry. But you don't know what it's been like. I've done a long stint. Now it's your turn – *your turn*, Maggie, and you're not getting off the hook.'

Maggie felt a strange stubbornness creeping over her; the more he opposed her, the more her desire to escape crystallised. She hadn't realised till now that she hadn't come for advice at all, but simply to get Stip to ratify what she was subconsciously longing to do.

'What about Ian? Why can't she live with him? They've got a big enough house – ' Something in Stip's face gave her pause, but then she rushed on. 'When they adopt their baby, they'll need her.'

'Shut your face, Maggie!'

Maggie shut her face promptly. Stip's rages, even as a child, had been rare, but cataclysmic and intimidating. 'You shock me. You selfish little wretch! Would you want to live with Ian, let alone with Lilian? She was always waspish, and if you think somebody else's baby is going to improve her you'll believe anything. Mum'd have to watch every step she took and every word she spoke. Why should she, Maggie, why should she, when she's got her own house and a daughter who owes her everything?'

'Everything – ?'

'Don't you know Mum more than half guessed all the time that you weren't at cooking school, and bore your secret for you, and the guilt of deceiving Dad, and then calmed him down when he found out?'

'He wasn't very calm when –'

'Maggie, listen. If it hadn't been for Mum, he'd have handed you over to the police.' She stared at him silently. She didn't doubt it. 'And she's never said a word or laid one wee claim

183

on you, and now you want to run off and leave her to rot with Ian . . . I can't believe it, I can't, Maggie, that's the truth. *Not even of you!*'

This last cut swift and deep. Maggie hung her head, crushed.

Chapter Twenty

Penicuik is many miles from the epicentre of the London theatre scene, but that would not, of itself, have kept Tanya and Maggie apart. Nor would their ancient quarrel. Scarcely a day – well, certainly not a week – had passed in all the years when Maggie had not thought of Tanya, wondered about her, and missed her vigorous lively companionship.

After Bruce's decampment Maggie had written, from Port Harcourt, a letter to Tanya, addressed to *Spotlight*, the casting directory, whose forwarding department had acted with commendable promptness and efficiency. Within a fortnight had come a lengthy reply, which Maggie hungrily devoured:

Darling, darling Maggie,

I must say it: sympathy – horrors – hands thrown up and eyes rolling, for your sake, you poor thing. Remember Miss Pross at RADA who used to say, for anything from a missed appointment to falling over a dead body, 'Horrors, darling! It's *horrors*! No, no dear, don't just stand there, REACT!' And 'react' with her meant throwing up your hands, rolling your eyes ... And that is what I am doing for you. And are you ready to do it for me? Here goes.

When you last saw me I was in love. With Joel. Right? And he was in love with me. Yes, he was. Perhaps you will say, at the end, well if he had loved you truly, etc., etc. But it is not so simple. Have you read *The Heart of the Matter*, where that poor Catholic couldn't make up his mind which of his two ladies to hurt and in the end did himself in and went to hell? (Does Graham Greene *believe* he went to hell, and if he does – or indeed if he doesn't – why does he persist to be Catholic?)

Joel was not a Catholic of course, but he proved you don't

185

have to be one in order to live in a this-world hell for loving two women at once. And in the end I saw it was tearing him into two bits. Besides, like in the song, every time we said goodbye, I died a little.

So I said goodbye to Joel for the last time, and I died a lot more than a little, in fact I went on dying for six whole months. It was tremendously awful – a real illness. Even when I began to recover I was very sickly and feeble and I think it's even lucky I was out of work at the time (though then it just seemed to make things worse) because I hadn't the strength to act. Oh, I did a few bits ... Since the new television channel started, the one with commercials, there've been lots of jobs, if you have absolutely no professional pride and just want to eat. I reach that point quite quickly I find. I helped advertise things like Mars Bars and Kelloggs Cornflakes and was even seen on big posters in the tube, glamorously puffing a Player's, which I got told off about by my doctor, who said at least Mars Bars only make your teeth drop out, they don't help to kill you. It was all as unlike acting as could be, but to be frank it was all I was fitted for just then, I was so degraded already with loss-of-Joel.

To think that without a miracle I would *never see him again*, that was the worst. I felt I could bear giving him up if I could just see him sometimes ... Oh, isn't it trite? Aren't all one's truest and deepest emotions just rubbishy-trite? When one is sunk in them or even remembering them, they feel like Dostoyevsky, but trying to tell about them they come out like Barbara Cartland.

And this is where I come back to you and *your* woe, Maggie, because I am here to tell you that one *does* get over it. If I can get over Joel so that it hardly ever hurts and I can look at, and go out with, and even go sometimes to bed with, other men, then you can get over your ex-Bruce. Because I still say, and now maybe you won't be angry at it, that you never were really *in it* with him, so having been married or not doesn't affect how long it will take you to get well.

What will, is how quickly you can bring Matt back to England and get on with your life that Bruce interrupted. I will help. Listen to how. I no longer live in a doss-house but a flat. In Primrose Hill, not overlooking but nearly. There's room for you. The place is always full of actors and other mad,

186

nice people and you will be sure to meet possible lovers/job-givers/playmates, you will have some fun and feel yourself getting back into your own true skin.

As to Matt, you must appreciate the terrible fact that I am now over thirty and bursting with frustrated maternal feelings, so he and I will help each other.

I don't know how you can bear not to be in England. I love it more and more the longer I live here. Of course I have an advantage over you. I know from experience how much it's better and more civilised than any other country. You have not tried living in any other country that could be called civilised so you can't compare. And this is a good time to be here. The war is left well behind and everyone is looking ahead and getting a wonderful excited feeling that stiff-necked and toffee-nosed old rules and patterns are being broken down and that people are at last going to be free to form new ones *for themselves* instead of accepting hand-me-down ones. You would love that feeling, Maggie. It's going to be a good time for women, too. Women are doing all sorts of jobs now. I would like you to come back from your exile in the jungle and share this adventurous time with me.

When you come (not if) we will spend several weeks just talking. Oh, I have learnt so much and changed so much since I saw you last! Mostly from Joel. No, I am not hankering but one should always make an accounting of what one has gained from even very sad and painful experiences, otherwise one feels only diminished. Joel used to say that everything that happened to people was caused by themselves. I got angry and said how could people cause themselves to be put into camps, etc. or be killed, and a lesser arguer might have given up then, in polite deference to my personal experience, but he persisted! Of course he had a most brilliant mind. He would sit there talking about things like personal dialectics and I would stop him irritably and make him translate into simple words (which he later said was good for him because he talked and wrote in such abstruse and erudite terms (!) that most people couldn't understand him). I remember I said, well how can people will themselves to be caught in an earthquake? And he said people who sit on a fault in the earth's surface, like in California, are such an obvious example of what he was talking about that he wouldn't even

187

mention it. I applied this (you may guess how unwillingly) to my parents. It came out that Joel was right, because they too knew that they were sitting on a fault, but they stayed there till it opened up and swallowed them. Because they preferred to believe that they were safe from the Germans, than to move out of their way.

So if this theory is right about lesser things, then you willed Matt and Bruce and Africa and all your experience there, just as I brought on to myself Joel. In which case all we can hope is that our deepest desires for our futures are better, since we neither know what they are nor can control them. For my part, I feel mine *are* better; you can tell I am very optimistic, especially when I go into my spare room which I now regard as putatively yours. ('Putatively' is pure Joel of course. I have many words like that which are his legacy. 'Irredentist' and 'recondite' are my favourites, though I can hardly ever find a way to work them into a conversation.)

At last I am going to finish but first I must just tell you that I've stopped puffing Players in the tube and munching Mars Bars on the telly and restarted to work properly. It's a no. 1 touring company, and not spear-carrying this time! Don't be jealous. Or, yes, do be jealous, let your jealousy move you here and challenge you to get back to the life you should have been living all these years.

So much love and lookings forward,
Tanya.'

At the time of reading this, Maggie was all but stunned with a new sadness, the sadness of wasted years during which her exile might have been cheered by letters like this. However that might be, she couldn't wait to be in touch when she got back to Britain, and she tried to be; but a tour by its nature goes on and on and its participants are virtually incommunicado while it does. Especially in this case, because instead of coming down to earth eventually in a London theatre, Tanya's company went abroad in the middle of the British tour and for more than six months she was in places like Germany and Italy, and then the company was whisked off to Singapore and thence to Australia. Postcards came and an occasional letter and from these it was clear that Tanya was up to her eyes in the sort of social life which inevitably accompanies tours of this sort where the visiting 'artistes' are fêted and lionised, a circumstance very much to Tanya's taste and in which she could not be blamed for revelling.

While all this was galling for Maggie, who was dying to see her friend, in a 'recondite' sort of way it was a relief. Tanya's offer of a batching-it, theatre-soaked lifestyle in her London flat had been all too tempting. And then there was her – Tanya's – rising-star aspect to come to terms with. They had started level . . . It was true Tanya was older, but that didn't make it any easier to appreciate her position three-quarters of the way up the ladder from Maggie's at the bottom. Maggie had an uncomfortable feeling that seeing Tanya again would not only involve odious and envy-making comparisons but would arouse all sorts of old ambitions and unassuaged hungers.

And suddenly, one summer morning, a telegram came from Tanya. Her play, partly re-cast, was coming to Edinburgh. Could she stay with Maggie?

Maggie was thrown into a turmoil. She was galvanised by anticipation and rushed about the house getting things ready. Every time she encountered her mother or Matt, she hugged them, crying, 'Tanya's coming! She's *coming*!'

'Who's Tanya?' Matt asked at first.

'She's my best friend. She's wonderful, you'll love her.'

'What do you mean, love her? Do you love her?'

'Of course!'

'How can you love another lady?'

'Why on earth not?'

'Did you love Tolly?'

'Yes. And Joan. And lots of people. But there's no one like Tanya, she's special.'

'So was Tolly special.'

'Differently.'

'Is Tanya black?' He often asked that still about people he was going to meet.

'No! she's – She's sort of bright red!'

'All over?'

Maggie hugged him again, laughing with joy. 'You'll understand when you see her.'

Mrs Robertson was excited too, in a quieter way. Her questions, too, were telling.

'She's almost a star, isn't she?'

189

'Almost!'

'Is it grand enough here for a real theatrical leading lady?'

'Of course, Mummy! She's got no side at all, not Tanya.'

'I hope she'll like me.'

'Don't you worry about that.'

'Will she be here at the weekend?'

'Yes. She's coming on Sunday morning.'

'Oh! What about Sunday lunch?'

That gave Maggie pause, but then she felt a great burst of happiness which swept all doubts before it. 'We'll have them all as usual, I'll make Stip come too, and she can meet them. She always used to say she wanted to meet my brothers.'

One of these at least was not so keen.

'What are you looking so fizzy about?' asked Stip suspiciously when she rushed round to tell him her news.

'My friend Tanya Zandler's coming to stay,' she cried.

'God, you sound like Milly-Molly-Mandy,' said Stip sourly. He recognised the threat of Tanya by instinct. 'And her imminence is what's lit you up like a Roman candle?'

'Oh, come on, Stip! I haven't seen her for eight years. She was my closest friend.'

There was a silence, and then Stip said, with unwonted spite, 'I just hope she's not too actressy, that's all. I can't bear over-made-up shrieky women. If she calls me "darling", I'll walk out of the house.'

Maggie was startled and chagrined. She'd expected him to be pleased for her. 'You've nothing to fear,' she said huffily. 'She's not that sort at all.'

'Is it today she's coming – the red lady?'

Matt was sitting on the foot of her bed, cross-legged, a gnome in a red flannel stocking-cap thing Maggie had never seen before. She struggled up out of sleep.

'What on earth's that on your head?'

'Grandad's bedcap.'

'I never knew he had such a thing,' said Maggie, blinking.

'It was a secret. Granny told me.'

Maggie stared at the tasselled cap and tried to remember her father.

190

'It's a good house for secrets,' Matt said. 'Not like the bungalow.'

'Does that mean you like it here better?' she asked unwisely.

Matt shook his head vigorously. 'Oh no,' he said, but quite cheerfully. 'I couldn't like anywhere better than with Tolly.' She saw him shiver and pulled him into bed. He had something under his pyjama jacket, a soft padding on his chest. She caught a glimpse of sharp blue between the buttons. Tolly's blouse. Would he ever discard it, discard Tolly? She suspected the former would fall to pieces, the latter herself have forgotten, before he did. Matt, unlike his father, was the faithful type.

'*Is* it today?' he repeated.

'Yes. I must get up and start making a super lunch.'

'Has she got any children?'

'No. She's not married.'

'Why not?'

'I don't know . . .'

Why not, indeed? Had the thing with Joel lasted, in its effects, all these years? Was there, nowadays, outside of fiction, a kind of passion which, denied propinquity, denied reciprocity, kept its effective hold on a woman's life for years? If there were, and if Tanya were a victim of it, Maggie knew with her head that she was to be pitied. Objectively she did pity her for such unrewarded thralldom. But subjectively she felt nothing but the profoundest envy. To feel like that! To *feel* like that! Even pain, even the aridity of loneliness and childlessness – no. Not that perhaps, Maggie amended as she held Matt tenderly under her wing. But to know yourself capable of a deep, passionate, *lasting* love . . . how un-shallow that must reassure you that you are! A real woman, painted in bright strong colours, not a bland pale thing like herself, whose strongest emotion ever, till now, had certainly been guilt.

She went to the station at 11 a.m. to meet Tanya, shaking with excitement. She had examined herself in the mirror before she left. She was incapable of judging how much she had changed, how she might strike Tanya . . . Her eyes were unmistakably more strained, her face thinner. That apple-cheeked bloom, the country-girl look she had been teased about at RADA had faded, giving place to a more fine-drawn and intense, a less –

191

well, less remorselessly *wholesome* look. The years in Africa had begun the de-appling, the months in Scotland had thinned and sallowed her face further. 'But at least I look more grown-up,' Maggie told herself as she stood on the platform under the grimy glass roof, staring up the track. 'After all, however much of a mess I've made up to now, it's been living, of a sort. Surely that's part of what matters.' Thus she tried to arm herself in advance against the impact of Tanya's vitality, the inner sureness that triumphed over *real* tragedies, *real* losses . . . Wasn't Bruce a real loss? No. There were moments in Maggie's life where nothing seemed quite real, nothing seemed ever to have truly touched her. Except acting . . . The worst and most testing experience she had ever had, she realised suddenly as the train came snarling in and she rushed to the barrier, was not the death of close relatives, the agony of childbirth, the shattering unexpected loss of a husband. It was being nine months out of work when she was nineteen.

A carriage door flew open a fraction of a second before all the others, and there she was. Vivid, alive, waving wildly before turning back to drag out case after case . . . Two men rushed to help before Maggie could get there. One produced a trolley, the other piled it high. Maggie arrived, breathless from running, and she and Tanya grabbed each other.

'Oh, Maggie –'

'Darling – it's so lovely –'

'How wonderful you look! How much more interesting now you are that little bit thinner! I thought having a baby made everybody more fat? All my friends who have are like plum puddings.' She hooked her arm through Maggie's and they walked up the platform while the two eager strangers toiled after them with the trolley. Others, less fortunate, simply gazed as they passed.

Tanya looked superb. You couldn't mistake her for anything but a successful actress. And she *was* 'bright red all over', or very nearly. A scarlet Wetherall suit with pale blue piping topped by a reversible scarlet and blue cloak which swung debonairely as she strode along. Shoes with long pointed toes and spike heels. Skirt very short, emphasising her thrusting, pretty knees. Plus a marvellous black velour hat with a wide soft brim, like a beautiful spy. Her hair was cropped short with points to the cheeks and was a truly stunning shade of red, almost magenta.

Her make-up made her look all eyes. Maggie thought she had never seen anyone so *swaggeringly* smart. She felt ludicrously proud of the impression her friend made in the sombre purlieus of Edinburgh station.

'You know I always used to think it was "plump hoodings",' Tanya was saying. 'I kept looking up "hoodings" in the dictionary! So tell, you said a party for lunch, who is coming? I hope it will be all your family. If po-faced Ian is not there, I shall die of disappointment.'

'He'll be there, and Lilian, and Stip. And if you dare send any of them up or make shocking remarks I shall drive you at once to the most straightlaced temperance hotel in Edinburgh and abandon you there.'

The car ride passed in a verbal kaleidoscope. It was as if they had not been parted for more than a few weeks, except that there was so much to catch up on; they scarcely scratched the surface of all that, though – it was just banter and nonsense at first. Tanya didn't talk much about her career, which Maggie already knew was on the verge of bursting into real brilliance. Nor would Maggie be drawn on the subject of Bruce, whose shade passed across the conversation in the time it took for a red light to turn green.

'Do you want to talk about him, get it out of your chest?'

'Off. No.'

'What do you mean, "off"?' Tanya asked, bridling.

'Off your chest, not out of.'

'I *said* "off"! I have not said "out of" for years, if ever! You know our producer is queer?'

'No?'

'Well, he is. And *he* says some most outrageous things. Last week I invited him to dinner with Oliver and another girl and I did everything nicely, with candles, and he looked at them and said in this madly camp voice, "My dear Tanya, fancy you still using *candles*! And *lit*, too – how kinky!"'

Maggie laughed, though she didn't get it. She was more interested in the name she'd caught.

'Who's Oliver?'

'Oliver? But you remember him! Oliver Britten. From RADA.'

Maggie did remember, quite clearly – a tall, rather intense boy with the face of an intelligent goat. South African, very hot

193

against apartheid at a time when nobody in England knew much about it, and among fellow-students who never gave a thought to politics or indeed anything but the theatre. She remembered him best from an occasion when they'd all gone to Shearn's vegetarian restaurant in Tottenham Court Road for lunch and Oliver had held forth about the iniquities of racialism while Tanya, still raw from her wartime nightmare, gazed into his face, forgetting to eat in the passion of her agreement. But he was talking, it seemed, exclusively about the blacks in South Africa; later in the same conversation he let slip some faintly anti-semitic remark which Maggie registered with amazement, glancing at Tanya and being glad to realise she hadn't heard . . . Odd to recall that now so vividly, her first realisation that people could be liberal in their own handpicked spots, while maintaining their pet prejudices in separate, unbreachable compartments . . .

This all flashed through her mind in the time it took to say, 'Of course I remember Oliver. What's he like now?'

'Oh! He is handsome as ever . . . beautiful long hands . . . He is interested in politics. For that I love him.'

Maggie turned to her sharply, her ideal of eternal, unfed faithfulness wilting and dying.

'Love him? Really love?'

Tanya threw back her head theatrically and closed her eyes. 'Really really love!' Her hat fell into the back of the car and she opened her eyes, laughed, and scrambled onto her knees to fish for it over the back of her seat. 'No more of that! You see how it makes my hair stand on end. Later I will tell what there is to tell of Oliver. He has been monopolising me rather. Meanwhile, give me instructions how I am to get off with your brothers.'

'Ian's spoken for. And Stip is terrified of actresses.'

'Ah. One of those. And Ian I am forbidden to shock. So perhaps I do my Calvinist matron? Have I time to remove my eyelashes and put on my high-necked dress and white orlon cardigan before lunch?'

The answer was no. The family were ready ranged in the drawing-room by the time they arrived, in fact Stip was on the doorstep to help in with the luggage before the car drew up.

He shook hands with Tanya rather gingerly and she lowered her eyes, not creating a particularly Calvinist impression since

194

she was wearing a great deal of turquoise eyeshadow and the aforementioned devastating false lashes, like black-pointed stars. Stip gazed at these in fascination for a few seconds, then hastily turned, gathering up enough luggage for three porters, and staggered up the steps.

Tanya turned to Maggie and fractionally shook her head.

'No,' she said softly. 'He is safe. I would be afraid . . . It will have to be Ian, after all.'

'Watch out for Lilian then,' Maggie muttered.

They went in. Ian was standing before the fireplace in a classic paterfamilias pose with Lilian sitting beside him. She was actually wearing a white orlon cardigan which made it very difficult for Maggie, who was feeling hilarious with nerves, to restrain herself. She managed to perform the introductions. Ian's eyes came to rest on the flapper-style, magenta hair.

'I hope you won't find us too conventional,' he said.

Tanya opened her eyes very wide. 'Why should I? I am not sure what "conventional" really means. I know I am not it, or you wouldn't have said that, but if it is something dull, I'm sure no one in Maggie's family could be it either.'

Mrs Robertson came forward from the bay window where she had been hiding. Her eyes were very bright as she appraised her guest. 'What a lovely girl you are!' she exclaimed spontaneously. 'I do love an actress to look like an actress.'

Tanya laughed aloud, swung her cloak off her shoulders with a flourish, pulled her beautiful-spy hat off and bowed.

Stip was standing in the doorway, gazing, as if Tanya's emanations might scorch him if he ventured too near. Ian by the same token appeared to be braced against a high wind. Maggie served sherry. Somewhat to her surprise, Lilian, who was normally all but teetotal, took one. This made Maggie give her a second look. She noticed now that Lilian had had her hair done and was wearing rouge. Or was it rouge? Anyway she was decidedly bright of eye and her carriage was even more upright than usual. She seemed to be containing herself with an effort. But Maggie forgot her in fascination with the conversation Tanya was having with her mother.

'Tell us about your play!' Mrs Robertson was saying eagerly. 'Am I to come and see it, or will it shock me too much?'

'Are you easily shocked?' asked Tanya. 'I must say, you don't look it.'

'Oh, but I am! How could I not be, at my age, and with the speed things are changing?'

'Things?'

'Everything! Styles. Of speech, of dress, of – I *love* your skirt being so short, just like ours in the twenties, but those shoes with their sharp pointed toes, won't they give you bunions? Oh, but that's nothing, of course! It's the changes in morals and what people talk about. When I was young, things altered slowly. One had time to accustom oneself. Except during wars. Hair and skirts shot up at a great rate in both the wars –'

Tanya gave a great, bawdy laugh.

'Oh! Oh dear, I didn't mean *that*, you bad girl! Anyway, so if your play is too strong, tell me at once, and I'll stay away and make you a nice dinner for when you come home.'

Tanya sipped her drink and considered. 'Does saying "bloody" shock you?'

'Oh, good heavens, no! I'm far past that.'

'Saying "Jesus Christ" as swearing?'

'Well, I won't say I like it, but it wouldn't keep me away. It's not words so much. It's moral attitudes. And ugliness. And being cruel.'

'There's no cruelty in this. But perhaps you would think it immoral.' She sat down and crossed her beautiful legs. Her skirt slid back to mid-top-thigh. Ian flushed and looked away. 'The girl I play is the hero's mistress, and he brings her into his home, and she tries to win the love of his daughter. I mean, the one he had with his wife.'

'And what is the wife doing meanwhile?'

'She is away. The daughter's supposed to be away too, but she comes back unexpectedly and catches her father with me. I'm very sexy and unprincipled but I am truly in love with this man and so I pretend to myself that *I* am his wife and the mother to this young girl. The man watches me talking to her and hugging her and trying to do the cooking and so on and he gets angrier and more mixed up and in the end I go that bit too far by wearing the wife's clothes. There is a fearful row. The girl calls her mother on the phone –'

'It sounds,' said Ian with unexpected joviality, 'not so much shocking as rather tedious!'

Tanya gave her lashes the tiniest flutter in his direction and said, 'I tell it better when the author is helping.' She turned back to Mrs Robertson. 'Do you think you would find it – tedious?'

'Not with you on the stage,' she answered promptly. 'In any case I usually find I can sympathise with things people do if they are, as you say, truly in love. However bad. Because after all, they are not responsible, are they, when they are in that condition.'

'You make it sound a bit like getting drunk!' said Ian in the same uncharacteristically jolly tone.

'No one chooses to fall in love the way you might choose to have *too many sherries*,' said Mrs Robertson meaningly. Ian's hands, engaged in pouring his third, paused fractionally but then continued. 'It's not the same at all. People in love are – not themselves. Anyone who has ever been in love knows *that*.'

There was a surprised silence. Mrs Robertson had replaced Tanya as the centre of attention. Maggie suddenly remarked, 'I'd always supposed the ability to fall in love as thoroughly as that had been left out of our family genes. What a relief to hear that there's hope for all of us yet.'

Stip abruptly flushed to the roots of his hair, and Ian suddenly cried, for no apparent reason, 'Bravo!' and cocked his sherry-glass stiffly in the air before throwing its contents down his throat. Maggie gazed at him in astonishment. So did Lilian.

Tanya was saying interestedly, 'Does that mean you would have sympathy with someone who committed a crime of passion?'

'Ah well now, you mustn't push my one little provocative view to extremes. Shooting people is one thing. Consoling yourself for a sad and futile situation as a married man's mistress by trying to make his child love you, and feeling at home in his house, that seems to me no more than an extension of wanting his arms around you.'

Maggie was to remember this scene all her life, and even then, at the time, she thought: 'When I am in my sixties I must remember to say something which forces my child to realise that I am a person, with a past and an inner life about which he guesses nothing.' And then she thought, 'If only, by then, I have *had* a past and an inner life worth talking about, and am not obliged to make it all up.'

The room was strangely silent. Maggie said, 'I must go and dish up lunch.'

197

Tanya tipped down her drink. 'I'll help. Do you use those place-tickets to show where everyone is to sit? I would like to arrange those.'

'Why?' asked Stip.

'Because I want to sit next to your mother,' said Tanya. She kissed Mrs Robertson. 'I love her and I am going to cry in a minute. You had better let me make the hooding, Maggie.'

In the kitchen, Tanya sank into a hardbacked chair and lit a cigarette. Maggie noticed that her hand was shaking and that she didn't look at Maggie straight away.

'Well,' said Maggie. 'Come on. First impressions.'

Tanya blew out smoke, sighed profoundly and pushed her fingers through her hair, making herself look, at a stroke, like her young, untidy, student self. 'My God, what a mixture of a family you have! But not at all as you described. That Ian. He is not the grim puritan as advertised. He is bubbling.'

'You noticed? But Tanya, he's behaving very oddly! I think he's a bit tight. All that grinning and rocking on his heels, like Malvolio cross-gartered ... and speaking of bubbles – ' She had opened the door of the old-fashioned fridge to get out the milk. Lying awkwardly on its side was a bottle of Möet and Chandon. She drew it out in disbelief.

'Can this be in your honour? ... Never! Something's happened, what can it be? Oh, wait! I think I guess.'

'What, what? Tell! I love it when people behave at a tangent from their normal selves!'

'It would explain Lilian, too, looking like Sarah after the angel's visit ... You see, they've been trying to adopt a baby, and they've had no luck so far, and I'll bet you anything there'll be an announcement at lunch!'

Tanya stared with her mouth open.

'Do you mean that some adoption agency would hand over to that thin-lipped, thin-hipped creature in there, the fruit of "full thigh and flowing breast?" '

'I *think*.' Maggie bent to open the heavy old oven door, sniffed the roast, and ladled some hot dripping into another pan for the Yorkshire pudding.

'Can I help?' asked Tanya. 'Give me an apron.'

Maggie gave her one, and also a bowl, an egg, some milk, some flour and a wooden spoon. Tanya got to work without much concentration.

198

'That mother of yours,' said Tanya slowly.

'You brought out something in her, within five minutes of meeting her, that I don't think any of us have ever suspected was there.'

'She and I are kith and kin,' said Tanya. 'Oh yes! Apart from age, nationality, race, religion and our entire life histories, she and I are basically the same.'

'Mix the egg in more before you add any milk. What do you think of Stip?'

'I don't know yet. He has this naked feel about him. I'm not normally scared of naked men, only when they think they are fully dressed.'

'What are you talking about?'

Tanya looked at her sideways. 'You didn't know?'

'Know what?'

'Darling Maggie, naive as ever. Never mind. *God*, this is hard work, haven't you a machine? Where is Matt?'

Maggie blushed. 'At Sunday school, actually.'

'*What?*'

'Don't make too much of it.'

'Seriously, Maggie, I am shocked! Whose idea?'

'His. His friends mostly go, so he goes.'

'You amaze me. This is going to be lump-hooding. Please let me use a whisk, at least.'

'Hoodings may be made with the aid of modern technology. *Puddings* are made with a wooden spoon. Here, give it to me. You decorate the trifle.'

'Ah! Glacé cherries and angelica – heavenly . . . I am longing to meet Matt. Are you a good mother?'

Maggie was silent, beating. After a while she said with some difficulty, 'I find I can't . . . I can't love Matt all the time.'

'I know mothers who hardly seem to love their children any of the time, except maybe when they're asleep.'

'But it's terrible, Tanya! I loved him every minute of the day and night in Africa.'

'But then you were not with him every minute.'

'It shouldn't matter. Now he's dependent on me for all his love, it's more important than ever that the supply should never fail.'

'It's impossible to love anybody *all* the time.'

Maggie straightened and said casually 'What about Joel, didn't you – ?'

'Ah,' said Tanya after a pause. 'Joel. Well, but I was *in* love with Joel, and as your sweet and intuitive mother pointed out, in-loveness holds all rules in obeisance.'

'Abeyance.'

'What's obeisance then?'

'Bowing down in worship.'

'So, that wasn't much of a mistake.'

'Did you really,' asked Maggie, in childish curiosity and envy, 'worship him?'

Tanya smiled and put the trifle, gloriously over-embellished, onto the middle of the kitchen table. 'Much more than God, anyway. I still think Joel was worthier of worship than that cruel bastard-god Matt's off learning about. You see, Maggie, although the heavens rained thunder-bolts and the ground opened up under my feet because of Joel, it wasn't he who made it happen. It was our situation, which I always knew. I always knew it must punish me terribly in the end, if I didn't run away in time.'

'But you don't wish you'd run?'

There was a long silence. Tanya sat on the table edge, one glossy leg swinging meditatively. Maggie sensed she was trying to project herself, actress-like, back into past emotion.

'Yes,' she said at last.

Maggie's heart lurched, then sank. It was profoundly important to her that Tanya should not regret this experience.

'I can't believe you! It must have given you so much – added to your armoury as an actress, if nothing else.'

Tanya looked at her enigmatically. 'I see you actually envy me that violent soul-shaking . . . Maggie, believe me, you might as well envy me the war, that filthy camp, my terrors and hunger and losses, my hatred of the Germans, and the awful, awful loneliness . . . Love for me in the end was pure pain, and something worse – shame. You don't know all that happened.' She lit a new cigarette and asked, without looking at her, 'When are you coming to the play?'

'Tomorrow night, of course.'

'I am good. It's a very well-written play and I am very, very natural in it. Do you understand why?'

200

She looked into Maggie's eyes challengingly through the smoke.

'You mean, you did something like the character? Going to Joel's home and trying to – get into his wife's skin?'

'I did that and a lot more. A lot worse. This shocking modern drama is a thin watery pastiche of the things I did in real, real life. I wonder what your sweet tolerant mother would say if she knew what ruthless and immoral things I did because of how much I wanted – how did she put it – his arms around me.'

Now through Tanya's smoke-narrowed eyelids Maggie saw the tears well out. She was appalled, and ran to hug her, thinking it was just an after-spasm which would be quickly over. But it was not just an after-spasm because Tanya was weeping from her guts and couldn't stop. In the end, Maggie had to get her up to her room, first going ahead to see that the coast was clear. By the time the guestroom door closed behind them, Tanya's eyeblack was smeared all over her face and the spectacular false eyelashes had come adrift. Later, Maggie was to find one like a crumpled spider in the folds of a tea-towel in the kitchen.

'This is the last,' Tanya gasped finally, sitting on the edge of the bed with a wet face-flannel pressed to her flushed and ravaged face. 'The very last time I shall ever cry over him. I am *amazed* at myself, Maggie, really – shocked at myself. Because it is, as I told you, long ago over, and this – disgusting display of female feebleness is nothing but a fluke. It is like when those stage hypnotists tell you that even after you wake from your trance you will react in a certain stupid way, quite unrelated to your true self, when you hear this tune or that phrase ... It was just the phrase your mother used. I won't say it in case it sets me off again ... Oh, really! How silly! How idiotic! And just when I am seriously thinking of marrying a proper, available, unmarried man.'

'Oliver ...?' asked Maggie slowly.

Tanya blew her nose for the tenth time and went to the dressing-table to put repairs in hand.

'Only now you will never believe that my love for him is genuine and that it is not just a sort of delayed bounce. There are different kinds of love. Nothing would lure me into that pit of snakes again! I don't *want* to be *in* love with Oliver. He is a good companion. He is intelligent – do you know how rare, for

201

an actor? And in bed he is good enough so I forget everything but my body. That has never happened to me before.'

'Not even with Joel?' She was ashamed of asking. But, sexually unfulfilled as she was, she couldn't help wanting to pry into the secrets of those who were not.

'With Joel I thought of Joel, and of what pleasures his body was getting from mine. It adds a dimension, no doubt. With most men one is thinking of one's lines or that one wishes one had left the heating turned on. Something goes off pop just below the navel and one thinks, "Nice!" and then goes on thinking of the other things.'

Indeed? Still, even a pop below the navel would be a fine thing, thought Maggie with a heavy sigh. This was not lost on Tanya.

'May one ask a deeply religious lady how Bruce was in that department?'

'A bit .. samey, really,' Maggie said evasively. 'I've nothing to compare him with.'

'Maggie? Have you never come?'

Maggie blushed. Suddenly it seemed her failure. She had a surprising need to *defend* Bruce over this. To be uninventive is not the same as being inconsiderate or untender. She was by no means sure, now, that another woman would not have found his love-making perfectly satisfactory.

'I'm probably – you know – frigid or something,' she said awkwardly, twisting her hands. 'I think I ought to go down and see to lunch.' She stood up, but Tanya stood up too. She put her hands on Maggie's shoulders and looked into her eyes.

'This is a very serious thing,' she said. 'I will ask you. Though I see you want to escape. When I said, have you never come, I meant literally – have you *ever* had an orgasm?'

'A what? – Oh. Is that what it's called?'

Tanya released her and turned away. 'Maggie, Maggie! don't you even *read*?'

'The wrong books, perhaps,' Maggie said, smiling, faintly through inner upheaval. It really felt like an earthquake, which brings long-buried objects to the surface to lie horribly exposed.

Tanya turned back to her. 'Yes, that is what it's called. Have you never, never had the feeling that something like a white pleasure-balloon was blowing up behind your pubic bone?'

202

'Yes, but only when I was asleep. Never in – in connection with anything physical.'

'Then you are not frigid. Do you masturbate?'

'Tanya! Heavens! Do you all really ask each other such questions nowadays?'

'If you are thinking such thoughts about frigidity it is time you learnt to be more open. *Do* you?'

Maggie struggled with the newly-uncovered look of things.

'Do you mean . . . Does sort of scratching count?'

Tanya's mouth twitched but she bit her lips firmly.

'Yes, if the "sort of scratching" produces that white bubble.'

'Well . . . Perhaps. Sometimes. By accident.'

'Oh my God, Maggie! You are a little bit incredible.'

Maggie shook herself free. 'Don't! Don't patronise me. I can't help it.'

'You were *in the theatre* for so long, and *married* for so long, and you don't even know the *words* for things . . . No. You are wrong, I am not a bit patronising you, but Maggie, listen. You must come to London. You must have some love, and some life. You must have some affairs, or one anyway. What is wrong with these Scots? A year, nearly, of being a grass widow, and – nothing?'

Maggie, still feeling prickly with embarrassment and inadequacy, moved to the mirror and combed her hair with a shaky hand, not noticing she was using Tanya's comb.

'My brothers are fairly typical of the sort we specialise in around here. Puritanical, or shy, or both, and then there's also the kind that drinks too much, and the rest seem to be either profoundly married or crippled with rheumatism.'

Tanya laughed her bawdy laugh. 'So the Scots' ardour is damped by the weather. One would expect the same to apply to London, but all that is changing. When are you coming, Maggie?'

'I don't think ever. How can I, with Matt?'

'How were you able to come back to England for visits, while you were in Nigeria?'

'We had servants there, one in particular, a lovely girl called Tolly who was a better mother to Matt than I could ever be.'

'And you left her behind because that made you feel inadequate.'

Startled, Maggie said, 'No! Not because of that.'

203

'So why? Why didn't you bring her and make yourself free?'

'You don't know her. She's – she's a tropical person. She would have been totally out of her element.'

'She didn't want to come?'

'She nearly killed herself because she wasn't coming.'

'Are you crazy, Maggie? Do you want to be tied for years to this house, to miss everything that is going on now? To miss your own life?'

'This is my own life. Being a mother and a daughter.'

'Oh! What a show of virtue! But you have just finished telling me you are a bad mother, and that this lovely tropical black girl is a good one. And as to your mother, she is self-sufficient, essentially. But perhaps *she* is against your being an actress?'

'She is very much for it.'

'*I* see. So who is against it? Stip?'

'Yes. As a matter of fact.'

'Stip doesn't want you to be a success because *he* isn't,' said Tanya shrewdly. '*Yet*. But he may surprise you all. Don't be held back by him, Maggie! Be a little ruthless for once. A little selfish!'

'For *once*?' Maggie burst out. 'I've been being ruthless and selfish since I was eighteen.'

'You were a little of both *at* eighteen. At twenty-two you changed into a doormat. Now your husband has wiped his feet on you and walked off. You are not going to lie there forever with his bootprints on your stomach, are you? Stand up and be yourself! Matt will thank you for it later.'

At that moment they heard the front door bang and Matt pounding up the stairs. Maggie leapt up guiltily, glad to escape from the welter of confused feelings Tanya had evoked. 'My God, look at the time –'

Matt dashed in and stopped short, blinking at Tanya as if confronted by a sudden blaze of light.

'She *is* bright red all over!' he exclaimed.

The tension broke and Tanya burst out laughing. She went straight over to him as he stood in the doorway and gave him a good hug. He bore it like a man, holding his breath against her strong musky scent. Maggie was staring at Matt, trying to see him through Tanya's eyes. Was there, objectively, anything special about him? Would he not look to a stranger like any little Scottish schoolboy with red hair and freckles, falling-down

204

socks and a grubby jacket, unique only to her . . . His life and hers were already growing apart. He no longer ran directly to kiss her. When had he stopped doing that – only a little while ago, surely? Now if she wanted a cuddle, she had to call him. Soon he would begin to evade questions, close in upon himself, shut her out . . . Other mothers had told her this was inevitable. That was why it was 'all right' to send them away to school, to cut the cord where it lay, withering anyway according to natural laws . . . Leaving her with what?

'Your hair *is* a funny colour,' Matt was saying to Tanya.

'Matt, don't be personal,' said Maggie.

'But I don't mind,' said Tanya. 'I dye it this shade,' she added to Matt.

'How?'

'When I wash it, I put some special stuff on that makes it this unusual colour.'

'What for?'

'To be beautiful and striking and make people look at me.'

'What colour is your hair really?'

'Oh, white,' said Tanya matter-of-factly. 'Come on, Maggie. The hooding will be reduced to a cinder.'

In the end they all went to the play, even Matt, for lack of anyone to babysit. He slept through most of it, but none of the others did.

'She's fantastic,' said Stip.

'Very impressive performance,' said Ian. 'I must say. And an excellently written piece as well . . .' Ian had stopped doing Malvolio and begun to address himself to fatherhood. Had Maggie loved him more, she could not have failed to find his approach to this watershed in his life very touching. It was clear that his feelings were altogether stronger than he was accustomed to handling, that his inner excitement and, perhaps, a certain unwonted insecurity were making him restless and nervous. This need for some outlet made him far more talkative than usual, more forthcoming. In the normal way he would almost certainly have been disapproving of Tanya's flamboyant and passionate performance. As it was, his reaction almost seemed to reflect some of her vivacity.

Lilian was going to the other extreme. She had retreated into herself; she sat through the play like a broody hen, intent not on the stage, it seemed, but on some internal drama. The baby, a girl, would be ready for collection in ten days' time. No wonder, Maggie thought, that anything as un-earthbound as a theatre meant little to her.

Mrs Robertson was openly thrilled by the play, though she said little. She clutched Maggie's arm in spasms throughout the performance, and held it tightly as they came out afterwards.

'Did you enjoy it, Mummy?'

'I loved every minute!' She leant to Maggie's ear and whispered, 'especially when I could imagine you were playing the daughter!'

Maggie was startled. 'Darling, I'm far too old!'

'Are you? . . . Possibly. Well, the wife, then.'

'I couldn't have done justice to Tanya's part.'

'No,' said Mrs Robertson with unflattering promptness. 'You'll never be any good in those glamorous parts. But the down-to-earth characters that we ordinary women can identify with, those will be your forté.'

Maggie looked at her sharply.

'What do you mean, Mummy? You're talking as if something had been settled.'

Mrs Robertson only smiled.

Chapter Twenty-One

Tanya left at the end of the week, blowing kisses and offers with equal spendthriftness. 'Come to London! Do it Maggie! Nothing adventured ... nothing won!' Maggie, chasing her train down the platform, cried: 'But how big is your flat? Where are the keys? How do you work the *heeeeating* ...?' Gone, with a thumbs-up and a red-lipped Cheshire-cat smile, as the train bent suddenly ... Maggie went home on the bus, confused, uprooted, planful.

Mrs Robertson stood by to continue Tanya's good work.

'It's a thing that's to be done, my dear one, or you'll go to your grave as bitter as any spinster. That's what you'll be, Maggie, an actress-spinster, your talent dried up in you.' She did not (she never had) mention the money, the deception, the burden of crime upon the soul which Maggie carried, crying out for its own redemption, the fulfilment of the talent so illicitly fostered, which might, in the last analysis, prove a sort of justification.

They talked ways and means, mother and daughter beside the fire. Other things were happening in the family, and they talked about these, too – Ian and Lilian's baby, which had arrived: a bald, bland, button-nosed female to be called Anthea Charity Robertson; Stip's suddenly-announced decision to leave the family firm at the end of the year and embark upon a career as an interior designer, a move which Ian disapproved of almost as much as Stip was going to disapprove of any equivalent move of Maggie's.

And they talked about Matt.

'There are three possibilities. Take him with you to London, and find a way to manage – an au pair, perhaps? But that will be very complicated for you. Or you could send him away to school. Or you could leave him here.'

207

None of these ideas presented itself to Maggie in any but the murkiest light. Watching her with the sympathy newly-established between them, her mother asked: 'Which seems the worst in prospect?'

'The school. The idea of Matt at boarding-school appals me.'

'Then we'll start by eliminating that. Why not leave him here with me?'

'That's the next-worst, by a small margin.'

'Thanks very much! So I'm as bad as a dreaded boarding-school?'

'The guilt, I'm talking about! I'd feel guilty every moment at wishing such a responsibility off on to you.'

'Ah. Well then,' said Mrs Robertson quietly, 'you had better take him with you. Adding more guilt would undermine you, and you'll need all your self-esteem where you're heading for.'

The flat in Primrose Hill, 'not overlooking but almost', was, despite its deficient view, a most visually stimulating place for Maggie's launch-pad.

It was, of course, redolent of Tanya – it smelt of her for one thing, something Matt remarked on at once, but it also recalled her in many other ways. The shiny bronze wallpaper, the glass-and-bead-and-paper-sculpted flowers. The cushions-of-all-nations filling every oblong surface and corner like an indoor herbaceous border, the crazy sunset-patterned rug on the wall, the green stage drugget, pegged to the floor, representing a lawn – the whole effect was of a garden somehow transmogrified into imperishable materials and brought indoors.

One of the long windows opened on to a sturdy square balcony over the front porch below, and here Maggie discovered something new and unsuspected about her friend. Those sophisticated scarlet fingernails were the tips of green fingers. Out of a random collection of barrels, boxes and big earthenware pots leapt and cavorted a riot of flowers. They did not seem just to be quietly growing. They resembled a sort of floral Olympics. The lobelias had decided they were a rambling species and were trying to clamber, all but panting with eagerness, up the parapet. Snapdragons opened great citron mouths to bite at geraniums swarming past them. African marigolds

208

glared through the fighting tangle as bright and aggressive as spotlights. Only a pink rosebush, crouching in a far corner, looked pale and weary from the struggle to hold its own.

'Matt, just look at these flowers! They're all about three times normal size.'

But Matt had no patience with such trivia. He had found the bedroom – Tanya's bedroom – and was busy pre-empting the largest bed he had ever set eyes on.

'You'll have to be careful if you're going to sleep there, darling. It looks like a valuable bed.' But Matt was bouncing happily with his large teddy (a present from his uncle Stip) and couldn't have cared less.

'Are we going to stay here long?'

Maggie was far from sure. She explored, and found one other room, currently cluttered with trunks, rails of 'wardrobe', wig-blocks, books, albums full of press-cuttings and stills and costume designs and other 'impedimenta of illusion'. 'Well. We'll stay till Tanya gets back from her tour. I'm blowed if I know where she'll put us, after that.'

And meanwhile, for the first time in their joint lives, Maggie and Matt settled down to live with each other in exclusivity.

It was the summer holidays. July and August stretched before them. Below on all sides of them stretched London, a super-market of new experiences waiting to be popped in their wire trolley. Maggie had dreamed of it, often – showing Matt all those mind-stretching places which she herself had found so entrancing when she had first seen them . . . But then, she had been eighteen, and Matt was eight. After a few weeks, Maggie was forced to the realisation that most of the wonderful cultural experiences she was offering her son fell on the stony ground of a child's innate resistance to everything his mother thinks it would be desirable for him to enjoy.

'But how can you want to go home? We've only been here twenty minutes!' she objected in the middle of the Geological Museum to which they had had recourse after Matt had found nothing appealing in the Natural History apart from the blue whale. 'But it's only rocks,' said Matt reasonably. 'Can we go home and watch TV?'

She took him to *The Dream* in Regent's Park. It rained patchily. One fairy slipped on the greensward and fell on to her bottom. Matt let out a shriek of glee and announced loudly that

209

he loved Shakespeare, but when nothing else of any interest occurred, began remarking that after all it would be better if they went home and watched TV.

The same thing happened, with variations, on an indefinite number of other improving occasions. Eventually Maggie downgraded their outings to places of more hedonistic promise, such as a trip up the Thames to Greenwich. This time the weather co-operated. Matt stood politely at the rail of the pleasure-steamer and turned his eyes wherever Maggie pointed; but after a while he excused himself and was later discovered below with his nose in a borrowed comic. Maggie felt exasperated and dragged him unwillingly on deck again, whereupon it grew dark and cold. By the time they tied up at Greenwich even Maggie was bored stiff. She chucked the return tickets into the river, irritably chalking up another failure, and they got a train back. Not Matt but Maggie sulked all the way. This wasn't turning out at all as she'd anticipated.

She took stock that night as she lay on the livingroom divan among the flower cushions where she slept. Why, when you come down to it, was she dragging Matt out on these educational excursions for which he was evidently too young? Could it be that she was afraid to spend a day alone with him at home, simply messing about together? It was she who needed the distractions, not he; she who needed to feel she was doing right by him, making a great effort to show him all the proper things. The trouble was, she had not grown up with her motherhood from its beginnings eight years ago. She felt she was embarking on it now for the first time. She was aware of her incompetence, her restlessness, her lack of dedication.

Besides, the flat was, for all its fascinations, an impediment to normality. It was not of her making. She was constantly anxious about looking after it; yet at the same time, there was little to be done, not only to it but in it. She couldn't even settle with one of the myriad books or records, because Matt found the sight of her sitting down in apparent idleness quite intolerable.

His eternal cry was, 'Do something with me!' That didn't mean, 'Take me out somewhere,' it just meant, 'Be with me while I do something of my own.' Even the newly-discovered delights of television paled if she were not watching it with

210

him. His demands were loving, peremptory, ineluctable and ultimately exhausting.

This sense of being bloodsucked by her own private insatiable leech had further ill effects. Matt had been what is usually called well-brought-up, which is to say he was trained to follow a régime which involved all the proper things: early bed and early up, clean plates and clean teeth ... Tolly had achieved all this effortlessly as if following immutable natural laws – children went to sleep when the sun set and rose when it rose, they ate their food because it was good and any bits left over she scooped from his plate with her fingers and ate herself, companionably. Hard crisp foods took care of teeth-cleaning ... Matt had no reason to rebel against Tolly because she made no rules.

Mrs Robertson had functioned quite differently, of course, but she carried a certain unquestionable authority, and when she said, 'Bedtime, Matt,' or 'What about teeth?' there was no arguing. As to eating, one murmur about fat on the meat or lumps in the porridge and she would clap her hands and cry cheerfully, 'Right! Off you go, Matt! Meal's over!' In a word, she expected to be obeyed. Maggie saw no reason on earth why Matt should take her word for anything, and sure enough, he didn't.

Mealtimes and bedtimes became, for the first time in Matt's life, battlegrounds. Why should Matt suddenly rebel against habits of a lifetime just because he was alone with Maggie? But he did. As if unerringly sensing her unsureness, he tested her, found her weak spots, and jumped on them.

Rows, real rows, began.

Maggie had never in eight years been really, deeply angry with Matt. She had never known what it was to want to hurt him. But when he refused to eat what she cooked for him, making ever more insufferable comments on the good, whole-some food; when he refused to go to bed and her indecision as to how to proceed in the matter led her to allow him to keep later and later hours; when he lapsed wilfully into sloppy, grubby ways, leaving his toys everywhere and refusing to be careful of Tanya's things – when, in short, she detected in him seeds of destructiveness and saw gleams of real devilment in his erstwhile innocent, beguiling eyes – she felt a deep and increasing frantic-ness which threatened to turn into violent anger.

211

Tolly had never raised her voice to Matt, let alone her hand. She had conditioned Maggie to the realisation that there was scant need of anger and punishment if the inherent expectations of the unborn for continuing love and closeness were fulfilled. But knowing something like that, and having the wellsprings of love and patience to put it into practice, are two different things. Every time Maggie heard herself shouting, every time she laid a forceful hand on Matt to shake or push or even slap him, her conscience would give her a return bout afterwards which left her feeling shamed and exhausted. After six weeks in Tanya's flat, Maggie was close to desperation, and Matt was beginning to bite his nails.

One morning they woke to the horrendous discovery that he had wet his bed. Tanya's bed.

It was no use saying anything. One glance at Matt's face showed how bad he felt. So Maggie lugged the huge mattress across two rooms and wedged it in the french window, doubled over, to dry and air, hoping against hope that there would be no stain. After breakfast she took him out to look at schools.

The local ones seemed to be all old-fashioned, high-walled, graffiti'd and as Matt put it, 'more like prisons'. He began to talk about Scotland as yet another green meadow left behind.

'You mean I won't be going back to Breckonridge?' he said. They were sitting in a local playground, he hot from swinging. 'Have you *told* Miss Frith that I won't be coming back?'

'You won't mind, will you? You never seemed to like it all that much.'

'I did like it, I did like it, I loved it! You never listen to anything I tell you!'

This sort of regulation ploy in the good old game of Getting At Mum had power to reduce Maggie, who had never played it and didn't know the rules, to the point of tears. She had listened to everything Matt said for the past six weeks, anyway, and to very little else because she had never worked out a way to be parted from him long enough to do or see anything on her own. It was so utterly unfair of him to say she didn't listen. She wanted to run away and stay away from him for hours, to make him sorry ... The mere thought of such a thought frightened her stiff the moment it escaped into her conscious mind, and she battened it down like a savage animal in the hold of her listing but not yet sinking ship.

212

Instead of running away, she said grimly, 'Matt, would you like to go to boarding-school?'

'What's it like?' he asked cautiously.

She told him. She found herself making it sound as frightful as she possibly could.

But before she'd got beyond the arbitrary food and not coming home even at weekends, the look on his face had so smitten her with shame that she suddenly broke off, pulled him against her, and hugged him as hard as she could, saying, 'Never mind, you're not going there. Just don't say I don't listen because I do. Now let's go home and watch TV.'

As they climbed the stairs and entered the flat, Maggie was thinking: 'Oh please let there be no stain!' As the door opened and the sun through the long windows hit her eyes, she blinked. Then she saw Tanya.

She was sitting on the divan, her face in shadow. Maggie couldn't suppress a gasp, not just of astonishment but of horror. Needless to say, this apparition was totally unexpected. According to Tanya's letters, her tour was not due to end till mid-October. Maggie hadn't even bothered to tidy up before they had gone out. The green drugget was littered with Matt's Matchbox cars and his plastic race-track, in sections. The breakfast dishes were still on the table. The place had not been dusted or swept for two days. And there was the king-sized mattress, doubled side-to-side, blocking the way to the balcony. Gaping at Tanya, all green-clad, coiled and crested like a beautiful chameleon, Maggie wondered whether she could, if she willed hard enough, make her turn the exact colour of the divan cover (bright orange) and thus disappear.

'Tanya – why didn't you – ' she began on a bleat.

Tanya, her eyes gone small and reptilian, said, 'You didn't tell me Matt is not house-trained.'

Maggie felt Matt shrink at her side and for a full long moment, hated Tanya.

The two women stared at each other with livid faces. Total strangers. Antagonists . . . It was a terrible moment. Then Matt pulled his hand free and started to run back down the stairs. At the bend he was heard to collide with someone. Through a sort of haze, Maggie heard a murmur of words. A few moments later he came back, slowly, carrying a telegram.

213

Stupidly, Maggie read it. 'Cataclysm. Coming home Sunday. Lay in whisky in magnums. I need it. Tanya.'

She looked up. Tanya still sat there on the divan, but her reptilian look had gone. Maggie could recognise her now, although the sudden change from fury to vulnerability – also highly uncharacteristic – unmanned Maggie even further.

'Tanya – what's happened? – I didn't know –'

Tanya's face, so austere with anger only a few moments before, abruptly crumpled. Matt took one appalled look and vanished into the bedroom, letting the door slam in an eloquent comment on grown-up women.

Tanya was hiding her face in a flower-cushion. She wasn't sobbing, just sitting there, green and poised, quite still with the cushion pressed to her face, the back of it indented by her tense red-tipped fingers. Suddenly she threw it down, turned her stretched eyes on Maggie and said,

'Christ! I'm ashamed! I hurt him. I'm a wicked, wicked cow. It was not being able to get out on to the balcony to see my flowers as soon as I came home. You've *no* idea what's happened – the most terrible, ghastly thing – Maggie – *I have broken my contract*!'

Maggie crossed the drugget, stepping over the toys, and sat beside her. 'I don't believe you,' she said slowly. 'How could you? Walk out? You'd be finished.'

'I know.' Tanya stood up. She was as taut as a wire. She evidently needed to walk about but the whole place was so cluttered that she couldn't. Maggie fell on her knees and began jerkily raking the little cars towards her and tipping them into their box. As fast as she cleared a space, Tanya used it for pacing.

'Listen. I've upset your son. That's more important than me ... No, it isn't. I've wrecked my career ... Oh my God, Maggie, what possessed me? What possessed me?'

'What happened?' asked Maggie, from the floor. She was torn between worry about Tanya, anxiety for Matt, locked in the bedroom with his shame, and her own shame at the state of the flat. Looking up at Tanya with all the insight and affection of their long friendship, however, she felt her priorities fall into place. If Tanya had broken her contract – unthinkable, unheard-of! – then it was entirely probable that she would never work in the legitimate theatre again because she would be black-

214

listed. Maggie swept the boy-rubble ruthlessly to one end of the drugget and got up and went to the cupboard where Tanya kept her few bottles. There was some vodka in there. She poured it out neat and gave it to Tanya, who merely stared at it with glazed eyes and then shook her head.

'I can't now ... I thought I would need to drink, but it's too awful for comfort ... Maggie, go to Matt, tell him I didn't mean it. Let me just get hold of myself a little, I seem to have lost sight of myself altogether ...'

Maggie hesitated, then obeyed. She shut the bedroom door behind her. Matt was sitting on the big bed with his back to her, his head bent, the exposed springs digging into the backs of his bare legs, holding his bear.

'Darling ...?'

'I couldn't help it,' he mumbled. 'It just came out in my sleep.'

She ran to comfort him, holding him tightly. 'Of course you couldn't. Of course you couldn't! And Tanya knows it too, really. She's awfully sorry she said that, she didn't mean it.'

'You talk about housetraining *dogs*.'

'I know. Please forgive her. It *is* her flat, and her bed, and we let her find everything in such a mess. It's my fault, not yours.'

A sob shuddered up his back and she felt tears, hot and salt, on her neck and shoulder.

'Will we have to leave now? Why did she have to come back?'

Maggie couldn't answer. She was struggling with her own tears. She just stroked him soothingly. The bear's rather hard nose was sticking into her ribs.

'Teddy's getting squashed.'

Matt pulled away and attended to his bear. A small movement in the doorway caught Maggie's eye and she turned. Tanya was standing there, looking, if possible, even more stricken than before.

'Matt. I'm sorry. I peepeed my bed once when I was *twelve*.'

Matt blushed deeply and did not turn. The two women exchanged signals: 'What can I do?' 'Nothing. Leave him now.' Maggie kissed Matt. 'Darling, I'm going to talk to Tanya. Don't sit on those springs too long, you'll have knitting marks up the backs of your legs.'

Maggie and Tanya cleared up the flat in silence. There

215

seemed no point in apologising for its state, and no way to do it anyway. When they got to the mattress, they stood one on each side of its arched bulk and their eyes fell, simultaneously and irresistibly, on the exposed hump. A faint brown line wavered round a slightly bleached patch. Maggie looked up at Tanya in a sort of anguish of apology, but Tanya said briefly, 'It couldn't matter less. Possibly.'

They lugged it back to the bedroom and on to the bed. Matt had slipped out somewhere, leaving the bear lying on the springs. Tanya found clean sheets and they made the bed together, a thing impossible to do without a kind of intimate domestic orchestration. Then Tanya sat the bear on the pillow.

'Look at the reproach in those beady eyes . . .' She sat down. 'Maggie, can I talk about me now?'

'Shall I make coffee?'

'I would choke . . . You know I have eaten and drunk quite normally for three days since it happened, and done my performances, everything – even laughed and joked. But on the train down, it hit me, right in the middle of a cheese sandwich, and I had to go and be sick.'

'You played to the end of the week?'

'Yes. To give the understudy time. It's such a huge part. I had nothing against her. I wanted to leave that same day, the day of the row, but she begged me, she was in panics . . . So I had to play three more nights and a matinée with the whole company knowing I was going to break my contract. They didn't speak to me, not a word, except Oliver of course, he had to, but you know, even he –'

They were sitting on the bed looking out at the rooftops at the back of the house. The garden, as in many houses 'gone to flats', was nobody's responsibility, and the sycamore seedlings had run wild; the tops of the young trees were now over the first-floor window sill. Maggie was struggling to catch some elusive memory. At the same time she was concentrating upon Tanya, empathising with her and yet somehow repelled, not any longer by what she had said to Matt (she fully understood that) but by the mere proximity of an actress who had broken that deepest of taboos. So she didn't have to ask why Tanya had been ostracised. Actors are creatures of instinct; in this sense, they are primitives, whatever veneer of worldliness they're thinly coated with.

216

'Tell me what happened,' she said once more.

Tanya heaved a profound sigh. She stood up and went out of the room, returning a moment later with a suitcase which she laid on the bed and began to unpack. Some activity seemed essential. Her hands busy with underwear and spongebag, a crumpled cotton peignoir and nylon balls of stockings, she told her sorry tale.

'It was all because of the way they were treating Oliver. The management. He was engaged to play the lead – my lover. Then during rehearsals they changed their minds and said they had to have a big television star in it because these days it is important for the box-office to have at least one TV or movie star. They offered to buy him off but he refused and insisted on his contractual rights to the lead and star billing, and then they started. Started to make his life a misery.

'When we began the tour, every time there was a poor house there would be loud remarks about how much better we would be doing with George Berridge, the one they still wanted to put into it. Representatives from the management came up from London to try to persuade Oliver to get out of the cast, and they would creep round the company doing him dirt and trying to convince everyone that his selfishness and stubbornness were spoiling our chance of coming into Town. Rumours started that we would have to cut the tour short and we would all be thrown out of work because there was no big name in the cast, I mean no name that meant anything in the provinces, because there, really, it is beginning to be all movies and television, and a London reputation cuts no ice.

'Of course I was completely and utterly on his side and I would get very abusive when this little creep from the management came sniffing around to *my* dressing-room. After a while someone must have gossiped to him that I and Oliver are living together because the creep kept away from me, but then I noticed everyone else was avoiding me too, and Oliver, and we realised that the message was getting to them. It was a strain. But still it was tolerable. At least, *I* thought so.

'That is, till last Wednesday. We were in Birmingham, doing three weeks there at the Alhambra, and to the Hippodrome came this other company, and who should be the star but George Berridge. And we had different matinée days, so of course, though without telling each other, every last one of our

217

company went to their matinée. And although it was a fine afternoon, it was a full house. A full house, Maggie – Birmingham – in the middle of August! *We* hadn't had a full house, even in the evenings, for months.'

Maggie could not suppress a groan.

'That night Oliver was late in. He'd left our digs before me on some pretext, which like a fool I believed – I knew he was feeling terrible and he hadn't said a single word to me since we all came, very silent and downcast, out of the dreadful play – and it *was* dreadful, a rubbish, a nothing, with just this one big name. And at our theatre they called the half, and then the quarter, and still he wasn't in, and the stage manager came rushing to me, where was he, and *I didn't know*. I was so frightened . . . And at the five, he suddenly reeled in. Maggie!' She put her red head in her hands.

'Drunk?'

'Yes. Terribly. The S M ordered him not to play, but he just shoved him to one side and went on just as he was, no make-up or anything, in his ordinary clothes. Luckily most of his scenes were with me and I could help him, but the girl playing his daughter was such a little *bitch*, she did everything she knew to show him up. When he was slow on his cues she would turn her head to the prompt corner, or turn away upstage as if unable to cope with this drunken fellow, and everyone was lurking about in the wings watching him . . . Once he started to talk nonsense, and I could see the S M was getting ready to bring down the *curtain* – imagine it, Maggie! I got to the wings and signalled him and then I surged back and started saying all Oliver's lines as well as my own, you know, that technique we practised at RADA, "I know what you're going to say . . ." The end was practically a monologue, but all the time I was thinking, what's the use, this is all they've been waiting for, he'll be sacked, and it was so bloody unfair because never, ever has anything like it happened before.'

She straightened up and closed the empty suitcase. 'Well, you can guess the rest. They jumped on him the next morning and sacked him and I said if he goes I go and they told me if I did that I would never work in legitimate theatre again and I said to hell with the lot of you. And that's it.'

'The last three days must have been purgatory for you.'

'Worse, in fact. Because purgatory is temporary and when I

218

came out of my anger, around Friday, and found everyone treating me like a leper, and Oliver gone, and realised these were probably the last nights I would ever spend on the stage, I realised this terrible feeling was for ever.'

They sat back to back on the bed for a long time. Maggie captured the vagrant memory like a flittering butterfly and gave it a scant glance – of course. The time she was sacked in Devon and cried all the way home on the train. But that was nothing. She had not been an established actress. And she was able to push it behind her and try again. For Tanya it was, indeed, a catastrophe. Unimaginable.

Tanya said, in a voice so weary that Maggie's heart smote her, 'I wanted to go on to the balcony and see my flowers. Have you been watering them?'

'Yes. They hardly seemed to need anything I could do for them. How do you make them grow like that?'

'I brought sacks of leafmould from the country. It has never grown anything before. No, don't come with me, Maggie, please. I want to be alone for a while.'

219

Chapter Twenty-Two

Maggie found Matt sitting on the bench at the top of the Hill, cutting at the wood with his penknife, not savagely but concentratedly, the way Tanya had unpacked. Maggie didn't restrain him. She sat with him till he'd finished the full-stop after the M.

'Let's go to a film.'

He stood up obediently but without looking at her and they walked down the Hill and into the 'village' in Regent's Park Road. At the very bottom of this was a Marine Ices place which sold ice-creams of every imaginable flavour. When Matt noticed that they were heading there, he perked up a little.

'Why *did* she have to come back?'

Maggie attempted to explain something of Tanya's dilemma in terms he could understand, but his mind was on ice-cream and a movie and pee'd mattresses and the possibility that he would not be sleeping in his king-sized bed that night, so he didn't listen much.

'Will she let us stay?'

'I don't know.'

'What if she doesn't?'

'We'll find somewhere else.'

'Where? Scotland?'

'No. London.'

'But where in London?

God alone knows! 'What flavour?'

'Green.'

After the film they retraced their steps up the street, stopping for fish and chips for three, though Maggie was fairly sure Tanya wouldn't feel like her share.

In the doorway of the flat, Maggie stopped. They had been gone no more than three hours, yet the flat was transformed.

For a start, the main room was restored to its original stylish neatness; all child-traces had been expunged, and Maggie's heart sank. But Tanya's voice issuing from behind the bedroom door instructed them to go into the spare room; and there marvels awaited them.

Gone the impedimenta of illusion, the general clutter; and in its place, two small pine beds, a chest-of-drawers and a washbasin (which must have been lurking there all the time). It was not a large room and two of them would find it restrictive, but it was a welcome and welcoming sight to the eyes of Maggie whose fifth viewing of *Snow-White and the Seven Dwarfs* had been marred by frantic thoughts of bed-and-breakfast digs at extortionate prices, or a total retreat.

Matt, however, had other views.

'It's wee,' he exlaimed in dismay. 'I'll fall right out of that wee bed! And where can I keep things?'

'I'll buy you a toy-box!' Maggie hissed. She headed for Tanya's room. 'Tanya! You're incredible! How in God's name did you – ?'

'Don't come in just now, darling,' came the voice from the bedroom 'The lock's bust.'

But Maggie was already half-way in, in enough to catch a glimpse of Tanya entangled in a sheet with a long angular other body which had its face coyly turned into the pillow.

'God! I'm sorry – !' she gasped, retreating.

'Never mind, love,' Tanya called equably after her. 'Put the kettle on, will you?'

Maggie, hot with embarrassment, did so. Matt edged round the partition into the kitchen area.

'There's someone else in my bedroom,' he said. 'I heard him.'

'Yes. It's a friend of Tanya's.'

'What are they doing?'

'*I* don't know. Getting dressed, perhaps,' she added boldly. 'They've been resting.'

'Resting! Are they babies?'

'No, indeed.'

The resters soon emerged, Tanya first, resplendent in a red velvet negligée. Her hair was no longer in its crest but suggestively tousled, her face, cleared of its make-up, looking a bit

221

bald, except that her eyes really needed no enhancement. They were no longer tear-bruised but almost manically brilliant.

'Talk about *coitus interruptus*!' she grinned. 'What's that delicious smell? Oliver, come on, don't be shy, it's only Maggie, and I do believe she's brought us fish and chips!'

Poor Oliver had no recourse but to creep forth, looking as if violence had just been done to him. He hadn't changed much since RADA days. Still the same tall, rangey figure, topping Tanya by a good foot, dark hair neatly combed around the long intelligent-goat face – just now, an intelligent, bright red goat. Maggie felt sorry for him. They shook hands, with much mutual avoidance of eyes. But Tanya was heartlessly laughing at their embarrassment.

'Oh come on, you two, it's nothing so dreadful! We should have put a sign up. Where's Matt? Listen, Matt, I want to say something private to you. Come with me.' And before he knew it he was being led away into the spare room, leaving Oliver and Maggie alone, heartily wishing themselves elsewhere.

'How have you been, Oliver?' asked Maggie with bright inanity, busying herself with trying to turn three portions of fish and chips into four.

'Okay till recently,' said Oliver. 'Er – I didn't mean – just *very* recently, of course.'

They both tried to laugh, then stopped. They met each other's eyes for the first time. Oliver's eyes were rather goat-like as well, a sort of topaz. There was no humour in them. They were the bruised ones now, and the shock they showed had little to do with Maggie's barging in.

'I was so upset by what Tanya told me,' Maggie said quietly. 'You must have been through a horrible time – both of you. Specially her.'

'Yes. If I'd been there, I'd never have let her do it,' he said stalwartly. But the histrionic note in his tone made Maggie suddenly doubt that. If women secretly like men fighting over them, how much more must men like women hurling themselves on to their funeral pyres? Maggie frowned, ashamed of jumping to such a conclusion. She had nothing against Oliver, except that it was through him that Tanya had immolated her career.

She changed the subject. 'Was it you who helped her transform the room while we were out?'

'Not only. She had a gang of us at it. That's typical of her, of course. Anyone else would be prostrated, but Tanya just gets to work.'

'What happened to the others?'

'Dismissed! She suddenly had a sort of – collapse of energy. I felt she wanted us to be alone, so I shoved them all out.'

'I'm sorry I came bursting in on you.'

'Well! Shouldn't have been at it at this hour – very antisocial. We knew you might appear.'

Maggie warmed to him a trifle, even though he was standing hands in pockets letting her do all the table-laying. There was very much a man-of-the-house feeling about him. She put the plates of fish and chips on the table and then said, 'Oliver, may I ask you something? Are you going to be living here with Tanya?'

'Sort of, probably, though I've got my own flat. Why?'

'Well, because –'

Just then, Matt and Tanya returned, hand in hand and looking very conspiratorial. Matt was grinning.

'Ah! Bisto!' Tanya cried. 'Well, anyway, ketchup. Can we have Naafi-type tea with it, and bread-and-scrape? Matt, you can have all my chips if I can have half your fish, without the batter. We actresses must watch our figures!' There was a sort of hiccup in the atmosphere, like an engine 'missing', and then she sailed round into the kitchenette. 'I'll make the tea. Do you like your new room, Maggie? Of course you'll need shelves and things, but it will do for the moment, won't it?'

'It's wonderful. But we'll have to talk about this matter of us staying on,' said Maggie.

Tanya's head popped over the partition. 'There'll be no talk – you're staying. That's settled. The only thing to decide is about jobs for all of us.' She glanced at Oliver. Fear flashed across her face for a split second and was gone, as if wiped off fiercely with a hot cloth. When she disappeared again, Maggie risked another look at Oliver. Tall and masculine-looking though he was, Maggie wondered how safe it would be to lean against him – really lean, with all the weight of one's troubled life. In her limited experience of actors, they were not, as a breed, much good for leaning on. Their preferred world was not the real one.

Throughout their supper ('Fit for a common man!') they all,

223

including Matt, chatted quite cheerfully of unimportant things, the undercurrents of deep anxiety held in abeyance. It was clear that Matt and Tanya had made it up. At bedtime Matt kissed her of his own volition and asked her to go and read him a story. This she did, while Maggie washed up the dishes and meticulously dried and tidied them all away, something she had never done after Matt's and her meals. Oliver meanwhile sat and listened to an LP of Fauré, limp as a cat with his feet up on a big square pouffe.

Then the three of them talked. Or rather, Tanya talked and the others listened, in Maggie's case quite bemusedly. It was not only the flat which had been transformed. Tanya had gone from an all-time low to a high. She was behaving weirdly as if nothing serious had occurred, as if she herself were quite likely to take off at any moment on some glamorous tour, while Oliver was perfectly sure of a job soon. As for Maggie, well, that might not be so simple, but Tanya had plans. She would introduce her to her own agent, get her into *Spotlight*, guide her back into the well-worn job-getting paths, and, though nothing could be guaranteed, there was every reason for optimism.

Throughout this monologue Maggie kept trying to catch Oliver's eye, but he was minutely examining the embroidery on an oriental cushion; when appealed to by Tanya for endorsement of one of her wilder flights of fancy, he obliged with affirmative grunts. Maggie began to feel she was the only sane one, the only one who realised it wasn't going to work, the four of them living together in a flat gone suddenly small. Especially with all the adults out of work and one at the point of ultimate professional crisis.

When Tanya flitted off to the loo, Maggie grabbed the brief opportunity to lean over, remove the cushion from Oliver's beautiful long fingers, and say, 'Oliver, why do you keep agreeing with her? She's talking pie in the sky.'

He glanced at her between narrowed lids, like one of Helen's hermit crabs peeping warily at the world from its haven-shell.

'Oh, I don't know,' he mumbled. 'Better than sinking into a slough of despond.'

He reached for the cushion but Maggie held it away from him.

'Oliver, listen to me! To begin with we can't all live here together. Matt's only a child, he'll drive both of you crazy. As

224

for jobs, maybe you'll get one, though word will get round about what's happened, but Tanya's going to be blacklisted by Equity, and *I* haven't worked for nearly ten years. Imagine the three of us trying to maintain our morale, or even our physiques ... How long is it since you were seriously out of work?'

Oliver shrugged uncomfortably. 'I've been pretty lucky.'

'Then let me inform you, it's hell,' said Maggie tersely. 'It'll be double hell for you if you're not used to it.'

'Charming of you to cheer me up,' said Oliver, rising as if to get away from her and going to put another record on. Maggie, remorseless now, followed at his heels. She was about to harangue him further when Tanya came bounding back.

'What are you two talking about behind my back?' she asked waggishly.

Suddenly Maggie felt defeated. If Tanya had anaesthetised herself with sex and false optimism, Maggie decided it was not for her to bring her back to agonising consciousness; yet she felt bereft. To see Tanya in this happy trance of unrealism was more alarming than the sight of her a few hours ago, feeling all the pain of her situation and reacting to it healthily. Maggie wondered when and why the change of direction had happened ... Out on the balcony, among the flowers, perhaps. Or making love to Oliver ... Making love properly, the way other people did, often seemed to have the effect of rendering all the problems of life somehow unimportant – irrelevant. But Maggie had always thought that this was a temporary dispensation.

Oliver took his leave at about midnight, well tanked-up and feeling no pain. None of them were by that time. Even Margaret had cast herself adrift from her normal anchorage to the bedrock of ineluctable fact. Margaret didn't often succumb to drink, staying obstinately sober on the sidelines hissing imprecations at Maggie. But tonight she lapsed, and Maggie was glad of it.

She washed up the glasses muzzily while Tanya lay draped on the settee, looking more than ever like some exotic species of lizard sunning itself amid heaps of bright flowers and stones. Maggie kept eyeing her warily. She was suddenly irremediably foreign, despite her addiction to English sayings and food ... Maggie felt her drifting away into her alienness at this critical moment and didn't know how to call her back.

They said goodnight to each other and Maggie repaired to

225

her new bedroom. Matt was sound asleep, but he had left his teddy in Maggie's bed to welcome her. Suddenly she felt quite maudlin. She picked the bear up and walked about the little room on tiptoe, cuddling him to her face. Her throat ached from holding back tears. The only person she could fix her mind on with any sense of comfort was – Tolly. Tolly! Tolly! she kept crying silently, as if the black girl had been *her* nanny.

Maggie and the bear went to bed together and in the night he came to life and she felt him standing by the bed, his beady eyes buttoned to her closed ones, waiting for her to wake up. In her dream she looked up at him and there he was with a shiny black face and a cup of tea in his paw, wearing a red dress and saying, 'Time to go to work, Madam!' But Maggie groaned in her sleep and hugged the real bear closer because she didn't want to wake to such impossible challenges.

Chapter Twenty-Three

Maggie found a local school for Matt. It was not ideal, but then, neither had the school in Scotland been ideal. It was a school, it was close by – close enough for him to walk there by himself after the first week – and it would have to do. Maggie did not precisely turn a deaf ear on his grumbles nor petrify her heart against his new-boy horror stories and occasional tears; but there is a certain subcutaneous toughness produced by the knowledge that there is no viable alternative. This second skin, below the very sensitive top layer, protected her from deep pain. Boarding-school would have been worse; they both knew that. Maggie found herself no longer entirely sorry she had burst out with that bogey-story that day in the park.

Matt's daily 8.30 to 4 absence undeniably relieved the pressure, both on Maggie and on the flat. Oliver, whether from tact or inclination, had refrained from taking up residence. He seemed to spend most of his days in the West End, job-hunting in whatever less than full frontal ways actors in his position did ('Ear to the ground in pubs and clubs mainly,' said Tanya). This all meant that the two women had opportunities for some of the 'weeks of talking' that Tanya had forecast in her letter.

Maggie had forgotten what unbuttoned confidences could do in the way of untying deep, griping inner knots. Curled up on the orange flower-cushion sofa, consuming endless mugs of coffee and glasses of cheap wine, she serviced Tanya's knots and let Tanya do a like office for hers.

She heard the full story of Tanya's Joel-misery, her struggles to recover, her slow recognition – due mainly to propinquity, for they happened to do two consecutive tours together – that Oliver might be, not a surrogate Joel, that was out of the question, but a pleasant, personable port in a storm. 'I need that more than anything now. A harbour. I am so very fond of

227

him, Maggie, honestly! Well, haven't I proved it? People who love each other properly have to make sacrifices for each other, don't they?'

Maggie, deep sunk into her rôle of uncritical friend (one she didn't play very well, and couldn't for very long) nodded sagely, careful, this once, to say nothing. Inwardly she thought that this was the key to the whole Birmingham incident. Tanya had evidently been proving something *to herself* about her commitment to Oliver. This somehow made a bad situation worse.

When Tanya ran temporarily dry, she leant back and listened while Maggie unburdened herself of the Bruce years, the traumas attending Matt's birth, Tolly, the African padding, the WC, Joan, and her teaching.

'How astonishing you succeeded so brilliantly at that,' Tanya said, musingly. 'I mean, astonishing to me because I couldn't do it.'

'Of course you could, if you had to.'

Tanya shook her head. 'I would rather be idle.'

'Why? Do you think there's something degrading in it?'

Tanya frowned. 'No . . . Not for other people. For me – well, I suppose it's a kind of inner, completely personal snobbery. I am a sort of theatrical aristocrat. I couldn't do *any* other kind of work without feeling degraded. But I don't flatter myself that is a good way to be. I admire you for the way you threw yourself into whatever came to hand.'

'At the same time, suppressing a profound organic contempt!'

Tanya chuckled ruefully. 'I can't help it, Maggie. You should have been an actress. I still think of you as one, I mean, *manquée*. If there is contempt in my feelings for you, it goes further back than your teaching career in Nigeria. Do you remember your understudy job, that you had before you married and left England? Well, your principal was in a company with me later and she told me all about how she got pregnant and was about to leave the company when one of the leads in the play fell ill and she was offered to move up into that very good part. Do you know what she did?'

'I can guess.'

'You guess right because you know how ruthless are true actors. She got rid of the baby and took the part and she has never looked back.'

'Are you saying that I should have got rid of Matt?'

228

'One *cannot* have everything in this life.' Tanya was silent for a moment and then added, 'You know, I've often thought that if I'd been willing to give up the theatre and settle down in Sheffield, where I could really have got to work on Joel – been available all the time – I could have got him away from his wife. I didn't, and not from any deep-grained morality in my nature either. I was prepared to break up ten marriages, to see her drop down dead, to do anything – except give up acting.'

And now it's given you up, Maggie thought. She had good reason to know it, better perhaps even than Tanya. In a typically generous gesture, Tanya had written some letters of introduction for her to managements and even to her own agent. The managements maintained a frosty silence. The agent had written back, not to Tanya but to Maggie. The letter had been brief and to the point.

'Dear Miss Robertson,
I have received, to my great surprise, a letter concerning you from Miss Tanya Zandler.
This actress no longer being on our books, however, I find myself unable to act on any recommendation of hers.
Yours sincerely.'

Mercifully Tanya was sleeping when this letter came and never saw or knew about it. But it had given Maggie a plumb-line with which to sound the depths of Tanya's professional disgrace.

Something of her thoughts must have shown on her face now, because after a short meeting of eyes Tanya turned hers away abruptly and got up. She often moved about during their talk-sessions. Now she drifted about the big room, finding small things to tidy, watering her plants with a long-spouted can ... Yes, thought Maggie, she has the look of a gracious, indolent lady of the manor. But what happens to the aristocracy when their stately homes are sold from under them to pay for their own improvidence or recklessness?

'I'd do any work in the world,' Maggie said suddenly, 'rather than be *deeply* out of work ever again.'

'That's all very well,' said Tanya, 'but how are you going to manage about Matt?'

After a pause, Maggie said, 'Well, I've been thinking about Tolly.'

'The black nursemaid you had in Nigeria?'

229

'Yes. If I were to get her over here, I could send Matt up to my mother's. He could go back to his old school and Tolly would take care of both of them and I could have him in the holidays. And then I could work. Properly.'

' "Properly" meaning in the theatre?'

'In it. Around it. Or not in it. I don't know. I just know I can't sit at home much longer. I'll go crazy. I *need* to work, Tan – almost anything, it seems to me, that disciplined me, that gave my life a shape, that satisfied my need to earn my own living in some sensible, productive way, would do. Not as well as acting, but as a better-than-nothing.'

'How could you bear to part with Matt for months on end?'

'I could. That's all. I could bear it better than feeling I was nothing but his mother and that I wasn't earning my own living. I've got to do *that*, in any case. Unless I'm prepared to send him to Bruce's old boarding-school, which is a spartan hell-hole, I soon won't have a penny of Bruce-money left.'

'Come out on the balcony with me while I water.'

Maggie stood well out of the way in the corner by the rose-bush, which was still sad and palely loitering. The rest of the strange jungle of flowers gurgled audibly as they drank; Maggie half expected to see them surge into renewed growth before her eyes.

'Do you think your Tolly would leave her little wooden hut for you?'

'It's more a matter of whether Joan would part with her, at this stage. I hear Tolly is invaluable as an assistant, especially with the younger ones. But I've been seriously thinking about writing to ask her.'

'How would you pay her fare?'

'I'd have to earn it.'

Tanya caressed the face of an angry-looking zinnia soothingly while she thought.

'What does your mother say to all this? What would your very white brothers say to a black home-help?'

'I don't know. My mother's view matters, my brothers' ulti-mately don't. I'll have to investigate.'

'Well,' said Tanya, 'I would do it fairly soon. It doesn't do to postpone essential decisions.'

Look who's talking, thought Maggie.

*

230

Maggie did two weeks' night-time washing-up in a trendy bistro in Chelsea to earn the money to buy a new outfit for Matt, a new blouse for herself, and the coach fares up to Edinburgh for a weekend. Perversely, Tanya saw nothing 'degraded' in washing-up. It was the sort of job actors do, when they're hard up; it wasn't a competing career. There was no question at all of Tanya joining her, however; she was too well-known. 'It would be death if someone recognised me.' But she always had a hot meal waiting when Maggie came home, late and tired and with shrivelled fingers; and it was Tanya who forced her to wear rubber gloves. 'You must take care of your hands,' she said. 'You may not be an actress just at present, but you are not to look like a washerwoman.'

At the end of the fortnight, Maggie and Matt went up to Scotland on the coach.

A tempered welcome awaited them. The whole family came to drinks on the Saturday, lunch on the Sunday. Anthea Charity, now ten months old, crawled straight to Matt, clutched at his knees, hauled herself upright and then let go. For several seconds she stood unsupported with a rather smug look on her little dumpling face before landing on her padded behind with a thud.

This was certainly the highspot of the weekend for Ian and Lilian and for the first time they unbent a trifle toward Matt, who was materially associated in their minds with this singular triumph. Maggie actually heard Lilian say, 'Seemingly she's taken a fancy to you, young man,' in a less than usually buttoned-up tone. The ice thus at least cracked, Ian directed a dignified word or two to him about school; his manner was schoolmasterly rather than avuncular but at least he didn't ignore him. And Matt, happy to see his grandmother and Stip again, behaved impeccably, so that Maggie was proud and not too tense.

Besides, by the time the formal ordeal of the Sunday lunch came upon her, she had already had a talk with her mother about Tolly.

She had not had the faintest notion what Mrs Robertson's attitude was likely to be to the radical proposition that she take a fairly unsophisticated black girl into her home. But Maggie hadn't reckoned with the vivid impression left in her mother's mind by Maggie's letters from Nigeria. These had been written,

231

sometimes dutifully, sometimes with the force of inspiration, once a week or so over the whole seven years. Mrs Robertson had kept them all, neatly filed, as well as several large albums of snapshots which inevitably included many of Tolly and the other servants. Tolly was thus not exactly a stranger to Mrs Robertson. She knew what she looked like and a good deal more about her, all of it good – even her attempt to kill herself because Maggie and Matt were leaving her – had done nothing to damage the warm feelings Mrs Robertson had, almost unconsciously, built up toward her over the years of her devotion.

All this apart, Mary Robertson was lonely, and getting to the age when the housework was an increasing burden to her and when the notion of a little spoiling did not come amiss. Long afterwards she would confess to Maggie that the very first image that came into her head when Maggie tentatively broached the idea, was a Hollywood-inspired one – a uniformed Tolly gently wakening her by drawing the heavy curtains to let in the morning sun, and arranging her against a lot of pillows for a treat she had not had for many, many years – breakfast in bed.

Later, of course, being the practical and cautious Scot she was, she thought it all over on a less frivolous level. The more she considered the idea, the more she liked it; but she was nervous about her sons' possible reactions.

After lunch on the Sunday, when Anthea Charity had been 'put down' as Lilian rather ambivalently phrased it and Matt had gone out to try the new roller-skates Stip had brought him, all the grown-ups settled round the fire over coffee and Mrs Robertson, after a nervous glance at Maggie, said brightly:

'Well! Maggie has brought me a very unexpected idea to consider. And I am considering it. Seriously.'

Ian, sitting in his father's wing-back leather chair as uprightly as ever Mr Robertson had, pointed his sharp nose at his mother like an alert gundog. Stip, who was seated on the carpet with his back against the arm of Maggie's chair, didn't appear to react. He had changed a lot. His hair was much longer than Ian would have dreamt of tolerating when Stip was working in the mill, and the clock-sided socks and all that went with them had vanished totally. He now wore tight jeans and a loose, rather raffish sweater over an open-necked peppermint-striped shirt. The sleeves were pushed up over his smooth, slight arms. His face was smooth too, the anxiety lines gone. He looked

232

very well and very happy; according to Mrs Robertson, he was beginning to make a local name for himself.

'What idea, Mother?' asked Ian warily.

Mrs Robertson gently expounded, while Maggie mentally shielded her own head with both arms, waiting for the explosion. It didn't come. There was a lengthy silence when the plan had been outlined. Lilian's eyes were fixed on Ian. Ian, one hand under his chin, was gazing with a deep frown into the fire. Stip, still relaxed as a cat, continued to play with some coloured pipecleaners he had bought for Matt, making a green and brown giraffe. He seemed not to be listening, but actually Maggie divined that he was waiting for Ian. They were all waiting for Ian. Ian, like or lump him, was head of the family, and it was not true that his opinion could be ignored.

'Well!' he said at last. 'If you are seriously considering the plan, Mother, I must try to see some virtue in it.' Lilian gave a little sound of surprise, but turned it into a clearing of the throat. Obviously she had expected him to hit the roof, both about Maggie's dereliction of duty as a mother, and about the importation of an alien servant. But Ian had changed, too, though not as obviously as Stip. He was in his mid-thirties now, his hair was thinning markedly, and if his outward style had not altered, his inner self had. He was a family man. Anthea Charity's advent had softened him, opened him up a little to new feelings, new tolerances. He was no longer so quick to judge nor so dogmatic when he did. 'What are the advantages from your point of view? That must be the first consideration.'

Eagerly, Mrs Robertson explained that she was feeling the need of help in the house.

'That's no problem. We don't have to send to Nigeria for living-in help; you've always refused it before.'

'But if Matt is to live with me –'

'Ah! *If.* I think *that*, and not this girl Tolly, is the heart of the matter. You must think this through, Mother. If the housework is getting too much for you, how will you feel about having a little boy – and not a particularly biddable little boy, if I may say so – about the place demanding your energy and attention?'

'That's quite different, Ian. It's a different kind of energy. Surely you can see that! There is something utterly wearing about hoovering and dusting and catering and cooking, for just my own self. I feel this house, not to mention me, are wasted.

233

With the wee boy living here both the house and I would have some purpose.'

'It's a heavy responsibility for you, Mother. Bringing up a child – well, that's what it comes to – at your age.'

'But Tolly would help me. He loves her. It will be like having the best sort of old-fashioned nanny.'

Ian turned to Maggie with something like his old austere, quizzical expression.

'Will it, Maggie? I doubt if it will. This girl has not had the benefit of an English education or a Norland Nurse's course. But of course only Maggie knows how different Tolly's ideas of child-rearing are to ours.'

'They are different,' Maggie admitted. 'In some ways, far better.'

'Oh?'

'In what way could they be better?' inquired Lilian in her high-pitched voice.

'They're more natural. More . . .' She searched for a word, but finally had to shrug and repeat, '. . . *natural*.'

'Is Tolly good at being firm?'

Maggie couldn't help laughing. 'Not a bit.'

'So what will happen when Matt is naughty?'

'It's such a hard question to answer. I never remember his being naughty, with Tolly.'

There was a baffled silence, into which Stip said quietly, 'What puzzles me is how this poor African girl is going to cope with our beastly climate, with our dark chilly houses, not to mention our dark chilly attitudes to children.' Lilian and Ian turned to glare at him, but he just stood his giraffe knee-deep in carpet-pile and said, 'You'll have to get your friend Joan to warn her properly, Maggie. You can't let someone raised exclusively in the tropics come to Scotland without a thorough briefing. It would be too cruel.'

'Of course I shall do that,' said Maggie.

There was a silence which seemed to be going Maggie's way, before Ian reached rather irritably for a cigarette (he smoked only when he was feeling tense) and said, 'And who's going to pay her wages?'

'I am,' said Maggie, with a confidence she was far from feeling.

234

'I should hope so,' said Ian with his old acerbity. 'Might one ask, how? Is your husband contributing to your upkeep?'

'Not exactly,' evaded Maggie. 'I shall get a job.'

'Oh, I do hope – ' began Mrs Robertson, caught Ian's eye, and stopped.

So Maggie wrote off to Joan the minute she and Matt returned to London. She said nothing to Matt, though she all but burst with the inner pressure of wanting at least to give him hints. He was having trouble settling at school and needed the comfort of dreams even more than Maggie did.

Meanwhile there was the little matter of the fare, should best come to best. After scanning the small ads in vain for several wasted days, on the Thursday she put on her least actressy town-clothes and went into the West End.

She didn't allow herself to stray into Theatre Mile, where stage photographers and agents' offices, familiar to her from other days, might draw her. Instead she visited a number of ordinary employment bureaux, there to register her very limited skills. No typing, let alone shorthand, of course. A good voice, a pleasing appearance, some native wit. What could she do with these? Receptionist? Demonstrator? Floorwalker? Telephonist?

One woman, and one only, told her to wait while she got a card out of a file.

'Would you mind a bit of market research, dear, just to fill in?' She looked up at Maggie, who shaped her face into the unbleakest mould she could manage.

'It sounds fine,' she said, in a passable imitation of Tanya's most affirmative voice.

When she got home, dying to talk to Tanya, she couldn't because Oliver was there.

Maggie had already acknowledged to herself that she was beginning to dislike Oliver. Today especially. He was so damned full of himself, regaling them with stories about promising interviews and an 'excellent' reading he had done for a 'fantastic' part in a new West End production which he believed he'd a good chance of landing.

'I've worked for the producer before, he knows perfectly well

235

I don't drink, good God, *me*! He'd heard about Birmingham, of course, but I explained the whole thing to him and he was bloody marvellous about it, terribly sympathetic.'

Afterwards when they had a moment alone, Maggie asked, 'Would his sympathy extend to Tanya, do you think?' Oliver looked at her and then pulled his mouth down. 'Going on a one-night bender is one thing,' he muttered. 'Breaking one's contract's bound to be quite another.' 'So what's going to happen about Tanya?' 'God knows!' He'd become noticeably less ebullient and made an excuse to leave shortly afterwards, though Tanya had clearly expected him to stay the night.

At supper Matt chattered about school as usual and this bridged the gaps in adult conversation, but he was oddly intuitive in some ways and he eventually fell into an uncomfortable silence.

The late September sun slanted through the long windows and fell on the pretty table Tanya always laid, complete with brightly-striped cloth and a posy in a silver salter she had bought (to Maggie's secret horror – it must have been very expensive) in Camden Town market. Tanya had been being very extravagant altogether of late, especially with clothes and, of all things, houseplants; she had obliged Oliver, not the handiest of men, to rig up new, narrow shelves across the windows and from these trailed curtains of leaves of all shapes and sizes. Charming as these were, they disturbed Maggie somehow – not just their unwarranted cost, but a feeling they gave as they accumulated that, like lace curtains, they were shutting out the world. Now the rays of sun arrived on the tablecloth, and on their faces, dappled and diffused, winking as if in collusion.

Into the silence Tanya suddenly injected a question.

'Matt! Listen. What if one morning you went to your school and there was the headmaster standing outside the gate –'

'It's a headmistress.'

'Whatever, don't interrupt! There she is, and as you come up with the others she bars your way with both arms, like this, and says,"Matthew Macrae, you can't come in." What would you feel?'

'Dunno,' said Matt, staring at her uneasily. There was about her eyes, her voice, a certain brilliant, trembling edge, like the brink of a weir.

'*Think*,' she insisted, transfixing him with her look. 'Imagine!

236

You, alone of all the children, are excluded. Forbidden. What would you do?'

Matt glanced at his mother for help, but she was watching Tanya anxiously.

'But why should she? I haven't done anything,' he muttered.

'Ah.' Tanya leaned her chair far back so the two front legs came off the floor, put back her head and closed her eyes. Anyone who knew her only superficially might think she was putting on a tragedy-queen act, thought Maggie, but she knew better. She felt very alarmed, and yet relieved. The edge was a precipice that she *wanted* Tanya to approach and look over; there was no going forward safely until she had.

'Come on, pooch,' she said to Matt. 'Bed.'

He came more willingly than usual. Usually he was magnetised to Tanya, but sometimes, as now, some strangeness in her had the opposite effect.

'What was she talking about?' he whispered as they closed the door of their room. 'Has Mrs Stanley rung up – ?'

'*No*, of course not! Tanya's just playing acting games.'

'Oh!' he said, relieved. And then, tolerantly, 'She plays games a lot, for a grown-up, doesn't she.'

'We all do.'

'You don't.'

'Yes I do. For instance, right now I'm rehearsing in my head for the new job I'm starting tomorrow.'

'How?' he asked, and then, sharply, 'What job?'

'It's a job asking people questions. I'll have to knock on doors or stop people in the street. I must think of something to say quickly or they'll shut the door or walk away.'

'Would you mind if they did?'

'Of course! Wouldn't you?'

'So what will you say?'

'GoodmorningsirormadamIwonderifyoucouldspareamoment toanswersomequestions,' she said rapidly. Matt laughed.

'They'll think you're potty,' he said

'Would you mind having a potty mum?'

'Yes!' he shouted.

After he was in bed and she had kissed him, he said in a whisper, 'Is Tanya a little bit potty, do you think?'

'Not more than most people. It's just that she's so sort of transparent, it's easy to see what's going on inside her.'

237

He frowned. 'You said once she was red.'

'She's lots of different colours. Just now she's sort of . . .' She screwed up her eyes. 'Black underneath and spangly-gold on top.'

'Like Tolly in her yellow hat,' supplied Matt unexpectedly.

Maggie opened her eyes quickly. 'Well, no – ' she began, but then stopped. She kissed him again and went to draw the curtains to dim the room. Might there be some degree of thought-transference between them? Tolly had been so much in the forefront of her mind, ever since she had written to Joan.

She went back into the main room. The sun was down now but Tanya had not got up from the table to light the lamps. This was not like her – she usually lit them before dusk, hating the dying phase of daylight almost as much as (Maggie had discovered long ago) she hated and even feared the dark. She was sitting now with her chin on her hands, staring out of the long windows. She stirred as Maggie came in and flashed one of her whitest, brightest smiles.

'Everything all right?'

'Yes. What about you?'

'Me? What do you mean?'

'Are you all right, is what I meant. Because I don't think you are.'

Tanya promptly got up and started clearing the table, but Maggie stopped her. 'Sit down, Tanya. Listen, I've got a job.'

Tanya froze for a moment. 'What kind? Not a –'

'No! Not a theatre job, of course not.' She was neither shocked nor surprised to see naked relief on Tanya's face. Naturally that would have been unbearable for her. 'It's something called market research. I had to go to some office in Battersea, they gave me a clipboard and a pile of questionnaires about people's lifestyles and about something called . . . Oh, some silly product, I forget its name, it's all nonsense but they'll pay me and I don't have to do it forever. Tanya. What about you, love? What are you going to do?'

'Oh, don't worry abut me! Everybody has bad patches. I'm going to ring Jean tomorrow.'

'Jean – ?'

'My agent!' said Tanya gaily. 'I haven't until now, because I wanted things to cool off a bit, but she'll soon rush into the

238

breach with something, even if it's not – *quaite* what Ai am accustomed to,' she finished in her U-voice.

Joan's terse airgraph arrived at the end of Maggie's third week of market researching. She had asked Tolly if she wanted to go and freeze to death in Scotland, among a lot of grim-faced strangers, big black buldings and sooty bushes.

'I did my absolute damnedest to put her off. Why shouldn't I? I've invested a lot in her. But alas for me and mine, Tolly is a one-woman woman, or perhaps I mean a one-child woman. When I told her you wanted her, I don't think she heard any of my bleak and scaremongering descriptions. She wept with joy and wrung her hands. She hasn't wrung her hands since you left.'

In short, she was coming. Maggie had only to send her a ticket or enough money to pay for one, and she would arrive within days.

And now at last Maggie might tell Matt. She could hardly wait for him to come home from school. She worked like a demon on her paper-work so as to have a whole evening in which to revel in his reaction. And he didn't disappoint her.

'Darling? Is that you?'

'Yes, Mum.' He sounded depleted. School was a grind for him.

'Come into our room. I've got something to tell you.'

He came trailing in. His shirt-tail was half out and it was fairly clear he had been duffed up again.

'Have you been in a fight, Matt?'

'Not a real one. Just pushing.'

'Just look at your bag!'

'Yeah. Someone bashed it against a wall, and it burst. It wasn't my fault.'

She hugged him, and pulled him down on her knee. She was still allowed to do that when there was no possibility of anyone seeing.

'Matt, what would you like more than anything in the world?'

He looked at her for a long time. She stroked his red hair but it wouldn't go smooth. Suddenly she felt her love for him like a piece of scorching-hot potato stuck half-way down, just behind her breast bone. How could she part with him? For

239

what had she made all those arrangements? To free herself to trudge round asking people silly questions and filling out forms? The pain from the lump of love brought tears to her eyes.

'Is it something bad?'

'No, no, good! Oh, do guess, Matt! Something better than anything, the best present you could have.'

'Could I lift it?'

'No! Not that kind of present.'

'Daddy.'

Idiot. You thoughtless bloody halfwit. Just because you don't care if you never see him again.

'No, darling. But you're warm in a way. It's a person.'

His face changed. 'Not – is it Tolly?'

'YES!'

He let out an inarticulate sound and threw himself on her. When he spoke again his voice was high and shrill and his freckled cheeks were flushed scarlet.

'When? When? When?'

'She's coming. I don't know when exactly. But you can start looking forward to it because it'll be soon.' But instead of leaving it at that, she had to go on. 'And when she comes, you and she are going to live in Scotland. You'll stay with Granny and go back to your old school and in the holidays you can come to London, or I'll come up to Scotland, and we'll do all sorts of lovely things together.'

His wild joy faded a little as he took this in.

'You mean I'll be living with Granny and Tolly and you'll be here?'

'Darling, listen. I have to earn money.'

'Can't you earn money in Scotland?'

'Not so well.'

He stared at her, all the excitement gone from his face.

'Would you rather be with Tanya than with me?'

'Darling, no. It's not like that.'

'What is it like then?'

'I know it's hard for you to understand, but I want a better sort of job. I want to do something interesting and exciting, something worthwhile. And there are more of those kinds of jobs in London.'

It sounded, even in her own ears, very thin. Drowned out, almost, by the sudden hollow sound of the warning bell.

240

Chapter Twenty-Four

They settled down, with difficulty, to wait till Maggie had saved enough for Tolly's fare.

Maggie discovered that she was quite adequate to the challenges of market researching. The work in general wore her out physically, at least until she got used to all the walking, bored her rather a lot, but afforded her not inconsiderable satisfaction. She could do it, she had one foot on the ladder of self-sufficiency and self-respect.

She did the legwork from nine till three, then devoted the next few hours to Matt and did the paperwork at night. This did not leave much time for Tanya, which both troubled Maggie and relieved her. Being in her friend's company at that moment did not give much subjective pleasure. Yet when, one Saturday, Tanya announced that Oliver would be coming to lunch and that it was a 'party' to which Maggie was invited, she was pleased.

'And there will be champagne,' said Tanya. 'Oliver got the part.'

'Are you glad?' Maggie asked.

'What can you mean?'

'You know what I mean. In your situation I might not like anyone having a job.'

'I am not like that.'

'Sorry. I thought everyone was.'

Tanya waited a moment while Maggie drank some coffee and then said, in a suddenly dangerous voice, 'You are just waiting for it, aren't you, Maggie.'

'Waiting for what?'

'For me to – to break down again. To have hysterics. To take to drink or something.'

Maggie put down her mug.

241

'I'm actually waiting for you to look as squarely at the situation as you're now looking at me.'

'I'm looking at you because sometimes one sees even old friends as if for the first time.'

'Oh dear! What have I done to bring this on?'

'You don't like Oliver, do you?'

Much startled by this unlooked-for turn in the conversation, Maggie blinked and said, 'Well –'

'I knew it.'

'Now, just a minute! Give me a chance. I don't dislike him, of course I don't! I just – wish – he would be a little more – supportive of you. He seems to me to be thinking mainly of himself in all this.'

'The best way he can help me is by helping himself,' said Tanya with unTanyalike sententiousness.

'How does that work?'

'Well, Maggie, when one is lovers with somebody, it is a partnership, so that if one person has work it is in a way as if both did.'

'I don't believe that's true in your case. What possible comfort can you get out of Oliver having a job when you haven't?' asked Maggie brutally. 'Anyway, I don't quite know what you call being lovers and partners. Doesn't that involve living together?'

'Tell me, Maggie. What is your definition of friendship?'

These swerves in topic were beginning to unnerve Maggie, but she answered as best she could off the top of her head. 'I suppose – giving support and – sharing things –'

'May I tell you mine? Friends are for making you feel good. And you are being a very bad friend this morning by my definition.' She got up with her dishes and walked statuesquely through into the kitchen.

'Why is Tanya being funny?' Matt asked when they had gone into their room to smarten up enough to match the arrange-. ments for lunch.

Maggie had long ago stopped trying to pull the conventional wool over Matt's eyes with platitudes when he showed this kind of acuity. She simply said, 'Tanya is having problems.'

'Worse than yours?' Maggie had begun, not without doubts, to confide at least the surface things to Matt as they lay in bed in the mornings for the routine fifteen minutes they allowed

242

themselves between the ringing of the alarm and getting-up time.

'In a way. You see, Tanya's never been married so she's always depended on herself for money. Actresses don't tend to save much, and as you see, she's wildly generous.'

'She mostly buys things for herself.'

'Only lately. Because she's unhappy. People often do that. But having us here at all is generous, Matt. I'm not paying rent, even. She wouldn't let me.'

She paused, reflecting. It occurred to her that her own situation in this flat was only tenable as long as she did conform to Tanya's definition of friendship, no matter what that was. As soon as she ceased to do so she would have to move out. At the moment, the latter seemed the preferred option; it was all getting too complicated, too wearing . . . Maggie simply didn't feel capable of coping with Tanya's problems on top of her own. Pulling the wire-bristled brush through her bushy hair and staring at herself in the little baroque mirror Tanya had hung on the wall for her, Maggie thought: I'll do my sums tonight. I can't keep us on what I'm earning now. How much would I need, not to do it well but to do it at all? More than I'll ever earn in market research, that's for sure.

When she emerged, nicely dressed, at 12.30, the doorbell was ringing. This was odd because of course Oliver had his own key.

'I'll go!' shouted Matt.

'Probably some man to read the meter,' Tanya surmised.

But it wasn't. Matt came back leading a total stranger, a slightly overweight young looking man of about thirty-five with dark blond hair neatly combed into a wave, and horn-rimmed glasses. He was sharply dressed in flannels and a rather loud tweed jacket. He glanced at Maggie, then round the room, and finally at Tanya. He gave the impression of wanting to shade his eyes.

'Hallo!' he said, advancing on her bravely with outstretched hand. 'I'm Ronnie Makepeace.'

'Are you really?' asked Tanya coolly. She allowed her hand to be shaken, and then waited expectantly. The stranger waited too. After what seemed like several minutes of silence, he repeated his name with a crestfallen inflection. Both women continued to look quite blank.

243

'Didn't Oliver tell you he'd invited me to lunch?'

Tanya shot Maggie a look which Maggie easily interpreted as one of bewilderment and annoyance.

'No, he didn't, to tell the truth. Who are you?'

'Really, that's too bad of him. How embarrassing. Well, I'm a sort of producer.'

There was a second's pause, and then Tanya opened up her petals like some exotic and possibly flesh-eating orchid in a time-lapse film. She covered the ground between them in one swoop, gathered Mr Makepeace up and bore him to the sofa where she seated him amid the jewel-cushions and had a glass in his hand before he had contrived to draw breath.

'But how very fascinating, Mr Makepeace –'

'Ronnie –'

'Ronnie.' she gazed at him, entranced and entrancing. 'Perhaps Oliver wanted you as a surprise for me! It is sweet of you to come. Are you producing Oliver's play?'

He gagged briefly on his drink.

'I say, this is terribly strong – No. Actually, I'm not.'

'So how did you meet him?'

'I produced him ages ago. In a farce.'

Tanya tinkled with laughter.

'Oliver in farce! Really and truly? Dropped trousers, curates in bed, lots and lots of doors? I can't imagine it! Can you, Maggie?'

She turned for one brief moment away from her unexpected guest and gave Maggie a frenetic, cross-eyed look of appeal. Maggie took the hint. Shepherding Matt, she melted away behind the partition and got on with the lunch – an act of pure unvarnished friendship to make up for her earlier lapse. She would have liked to be around herself if, as Tanya all too clearly hoped, this was some kind of ad hoc casting session masterminded by Oliver.

But after about ten minutes she detected through Matt's chatter an altered note in Tanya's eager voice, and soon she heard her footsteps approaching the kitchenette.

' . . .Must just glance at the *petit marmite* . . .'

The *petit marmite* was in no need of glancing at – Maggie had everything well under control – so she turned to wave Tanya back to Ronnie; but Tanya's face was a study in disgust and disappointment. She wrote in the air the letters 'N.B.G.'

244

'Why?' Maggie mouthed back.

'Left the theatre. Gone into television.'

'What's wrong with that?' Maggie whispered, making a great noise with the dishes.

'Darling, don't play Cinderella!' Tanya cried suddenly, nearly making Maggie drop the plates. 'Go and talk to Ronnie while Matt and I deal with the garlic bread!' She was writing in pencil on the shiny top of her small easiwork, 'BEC. HE'S IN TV *NEWS*'.

Maggie snatched the pencil, scrawled a four-letter word and scurried out to keep Ronnie from feeling neglected. Her main feeling was one of annoyance with Oliver. Why on earth had he lumbered Tanya with this perfectly useless stranger who would only spoil their intimate little celebration without even the possibility of being of the least help? Probably some aberrant impulse, born of Oliver's total insensitivity to Tanya's basic needs ...

She chatted to Ronnie politely. He was rather nice, in a boyish, self-satisfied kind of way. He sat with his knees apart and the soles of his shoes together, expounding about the still comparatively new and innovative news service provided by Independent Television, which, he rather smugly explained, had broken a lot of fresh ground, and 'really made the old stick-in-the-muds at the Beeb sit up'. Its newscasters were not mere ciphers but personalities in their own right; its reporters had developed a new technique of street interviewing and hard-hitting questions; and on top of that, they were giving radical new opportunities to women.

'Why, have you any female newsreaders?'

'Newscasters,' he corrected her. 'No, not so far, but we do have a woman producer – Welsh, swears like a navvy –'

'She doesn't sound very feminine.'

'No reason why women shouldn't swear if they feel like it, it's an aspect of equality. And of course, we were the first to have girls as reporters.'

'Oh yes,' said Maggie, 'I think I've seen one. She always seems to do the sillier stuff.'

Ronnie bridled visibly. 'No, no, nonsense! Well ... of course it's more appropriate for a woman to do the fashion shows, the royals, the human-interest stuff and so on –'

'That's what I meant.'

245

'But she has to be ready to tackle the hard news too! Take yesterday,' he said, settling into his chair with a wriggle of his quite large behind. 'That plane wreck. Fantastic! Came down smack on a village, mercifully not far from London. And at tea-time. What luck! We just managed to rush a crew out there, do an into-camera piece and interview some witnesses, and rush the film to the lab by DR in time for the early bulletin –'

'Did a girl go out on that story?'

'What? – Oh, yes! that's what I was going to tell you. Great stuff. There she stood in her sweater-and-pearls and not so sensible shoes, in this smashed-up village street in the midst of all the wreckage and bodies –'

'Bodies?' asked Maggie in horror.

He drooped a little. 'Well, no. To be truthful, the actual bodies had all been cleared away before she got there. But for all you could see on the screen, it could easily have been *bits*, mixed up with all that rubble.' He was so carried away, he didn't notice how Maggie was looking at him. 'Of course, the news editor wouldn't have sent her on a story like that, only there happened to be no one else in the newsroom. And in the end it worked out marvellously. Cameraman had the sense to do a couple of cutaways on her face. She looked really, you know, stressed, *moved*.' His cheeks swelled like pink bubblegum with pride. 'You'd never get any of those po-faced male repor-ters at the Beeb showing a bit of sentiment on a story, they're like so many bloody automatons.'

'What experience do you have to have, to be a reporter on TV?' Maggie asked, her curiosity at last aroused.

'It's astonishing what varied backgrounds our reporters have. One or two old lags from Fleet Street, of course. Couple of ex-lawyers – great training for grilling the politicians! We've got a new boy straight from Oxford, but he's not up to much, bit wet.'

'But the girl?'

'We've got two. One graduated to us from steam radio. The younger one, who did the plane-crash, I think was in show-biz.'

Maggie sat up. 'You mean, an actress?'

'Yes.' He seemed defensive. 'Some quite serious people get stage training. Why not?'

'No reason. None at all,' said Maggie thoughtfully.

*

246

Oliver arrived at last, glowing with triumph and an armful of flowers and quite oblivious of having blundered. They had a rather brittle little lunch party round the revised table, but the champagne, Maggie noted, stayed in the fridge. Then Maggie prepared to remove herself and Matt, as she had earlier promised.

But Tanya had abandoned her plans. She came into Maggie's room and whispered, 'No post-prandial beddy-byes today. You might as well stay for coffee, not to mention helping with the dishes.'

'Don't blame Oliver. Perhaps he didn't know Ronnie had changed jobs.'

'Of course he bloody well knew! Wait till I get him alone.'

Ronnie took his time, but he left at last. Maggie saw him down to the front door and they shook hands.

'Thanks for telling us about your work,' she said. 'It was all news to me.' He laughed uproariously at her little joke. She felt a bit sorry for him. He must be pretty thick-skinned not to have guessed how Tanya felt.

'Why don't you come along one evening and see for yourself?' he was saying. 'We're just near the Aldwych. Come on Friday, I'll take you up to the studio and you can watch the late bulletin go out. It's quite exciting.'

When was the last time a man had asked her out, even on this basis? A hundred years ago?

'All right. I'd like to.'

'What about bringing your boy?'

Now Maggie definitely warmed to him.

'Thank you, that is kind of you. He'd love it, I'm sure.'

She went back up the stairs slowly, pondering. As she reached the landing outside the flat, Matt came out.

'They're fighting,' he said

She listened. The voices inside were not unduly raised. 'No they're not –'

'They will be soon. Tanya's cross.'

God, I wish I had my own place! she thought. It was very difficult, living tangled in somebody else's fringes. As she and Matt crept along the wall of the big room like mice, trying to be invisible, she felt as if they were cutting through some tangible atmosphere. At the far end, Tanya and Oliver were sitting opposite each other, not yet shouting, quite.

247

'He's not even in the business any more! How *could* you have thought he'd be any use to me?'

'My dear darling girl, *because* he's "not in the business". You've got to face facts.'

'What facts? *What facts?*'

'Ronnie is in a position to help you.'

'Help me *how?* I don't understand what you're talking about!'

As Maggie and Matt reached, and slid through, their bedroom door, Maggie heard Oliver say:

'Their older female reporter is leaving, and they're going to hold auditions for –'

Maggie shut the door swiftly. It was insufficiently thick to cut off Tanya's barely-articulate shriek of fury:

'Audition? Me? To interview people in the *street? Are you completely* –'

Matt was looking at her philosophically.

'You see?' he whispered. 'I told you.'

248

Chapter Twenty-Five

Maggie was glad she hadn't got to ask Tanya to babysit that Friday night. It was nearly a week since the lunch-party but the mood was still strained. Living with a person in Tanya's state of mind is fairly hard graft at the best of times and Maggie's times were not of the best; she was finding it increasingly difficult to show proper sympathy and to fulfil Tanya's criteria of friendship – especially since she suddenly found herself playing pig in the middle, with Oliver trying to get her on his side.

'I simply couldn't come to lunch and celebrate my new job without doing something for Tanya,' he explained to Maggie over the phone. 'Why can't she realise she'll have to gravitate into some other branch of the media? She'll never get another legitimate acting job as long as she's blacklisted by Equity. Our agent told her so very frankly when Tan phoned her.'

Tanya had not told Maggie about this, which indicated that her conversation with Jean had been pretty harrowing. But she chewed over Oliver by the hour.

'How dare he! Yes, that would just suit him, wouldn't it, if I were in a different profession. A good steady income to bridge *his* out-of-work patches!'

'Tanya, I don't think he's even thought of that. He just wants to help.'

'Oh! Has he been getting at you behind my back?'

'No!' lied Maggie. 'Of course not. I just don't see that he's done anything so awful.'

'I thought you didn't like him!'

'Well, to be honest I like him a bit better now.'

'– Now that he's come over to your side and is trying to push me into some bloody boring, un-me job –'

'Trying to help. Trying to get you to face facts –'

249

'*Shut up*, Maggie! I don't notice *you* facing any of *your* facts!'

'What does that mean, if anything?' asked Maggie, getting heated despite her best intentions.

'Do you think you're going to be able to muddle on like this for ever? At least I haven't got a child to worry about! At least I'm viable on my own!'

'For how long?'

'Well, I've got this flat – I could get six pounds a week for your room –'

She stopped cold, but only for a moment.

'No. I don't mean that. I know very well I need you as much as you need me and that no stranger would stand for me, let alone pay me.'

'Yes, they would. Tanya –'

'Shut up, Maggie,' she said again, but in an entirely different tone this time. She was looking at Maggie sideways, a sheepish, appealing look. 'Don't take me up on every word just now. I'm not myself, you know I'm not.'

'Okay. But, love, I am aiming to get out of here and stand on my own feet. I want you to know that.'

'I don't want you to go. I'd go crazy without you. Cra*zier*, that is.' Now she turned her head and looked straight at Maggie, and then suddenly gave her a hug. 'God, I'm rotten. I'm a lousy bitch. I think I really am half-mad at the moment. I haven't set foot in a theatre for six weeks and it's killing me –'

'I know. Don't apologise. It's amazing the living arrangements are working as well as they are. I don't take them for granted for a single moment.'

'Nor do I, Maggie,' Tanya said with utter sincerity.

A little later, Maggie mentioned that Ronnie Makepeace had invited her to go down to ITN that evening and watch the news go out.

'What made you say you'd go?'

'I want to. It'll be interesting. Besides, he invited Matt to go and he'll like it.'

'He'll probably be as bored as I would.'

'How can it be boring? News can never be boring.'

'You wait and see. Maggie –'

'What?'

'Did you find him attractive, that fat young-old man?'

'Ronnie? No. Nice. Not attractive.'

'How *do* you manage?' Tanya asked curiously.

Maggie didn't have to ask what she meant. She sighed.

'What you've never had, you never miss.'

'God!' exclaimed Tanya. 'What a dreadful thing to say, after seven years of marriage! I wish I could find you a nice chap.' Maggie said nothing. She wished so too. But Tanya's life was drawing in around her. She seldom went out except to the shops; she seldom saw anyone. It was as if, now that she was no longer an actress, she felt naked, and insecure, and ashamed to show herself.

Ronnie was waiting for Maggie at the reception desk of ITN, which was on the seventh floor of a huge building on the corner of the Aldwych and Kingsway.

'Luckily it's a light news night,' he said, 'I've got time to show you round before the rush starts. Hallo, young man,' he said avuncularly to Matt.

'Hallo. Will we see Robert Ottaway?'

Maggie stared at her son. So far as she was aware, he never watched the news.

'Ah! Are you a fan of Bob-the-newscaster or Bob-the-four-minute-miler?'

'Four minute miler,' said Matt shyly.

'Well, you're in luck. He's on tonight. Come and meet him.'

Matt grinned and gave a little hop of excitement. Maggie, bemused at this evidence of her son's private enthusiasms, gave his hand a sympathetic squeeze, but he at once took it from her grasp and walked ahead of her after Ronnie, who led the way into a huge square room full of desks, partitions and very busy people. The place was a blaze of light and a riot of sound, mainly mechanical – typewriters and tape-machines clicking continuously – but there were also voices and footsteps and a general air of strongly motivated, efficient action. Maggie looked round as she moved through it all. It was just as she might have imagined a television newsroom if she had ever tried to. She liked it. She liked the bustle, the feeling of purpose, and something else: she felt this room was some kind of fountainhead, a source, a kernel. It gave her a sensation which was the precise opposite of what she had so often felt in Nigeria. It had a quality of intensity not unlike what one felt in the theatre.

251

Tanya *would* like this, Maggie thought. She wouldn't be bored. No one could be.

Ronnie was solemnly introducing her small red-haired son to a smallish, red-haired young man with a likeable monkey-face and a warm, crookedy smile. He had a desk to himself and seemed to be in the midst of piles of paperwork, but nevertheless he took time out to chat to Matt in a man-to-man fashion.

'I don't get in too much serious running these days, except when a policeman comes up here and asks me to *run* down and move my car . . .' 'Could you beat Roger Bannister?' 'I doubt it! Are you keen on running?' 'I don't know – I've never tried.' 'Well, try. You're the right shape.' 'Am I?' 'I should think so. Just put on trackshoes and run, a bit further every day. Do you live near a park?' 'Yes.' 'Well, then, you're in luck. Are you going to watch our bulletin?'

Matt gave Maggie a look of confusion. She nodded. She herself was one big smile, like Tolly's body-smiles, of pleasure at this encounter – Matt standing there so straight, his shyness melting, and the famous young man speaking to him so kindly and yet so unpatronisingly . . .

'Well, keep your fingers crossed for me. I make mistakes sometimes.' He gave Ronnie a wink. Matt asked solemnly, 'What mistakes?' 'Well,' said Ottaway, 'the other night instead of saying "Royal Horse Artillery" I went and said "Royal Arse Hortillery". At least,' he added, 'I said it at rehearsal. Now I'm terrified every time it comes up that I'll say it on transmission.' Ronnie and Maggie were laughing; Matt, innocent of the word 'arse' (he always said 'bottom') was baffled. Bob Ottaway shook his hand again and Ronnie led them away, still chuckling.

'Super chap,' he said. 'No side whatever. Look, these are the AP and Reuters tape machines, where a lot of our input comes from . . .' He tore a strip of tape off, glanced at it and handed it to Matt. 'There now, you can tell your grandchildren you were the first to learn the historic news that the Queen Mother opened an old people's home today . . .' Matt stared at the tape, frowning. Ronnie was moving them on. He showed them the various newsdesks, subs' table, script-writers' corner and eventually the reporters' area near the windows.

Until that moment Maggie hadn't let herself know exactly why she had been so eager to come, but when she was

252

introduced to a woman in her mid-thirties called Jennifer who was soon leaving to go abroad, it clicked.

She looked at the woman closely. This one had never been an actress. She knew that at once. This woman was of another species altogether, deep-voiced, calm, effective, yet without any flamboyance or that trace of exhibitionism which characterises stage people; Tanya had an overdose, but even Maggie, in her quiet way, had some of it.

'How do you like working here?' she asked casually.

'It's been great fun, but it was just one – of those things,' replied Jennifer, laughing somewhat enigmatically.

'Who's going to get your job?'

'I wouldn't know. Whoever it is, I wish him luck.'

'Him?'

'Oh, sure. One female around here is enough for the trivia. They'll get another man.'

Ronnie coughed uncomfortably.

'No, no, nonsense,' he said brusquely. Jennifer cocked her eyebrow at him, gathered up her coat and said, 'I'm off. Don't let them cut my mother-of-ten-in-a-council-flat down to nothing, will you? By the way, she's not RC. She's just the old lady who lived in a shoe.' She gave them a salute and clacked away on high smart heels.

'The old lady who lived in a shoe?' repeated Matt.

Ronnie grinned. 'The one who had so many children because she didn't know what to do. Come on, I must go up and watch some rushes and you can come too. The editor's not here tonight. When the cat's away!'

'What cat?' asked Matt in the lift. It was all getting a bit much for him.

'It's just a saying, darling.'

'Where are we going now?'

'To see some films.'

He perked up at this, but for him the actuality was disappointing. It was relays of uncut news film relating to news items as varied as cricket in New Zealand and a strike in a car-factory in Dagenham, all of it, from a child's point of view, as dull and incomprehensible as mud. Maggie, however, found it thrilling, and listened alertly to all the technical talk going on round her about lead-ins, shot-lists and footage; she watched Jennifer's overburdened council-house mum, actually not out of concern for the poor worn-out creature but to see how Jennifer had handled her. The interviews all interested Maggie. At one point there was film of a young man speaking straight into camera from outside Transport House.

'Is he reading something, or has he memorised it, or what?' she whispered to Ronnie.

'Just off the cuff, I think,' Ronnie replied.

Maggie sank back thoughtfully in her seat. You'd have to do plenty of homework. She'd never taken more than a passing interest in news and current affairs. She would go out first thing in the morning and order *The Times*, the *Telegraph* and the *Manchester Guardian*, plus all the posh Sundays and a couple of weeklies as well. She would put herself through a short crash-course without saying a word to anyone. In the meantime she would cultivate Ronnie and keep her ear to the ground. Jennifer wasn't leaving till the end of October. She had time, but not much.

Chapter Twenty-Six

'Crumbs, mate,' said Tanya, doing her Cockney bit, 'Get a load of you! What are you all tarted up for?'

She was lying sprawled on the orange settee, only now instead of looking like a green chameleon or a bird of paradise she looked dark and rather sinister, like a millipede. She wore a shiny black tunic and tight black trousers. Her hair was growing out of its henna red and the roots were unmistakably grey. She was not wearing make-up and this was, to Maggie, the most disquieting thing of all. She looked almost middle-aged.

Maggie by contrast was – not tarted up in any actressy sense, but got up, certainly, to look her very best in a different way. She had studied the part of woman reporter and dressed it to the life. Her bushy dark hair had, for once, received the attentions of a skilled hairdresser, who had trimmed and tamed it into a neat but feminine cap. She wore a brand-new two-piece (bought with almost the last of Bruce's money) in Swedish heavy cotton trimmed with black braid, fitting to waist and neck, with long, tight sleeves, and little buttons fastening closely enough to do justice to her bust without drawing attention to it. She wore small pearl earrings and a cameo. Her make-up had taken her half-an-hour. She had borrowed Tanya's lip-brush to make a perfectly clean outline, had done her eyes with extreme care to give a vibrant, understated effect, and powdered down her naturally high colour. She now felt that her appearance matched the immense amount of preparation she had put into her mind.

'Where are you going?' asked Tanya, who had been told nothing.

'To an audition.'

Tanya slowly sat up and put her bare feet on the drugget. 'What did you say?'

'Not for a part, Tanya. Don't worry, I probably won't get it, but please wish me luck.'

'Tell me what you meant – an audition.'

'It's for ITN. To be a reporter on television news.'

Tanya stared at her as if seeing her for the first time.

'Ronnie Makepeace.'

Maggie nodded.

'You didn't tell me a word.'

'You haven't been exactly inviting confidences lately.'

'You might have forced it on me. It wouldn't have been worse than finding out you've been keeping secrets.'

'It's not that at all! It was sheer superstition. Talk about it, hope for it openly, and you don't get it. *You* know.'

Tanya looked at her. Then she got up, crossed the room, kissed Maggie on both cheeks with dry, cold lips and said, 'Good luck. I feel you will get it.' She turned and walked back to the sofa and lay down again on her face.

Maggie hesitated, then said to the still figure of the millipede among the flowers, 'If I'm late, will you give Matt his tea?'

'Yes.'

Oh Tanya, I'm sorry. I'm sorry! But I can't help it – I've got to. And it's not the theatre.

The audition was quite unlike any she had ever done before, and not merely because no acting was involved. She had to sit at a desk under bright lights (one of them, like a third-degree lamp, seemed to strike straight into her eyes) with the dauntingly huge television camera shifting its monstrous bulk fractionally in front of her as if settling itself for the pounce. At a signal, she had to launch into a news bulletin, previously prepared by herself.

Of course there was no teleprompter. She had been instructed either to read the bulletin, or have memorised it. So, she memorised it – the whole eight minutes. And the catch was, the news had to be fresh. She had written, learnt and repeatedly rehearsed the final bulletin only the day before, shut into her room from 9 a.m. till tea-time and in the landing bathroom late at night after Matt was asleep.

Thank God for her rep-trained memory, her RADA-trained poise. Twice she dried up and twice she got out of it so smoothly

256

that from an observer's point of view, everything went like clockwork. Then, just as she thought it was over, the totally unexpected happened. The phone on her desk rang.

She stared at it for a timeless second. Somehow she had assumed it was a prop. She picked it up, as she would have done on a stage.

'The Prime Minister,' said a voice in her ear, 'has just had an attempt made on his life. A postal bomb. No more details yet. Programmes will be interrupted.' The line went dead and so did Maggie's brain.

But it quickly revived. Was it true? She put the phone down, her face shocked. She turned back to the waiting monster-eye with its glimmering grey pupil and said, 'Some extremely grave news has just reached us. Someone has tried to kill the Prime Minister by sending him a bomb through the post.'

This sentence all but undid her. A mental picture leapt to her mind. The bomb, shaped like a Christmas pudding, gift-wrapped with just the sputtering fuse sticking out, was sitting on Harold Wilson's breakfast plate next to his fried egg. 'I wonder what this can be!' he cried gaily, reaching out . . . Her face fought to break into a shriek of laughter. That battle with difficulty won, she found she had already said the bit about programmes being interrupted and that nothing untoward had happened.

She still had a funny end-piece in front of her, and she nearly lost her head and read it – it was such a good one, she had combed yesterday's *Mirror* to find it. But before she could commit this monumental boob, the bright lights went off, a grinning face appeared above the monster, and a disembodied voice said, 'Well done! Could you come through into the control-room, please?'

It was over.

Ronnie met her outside the control-room door, his cherubic face beaming.

'Smashing,' he said. 'The editor's delighted. You looked great on screen too – marvellously photogenic, aren't you?'

Maggie blinked. 'Am I?'

'Ever done any filming?'

'Chance would've been a fine thing – no.'

'Well, it's my bet you'll be doing plenty from now on. No, I

257

shouldn't say that, it's not absolutely final, but you're certainly well ahead of the field so far, and we've only two more to see.'

'I thought Jennifer said they'd be looking for a man.'

'That's as may be. They – we – are looking for the best man for the job. And if you're it, lady, you're in.'

Tanya knocked on her door at eight o'clock that night.

'It's for you – Ronnie,' she said.

As Maggie emerged, Tanya added, with a lipstickless ghost of one of her wide clown-smiles, 'Bad news comes by letter. good news by phone.'

Maggie rushed to the phone with a sense of something like panic. Could it be true? Could her whole life be on the brink of a fantastic change for the better?

'Hallo?'

'How does it feel to be ITN's new girl reporter?'

'WOW!'

'What did I tell you? You can come in tomorrow morning to talk terms. Two months' underpaid training trial and then a year's contract. I'm not supposed to tell you this but the sum you'll be offered is £1,500 a year.' Maggie gasped. 'Well, and before you start making enquiries among your male colleagues, no, it's not what the men get, and I personally agree that's not fair, and if you put it to the editor that you've got a child to provide for, yes, he just might push it up to seventeen-fifty but *no higher* so don't press your luck, though he was very, very impressed with you. When will you come in?'

'Ten o'clock,' croaked Maggie

'Make it eleven and I'll take you to lunch at the Wig and Pen afterwards, to celebrate. You were my candidate, after all, and you've done me proud.'

Maggie turned away from the phone and found Tanya staring at her from across the room.

'You got it.'

Maggie nodded, speechless.

'Congratulations, darling, I'm so glad for you.'

'Thank you, Tanya.'

Tanya hesitated, then approached her, almost shyly.

'Let me touch you, for luck.'

She touched Maggie's hand which was still resting on the

258

telephone. Maggie turned up her hand and grasped Tanya's and held it tightly. Suddenly all the joy, all the excitement, all the triumph and relief were gone, submerged and drowning in Tanya's ruin.

In all the weeks, since the day she'd returned in disgrace, Tanya had not cried, or if she had there had been no sign nor sound of it. But now her great grey eyes overflowed with tears and she collapsed into Maggie's arms, weeping rawly and bitterly.

'Oh Maggie! Maggie! I am finished!' she sobbed.

'No, Tan, you're not. You're not. Nobody on earth is nothing but an actress, there's always an alternative. You must try. You could have had this, but I've taken it, and I know that hurts like hell, but there are other things.'

'Name one. Just one!'

Maggie wracked her brains in vain for something that would not infuriate and insult Tanya. In the end, all she could think of was Joan's words: *A woman who works is by that alone better than one who doesn't.* 'You must work at something. It doesn't matter what it is. You've got to prove to yourself that you *can* do something other than act.' A fresh outburst of sobbing interrupted her, but she held Tanya tighter and forced herself to go on, throwing tact and gentleness to the winds.

'Take over my job as a market researcher. Shush, listen. You'd do it standing on your head. Act it. I did. All jobs are partly acting if they're not natural to you. Do it for a few weeks. Keep your ears and eyes open. Once one is out on the work-beat, other things come along, openings, opportunities ... Watch the newspapers. Put the theatre right away from you.'

'I can't. I can't! It's all I am, it's all I know, it's all I want!'

'Tanya, listen to yourself. You sound like a tragedy-queen. You're saying what flatters you, what keeps you inert. What makes it pointless for you to fight, to try, to keep going. If you keep saying things like that to yourself, you really will be finished, you might as well kill yourself and have done with it.'

Tanya abruptly stopped crying and, after a moment, extricated herself from Maggie's arms. She looked a wreck, and a middle-aged wreck at that. Maggie felt shocked, partly at her own brutality. But something wilful and angry and loving in her kept her from withdrawing a word.

'How did you know I was thinking of it?' Tanya asked.

259

There was a silence. Then Maggie said, quite untruthfully, 'I just did.' In fact she had not consciously had a notion of it and the thought that Tanya had been considering such a thing shook her to the core. But she maintained a calm face and turned the admission to the advantage of her main thrust: 'That's why I'm talking like this. A drastic remedy for a drastic situation. It's kill or cure, Tanya. You've got to move away from where you are now, right in the opposite direction.' She had a fleeting memory of Aunt Helen, saying, 'Pull me up, dear, I'm sliding!' She had not been able to save Helen. And had Helen's disease, in fact, had more of a grip on her body than Tanya's had upon her psyche?

Tanya, after staring at her through that ravaged mask for another few moments, turned abruptly and walked the length of the big room and out on to the balcony, ignoring the fact that it was dark, that it was raining and that she was not wearing much. Maggie let her go, lit the gas fire and had a drink waiting for her when she returned, after a quarter of an hour, damp and shivering but with a better colour. Maggie wrapped something round her friend's shoulders and sat her in the warmth and put the scotch in her hand. She had one poured for herself and sat on the sofa with it.

'Well?' she said after they'd both had a swig.

'I decided not to throw myself off.'

'Just as well, you'd only have managed to break a leg from that height.'

'Of course, I could climb up on the roof.'

'The roof! Are you trying to kill yourself, or what?'

Tanya managed a faint snort of laughter. She put the rest of her drink away and set the tumbler on the coffee table with a little bang.

'I was acting my socks off, wasn't I? And not very well. But the awfulness of my position is not put on, Maggie.'

'Do you think I don't realise that?'

Tanya leant back in her chair and stared at Maggie.

'I am in your capable hands. What do I do first?'

'Go into your room and do something firm about your face.'

'And then?'

'Go to the bathroom and ditto-ditto your hair.'

'And *then?*'

260

'Then I'll tell you how to do market research. You'll have to start tomorrow.'

Tanya sat up, aghast. 'Tomorrow! I can't!'

'If you don't take over my work-load, you'll lose the job. You'll have to work double to make up for the last two days when I haven't done one interview. I'll come out with you tomorrow afternoon and show you the ropes and do a few with you. Maybe we'll fake a few more tomorrow evening – I've never faked, but lots of the other girls do if they don't get their quota done. Tanya, I promise it's not so bad. If I can do it, you can.'

'Maggie, will you hate and despise me if I say it is different for you?'

'Because I've never known success on the stage?' said Maggie calmly. 'Believe me, I'd swop my whole life so far, except Matt, for just one week of being you, playing leads at the Vic. You've *had* all that in both senses. Lucky you, in one way – bloody unlucky you, in another. That's it, chum, that's life. Now get off your royal arse hortillery and get on with it.'

261

Chapter Twenty-Seven

Maggie and Ronnie Makepeace went to the Cock Tavern in Fleet Street to celebrate Maggie's maiden appearance on the bulletin. It had been broadcast at 5.55 to approximately three million viewers. So when Ronnie led her into the main bar, she was faintly surprised that nobody seemed to recognise her, let alone give her a standing ovation.

Ronnie sat her in a booth and ordered them both a scotch.

'Very good little piece for starters,' he was saying for the fifth time. His cherubic face beamed at her across the checkered tablecloth. 'Editor was quite chuffed. Word came back from the crew that you were at least sufficiently professional about it to escape their scorn, and that's quite something. The cameramen all dread new reporters and think it's their task to break them in.'

'Oh? I thought they were being rather helpful.'

'Any marked eye-rolling or speaking to you very slowly as if you were half-witted?'

'No.'

'Great! Good sign, means they've taken to you. That's a big hurdle. And nearly three minutes' air-time on your first story!' He rubbed his hands gleefully. 'Maggie, you've taken off.' He grinned at her and put his warm, chubby hand over hers for a moment. 'Having lit the blue touchpaper, I've got nothing to do but stand well back from now on.' She saw a slight alteration to his expression; a sort of interrogative look came into his eyes as if he'd heard some odd sound or had a sudden, unexpected pain. She was to remember it later, that first little indicator of impending love, like the first throat-tickle heralding a fearful cold.

They got down to ordering dinner, and while waiting for it he began talking, very tentatively, about her personal situation.

262

'How are you managing about your boy? Is Tanya looking after him while you're at work?'

'Well, sort of. I don't like to impose on her, she's got her own problems. When she's going to be in, she babysits . . .'

'And the rest of the time?'

'Catch as catch can with various makeshifts,' said Maggie evasively. The truth was that when she had to, she left Matt in the flat alone with the television and left her key with a woman who lived in the basement – quite a decent sort, but old and with a gammy leg. She was not happy about it, as was proved by her unwillingness to tell Ronnie she did it. 'Anyway,' she went on hurriedly, 'it's not for long. Matt's old nurse-maid that he had in Nigeria is flying over next week, and after that they're both going up to stay with my mother.'

'Where's that?'

'Outside Edinburgh.'

Ronnie was frowning. He looked down at his potted shrimp, squeezed his lemon wedge over it, and then looked up again. The frown was still there.

'Isn't that an awful long way away?'

'Yes, of course it is, but what else can I do?'

After a few moments Ronnie said bluffly, 'There's nothing to be ashamed of in wanting to be free to work.'

'Do I sound as if it were only that?'

'How long is it since you had a job you cared about?'

'I quite cared about my teaching.'

'But you're really an actress.'

'It's been years since I had an acting job.'

'You're entitled to a career.'

'*I* think so.'

'Besides, you have to earn a living.'

'Yes, that's for sure.'

'So it's all right, then.'

'That's what I said.'

' – Except that naturally you're dead worried about what's going to happen to your relationship with Matt.'

There was a startled silence from Maggie. Then she said, 'No, I'm not. I'm worried about whether I'm doing the right thing by Matt just now, but nothing can harm my relationship with him.'

Ronnie looked at her very seriously. He didn't often look

263

serious, despite his owl-like features, but when he did – at that moment and later – Maggie was instantly put on the alert. Ronnie might be somewhat gauche, even lightweight most of the time, but he could grow quite steely when he felt sure of his ground.

'Listen, Maggie,' he said. 'I'm not married and I haven't any kids but I know this much, it's bloody rubbish, what you've just said. Surely you're not kidding yourself that just because you're someone's mother, they'll always love you and be close to you. You've got to keep working at it, steadily, or you risk losing it.'

Ronnie was ringing the bell. He rang it loud and clear, but Maggie chose not to hear him. There was no sense or truth in crying later, 'It wasn't fair, I didn't know!' And when the bills did come in, years later, she wouldn't have dared to mention the man – a total stranger – who at that moment in the conversation, walked past the booth, paused, turned, came back, and, leaning over the table, remarked, 'Didn't I see you on the box tonight? Nice story if I may say so!' – smiled pleasantly, and went on his way.

A week later, Maggie saw Matt and Tolly off at King's Cross.

She had tried to have a talk to Matt the night before, but he had been so excited about Tolly's arrival, due at ten the next morning, that he couldn't think beyond that. She had said, 'We'll see each other often, and if you ever need me – ' He had said, 'Will she be the same? Will she bring me some coconut? Did you get her a fur coat?' Maggie said, 'I'll love you every minute and you can phone me whenever you like.' Matt said, 'Which room at Granny's will she sleep in? Will I sleep in the same room with her? Can she really read now?'

They met her at the airport. She took their breath away, both of them – Matt's because she was just the same in his eyes, Maggie's because she was utterly changed. She walked differently, talked differently, met the eye differently. Joan had 'grown her up', firmed and extended her. She was strong enough to have mastered the ways of white men without losing what was essential of her self. One hour with her and Maggie knew she had done well to bring her – well from the viewpoint of her own selfish purposes. She had come a very long way from the

264

shy, half-wild girl who had struggled to save her babies in the forests of Nigeria.

But she was nowhere near sophisticated enough to resist the delights of London, especially culinary ones. Maggie had arranged a meal in Fortnum's restaurant which climaxed with a Knickerbocker Glory apiece. Tolly was so excited, so beset by newness, that she glowed, and wrung her hands so much that Maggie had to keep disengaging one to clasp it round the long spoon and guide its probings through the rainbow layers of exotic sweetness.

'I'm so happy! I'm so happy!' Tolly kept saying.

'You used to say, "Tolly so happy",' said Matt, teasing. He, too, was glowing.

'Mrs Joan teached me not to talk so pidgin,' Tolly said proudly.

She leant over again and again to kiss Matt, until he told her strongly to stop it. Then she turned to Maggie.

'You didn't forget me,' she said, her eyes brimming with tears. 'I always think, soon you forget, but you remember.'

She had brought them presents. There was even a gift from some of Maggie's old pupils, two little wooden candle-holders. She brought love and a letter from Joan. Joan, too, was a bell. Her letter read, in part, 'Now don't you let Tolly take Matt over from you altogether. She will, you know, given half a chance.' But Maggie only glanced once at this letter, in Fortnum's ladies' room, and promptly lost it. The bell was deafening her as it was; she needed no amplifier.

They went to an early matinée of a children's film, which Tolly adored, and then by taxi to the station.

At King's Cross, Maggie was suddenly faced with the separation as an actuality. Half-way to the buffet for sandwiches, chocolate bars and apples, she stopped cold. The concrete under her feet struck a deathly chill up her legs as if she were barefoot; the gloomy brickwork and the smell of diesel oil and beer filled her eyes and nose with desolation. *What am I doing?* she asked herself. *I'm sending him away. I won't see him again for weeks. I won't see him ever again as he is at this moment. He will change and I won't know him. I'll recognise him but I won't know him. I must be mad. All this so that I can cover fashion-shows and interview dozens of nine-day-wonders on the box?*

But a voice inside answered her firmly. *No. You're doing it to*

265

be free, to make up for your lost life, for the satisfaction of independence. To give yourself a person and a story you can look back on when you're old. When Matt has grown up it will be too late for you. You have to do it now. He won't suffer for it – look at him, he's in love! And you're not and you never have been and soon you'll be thirty.

It was Margaret. Incredibly, for once, Margaret gave her, not the advice of the puritan conscience she bore like a burr embedded in her flesh, but the advice of clamouring egoistic selfhood that she wanted to hear. Their roles were reversed; it was Margaret's turn to be afraid of the future. So, ironically, while Maggie was listening to the warning bell, it was Goody Two Shoes Margaret who muffled its clapper.

Maggie got to the buffet, bought the provisions, added magazines and pencils and jotters, and rushed back to Tolly and Matt, who were already climbing into the Edinburgh express. Tolly, enchanted by all she saw, was running her hand over the moquette seats and admiring the other occupants of the carriage openly. Matt was suddenly silent. The facts of the situation were not so clear to him as to Maggie, but he too had been hit by the impending parting.

Maggie sat by him and resisted the temptation to take his hand.

'Matt – ' she began.

He turned to her with abrupt determination.

'I want to be called Matthew,' he said. He pushed his voice out so hard that it shrilled, and he flushed under his freckles.

Maggie was dismayed. 'Why, darling? We've always called you Matt.'

'I don't like it. It sounds like a doormat. It sounds like what the cat sat on.' She tried to laugh but stopped – he was utterly serious. 'It's babyish,' he finished.

She looked at his small red head outlined against the moving platform bustle through the train window. He was turned in profile to her and she saw that there was nothing babyish left about him, even the tears he was holding back; he was all boy now and had inherited his parents' strong will to fight for all the wrong things.

'All right,' she said. 'When I write my first letter to you tonight, I'll begin it, "Darling Matthew".'

'And Tolly mustn't call me Matty.'

'That's between you and her.'

It was time. She gave him the permitted goodbye kiss and suddenly he flung his arms round her and she thought, *It's wrong. I can't. This is what matters – I don't matter except to him.* But it was too late. The train was about to start. The pre-programming took effect. She hugged Tolly, scrambled off the train and stood, with the noisy door-slams up and down its length crashing in her head with the finality of little deaths.

PART FOUR

Chapter Twenty-Eight

Tanya flopped at market research. She hated the part too much to play it well. All she succeeded in doing, in the few weeks she kept at it, was to prove her original contention that in hard times, aristocrats can more easily move into the gatekeeper's lodge and breed cocker spaniels than leave their manor altogether and take up factory work in the city.

So, first, she married Oliver, and threw herself into the role of appendage to a successful actor. Hopeless, of course; her ego wilted and she saw more disaster up ahead if she did not take urgent action. So, next, she had a baby, and tried to be satisfied with sublimation.

The baby, Imogen, was an excellent child in every way who would have afforded full satisfaction to her mother if anyone could. But as Tanya confessed to Maggie, 'She's not a human being yet. I love her and she occupies me, but it is no substitute for acting, only an excuse for not. An excuse which is wearing thin now she is weaned-thanks-God ... And you, Maggie,' she added severely, 'you are not helping me. Having you in my old flat living a life of bells, balls, balloons and tinsel in something suspiciously like the limelight is driving me to desperation.'

Oliver's play in the West End ran and ran and he became somewhat famous. *His* little lapse in Birmingham was forgotten. Tanya's was not, and it looked as if it never would be. One night Tanya was in the Buckstone Club behind the Haymarket, having a drink by herself at the tiny bar while waiting for Oliver. It was one of her exercises in self-torture. All the members of the club were theatre people and the atmosphere was pure theatre. It was akin to a starving pauper sitting in a hotel grill-room watching people eat and smelling the rich food. Some old friends spoke to her and other old friends avoided doing so

271

But one perfect stranger who had drunk too much lurched against her and said, 'Oops! Sorry, darling. Well! – if it isn't Little Miss Blacklist herself! What are you doing in here? *You're* not in the business any more.'

When Tanya recovered herself she was out in the street, running, with some recollection of red wine pouring down a puffy white face and a sense of a wild release of energy.

That night she didn't go to her own home in Oliver's flat, but went to Maggie's flat which had once been hers. She drank scotch and wept and raged and drank coffee and calmed down and then drank more scotch and wept and raged some more. Maggie was dumbfounded and appalled, and yet, oddly, relieved. This was Tanya, the real, disabused, fighting Tanya. In the early morning she thanked Maggie, had a bath and went home. And from there she swung into action.

She began gathering around herself a group of actors she had known since RADA, whose talents she had registered in her efficient personal filing system. With them she formed an ad hoc commonwealth company. It mounted economical productions of small-cast plays with good parts in them for Tanya. There was no way she could get legitimate theatrical dates, but there were plenty of venues which could be booked for a few nights. She got Oliver, who was in the money, to buy her an old reconditioned motor-caravan, painted the name of her company – 'TANTOURS' – on its sides, and drove her troupe around the Home Counties often with Imogen in her carrycot in the crowded body of the van amid the wicker costume skips and makeshift scenery. They shared the take, dossed down wherever they found themselves, and worked like slaves.

Things were very tough for the first two years. Equity did its best to delegitimise the company completely and there were professional risks involved in being a member of it; but though there was a lot of fluidity, some of the originals stuck as a nucleus. The standard was quite high to start with and improved steadily. They began to get bookings in fringe theatres around London and to be offered new plays by aspiring young writers. One of these, in their third year, transferred, although without Tanya.

But Tanya's name was no longer mud with the theatrical establishment. The unofficial ban on her company was quietly

272

dropped, and it was bruited in the Equity Council that she herself might be re-embraced into membership if she played her cards right.

When she got wind of this, she let it be known that the Equity Council could get stuffed.

Oliver was horrified, and not only because he rather saw himself *on* the Equity Council some day; he badly wanted Tanya to come in out of the cold because until she did, he foresaw that he would stand precious little chance of a normal home-life. Oliver was not a self-sufficient being. Maggie sometimes suspected that he might not have married Tanya had he not had good reason to suppose that her career as an actress was at an end, freeing her for a new one as adoring helpmate. Perhaps, by the same token, Tanya would not have married Oliver, had she realised that her need of a port was only to be temporary, until she had navigated herself clear of the storm. At least, so Maggie privately thought. She had no confirmation. Tanya was not as free with her confidences as she had been when she was single.

Television news reporting is a glamorous, well-paid and presti-gious occupation, excellent for the ego and the appearance. Over the next six years, it made a new woman of Maggie. She left behind her careless, rural ways and became crisp and smart She exuded an air of self-confidence, even of sophistication All obvious traces of the old naivety, the undermining guilts and self-doubts, had vanished.

In her thirst for the deeper satisfactions, she sucked her situation dry. She convinced herself that she had reached a level of fame and status higher than anything she could have achieved as an actress. After all, she was at the hub of affairs, or at least the reporting of them. What comparison could there be between arousing phantom emotions in audiences of hun-dreds, and imparting solid, vital information to millions? She even assured herself that in her small way she was helping to mark the beat of history.

With all this ego-boosting, it was easy to ignore the all-obliterating drawback of her metier and her medium, the fact that it was all entirely ephemeral.

Theatre at its best can leave a mark on the memory which

273

is indelible. Television news – however dramatic or brilliantly presented – leaves no mark whatsoever. It flicks past the eyes and is irretrievably, almost instantaneously, lost.

During her time at ITN, Maggie did many interesting, and even some seemingly significant, things. She forged her way intrepidly through crowds of angry strikers, set the scene at disasters, delivered hard-hitting questions to politicians, trade unionists and princes of industry, and more ingratiating ones to film stars, authors and ballerinas. She conducted innumerable fearless *vox populi* interviews on burning (or lukewarm) topics of the hour. She even – her greatest coup – waylaid, outside the Mother of Parliaments, a certain Mighty Russian visitor, whom no other reporter, male or female, had got anywhere near.

What it all added up to, actually, as she was soon to realise, was no more than a damned good job which afforded her a lot of fun and kudos. As to doing any ultimate good, or earning an honourable place in anyone's memory or in any annals whatever, she would have done better to tour in an underpaid, understaffed theatre company playing village halls and schools before audiences which would not otherwise see any live entertainment. That was what Tanya did. And whatever Tanya lacked, then or later, it was not job satisfaction.

As to Maggie's love-life, that, too, was on a superficial level. Since Tolly's arrival, Maggie had been, to all intents and purposes, a single, unencumbered woman. Tanya's flat, which Maggie had taken over, was a suitable background, and she made the most of it, entertaining quite extensively. Her new status and neo-sophisticated exterior inevitably attracted men of all sorts, some of whom were quite interesting and some quite attractive. Occasionally Maggie encountered one who was both, and when that happened she felt duty-bound to embark on an affair. After all, this was the swinging sixties. She could scarcely eschew sex totally for fear of seeming, even in her own eyes, a freak.

But it took more than the pressures of the permissive era to convince Maggie that she was actually in love with anyone for longer than a few weeks. Margaret, tense and wary, stubbornly refused to swing. Every time Maggie let a man make love to

274

her, Margaret curled herself up tight, muttering grimly, 'This is *all wrong*. How *can* you? No, really! Well, don't expect *me* to respond.'

To compensate, Maggie put on a tremendous act of glossy worldliness. So convincing was this act that it got her into quite a few tight corners; but after a while she developed a means of categorising men, which saved her from the grosser encounters and blunders.

Her method evolved from a chart-thing that she'd filled out during her market research days, aimed at giving her 'instant perception of motivating factors'. Briefly, it assigned colours to people's characters. She had always thought of Tanya as red; she was intrigued to discover that the makers of the chart agreed with her. Red women, then, were all right from Maggie's point of view; but she learned to avoid red men like the plague. Red men were domineering, flamboyant, go-getting, macho. Like Bruce. They scared the wits out of her, not least for the insecurity often lurking pinkly beneath the red surface. Maggie preferred green men.

Green men were quiet, self-sufficient, intelligent, analytical; often shy; usually gentle. They needed bringing out. The trouble was, when she had brought them out she usually wanted to put them back in again, because brought-out green men can be very hard to control.

Blue men, she realised ruefully, were the ones she ought to aim for. Ronnie, for instance, was very blue. He was neither aggressive nor withdrawn. He was the caring kind, outgoing, never really happy unless he was doing something for somebody. Kind and generous to a fault, he could not credit that anyone could be less so, which meant that if Maggie was impatient or ill-tempered he could not just let it roll off him, but was profoundly hurt. Ronnie became a problem.

At first he was content to look after her within the company. He virtually nursed her through her first year at ITN, steering her past the dangerous shallows of cameramen's temperaments, news-editors' callousness, fellow-reporters' suspicions and jealousies, subs' cattiness and newscasters' rapier wit. He covered up for her initial ignorance or occasional blunders, took her part in editorial meetings, and when she was ready to handle them, pushed some serious stories her way to build her reputation. In short, he was her staunch friend, and she was touched

275

and grateful. But when he began to show signs of a different kind of caring, she had to control the urge to flee.

Not that it was possible to flee far. She saw him nearly every day at the office. By the time their 'affair' (which wasn't one) became the gossip of newsroom and viewing theatre, Maggie was already an entrenched feature of the ITN scene, onscreen and off, and people who had taken the trouble to get to know her at all well shook their heads over Ronnie's misplaced passion.

'Hasn't a hope, poor bugger,' was the general opinion. 'Just not Maggie's type.'

It ended in Ronnie leaving ITN and moving sideways into television drama. This unfortunately meant that for much of the time he was still working in the same large building as Maggie; for months after his removal from ITN he seemed to go out of his way to bump into her in lifts and foyers. His round face would always light up, his mouth stretching into a happy and forgiving grin. These encounters upset and irritated Maggie terribly. The truth was, she longed only to be shot of Ronnie and his doting love. She knew she didn't merit him, and was almost maddened by her inability to love him even a little. The sight of him stirred deep unfaced fears in her heart.

Was she never going to fall into the pit, as Tanya had called it? Had it been writhing with snakes – as, to watch others struggling in the devastating toils of love, she realised it probably was – she would still have longed with all her being to jump down there, where Margaret would be crushed to speechlessness by some emotional boa-constrictor and where Maggie could, not despite but because of her sufferings, emerge from her heart-frozen isolation and join the human race – or even the animal kingdom.

Sometimes she tried to convince herself that she was lucky to be above the scrum; but this was like a deaf person trying to feel lucky because he is spared all ugly or distressing noises. Maggie felt, knew, herself to be subnormal, emotionally retarded, physically deprived. Sometimes she would lie in bed, after some profoundly unsatisfying sexual encounter, and while her satiated partner snored at her side try to trace this unfillable emptiness in her loins to its source. Was it Bruce? Was it her father? Or was it just some ineffable, basic coldness in herself?

Ronnie's eventual departure for the BBC relieved only the surface anguish of these gnawing doubts. But in any case they

276

were nothing to the doubts which, as the years went by, increasingly and excludingly plagued her about her son.

Matt was by now a stocky, well-built Scot of fourteen. He had turned out to be a sensible and pragmatic child, who had adapted admirably to the various twists and changes in his fortunes. He managed to enjoy himself tolerably wherever he happened to be – in his grandmother's home, his base, as solid with love and routine as with old, weathered stone; at school, where, though no one could have called him a brilliant scholar, he had loads of friends and could always shine at sports; in his mother's London flat, where he could have a healthy wallow in treats and hedonism from time to time; and at his uncle's. Not his Uncle Steven, oddly enough – his Uncle Ian.

Ian was now smoothly bald, but otherwise little changed to look at. Inwardly, however, he was a very different man. And this deep modification was due in large part to his once-despised nephew, a turn-up for the books which had caused quite some subterranean bother in the family.

Lilian resented Matt. She felt, not without cause, that Ian favoured him over their own child. Anthea Charity, now a tubby six-year-old, regarded Matt as a god. Matt, naturally, had no time for her, which fuelled Lilian's dislike. Her feelings toward Maggie, who had dumped this little cuckoo, if not right into, at least adjacent to her nest, were less than sisterly. She was quite incapable of watching her on television without giving vent to some spiteful remark, which in turn irritated Ian, who was secretly rather proud of Maggie's renown.

Stip was also upset by Matt's orientation toward Ian. Before the boy had come back to Scotland, Stip had cast himself firmly in the role of favourite uncle, but it hadn't worked out that way.

Matt, to tell the truth, found Stip at close quarters strangely off-putting. His increasingly colourful clothes, language and manner created deep embarrassment in Matt, made him squirm somehow. Stip liked Matt to come to his house to visit him, and Matt hated Stip's house. He hated all the bright colours and exotic touches. He once told Maggie that it was like being shut into the parrot house at the zoo. Considering that Matt had been surrounded by vivid colours and people all his life, it was surprising that Stip's brand of extravagance grated when

277

Tanya's, for example, didn't. But it was different with Tanya. Matt could only explain it to Maggie by saying, 'Well, but she's a woman'. Had he met Stip in London he might not have reacted against him; in a small town outside Edinburgh, a come-lately exotic like Stip did not fit.

Ian, on the other hand, did. He fitted perfectly. In his three-piece suits, with his rather strict old-fashioned manner and his conventional household, Ian fulfilled some deep longing in Matt for order and solemnity which he had probably been born with and never had a chance to fulfil.

His own home with his grandmother and Tolly was a strange mixture of cultures and influences. His grandmother satisfied his notion of what grandmothers ought to be. She, too, fitted. Tolly was something else. She didn't fit at all, she never really tried to, and nothing could have been more exotic and extraordi-nary than a beautiful black girl in those surroundings. If the neighbours turned to glance at Stip in his espadrilles and his yellow linen suits, how much more did they gawk at Tolly, who, when she first came and for some time thereafter, was the only black person for miles. But in Matt's eyes Tolly was beloved beyond criticism, all the more because for so long he had lost her and then, miraculously, had her restored to him, in a new setting but in herself unaltered, immutable, like gold. Like gold she had lain buried for an aeon of his short existence, and been rediscovered as bright as if new-minted.

Mrs Robertson had taken one look at Tolly in the flesh and realised two things simultaneously. One was that she was going to love her like a daughter, and the other was that to put her into any kind of maid's uniform, as she had vaguely planned, would be a travesty. She knew from the photographs that Tolly had submitted to a type of servant's dress in Port Harcourt, but here in Scotland she must be as she was born to be, African.

But Tolly had brought only the subdued quasi-European clothes she had had to wear until now, and certainly nothing more ethnic was available in Edinburgh at that time. Stip came to the rescue. He returned from his next trip to London with great swathes of Liberty prints in silk and cotton and fine wool. With these he draped Tolly, pinning and tucking as if she were a suite to be upholstered or a rather complicated window to create exquisite curtains for. Soon she was delighting the eye of all beholders – all unbiased ones, anyway.

278

And if these did not include Ian and Lilian, Tolly remained happily unaware of it.

By one of life's odd twists, the unhappiness, the disorientation Joan and Stip had foreseen for her, caused by the beastly climate, the measureless gulf between this life and the one she'd been born to, scarcely touched her. The long flight which she'd endured in silent, stoic terror was to her a sort of magic carpet ride to another planet. To find, when she got there, that not only could she still breathe and move normally, but that the inhabitants of this strange alien world were not odd-shaped and hostile but familiar and gentle and funny, was enough for her at first. And hard on this relieving discovery came wonders. Great buildings and shops and films and delicious confections, huge lumbering buses, a swift, exciting train (no real travel-fears could affect her after the agony of being suspended far above the ground).

And Matt. Her child in all but the flesh. The miracle of seeing him again, being given him to care for . . . She would have lived in an igloo menaced by howling demons for that privilege, that bliss.

Besides, she knew that what she had left behind was – despite all Joan's efforts to integrate her and give her purpose and a wider horizon – the eternal status of an outcast. Here on her new planet she still had no tribe, no people of her very own; but not only did this represent no actual change in her fundamental condition, it was less gnawingly painful to her than to see her own constantly around her but to know herself forever cut off from them.

All this would have been enough. But there was more. Her new family was extremely good to her.

Mrs Robinson, settling delightedly into a new life-style based upon cossetting, was increasingly her own woman, indifferent, or at least indulgent, towards Ian's prejudices. (This in itself was a secret source of pleasure to her. He was so like his father! – and she had never been allowed to distance herself from *his* bigotries.)

In a way, perhaps, her adoption of Tolly and her refusal to modify her or force her into any kind of conventional mould was a gesture of independence toward her own, and indeed her clan's history, and it was one she enjoyed so much that she could not maintain a shadow of disapproval for Maggie, who

279

was the author of this new chapter in her life's story, which she had been sure was – in terms of change – ended. Of course she knew, and if she hadn't Lilian would constantly have reminded her, that Maggie was being selfish and unmaternal. But she didn't care. She adored Matt in a way she had never adored either of her own sons; after a few months of having him in her home, she could no longer imagine it without him. Ian's constant solicitations during the first months about 'how she was managing' and 'whether it wasn't all too much for her', she turned off with increasing vehemence.

'He is not the slightest trouble in the world,' she kept saying, and when the enquiries were irksomely repeated she lost her temper at last and said tartly, 'I wish you and Lilian would stop implying that I am making some heroic sacrifice in having Matt. I will begin to think your own child is not making you happy if you go on behaving as if children are such a monstrous burden.'

Perhaps this was part of what caused Ian to look with new eyes at Matt. For the truth was that Anthea Charity, as she emerged from babyhood, was not proving the unmixed blessing, or affording her parents the unblemished reflection of themselves, that they had naively anticipated. She was actually quite a handful, combining all the less endearing wiles of femininity with an iron stubbornness which could drive her father into a fury. It was on the day when he actually heard himself shout at her – she was barely four years old at the time – 'We should have chosen another wee girl, I can see, and left you where we found you!' that Ian realised he had never really known himself or what cruelty he was capable of.

The awful remorse he felt after this episode led to a whole reassessment. He had been so certain of himself all his life, so sure he knew what was right and could do it at all costs, so confident in advance that he would be a better parent than those he saw around him, and than Maggie in particular.

Now, in his shame at having allowed himself to be so savagely cruel to Anthea (not that she had been noticeably affected) he was further tormented by memories of the open contempt he'd shown over the years for Maggie. One episode in particular returned to sting him – the occasion when Matt had pulled the tablecloth. In daily contact with the ineluctable realities of infant villainy – the pulling of the odd tablecloth was as naught to some of the devilments Anthea got up to – his native honesty

280

showed him up as having been a prig, and an uncharitable prig at that.

He couldn't make it up to Maggie. Even if she had been around, that would have been asking too much of him – his relations with her were long ago fixed and to unfix them now would have meant humbling himself, even in his own eyes, more than he could bear. But he could salve his conscience in another way. He could withdraw his personal doom of excommunication from Matt, forget the near-shame of his birth, the true shame of his parents' divorce, and his semi-orphaned status in Scotland. He could start treating the boy as a human being and, incidentally, as his own close kin.

The moment he began to do this, he found in Matt, if not a kindred spirit, at least a personality he could easily respond to, and in his own way, in due course, grow very fond of. He liked Matt's unmistakable maleness, his affinity for boys' toys and boys' concerns. He approved of his love for games and especially running. But it was when he took him down to the family mill and showed him over it that Matt, all unwittingly, forged a true bond with his uncle.

Ian was oddly moved by Matt's immediate interest in the great pulp-vats and rollers and drying rooms, his sensible questions about how the watermark got into the paper and where the raw materials came from. The paper trade was falling off sadly at the time; there was a huge drop in demand, especially for quality paper, and with lumber climbing steeply in price Ian was going through a period of intense anxiety about how to maintain the family concern – not just at its former level, but at all. It was a terrible thing for him to contemplate – the possibility that, of the several generations of Robertsons who had owned and steered the mill through many vicissitudes, *he* should be the one at the helm when it foundered.

The eagerness of this boy, the nearest thing to a male heir he would ever have, raised his spirits. He took him down to the mill often, made him familiar with it, let him play there. He introduced him to his staff and workers as 'my young nephew Matthew'. These visits had a fundamental effect on Ian which for years he never confided to anyone. For some time before they began, he had been angered and dismayed to find that every time he approached the mill, or looked down on it from the road above its riverside position in a fold of the hills

281

as he had done since childhood, his imagination – which had certainly never caused him any problems before – showed him the building stark and empty, its windows out, its chimneys cold, the pointing on its brickwork crumbling ... deserted, in fact, like so many other mills of various kinds whose dead hulks littered riversides all over Scotland and the North.

But for some reason Matt's advent and interest, his small sturdy figure meandering about the place, chatting curiously, drawing on the scrap, gazing at the machinery as if willing it to go on working, heartened Ian. From then on, the unpleasant dreamlike affliction he had experienced looking down on his mill no longer troubled him. He was able to recover his normal phlegmatic and pragmatic approach to his difficulties, and though these grew worse, not easier, the future had become a matter for practical endeavour, not a waking nightmare. He was working now to keep the enterprise going, not just for his own pride and the family's, but for a solid, practical reason of the sort he was well constituted to act on. He had decided to hand it on to Matthew.

He said nothing about this intention. Although with some unease of conscience, he didn't even tell Lilian. He just quietly altered his Will. He left Anthea well provided for, but he bequeathed the business to Matt.

And having done so, it became necessary to interest himself in the boy's education. While Maggie's back was turned (which of course it usually was) Ian took Matt up in the car to the Open Day of Glencora, Bruce's old school in the Highlands, and successfully sold him on the place, lock, stock and playing fields.

Mrs Robertson was furious, and in her new mood of independence none of her customary inhibitions restrained her.

'How precisely like you, Ian! A typical piece of Robertsonian high-handedness. And under-handedness as well, which is less typical.'

'I thought the boy should have a chance to make up his own mind about the possibilities. After all, it was his father's wish –'

'Don't add sententiousness to your faults! His father's wish, indeed! What value have the wishes of an absconder? Besides, what is weighing with you is not his wishes but his money, and don't tell me *that* hadn't come into your considerations!'

'In fairness, Mother, I would have contributed if it had been

282

necessary. I was willing to show him other good schools if he had hated this one, but he didn't.'

'You saw to that!'

'The school itself saw to it. It's a marvellous place. Any boy would think himself fortunate –'

'Especially if he had an uncle at his elbow, brainwashing him!'

'I'll not deny I wanted him to take to it, but I'd very little persuading to do, I promise you.'

'Why didn't you ask me first? Why didn't you ask Maggie? You know she hates the idea of him incarcerated in that dreadful place!'

'It's not a dreadful place at all, Mother. I'll take you up there to see for yourself. And Maggie too, of course, in the unlikely event of her being able to spare the time,' he added, with more than a glint of his old edge.

When her mother's SOS reached her, Maggie was in the throes of preparations for her first trip abroad for ITN

She had been manoeuvring for it for months. Her male colleagues seemed to go abroad constantly, and not just to war zones – Maggie hardly aspired to be a war correspondent, her news editor was reluctant to send her out even on industrial stories if there was a male reporter available. But when it came to a film-star wedding in a minor but charismatic sheikdom, she felt her moment had come.

The male reporters, despite their Pavlovian sneers about the wedding, were jockeying for the assignment, which promised all the hedonistic delights reporters love to hate. Battle was joined. In those pre-Lib days a woman worth the name instinctively knew how to balance her disadvantages by turning on the charm. Maggie shamelessly wheedled the news editor, snoozled up to the head producer and boldly bearded the editor in his lair. To the undisguised disgust of her male colleagues, these tactics triumphed. She got the story.

Filled with glee and anticipation, Maggie rushed out to shop and organise her journey and have her shots. She booked a hair appointment and then rang her friends with the news. One of the foremost of these was a man called Derek, a film publicity director who was doing his best to get her into bed, so far

283

without success, chiefly because he was too 'red' (or rather, reddish-blue, sort of mauve in fact). But that didn't mean she didn't like him and was not quite pleased by the prospect, which he promptly offered her, of an evening out to celebrate.

It was when she was going to have her bath that she found the morning's letters, jammed into her dressing-gown pocket earlier and forgotten because she had slept in and been racing to get ready for work. She sat on the loo-seat while her bath ran and opened the one from her mother.

As she read it, she stiffened, and rose slowly to her feet. So it had come to this! – Ian had dared, behind her back, behind their mother's back, to coerce Matthew into opting for Bruce's bloody school!

'Ian has been in touch with the solicitors,' Mrs Robertson had written, 'about the trust, and there seems to be no impediment there – they are in touch with your ex-husband [she never referred to Bruce by name] and he has written to the trustees, to Ian and to the school, from some address in Minnesota. He is in full agreement with Ian's plan. Darling, I don't want to worry you, I know how busy your life is, but frankly I am afraid ... I seem to have lost control of things ... my nightmare is that the doorbell will ring and I will go out to find *him*, come back from America to take my darling Matty away. If not him, then Ian will do it. It is as if they were in league to rob us, you and me. I don't want him to leave home and go to that horrible, spartan place. Do you? If not, please, my dearest, come and try to stop it.'

Maggie looked up from the letter and the steamy old-fashioned bathroom was jittering before her eyes. She was to leave for the Gulf in three days, for two of which she was on duty. Perhaps she could arrange a swop? Pulling the plug on her bath, she threw on some clothes and drove down to the office.

Mac, her male-chauvinist news editor, was in the thick of preparation for the evening bulletin, but he accorded her a short, sharp two minutes.

'Listen, Mags,' he said before she could pass the half-way mark in her appeal, 'this is not some pissy office where you can drop off the roster for a week and no one will notice. It's a news organisation. I wish I could say I cared a bugger for your sob story but I don't, I haven't time or energy. You're on duty

284

tomorrow and Saturday and if you don't show, no one'll make allowances. You scraped home for the wedding story by a whisker. This is not the time to put yourself in wrong with the editor, or with me either.' He spent several moments irritably shifting papers about his desk, while Maggie, who knew him of old, stood waiting, and then he snapped, 'Look. I'll pull Wally in tomorrow for the demo at Dagenham, he'll do it better than you anyway, and I'll scrub the auction story. That's all you were down for. Of course if anything urgent comes up I'll be in the shit and you'll be right beside me.' He submitted to Maggie's hug with apparent impatience, patted her bottom affectionately, and told her to piss off.

Maggie rushed home, threw some things into a case and took a taxi to Kings Cross. She forgot all about poor Derek.

Chapter Twenty-Nine

Sitting in her first-class compartment, watching the country-side flash past, Maggie steadily – almost deliberately – worked herself up into a fury of indignation against Ian.

How dared he! How dared that toffee-nosed, canting prig, who had done his level best to put her down all her life, try to take over her son! It almost passed belief. It was as if Ian felt himself *in loco parentis*. She'd noticed signs of it when she'd been up on visits; she had noticed, with narrowed eyes, Matt's increasing mention of Ian and the mill during his stays with her in Town. Their obvious and deepening affinity baffled her, she disapproved instinctively, but under prevailing circumstances there was little she could do. In fact Margaret tersely hinted that she should be grateful. In all honesty she could no longer hide from herself the fact that Stip was not well cast in the rôle of surrogate father. But she didn't fancy Ian in the part either, she never had, and if he was going to assume parental rights, she was not going to stand for it.

As she stepped out of the taxi at the front door of her old home, she looked every inch the successful career woman, as smart, if not flamboyant, as ever Tanya had. Well-coiffed, high-heeled, immaculately suited and with her war-paint refreshed in the back of the taxi, she marched up the swaybacked stone steps, with strong-principled purpose and the full anticipation of moral victory in every line of her. The contrast to a previous occasion, when bedraggled and guilt-ridden she had dragged her scuffed suitcase up the steps after a night of terror on the train, flashed across her memory and lifted her head a fraction higher. She was her own woman now, self-made, confident and free. She could cope with brother Ian with one hand tied behind her. That was her honest opinion, and Margaret didn't contradict her. The long, commanding ring she gave the brass-

286

rimmed doorbell sounded nowhere but inside the house. Yet again, she ignored the one that was jangling in her head, struggling to warn her.

Tolly answered the door. Her face lit up and she threw her arms round Maggie.

'How good you've come! Madam will be so happy!'

Maggie of course was no longer 'Madam' to Tolly; that prime courtesy was reserved for Mrs Robertson. She hardly knew what to call Maggie. She called her 'Mummy' in front of Matt and 'you' to her face. Their relationship was a little strained nowadays. If Tolly allowed herself to disapprove of Maggie in her secret soul, it was not something either of them was prepared to acknowledge.

'Where's Matthew?'

'Of course at school.'

'Ah, yes. Of course.'

'Madam is in the garden. You go, I bring tea.'

'Coffee for me, please, Tolly.'

'Madam doesn't like coffee only after dinner.'

She said it with great firmness, and then turned and walked away, carrying Maggie's overnight bag. Maggie watched her go, her beautiful graceful hips swaying unselfconsciously in their bright folds of cloth. She wanted to call after her plaintively, 'Couldn't *I* have a cup of coffee?' but somehow she didn't. It was extraordinary that this tiny incident should have made the first small hole in her full-bellied sail of self-righteousness. She almost felt the wind leaking out of it, though she couldn't yet begin to understand why.

She walked through the quiet house, through the kitchen and into the back garden. It was looking its best, full of all the spring flowers which were over in London, especially the parrot tulips, always her father's pride and now a self-renewing memorial to him. Her mother was moving about the paths with a pair of scissors, dead-heading the narcissus and daffodils. Maggie stood watching her. She had taken on a new lease of life. Her figure looked more pliant, her hair was more softly arranged; she no longer wore the dark dresses she had always favoured, but paler ones, as if to match the decor of her house, or perhaps her changed life . . . Today she wore a very pretty pale lavender skirt and matching blouse, with its sleeves casually turned back on her forearms. From a short distance one couldn't see their

287

wrinkles. Her feet were bare and thrust into mules . . . Maggie couldn't remember ever seeing her mother outdoors without stockings. It gave her a strange turn to see her looking so youthful. It made one think of Sarah in the Bible. The miraculous gift of a latecoming child . . . Was it really Matthew, Maggie's son, who had achieved this? If so, in adding so much to his grandmother, what must inevitably have been subtracted from his mother . . .?

'Mummy.'

Mary Robertson looked round, unstartled. She must have been half expecting Maggie's arrival. In her face Maggie could see that all was not well with her; the anxiety in her letter was repeated in her eyes and around her mouth.

'Darling! You came! How good of you . . .'

They embraced. Maggie smelt the light scent in her mother's hair.

'It's not good of me at all. You smell lovely, Mummy.'

'Well, when one has a child around, one has to be careful. I read the most awful article in a magazine about how old people often smell. It was actually called "Stinking Grannies". Can you credit it? It upset me so much, I started having two baths a day and dousing myself with perfume until Steven told me I smelt like a – well, that's quite enough of that! You must be tired, darling. Do you want to sit indoors?'

'No, out here. It's looking so beautiful.'

'Tolly does it, all but mowing the lawn, Matthew does that. What a feeling she has for flowers! And just look at Dad's tulips, they get better every year . . .'

They walked round and round the little garden, arm in arm, and spoke of unimportant things until Tolly had brought out the tea and arranged it on the garden table. She had brought a cardigan for Mrs Robertson, and when she put it round her shoulders Mrs Robertson caressed her hand fondly, calling her a dear thoughtful creature.

'Why only two cups, Tolly, aren't you having tea with us?'

'No, Madam, I go to the shops. Something special for dinner.' She beamed at Maggie, who suddenly felt better, though why she needed to she wasn't sure.

When Tolly had gone in, Mrs Robertson poured tea and said, 'Now we must get down to business. Matty will be home

288

soon, it's his weight-training day or he'd be home by now. What do you intend to do?'

'Do? I shall simply tell Ian that I don't want Matt to go to Glencora. That'll be the end of that.'

Mrs Robertson handed her her tea without speaking.

'Won't it?' asked Maggie.

'I don't know, dear, I'm sure.'

'What do you mean?'

'Just that Ian is behaving as if the whole matter were settled. And so is Matty.'

'Well, it isn't. It can't be, when I don't approve, and you don't.'

'*My* disapproval – very freely expressed, I may say – has made precious little mark on the situation so far. Of course, I'm old. I'm also a woman. And as I've spent my life finding out, this is not a country or a society where the views of the female sex are taken much into account.'

'That's absolute nonsense, Mummy. You must remember that I got custody. My sex is immaterial – the last word is mine.'

'I only hope you're right, darling, that's all,' said Mrs Robertson. But she didn't sound hopeful, and Maggie was soon to learn why.

Matthew came bounding out a few minutes later. He had grown yet again since Maggie had seen him during the Easter holidays, or so it seemed – perhaps it was the effect of a new blazer bought prudently a size too big. With his long trousers and his long hair he looked – as he had looked, every time she had re-encountered him since the day she had parted from him six years before – strikingly new, familiar yet different, making an impact on her eyes and heart which thrilled her afresh each time. Only part of the thrill was pride. The other part was disquiet amounting to fear, but that part she ignored.

'Hallo, my darling!'

'Mum! Hey, wow, when did you blow in? I like your dress.'

'First give us a kiss.'

He kissed her, then turned and kissed his grandmother so she wouldn't feel left out.

'Did you come by train? Was it the diesel express, the new one? I read they go at ninety or something. Gran, guess what, I did it! Fifty pounds!'

289

'Darling! Not over your head? You shouldn't, you'll strain yourself –'

'Oh, don't worry, we're supervised, they don't let us lift anything over our heads at our age . . . But I did the fifty up to my shoulders, watch – Ugghhhh – ' Flinging off the blazer and flexing his muscles he did a passable mime of a mighty weight-lifter hoisting a huge laden bar to shoulder height. He bared his teeth and grunted and all but sweated with the strain. He even managed a realistic stagger or two before he 'dropped' it on his toe. Then he danced about clutching his foot and howling. Both women roared with laughter at this comic performance. Good God, he's an actor! thought Maggie. It was the first time she had seen signs of it – his weight-lifting triumph must have unbuttoned him. She felt a surge of maternal excitement. A new facet, a new development! And yet the pleasure was vitiated because it had happened behind her back. No, that wasn't what she meant . . . in her absence.

He helped himself absentmindedly to every bit of food Tolly had put on the tray, chatting away, chiefly to Mrs Robertson, about his day, and when the plates were empty he excused himself and started indoors. Maggie, watching him as if bemused, would have let him go; his presence had made her forget what she was there for. But her mother gave her a strongly meaning look and she called him back.

'Matt, come back a minute, I want to talk to you.'

'What, Mum? – sorry, but I've got to do my homework.'

'Just for a minute. Sit down . . . Listen. Granny tells me that Uncle Ian's railroading you into going to boarding-school.'

He frowned. 'What's railroading?'

'Pressuring.'

'Well, he isn't. I want to go.'

'You used to hate the idea.'

He looked surprised. 'When?'

'You remember! When you were living in London.'

'Oh, *then* . . . But then I was a baby. Besides, I hadn't seen it.'

'What's so attractive about it when you do see it?'

'You should get Uncle to take you there, Mum, it's fantastic.'

'I'm quite capable of going by myself. And I would, if there were any real question of your going there. But there isn't.'

An expression she well remembered settled over his face, a

290

look of mulish incomprehension. It made a greater impact because only a moment before he had been looking so open and happy.

'But I *want* to go.' He flashed her a look under his rather beetling red eyebrows which plainly said, What are you interfering for?

'Why, Matt?'

'*Matthew.*'

'Sorry. Why, though?'

He sighed heavily and glanced over his shoulder at the house. Maggie was obliged, by this simple gesture, to realise that within a few minutes of her arrival she had become a bloody nuisance. Only a stubbornness equivalent to his prevented her backing down on the spot.

'Come on, tell me.'

'I like the look of it, that's all. It's got a simply smashing outdoor track, and a new gym that's more like a stadium. You can do squash there and badminton. There's 9-hole golf, even, and riding. But the main thing is track. They win everything. The hall's simply full of trophies.'

'I thought the main point about going to school wasn't running round tracks but sitting on your bottom studying.'

'They get masses of people into Oxbridge every year,' said Matt defensively. He pulled back his cuff, displaying a rather magnificent watch which Maggie didn't recognise. 'Ten past *five*, Mum, and it's my heavy maths night. Listen. You should go and see it.' Then he hurled his dart. 'You're just prejudiced because it's where Dad went.'

Maggie stiffened. 'Who said that?' As if she didn't know!

Matt flushed as red as a turkey's wattle. 'See you later,' he said, and bolted.

'Matt, your blazer!' called Mrs Robertson, but he affected deafness. She bent down, picked the blazer up from the grass and smoothed it across her knee, then met Maggie's eye and shrugged. 'See what I meant?'

'How dare Ian tell him I'm prejudiced against the place?' muttered Maggie. She herself was flushed and prickling with a mixture of anger and chagrin. 'Where did he get that watch?'

'Ian gave it to him last week.'

'What the hell for? It's not his birthday! I was going to give him one when he's fifteen!'

291

'He really needed one, darling –'

'Why didn't you tell me?'

'What, that he needed one or that he'd got one?'

'*Why* did Ian suddenly give him a watch anyway? What was it in aid off?'

'Well, I rather gathered it was to – to celebrate their agreement that he should go to that school.'

Maggie stared at her mother. She felt quite winded.

That evening after dinner, and following another bootless attempt to talk to Matt, Maggie took a taxi to Ian's.

Lilian answered the door to her. Their house was new and highly decorated, as befitted a man in Ian's position. Everything in it bore Lilian's imprint. There was no sign downstairs of child-occupancy other than a portrait of Anthea Charity, a life-sized studio colour photo printed on simulated canvas to look like an oil painting. It had a gilt frame and a little light over the top of it.

'Come away in, Maggie. Ian's expecting you,' said Lilian frostily.

'Is he? How odd, nobody knew I was coming,' said Maggie, taking off her coat to reveal her fashionably brief dress and long boots. Lilian glanced down and up again so quickly her eyes practically bumped into her eyebrows.

Ian was in the living-room, working at his desk, the same rolltop one which had been their father's. He looked extraordinarily informal. He was wearing a V-necked pullover and an open-necked shirt. His hair (what remained of it, round the back and sides) was neatly brushed, but a shade longer than usual, Maggie thought. He looked distinctly older, and just as distinctly mellower, and when he stood up to receive her she noticed on his face – not the gimlet-eyed challenge she had been expecting to see, but an apparently guileless and even welcoming smile.

'Hallo, Mags. I had a feeling you might come.' And before she could gather her wits, he had pecked her cheek and was leading her to a chair by the tiled fireplace. 'Aren't you a wee bit chilly in that minute garment you're wearing? Not that it isn't very fetching, isn't it, Lilian? I can't think why you don't buy yourself a mini-skirt.'

292

Lilian, seeing he was in one of his rare teasing moods, contented herself with a thin smile. 'I'll make some coffee,' she said, and tactfully took herself off.

Ian sat down opposite Maggie, who was struggling to recover her poise and her impetus after stepping, so far, up a step that wasn't there.

'I know why you're here,' said Ian.

'Naturally.'

'You're upset that I've butted in about Matthew's schooling, and – wait a sec – I don't blame you. Now. Would you like to get your say said, and then listen to mine?'

He was still smiling, not in barely concealed triumph, but in what looked like genuine mollification and even sympathy. Maggie felt nonplussed. She had worked herself up for a real row and it was all too clear Ian wasn't going to fight.

'Maybe as you made all the moves, you say your say first.'

'All right. Here goes.' He leant back in his armchair and folded his hands across his stomach. Maggie, staring at him, seeing him in this conciliatory mood for the first time, also saw him for the first time as rather good-looking, despite his bald head and sharp, narrow features. He was healthy and firmly muscled; his hands were well-kept, the hands of a capable, disciplined man who can turn them to anything within his sphere of action. His forehead and eyes showed signs of stress but his mouth was neither bitter nor complaining. A man who bore his lot with dignity and even a certain amount of good cheer. There was even a hint of kindness ... Luckily for Maggie, she didn't realise yet that for this, too, her son was responsible. Matt had been putting in quite a lot of adding-unto around Penicuik.

Ian talked. He talked very seriously and reasonably for about half an hour. He told her how fond he had grown of Matthew, how much he was forced to admire Maggie for the way she had brought him up to the age of eight when he'd come to Scotland. He even confessed some of his own shortcomings, his own regrets for not having recognised the difficulties of bringing up children. Not a word of reproach escaped him for any of her decisions or for any dereliction of duty in recent years, for putting her career first – in fact he said she had done the right thing in realising the impossiblity of bring up a child alone in

293

London. Her decision had brought great joy into their mother's life and – he added with disarming frankness – into his own.

He confessed that he regarded Matthew more as a son than a nephew. He realised he'd acted high-handedly about Glencora, but he had done it out of genuine concern for Matthew's welfare, and had not consulted her – he conceded she might well find this unforgivable – for the same reason, perhaps, that Maggie herself had sometimes done things without asking their father – because she knew he would say no.

'I don't need to tell you,' he said almost diffidently, 'how impossible it can sometimes be, to contemplate a blank refusal for something you want very much. A really first-class start for Matthew is – I mean, it's become, recently – a dream of mine, something very fundamental and very – vital.'

And then he told her, in the strictest confidence, of his plans for Matt, how he had changed his Will, how he hadn't even told Lilian yet, but that he was telling Maggie because he felt, however impertinent it might seem to Maggie, that he had earned a real share in Matt, that they had something to give each other, he and the boy. He laid no dramatic stress on the magnitude of what he, Ian, had to offer; but it was suddenly crystal clear to Maggie what this amounted to – Ian's whole past for Matt's future.

Maggie sat in Ian's leather-look wing chair, listening in cynical silence to her brother's long monologue. She believed the surface things, that Ian wanted Matt to go to public school and on to a good university because he had him in mind to take over the family concern. She had no difficulty in believing that, because she knew Ian's dedication to the mill and the business and to the family name. (It even occurred to her to wonder at what point he would hint that Matt might alter his surname to Robertson by deed poll.)

What she couldn't credit was that Ian had had a genuine change of heart. She could only suppose that he was going through this extraordinarily well-worked-out line of sales talk to get his own way, to undermine her resolve and her hold upon Matt's life so that he could take him over. He had realised that his previous technique of patronising and belittling her would no longer give results, and was going a more subtle way to work.

In a word, he was still trying to put her down. The old pattern

294

had shifted slightly; it had not basically changed. The new mellowness and generosity were nothing but a ploy. Maggie had come to do battle for her son, and to win an old war against her brother. This new approach, though it had disorientated her at first, must not be allowed to triumph.

'Have you finished?' she asked at last.

'Yes.'

'I want to ask you a question. You've taken a flattering interest in Matt, you've more or less adopted him, or at least you're trying to. Would you have done that if you'd had a son of your own?'

Ian stared at her thoughtfully for some time.

'I'll be honest,' he said. 'I don't know. It would depend on what sort of boy he was. I know now that there's no guarantee that children will fulfil the rôle you have in mind for them. You can't mould and shape them, as I thought – arrogant as I was, before we got Anthea. Matt, though he's not mine, is the sort of son I would have wanted. *I* didn't mould him, it just happened. I can't feel proud of him. I'm just grateful.'

'Grateful? To whom?'

'God, and you, I suppose. I'm not even sure in what order!'

Maggie turned her head away. It damaged her certainties and her resolution to hear Ian talking so uncharacteristically.

'Maggie. Let me take you up to see the school.'

She swung back to the attack.

'Why should you bother, when I'm "prejudiced" against the place because Bruce went there?'

Ian had the grace to look heartily embarrassed.

'I'm sorry I said that to him.'

'So you should be! And that's probably only a fraction of what you've said to try to undercut my authority with him.'

'No, Maggie! That wasn't my motive –'

'Oh, stop it, Ian! Are you trying to fool yourself or me? Of course it was your motive, what other could you have? You have a blueprint for my son which you're quite determined to carry out, come hell or high water. Well, you're not going to take him away from me. Legally you haven't a leg to stand on.'

Ian looked up sharply.

'Take him away from you! But I haven't the slightest intention –'

295

'Oh, not the very slightest! You're just planning to do the one thing I have set my face against.'

'But *why* have you set your face against it, without even looking – ?'

'I don't believe in boys' boarding-schools, it's a totally unnatural life. It breeds a type of man I can't bear.' She said this in the full recollection that Ian had been to one.

Ian was pacing the floor, looking loose-jointed with agitation. Maggie had never seen him in such a strange state.

'Maggie, *no* system of education, no sort of upbringing – no family or religious or any other influences – "breed" a particular sort of man. It depends on the basic material you start with. Public schools can produce all kinds of men, it always has. If you're thinking of homosexuality –'

'I wasn't –'

' – you can forget it in Matthew's case. That only proves my point, because the most conventional upbringing without a boarding-school in sight can throw up one of those. *As you and I know.*'

Maggie stared at him, shocked to dumbness. Could he mean what she thought he did? Not only was that unsayable, it was unthinkable. She had never allowed herself to recognise it. But Ian was going on remorselessly.

'It's time we faced the fact, even if we don't speak of it except between ourselves. Personally, watching Steven's . . . development, if that's the word, as a human being, following his own tendencies good and bad, has taught me a great deal. I wouldn't have believed I could tolerate or accept such a thing in the family – *my own brother*! Well, it still shocks me, I can't deny it, but it's taught me to realise that it's what a person basically *is* that counts, and that will out, somehow or other, whatever sort of influences he's subjected to. Maggie . . .' He sat down again, facing her, his knees apart and leaning forward as if trying to contact her physically. 'Please listen to me. Matt is fourteen. He's essentially formed. He is what he is. It would take some catastrophe, some tragic cataclysm, to harm him basically now. Not that that means I'd want to send him away to an institution where he'd be lonely or unhappy, God forbid! I honestly believe he'll love Glencora. It's his kind of place. Not yours or mine, Maggie – Matthew's. He's a real boy, athletic, grubby, independent, *physical* . . . None of *us* is like

296

that. I sometimes think all children are like adopted children. They are all *themselves*, with little or nothing to do with what their parents bequeathed to them in the way of genes *or* nurture. You let him go six years ago. You opened your hands, for his sake, and let him go. You did right. Now open your hands again.'

If I open my hands once more, I will lose him forever, thought Maggie. I've nearly lost him already. I saw it, I felt it, in the garden this afternoon. and it is not just a matter of his freedom, his individuality. He's not yet ready to be his own person, responsible for himself. You want me to open my hands so that he will fall out of them and you will catch him. If I lose him, you will gain him. He will become your son, not mine, and then I will be left with . . . with nothing. With television news.

Yet somehow the fight went out of her. Querying it in her mind afterwards, she realised it was because she was forced to acknowledge that she had begun the process of forfeiting Matt long ago. Not just six years ago when she had chosen to have a career instead of being a full-time mother, but fourteen years ago, when she had let that black nurse, in the hospital in Lagos, pluck him out of her arms. Or before that, even – when she had gone limp on the pink chenille and yielded herself instead of yelling, 'Stop!' and meaning it.

297

Chapter Thirty

After Maggie returned from losing her battle with Ian, she tried to plunge into work, discovering only then how profoundly unrewarding TV news reporting is. Her days' routine, formerly so 'glamorous' and 'prestigious', suddenly seemed to her meaningless, trumpery and boring. Not for the first time, perhaps, but for the first time maddeningly, she became aware of the long hours of idleness she whiled away with newspaper reading, newsroom gossip, crosswords or drinks in the pub, during alleged working hours, waiting to be sent out on a story. She went off all her colleagues, with the exception of Mac, her news editor. And even he . . .

'Mac, I'm fed up.'

'What's wrong, love.' (He happened to be in remission between bouts of bulletin, and therefore inclined to be mellow enought to endure female reporters' whims and whinings.)

'I get nothing but trivia.'

'What total balls. You're an unappreciative silly bitch. I gave you a strike story only last week.'

'Last month.'

'Was it? – Well, what about Sir Laurence and Lady O? You had hot pants for that.'

'I'm sick and tired of theatrical stories.'

'Oh, come on. After you campaigned for months to have West End first nights treated as new-stories on a par with local wars, Middle East assassinations and international Cup Finals?'

'I was wrong.'

'You, dear? Wrong? What's this, the change before the death?'

'Don't be horrible to me, Mac. I need to get my teeth into something. I'm bored.'

Mac bridled visibly. Then his eyes grew small and malevolent.

'If by that enigmatic remark you happen to mean, bored with

298

your *job*, Maggie dear, I would, in *your* size fives, keep quiet about it. If you care to glance through the newsroom windows you will doubtless see crowds of wild-eyed women tearing each other to pieces for your job. Also you might ask yourself how sure you are that the Great British Public isn't getting just a shade bored with *you* after six years of seeing you on their screens, not to mention the big boys Upstairs who – it's just possible – might at this very moment be remarking through the cigar smoke round the board table that that Robertson girl is getting a bit past it for a "girl" reporter.'

That shut Maggie up. The mere thought of losing her job had the power to terrify her. Being an actress out of work is bad enough. Being a no-longer-girl reporter on one of only two television channels is very much worse. There is little question of moving sideways, and Maggie did not flatter herself that she was fit to move up to some more demanding job such as production or newscasting. It was a one-off job which, by incredible good fortune, had lasted until she had become a fixture. How long it could go on lasting, before she was really too old or until she made some blunder which gave the 'big boys Upstairs' an excuse to replace her with someone younger, more nubile, better educated or just better at the job, she dared not think. She told herself that she'd just been letting off steam to Mac, that there was no excuse to be bored or dissatisfied and that, therefore, she wasn't.

But she suffered increasingly from malaise.

She began to live not in the present but in the past. She had chucked Derek (or he her, it hardly mattered anyway) and not replaced him, so she was alone at home a good deal more than previously. Of course there were the usual press parties and she still went to the theatre, but in the mornings before she went in to work or on her days off she did a good deal of just sitting about. The balcony, once Tanya's floral Olympic stadium, was now just a balcony with some window-boxes sporting an ordinary assortment of unambitious geraniums. Only the pink rose in its corner looked happier than it had, now the fervid competition had gone. Maggie would sit out there by the hour when the weather allowed, gazing over the rooftops and the trees, the lady rose nodding its commonplace blooms sympathetically at her shoulder. She reflected endlessly on the months she had spent in the flat with Matt when he was little.

299

Even their fights she relished in retrospect. The disharmonies and discords of her brief motherhood solo had a kind of nostalgic echo.

Then a new memory was added. In the summer holiday prior to Matt's first term at his faraway highland school, she took him to France. They drove to Brittany where they lazed on the beaches, went sailing, ate divinely (though Matt was rigorously conservative at first) and in sum, had what might seem to have been a very successful holiday.

But, however oddly, Maggie tried *not* to think about it as she sat on her balcony in the September sun. Matt had been a good companion. He was charming in his schoolboy way, his manners were good and he'd been quite chatty and appreciative. She had enjoyed showing him things and sharing new experiences, tastes and places with him. But she hadn't been able to feel any intimacy with him. She had felt like his aunt or his godmother, taking him out for a special treat. At the time she had thought she was enjoying it as much as possible, having looked forward to it with all a child's devastating nervous excitement. But looked back on, it had the aura of a heartbreaking failure – a spiritual disaster.

Her son stood on the verge of manhood; Glencora (Ian had said characteristically) would 'make a man' of him. Each future holiday would bring her an expanded human being of whom she knew less and less. Effectively, when she kissed him goodbye on that same damned platform at King's Cross, she had kissed her 'little boy' goodbye for ever. She had lost him. Given him up. And for what? For his own wellbeing, Ian would say. And certainly *Matt* didn't seem to be the worse for the lack of her. He was fine. Who knows how much less fine he might have been, had she kept him close to her, seen him every day of his growing-up, been his mother in the real meaning of the word, instead of . . . farming him out? He might have been a neurotic, a misfit, a delinquent . . . At least she hadn't given herself the possibility of damaging him . . . And for herself, she'd been free, she'd had a good time, she'd made a name of sorts for herself. She'd made a good living, had 'kept' Matt and herself, depending on no one in *that* way. Now, in her mid-thirties, she had no actual need to feel so empty and ashamed, such a failure. Why did she?

Brooding at home, slacking at work, relishing nothing, not

300

even the primitive pleasures of food and drink and sun and sleep that had so often consoled her at bad times in the past, she felt herself dwindling in her own eyes into a sort of premature decline – mental, moral and physical. She wondered who she should take her trouble to – a doctor? A psychiatrist? Neither appealed. Her mother . . .? No. Her mother was now to see as little of her grandson as, for years now, she had of her daughter. When she did see her, she had a right to expect a smiling face and no deep discontents. So Maggie went to Tanya.

Tanya was between productions. This was fortuitous from her point of view as well as Maggie's – it had afforded her the time not only to have an abortion but to rest a little after it.

'Thirty-nine, I have to get myself pregnant . . . No, darling, I couldn't. One is enough. Besides, I am on the brink of a breakthrough into the legitimate fully paid-up Equity-blessed West End in the best new play for a generation. And besides . . .' Here she stopped. She was sitting up in her luxury double bed – actually a four-poster she had commissioned and paid £1,000 for. Well, Oliver had paid the £1,000. That was somehow in Maggie's mind as she sat under its red silk canopy and looked at Tanya propped up on pillows, looking a bit like Elizabeth the First, with her red hair very short and roughish as if she'd just removed a magnificent wig.

'Besides what?'

'I gave you all the besideses.'

'No, you didn't, there was going to be one more. Not that you need to excuse yourself to me. I won't reproach you.'

'So why are you looking so funereal?'

'It just seems a little sad. Ginny's such a beautiful creature. Obviously you and Oliver are the sort of couple who should be paid a bounty by the state for every child you give birth to.'

'Ah. But then, the one I just got rid of would not have attracted the bounty.'

It took Maggie a minute to figure that one out.

She was not as naive and easily shocked as she had once been. Even Margaret had evolved with the naughty times. But this did shock both of them. They tried not to show it. Tried, and evidently failed. Tanya smiled somewhat wanly.

'Oh, Maggiekins, your face! – Don't tell. Nobody knows. Not even *him*.'

301

'Who – ?'

'Oh, darling, does it matter? It was a bit of an accident, I mean in more ways than one. He is not important. Just as well, perhaps, or it might have hurt more to give up having his baby.'

'Does Oliver guess you had an affair?'

'There is nothing to guess at now. It's all over. All, all over. I will never be a bad girl again.'

'Why were you?'

Tanya looked away and shrugged, 'I can't answer. Things can happen that you don't plan, but they don't just erupt out of nothing. There is always sub-text. The sub-text of this was to do with me and Oliver.'

'You were never really "in it" with him, were you?'

Tanya shook her head slowly. 'We married to fill out the missing bits of ourselves. That doesn't have to be a bad reason. But you see, I'd *been* "in it". The contrast between that infernal blaze of feeling and keep-the-home-fires-burning was just too much. It's why one mustn't start taking Lucy.' Lucy was the current slang for LSD. 'Everything seems drab after it. Probably if I hadn't been so busy with the company and Ginny and everything, something like this would have happened long ago.'

'Does Oliver know you had an abortion?'

'*No*, Maggie. Oliver doesn't notice things like that.' Things like what, thought Maggie. *Were* there any 'things like that'? 'Oliver thinks I've got flu. He doesn't even notice the waste-paper baskets aren't full of Kleenex.'

This was supposed to raise a laugh, and when it didn't Tanya turned her antennae in Maggie's direction and at once realised she had not come to console her on her bed of pain.

'What's *your* trouble, Maggie?'

'Oh, you don't want to hear –'

'Yes, I do. Distract me from my remorseful thoughts.'

So Maggie did her best to explain. Tanya knew about Matt, and about Maggie's feelings, more than anyone else did, anyhow, but it was all so amorphous and hard to express in words that it was hard for her to be wise and helpful about it. For her part she could not but think Maggie had made the correct decisions all along, and as she was herself a natural-born decision-maker she had learnt early that even right decisions brought their own inevitable clawback in the form of fruitless regrets or disadvantages.

302

'Listen, Maggie,' she said at last when Maggie stopped talking. 'If you want my opinion, your trouble is not with Matt at all. It's not even with your work, though perhaps that has been dragging on too long until it's not a proper challenge to you any more – you are just getting stale, like in a long run. That's a practical matter which you'll just have to tackle one way or another. But your "malaise" as you call it is caused by something you're not even thinking about, which in my present dubious situation perhaps it's indelicate to mention, but it's actually sex.'

Maggie heaved a profound sigh. 'Tanya, it is time you knew. I don't really like sex.'

'Oh, I know you think you don't.'

'Isn't that the same as not?'

'In my view, like in *Tea and Sympathy*, "with some people there has to be love". You've never been "in it", Maggie. Admit.'

'I admit . . . Too late now.'

'No, darling, it isn't. You're a late developer.'

'Oh, Tan, I've been comforting myself with that old bromide since I was twenty-seven!'

'Well, just look how long it took to turn you into a smartly-dressed, self-confident, sophisticated woman of the world!'

'Don't make me laugh.'

'Of course *I* know it's all an act, but it's a wonderful performance.'

'It's a performance I'd love to bring down the curtain on for ever. I despise myself in it. It's nothing to do with me at all.'

'What does that matter? You're an actress.'

'No. It's time you knew that about me, too. In your terms I'm a rank amateur.'

It was still September – the end of it – when Mac called her in to the office on her day off and said, without preamble. 'You wanted a story to get your teeth into, so here is one.'

Oh, make it abroad! thought Maggie. The trip to the sheikh-dom had been total bliss, taken her right out of herself, but it had only lasted three days, and coming down off that 'high' had been almost worse than not going at all.

But Mac was not talking about Roving Reports or anything

303

glamorous of that sort. What he was talking about sounded incredibly dull and heavy to Maggie.

'. . . isolated on estates,' he was saying, his eyes aglow with enthusiasm. 'Not just council estates, private estates too, even very posh ones. There they all are, poor cows, no grans and aunties any more to share the load, thigh-deep in kids, and they're getting fat through eating their heads off for lack of something more interesting to do. So their doctors put them on these pills. They're supposed to be appetite suppressants, but they actually make you high. So instead of taking one a day or whatever, some of these women are stuffing them down like Smarties and winding up in funny-farms. There's a big scandal about it in today's *Express*.'

Oh gawd, thought Maggie, and she would have groaned aloud and tried to wriggle off the hook, only nowadays she was inhibited from complaining.

'So who am I to interview?'

'Well, I've found you a couple of women who've been taking these things, one's just getting over a breakdown, another's being divorced. But what we really need is an expert on the social side of pill-popping. An egghead of some sort.'

'How shall I find – ' began Maggie lethargically.

Mac abruptly lost patience.

'Maggie, you've been at this job for six bloody years,' he shouted, attracting the attention of all the subs, reporters and script-writers in the newsroom. 'If you still expect to be tit-fed, I'll ask the editor to advertise for a wet-nurse, but I don't think he's going to like it, somehow!'

'I only meant –'

'Oh, piss off out of here, will you? Pretend you're a real reporter for a change and do a little of your own digging!'

Maggie crept home with her tail between her legs, humiliated by Mac's public outburst. She took her usual remedy and phoned Tanya.

She had no real hope, she was only ringing for comfort, but to her incredulous relief Tanya, after only a moment's hesitation, said, 'Yes, I do know someone in that field. Now there is a coincidence.'

'Oh, Tan, thank God, I'm saved! Who?'

'Can't you guess?' Tanya's voice sounded odd.

'No?'

304

'It's Joel.'

'*Joel?*'

'Yes, Joel. My ex Joel. He has a Chair at London University now, in sociology, and that happens to be his speciality – drugs and alcohol.'

Maggie was so relieved she didn't stop to think too deeply. 'Can you put me in touch with him?'

'Me? Are you mad? Of course not. You must do it yourself. I have not been anywhere near him for twelve years.'

'So how do you know he's moved from Sheffield?'

'One gets to know these basic things, that's all. One has to know the places to avoid. It was comparatively easy to avoid Sheffield. It's much more inconvenient to keep outside a two-mile radius of London University.'

Maggie thought this was a sort of wry Tanya-joke, and laughed. 'Okay, I'll phone him now.'

'Now?' Tanya sounded startled, almost frightened.

'Yes, now, this minute! I've got to lay him on for tomorrow morning.'

Tanya didn't say anything for a moment, and then she muttered, 'How – unimaginable.'

'What?' asked Maggie, impatient to get on.

'That I am talking to you and that in a few minutes you will be talking to him.'

'Well, I see nothing unimaginable about that,' said Maggie with marvellous crassness. 'Shall I ring you back later and tell you how it went?'

Another long, unaccountable pause, and then Tanya said firmly, 'No. Thank you. Please don't tell me anything about it except when *not* to switch on television. Do you know his surname?'

'Oh my God! No.'

'It's Langham.'

'Professor Langham. Nice name.'

'I always said so, even before the professor was added.'

Maggie quite easily located Joel's office, or rather the university switchboard did. It gave her a strange feeling, listening to the ringing, and when she heard him say, 'Hallo, Langham here,' she realised why. For many years this man had lurked in her subconscious at myth-level. What she was doing now was akin to dialling Olympus, or perhaps the nether world. This

305

man, this presumably quite ordinary, quiet-voiced man, had extraordinary power, the power to inspire passionate, lasting adoration. In Maggie's love-starved life this invested him with a quality she couldn't pin down, something – rarified, almost fabulous. She found her breath fluttering; she felt like a young girl talking to a famous man, and when she began the conversation she stammered. Then she pulled herself together firmly.

She made the appointment, hung up, and sat still, wondering why she felt so excited – so ... well, almost conspiratorial. There was nothing underhand about it – was there? And then she remembered that she had met him before years ago, and that the natural thing would have been to remind him of it.

Chapter Thirty-One

She laid on the crew for 8.30 a.m. at his home. It didn't make her very popular because camera crews don't relish early starts any more than, say, actors; but the funny thing was that Maggie, the worst getter-upper on earth, rose that morning willingly and cheerfully. If 8.30 was the only time Joel Langham could manage, due to a dayful of lectures – so be it.

She sat in the sun in her little car outside a rather imposing old house behind the Finchley Road, looking at her face in the driving mirror and afterwards, more closely, in the mirror of her compact. It seemed to her that she looked better at thirty-five than she had at twenty-five. (As indeed she must have done – at twenty-five she'd been bush-haired, sack-line dressed and etiolated, fighting ol' daybed in Port Harcourt.) 'I now look as if I know who I am, at least,' she thought.

She was early. Why had she come so early? The crew would not arrive for half an hour. She sat behind her wheel, oddly reluctant, for all her eagerness, now the moment of meeting was upon her. She would feel a complete fool if he recognised her. But surely he wouldn't.

But he did. She saw it in his face the moment he opened the door. And she would, as they say, have known him out of thousands. There was an immediate small shock of mutual recognition between them. It had the effect of a frisson, exacerbated by the fact that he was in the process of shaking her hand and the motion of it stopped abruptly without his releasing her.

'I've seen you somewhere before.'

'On screen, probably.'

'I don't think so. I have a feeling of knowing you behind the face.'

Later, Maggie was to compare her feelings from this time forward until she left the house with those of a long-term

307

prisoner pacing his cell for the ten thousandth time who, reaching the door, finding it mysteriously open, is too frozen with incredulity and even fear at first to walk out into open air, normality and freedom. Later still, she would think of it as more closely analogous to a fledgling which has reached term in its cramping egg, and whose struggling beak and wings and feet force the claustrophobic shell to crack and fall away.

In a certain sense, she was a 35-year-old virgin. But virgin or not, she was a mature adult – her reactions were not those of a tremulous young girl to the onset of her first sudden deep affinity. She had lived through all those years, she had observed other people, she had read and acted in plays and all this and more had taught her what love was supposed to be like and how people in love were supposed to feel and behave. So that when she looked into this already-familiar face, realised that he was actually no more than moderately good-looking in a tall, beaky, bespectacled, professorial way, yet at the same time sensed a profound meaning for herself in everything about him – she could not avoid the implications. She could not help sensing at once her own dangerous vulnerability.

She took instant refuge in a theatrical cliché – 'wildly attractive, my dear!' She was still able, at that stage, to pretend to herself that she would say this, lightly and gaily, to Tanya. What she would not say to Tanya was that he was green. Green as grass. That feeling of being looked out at from some well-fortified inner world, the self-knowingness, the gentle eyes and hands, yet with a sharpness, a strength . . . And suddenly she remembered that she had once offended Tanya by remarking, only half in fun, that Joel made her think of the Mekon in *Dan Dare* – the egg-headed, pea-green Mekon . . . The ludicrousness of this thought tickled her unexpectedly and she gave a laugh, strangled at birth, but out before she could stop it, a laugh which had in it a measure of pure happiness.

'What's so funny?' he asked without truculence, taking her coat.

'For a moment you looked – green.'

He turned to stare at her comically. 'Green!'

'It must have been the light,' she said hurriedly. 'Through the trees.'

' "A chance light meaningless shines" – and I am green. Unless you meant metaphorically. Come through.'

308

He led her across a square hall and into a large, high-ceilinged living room at the back of the house. She paused fractionally in the doorway. One glance was enough to tell her something she hadn't even thought about until this moment but already it had its fundamental importance. There was no woman here. The room was all male, all intellectual, all green, green, green, with its evidence of music loving and book loving, brain-work and lack of obvious show. The colours had a quiet, thrown-together look, infinitely pleasing to her eyes, like himself. The remains of breakfast on a tray was unselfconsciously resposing on a small table in front of the open french window. Beyond was a small garden with a fork stuck into a half-dug flowerbed.

She stopped. 'Oh, look – a robin!' she whispered, pointing.

Joel turned and looked and they stood together in silence until it pleased the robin to fly off.

Later she was to remember what Tanya had written in her letter: *Aren't all one's truest and deepest emotions just rubbishy-trite?* A bloody little Christmas-card robin perched on a gardening fork! Yet when they turned back towards each other, they were both smiling; some inevitable initial barrier had been painlessly crossed, or rather – had simply dematerialised. All at once they were at ease with each other. Maggie almost forgot the Tanya connection. She sat down beside the table and touched the handle of the knife.

'You haven't finished your breakfast,' she said 'I interrupted you, coming so early.'

'Don't worry about that. Would you like anything? Coffee?'

'I had one before I left home, thank you.'

'So have another.'

'Will you join me?'

'Have we time?'

'Perhaps we ought to do a little preliminary chatting.'

'All right.'

He sat down in a wing chair facing her. Because she wanted so badly to stare at him, she turned her head and looked instead at the garden. The sun was shining all over it. He obviously loved it and worked in it often. Perhaps he'd been out there already this morning – the soil where the fork was stuck looked freshly dug. He must, she thought, be one of those most admirable beings, an early riser.

309

She allowed herself another quick glance. She had not noticed what he was wearing; now it was important because, imagining him in the garden in old clothes, she had felt herself so full of a sort of fascinated tenderness (a professor – in wellies!) that she needed an antidote. Now he had on a grey hopsack suit, button-down shirt and blue university tie. Out there in the garden, earlier, he must have glanced at his watch, stuck the fork into the earth and hurried in to wash and change. Because she was coming. It made her feel almost sick with some incomprehensible emotion to realise that she had already, in advance of their meeting, had a direct effect upon him.

A linen napkin lay crumpled on the tray. He had put it there when she rang the doorbell. She looked at it, positively savouring the realisation that she longed to pick it up and put it to her face.

'Well? Let's do our chat. How many questions are you going to ask me?'

With an effort she recalled what she was doing there.

'Unfortunately not many. The whole story, including the women, will probably be cut to no more than two or three minutes of screen time.'

'Good God!' he exclaimed. 'My life's work condensed into an Oxo cube! It hardly seems worth it.'

'That's the way we have to work, I'm afraid. It's news, not documentary or feature.'

'Three minutes . . .' he mused. She watched his hands tapping the arm of his chair and remembered Tanya saying they held magic. She could well believe it. She remembered the time when she had been so hungry for love and the freedom to express it that she had longed to kiss and caress everyone she saw . . . Something of that longing, so long dormant, rushed back to her, but the urges were more exclusive now.

'Well, I suppose one must aim to encapsulate, in that short time, the boredom and loneliness of urban domestic blight. Under equivalent conditions, men turn to drink. Woman are often afraid of the – grossness of alcohol. Pills seem more refined.'

'How widespread is it?'

'Are you going to ask me that on camera?'

She liked his knowing the terms of her trade. 'Yes.'

'Then do you mind if we don't rehearse? I think I'd do better

310

spontaneously. Like most teachers I have a horror of repeating myself before the same person. I'll keep it brief.'

'Well! That's the end of the chat, then.' She tore her eyes away and looked once more round the room. 'This is a very pleasant flat,' she said with a good imitation of casualness, though every detail was a clue to him and thus vitally interesting to her.

'Yes, I was lucky. I took it as I found it.'

'How long have you been living down here?'

The moment it was out, a spasm of shock turned Maggie rigid. She actually clenched her jaw and shut her eyes for a second, which was as long as he gave her in which to hope he had not noticed her gaffe.

'Two years. How did you know I used to live up North?'

One of the symptoms of love is that one does not willingly lie, and Maggie had, over the years, lost her early skill as a dissembler. She gazed at him like a guilty child, unable to think of a word to say. Suddenly his face, bland and quizzical a moment before, snapped into a frown.

'What did you say your name was?'

'Margaret Macrae.'

'Wait a minute. You're not Margaret at all. And you're not Macrae, or you weren't. You're Maggie – Maggie Something – Robertson, that's it! You're Tanya's friend, and that's where I met you before – that day in Sheffield.'

There was a silence. Then Maggie said, 'I didn't think you'd recognise me.'

'But you weird girl! Why didn't you tell me on the phone that we knew each other? Come to think of it, you must know me pretty well, by report.'

Maggie felt her head might burst from the pressure of the hot, shamed blood in it. She couldn't have managed the whole thing worse if she'd tried. Now she was caught in a trap. She must either betray some essence of Tanya's confidence, or embark upon an endless string of lies.

'I'm sorry. I really don't know how to explain.'

'Do you still see Tanya?'

'Yes.'

'Was it, by any remote chance, she who suggested that you interview me?'

To hesitate would make it worse.

311

'Yes, it was, as a matter of fact. You see, she'd heard that you –'

'That I'd – what?'

'Moved to London. Changed universities.'

'Is that all she'd heard?'

'What do you mean?'

'I just wondered if she'd heard about my divorce.'

After a moment, Maggie replied carefully, 'If so she's said nothing to me about it.'

'I don't see how she could have heard about it, actually. It wasn't in the papers. Unlike her wedding,' he added with a sardonic note in his voice.

They fell silent. What must he be thinking? thought Maggie frantically. He'll think Tanya sent me to spy on him. He might, with the irrepressible vanity of men, think she's still in love with him, that she's waiting breathlessly to feast on all the details I shall bring away from this encounter. I must let him know that she's no longer interested in him, I must be able to tell her truthfully that I didn't betray her in any way.

She opened her mouth to embark upon some more or less doctored version of the truth when he interrupted her.

'You know, this is really quite extraordinary,' he said. He was peering at her closely through his glasses, as if she were some object of intense scientific interest to him. 'You have a kind of – well, I don't know how to express it. A kind of legendary quality in my personal filing system. Until that day, you'd been a name without a face. Then you got a face, but still you didn't have a real identity. As a matter of fact, that day you were rather in the way.'

'Yes, I was well aware of that.'

'If we let you feel it, I apologise.'

'A little late for remorse on that score!'

He gave a little snort of laughter down his nostrils like a horse's sneeze. Hardly a thing of charm in itself, but it delighted Maggie. She realised that she had a basic awe of him because he was an academic, and Tanya had said he was brilliant. The fact that he was capable of what amounted to a giggle, albeit a strictly masculine one, enchanted her.

'At all events, subsequent to our meeting you took on quite gradually a firmer and clearer reality, over the period when I was still . . . with Tanya. She talked a good deal about you.'

312

He paused, still gazing at her. 'I've suddenly realised, I mean this second, why I, who am probably the most private person you'll ever meet, don't mind that you know so much about me. It's because you don't have an advantage over me. I know a lot about you, too.'

'What do you know?'

'May I tell you? It's all, as you said, long ago and far away.'

'Go on.'

'I know about your career, and your love-affair, and your marriage, and your quarrel with Tanya.'

She sat feeling as if he were undressing her and trying not to be clear in her head about how deeply she was enjoying it.

'Do you mind?' he asked.

'I haven't decided yet.' Then something occured to her. 'The quarrel . . . How much did she tell you about *that*?'

'Ah. As to that, she was rather vague. Although I was left in no doubt that she was profoundly hurt by it, and by the long breach which resulted, all the time you were abroad.'

A silence fell. Now she had no desire to turn her eyes away, but stared back at him, free to do it because he was staring at her.

'You've changed a good deal,' he said.

'I've grown up.'

'You've become more adult looking, of course. But also there's a veneer . . . Rather a pity. But I suppose inevitable. Have I changed?'

'Not much. You've gone grey.'

He passed his hand over his head rather self-consciously, and then said something that startled Maggie.

'Tanya once told me her hair was grey under the dye. Is that true, or was she just being dramatic?'

A belated surge of loyalty to Tanya stiffened Maggie's face. He saw it at once and said, 'Sorry, that wasn't a very generous thing to say. But, as another who has been close to Tanya, I've no doubt you must have suffered from her dramas as I did.'

'There's something I really must make clear to you about Tanya – ' Maggie began.

Just then the doorbell sounded. They both started.

Joel rose. 'That must be your crew,' he said. He looked at her from the door. 'We'll continue this conversation anon,' he said drily.

313

The interview went smoothly. Happily she'd done her homework and prepared her questions in her usual methodical way, leaving nothing to chance. Joel gave an impeccable interview. All the time the crew were there, Maggie felt them as intruders, and she sensed that Joel, too, was waiting for them to leave. Yet the break in her strangely intimate conversation with him restored her consciousness of her vulnerability. Even while longing to be alone with him, she feared it.

Nobby, the cameraman, gave her the thumbs-up, the gear was unplugged and folded away. They were due at another story on the far side of London in an hour.

'Coming with? We could drop you at the office on our way –'

'No thanks, Nobby, I'm mobile.'

The crew departed. Maggie stood in the middle of the room while Joel saw them out. Her heart was beating urgently, yet she felt strangely lax and will-less. She had to force herself to look at her watch as he returned.

'Do you have to leave straight away?'

'I – I don't know. May I ring my office?'

He gestured to the phone on his desk. To use it she had to sit on his chair, a wide wooden one with a worn leather inset seat. Dialling, she wondered how much of the furniture in this room dated back to Tanya's time, whether familiarity and association would invest it with the same importance for Tanya as it seemed to have now for Maggie, seeing it for the first time but wanting to touch everything because it was his.

Mac informed her that the first pill-popping wife was laid on for 10.45. In Dulwich. Dulwich! It would take a good hour to get there, more if there were traffic . . .

'Well? What about that coffee?'

She turned with a bright smile, which masked a suddenly-born determination.

'I'm afraid not. I must be off.'

She thought he would try to persuade her, but instead he just nodded. She crushed down irrational, overwhelming disappointment. *Press me to stay! Just some polite formula . . . That's all I'll need.* But he stood silent, waiting for her to get up and go past him into the square hall where he'd hung her coat . . . She found she needed some incentive to move. She was simply sitting there helplessly. The coat. Yes. She would let him help her on with it and that would involve his touching her. She

314

jumped up gauchely, hunted for her bag, found it, and preceded him into the hall. The front door loomed before her, a symbol of parting. Once it closed behind her, there seemed no earthly reason why they should ever meet again.

He didn't help her on with her coat. He simply handed it to her, and watched while she slipped it on unaided. The silence between them was stretching to unnatural lengths.

'Thank you very much for agreeing to – ' she began, holding out her hand.

He ignored it.

'You're not going to get off quite so lightly, you know.'

She dropped her hand and stared at him. She could think of no response. She couldn't even ask him what he meant because she knew.

'I'm terribly afraid you've misunderstood the situation,' she said at last.

'I haven't misunderstood it, or understood it. I am very curious about it. Are you sure you haven't got a few minutes?'

After a moment's meeting of eyes, Maggie silently took her coat off again and he hung it up. He led the way, not back into the living-room, but into the kitchen. It was an expensive modern one which must go with the flat – it wasn't his taste, she knew at a glance. It had a sort of bar jutting out into the room, with two high stools and a bright red tiled top. She sat on one of the stools while he went behind the bar to the cooking area and plugged in a kettle.

'What precisely is it you're afraid I've misunderstood?'

She licked her lips. 'I'm in a very awkward position.'

'I can't quite see why.'

'Tanya's my best friend. Now as then.'

'So?'

'I wouldn't want you to think – because, in all honesty, it wouldn't be true – that Tanya, who is now married and who long ago – well –'

'Recovered from me?'

'Yes,' said Maggie firmly. 'It would hurt her to think that *you* might think she was – very subtly trying to . . .' She stopped, unsure whether she was clarifying things or making them worse.

'Re-establish contact,' he finished for her. 'I don't think that would have occurred to me.'

315

There was a silence for some moments. His hands were busy with mugs and spoons.

'Has she any children?'

'A little girl. Imogen.'

Joel put a mug of coffee in front of her. 'She always said she would name her daughters after Shakespeare's heroines, but I understood the first in line was Perdita,' he said ironically.

He hiked the second stool round the end of the bar and sat facing her, their faces about a foot apart. Across the aroma of coffee she could smell him. She was very sensitive to men's smells. Bruce had smelt of sweat and brilliantine and tobacco and sometimes scotch. Joel smelt of shaving soap at the moment. What was there in that to make her lean backwards in case she should lean forwards and kiss him?

'It is quite uncanny,' he said slowly, 'how well I feel I know you. Perhaps I have seen you on the screen. While you were doing the cut-aways I was watching you. It can't possibly be that I've only seen you once. You're familiar.'

'And you to me. No doubt because of Tan.'

'No doubt.' He continued staring at her for a moment, then took a drink from his mug. 'I can't help wanting to know about Tanya, though of course it's all so long ago now. She was a very important part of my life.'

'Well, why don't you get in touch with her? After all this time, what harm could it do?'

'Probably none at all, but personally I'm not prepared to take the slightest risk.' His expression and his voice were tinged with wryness. 'We really caused each other a great deal of anguish. In addition she wrecked my marriage, albeit by remote control. I've no desire to do the like for hers.'

'Wrecked your marriage?' asked Maggie. 'That wasn't my impression.'

'Or mine – at the time. But by an irony of monumental proportions, some years after Tanya's departure from my life, my wife . . .' He abruptly stopped talking, and sat for some moments looking out of the kitchen window. Maggie didn't move. She knew exactly what was happening. He had caught himself talking too freely to her. She had had this experience before with green men. She longed for him to decide to trust her, and to go on. At the same time she hoped he would stop, because here it started: the putative treachery to Tanya. If Joel's

316

wife had, for example, found some letters, or in some other way discovered about Joel's long, fraught affair with Tanya, and had left him on that account, it was something Maggie would have the greatest difficulty – given the quintessential openness which had always characterised her relationship with Tanya – in keeping back. It was too interesting, too – germane. She actually thought the word 'germane' and then realised she had learnt the word, indirectly, from Joel, for it was one of Tanya's Joel-words. So was 'putative' . . . She felt the laugh breaking out again and buried her nose and mouth abruptly in her hands.

He looked swiftly back at her. '*Now* what's amusing you?'

'Oh, I don't know! This whole situation is – one must laugh so as not to cry.'

He stared at her with his lips parted in astonishment, as if he'd heard an echo.

'That's Tanya,' he said. 'That expression. Straight from her Jewish half.' And she realised that it was. Tanya was like a shuttle, passing back and forth between them as they wove their own bit of cloth. A bit which, as abruptly he looked at his watch, seemed destined to be too short to make any warming garment out of.

'I'm late for my first lecture.' he said. 'I must go.'

It was over. Maggie tried to feel relieved that they hadn't really touched on anything dangerous – she could tell Tanya all of this, if she asked. All except, of course, Maggie's inner turmoil. The situation was too difficult for her, she was out of her emotional depth, she who had never learnt to swim. She found herself hurrying into the hall, as if eager to escape.

Now it was he who put out his hand, and she took it, and he instead of shaking it normally simply held it in a way that sent a shaft of physical feeling straight through her to her loins. She became motionless to experience this better. I have only just met him, she thought. How can it be that I am feeling for him something I never felt for Bruce or any other man in my whole life? I want him. I would go to bed with him this instant if he showed me by the slightest hint that he wanted me. *But he is*, she realised suddenly. That's just what he is doing.

And at this, Margaret came to her aid, pulled her hand out of Joel's and said, with commendable briskness, 'Well, it's been very interesting to meet you again. I'm sorry for the small

317

deception, it had something to do with loyalty I hope you understand.'

'Oh yes,' he said evenly, still gazing with a cool green hunger into her eyes. 'I understood that part from the outset.'

Margaret contrived an almost formal smile and got her out to her car. Maggie, like Lot's wife, could not resist the urge to look back. He stood in the doorway at the top of the steps and did not respond to her falsely insouciant little wave. Margaret it was who got the car moving and drove it away. Maggie was still stunned by the first heavy blow of desire.

Chapter Thirty-Two

She reached home that evening after a long but by no means exceptionally heavy day, in a state bordering on exhaustion. Not for a minute, even while interviewing, had Joel Langham been absent from the forefront of her mind. The realisation that she would never, other than by some crude manoeuvre or unimaginable accident, see him again, was what had tired her to the point of making her unsafe behind the wheel of her own car, barely able to climb the single curving flight of stairs to her flat. Even the sound of the phone ringing shrilly and demandingly behind her front door did nothing to galvanise her. Indeed, she half-hoped it would stop before she could reach it, and moved so slowly that she expected it must. But it didn't

'Hallo.'

'Maggie. Where in the name of God have you been? I've been phoning you all the damn day.'

A pang shot through her at the sound of Tanya's voice, an all-too-familiar pang of guilt. There was no opportunity to analyse it, only to feel an answering, and equally profound, resentment at it, for whatever had happened this morning had not been her fault and she had done her best.

'Just working,' she answered. It sounded, even in her own ears, like a retort. 'Why didn't you ring me at the office?'

'Do you think I didn't? I rang there four or five times this morning. Maggie, you don't know what a terrible day I've had.'

Stupidly enough, she had a sudden hope that all this had nothing to do with Joel, and said, 'Why, what's happened?'

There was a silence and then Tanya said slowly, 'Don't drive me mad, Maggie, please. Did you see him or didn't you?'

'I thought you didn't want to know anything about it.'

'I thought I didn't, but I do. I've been half crazy all day, thinking about it. Tell, Maggie. Tell.'

319

'Let me get my coat off.'

She did this, her mind racing. Tanya knew her so well. She knew every intonation in her voice, every nuance in her behaviour. If Maggie were not the very soul of caution at this point, Tanya would guess at once. No. Not caution. Deceit.

'He was absolutely right for the story. I'm really grateful to you for putting me on to him.'

Tanya emitted an exclamation that was like a gasp of passion.

'What are you talking such nonsense for, as if he were anybody? Tell me about *him*, will you?'

'I am. He was very n-nice.' she found herself stammering, the word was so inept. 'I got there early and we had a pleasant talk –'

'What about?'

'Oh, just – a preliminary chat –'

'Maggie,' Tanya said tensely, 'you're frightening me. What's wrong? Is he ill? Has he got old? You're keeping something back.'

'He's perfectly okay. He lives in a very nice flat off the Finchley Road. His hair is white but other than that he doesn't look old at all. He has a garden and a rather swish kitchen and he obviously looks after himself very well.'

'Looks after himself?' And then it came, like the crack of a whip. 'Where's Sonia?'

'Who?' (Though she knew.)

'*Sonia*! His wife. Wasn't she there?'

She had to be truthful – or nearly. 'He's living alone.'

Tanya let out her breath with a long hissing sound.

'That means she's gone!' she whispered. 'She would never have let him move down to London without her. She's gone, dead, divorced, what does it matter? He's free.'

'But you aren't!' cried Maggie. It came out louder than she had intended, and with an almost harsh edge. Not that it mattered – Tanya didn't hear it.

'Maggie, tell me the absolute truth! Did he mention me?'

'Why should he?' Maggie heard the lie-by-implication emerge and knew she had entered the web and was already stuck fast to it.

'I thought he would recognise you and realise the connection.'

Oh! So that was the plan. Subconscious, maybe, but a plan.

320

And during this long day it had surfaced. Tanya was now hiding nothing from either of them.

'Absent-minded professors don't tend to recognise people they've met once, a hundred years ago, when they see them again in a totally different context.'

'Joel is not absent-minded in the least.'

'Well, his mind, on the occasion I met him, was certainly absent from me, being focused exclusively on you. I never supposed he even glanced at me in a seeing way.'

There was a long pause. Maggie felt electrified by her deceit.

'Well,' said Tanya, sounding a fraction less tense, 'So that's good, really. It would have been awkward if he had recognised you, he might have thought we'd cooked up the whole encounter between us . . . You've managed to find out what I most wanted to know without in any way compromising me. It's I who have to be grateful, Maggie. And I am.'

Maggie felt suddenly aware that she was frightened. The fear had started at the very beginning of the conversation.

'Wait a minute, Tanya! What difference does it make to you, whether he's still married or not?'

'Let's just say that I no longer have to keep outside the two-mile limit,' said Tanya. 'Goodnight, Maggie. And thanks.'

Maggie sat still, with the receiver unhung-up in her hand. The purring sound of the dial tone stopped after a bit and then she remembered to put it back on its cradle, very carefully as if it might break. She crossed the room to sit on the flower-sofa. She was empty and she tried to contemplate food or a comforting hot coffee, or a proper drink, but she couldn't face any of it. She simply sat there, quite limp, until it grew completely dark outside. She had never in the whole of her life felt so forlorn or so afraid of the future. Her eyes were open and fixed on the opposite wall on which hung one of her African souvenirs, a round, blackwood shield with a crudely-carved face as a boss in the middle. It had eyelids but no eyes, just slits. After darkness fell and she could no longer see the shield or the face properly, the wooden eyelids opened and the eyes began to stare at her, gleamingly. When that happened, she got up quickly and went to the phone and phoned her home-number in Scotland. Tolly answered.

'Mrs Robertson's home.'

'Tolly, it's me.'

321

'Yes. I was thinking about you.'

'Were you, Tolly? Why?'

'I don't know. Are you well?'

'Tolly . . . I need you. I want you to come down here for a week or so. Can my mother spare you?'

There was a silence and then Tolly said, 'I like to come. But Madam very sad now Matty go to the big school.'

'I only want to borrow you, Tolly.'

'If I could come, I come. But Madam need me more.'

They talked for a few more minutes, exchanging news about Matthew, who had written a special letter to Tolly. She fetched it and read it slowly and proudly to Maggie. It was a most intimate and funny letter, full of detail, much more so than the brief one Maggie had received. Maggie tried desperately to keep control until the phone-call came to a natural end, and she succeeded, more or less; but as soon as she hung up she burst into a storm of weeping. She had no idea why she was crying, except that she felt utterly wretched, ashamed and alone. She felt robbed, but that was absurd. What she lacked, she had given away. And now – this. Joel. Tanya's Joel.

Her tears come to a hiatus, rather than an end, and she went round into the kitchenette and bathed her face at the sink. Then she went out on to her balcony. The pink rose alone still had a flower on it; all the other plants were dying back. Maggie thought of the time Tanya had come out here and used her flowers to help her decide that life was still worth living. Maggie touched the face of the rose, which glimmered palely in the semi-darkness, and smelt it. Its perfume was so gentle and so sweet, it consoled her a little. It restored to her some sense of proportion.

'I can't have fallen in love with him,' she said aloud to herself. 'And even if I have, it can't go very deep. It has no roots so it will soon die of neglect.'

But, in the first place, she knew that in some strange fashion her relationship with Joel did have roots. That they went down through Tanya and not through herself did not invalidate their strength. Next, she did not get any comfort from reflecting that if she never saw Joel again that aberrant feeling she had conceived for him on sight would wither. No doubt it would – nothing lives unfed. But she felt she would rather go through any pain than relinquish it. She wanted it, she wanted it to

322

develop; she felt, even at this nadir, that something had become part of her that made her more alive and more in touch with herself than she had ever been in her life, except, perhaps – and here was a queer thought – in the moment of giving birth to Matthew. The raw pangs had cut straight through the padding layers of her civilized conditioning and united her with the primitive sources of feeling and being. Thinking about Joel was an emotional equivalent to that agony, and welcome to her in precisely the same way. Something was being born that tore her but that would make her normal. No longer acting life, but living it. She wanted it. She wanted it, no matter for the pain. Her whole soul and body cried out, not even so much for the particular man, but for the feelings he had woken in her, the commitment to life that he had seemed to promise she might find through him.

And she was not going to get him. There was no way she could see that it could happen. She was going to be this hard-edged, enviable, empty failure for ever.

She stood straight in the darkness of the balcony with the night wind in her face and understood what had brought Fiona Dalzell to the pavement's edge.

Maggie got through the next three days with difficulty. Mac, the allegedly tough, crass, insensitive newsman, noticed almost at once that something was wrong.

'You're very lacklustre these days, Mags. What's eating you?'

'Nothing, Mac. I'm okay.'

'Well, if that's the case, cheer up, for God's sake. You're droopy-drawersing about the place looking like a wet week in Wigan. Even the editor's noticed.'

'That I don't believe.'

'Why not? He's very much on your team.'

'My team? What on earth does that mean?'

Mac turned evasive. 'We all need a team in this harsh world, Maggie.'

'Which harsh world are you talking about?'

'Well, I might be talking about the world at large, it would still be true.'

'But you're not, you're talking about our little world right here on the seventh floor of Television House.'

323

'He who runs, as they say, may read. Now pull your socks or any other garment that happens to be down, up, and get yourself out and do some sparkling street interviews on the prospect of yet another election.'

'Another election! God, what a bore!'

'Now, now, Mags, mustn't get peevish. And if we're really bored, we must hide it. Must we not, Maggiekins? Don't say I didn't tip you off to the need to be an extra-good little girl reporter just now.'

The bell rang but it was muffled. It wasn't just the prospect of a new election that was making Maggie feel up to her knees in a bog, unable to respond energetically or with her old enthusiasm to anything. Nothing seemed to matter, if she couldn't have what she wanted. And what she wanted – the only thing that mattered – was to see Joel again.

She had seen him of course in the rushes theatre when the pill story was being cut. He looked so wonderful on screen, he spoke so well – she marvelled that the film editors and producer didn't break into applause. She had sat riveted to the monitor in the newsroom during the relevant bulletin. But then it was over. Even his shadow had vanished. Turning from the set to a Joelless life, she suddenly knew how Tanya had felt about little deaths at parting.

After that began a painful blank, stretching ahead presumably into infinity. The need to get in touch with him grew and gnawed on her nerves like toothache, and there was no way she could assuage it. And she had no one to share it with. She felt lost and friendless. Somehow Tolly's refusal to come – even though Maggie was quite uncertain why she had wanted her to – had been the last straw. She seemed to shrivel like an unwatered plant. She could scarcely drag herself about.

One night, five days after her meeting with Joel, she arrived back at the flat after the late bulletin to find Stip sitting on the doorstep.

Never in all the years had she been so glad to see him. She flung herself into his arms and stood there under the porch hugging him desperately. He held her with a puzzled air and patted her and eventually, when she didn't release him, muttered into her ear, 'What's got into you, then? "Jenny kiss'd me" is one thing, but it doesn't say she hugged me to death.'

Wordlessly she led him up the stairs and sat him on the

324

orange sofa. It was getting shabby now; Stip in his glamorous clothes put it to shame. He looked as flamboyant as ever Tanya had, sitting there among the cushions with one pale blue leg crossed over the sagging arm . . . Her exotic, homosexual, adored and desperately needed brother.

'Drink?'

'Yes please. I've been sitting out there for an hour.'

'Why didn't you let me know you were coming?'

'Wanted to surprise you – idiot me. Should have remembered what incredible hours you keep.'

She put some bottles and a glass before him on a tray and watched him mix himself a pink gin. He offered her one with a gesture, but she shook her head, her eyes fixed on him. Perhaps he was heaven-sent to help her in her hour of despair? Would he be able to? She moved over to sit beside him, hugging his free arm, rubbing her face against his blue linen shoulder, kissing his cheek.

'I like this show of affection, I must say!' he remarked, leaning back as if basking in the sun. 'What's behind it, though?'

'Can you stay? I've got the spare bed made up.'

'Just tonight.'

Her face fell. She drew back as if he'd snubbed her.

'Why? Why not longer? Oh, do stay with me for a while, Stip, I need company!'

He looked at her narrowly for a moment and then leant forward and put his drink on the table. 'Sorry.'

There was no appeal against the finality in his voice. Her own voice gone toneless with disappointment, she said, 'What are your plans?'

'I'm going to Paris.'

'For how long?'

'For good.'

Maggie had not thought it possible for her to feel any sadder or more abandoned, but there is always a lower rung on the ladder of misery. She stood up and went to the long window, gazing out into the street. After a while he came up behind her.

'What's wrong, Mags?'

'Nothing. Why are you going to Paris?'

'To work for this chap I met on holiday last summer. He's an established designer. Really fantastic talent. His own offices in Montparnasse and everything. He's asked me to join him.

325

It's an incredible chance for me. Even Mum thinks so. She says there'll be – how did she put it? – "more scope for my talents in a more cosmopolitan milieu".'

Maggie turned abruptly and looked up into his face.

'And apart from his offices and the quality of his designs,' she said, 'is this chap a nice chap?'

Stip's colour came and went, but his eyes did not flinch.

'He's somebody very special,' he said.

Maggie slowly nodded. She examined her innermost heart and was relieved to discover that she was unambiguously glad. But when she'd gone to bed and he came in to sit on its edge and chat, as in the old days at home, she felt the gulf between them – simply in the fact that she couldn't say, 'Listen. I'm in love, too.'

She put on a good show the next morning when she saw Stip off at the airport. She had never seen him look so ebullient.

'I feel as if my life's just beginning,' he said exultantly. 'I know now how you felt when you first came to London – as if you'd found your right place, as if you'd broken free. I don't blame you any more.' He kissed her. 'Go to visit Mum as much as you can, Mags. She's awful lonely now Matt's gone.'

'Of course I will. Don't you worry. Go off and enjoy yourself. It's your *turn*.'

Their eyes met. 'Yes,' he said, 'I think so, too.'

There was some hanging about which is usually destructive of good partings but in this case Maggie didn't care. She wanted to keep him as long as possible; she felt time as a moving belt pulling them inexorably apart, and clung to him like a child until the last precious moment.

'You're okay, aren't you, Mags?' he asked when it came.

'I'm just fine!'

And she waved to him until he disappeared and then stood, hollow with loneliness and despair and an unacknowledged but powerful resentment. There went her last beloved person, leaving her behind.

Out of sheer habit she phoned the newsdesk before leaving the airport in case, and discovered, to her dismay because she felt so terribly tired suddenly, that a famous screen couple were

326

stopping off on their way to somewhere or other to make a film. A crew was on its way. She was to wait in the VIP lounge.

The plane was late. Maggie and the crew sat for two hours amid the hideous zig-zag curtains and squodgy furniture. The crew passed the first hour in generalised moaning, and the second in devising ingenious ways of padding their expenses.

'Here, Maggie, don't sit over there all on your tod – you're a party to this, you know!'

'No, I'm not.'

'If Joe and I put in for a four-course dinner here tonight, obviously you'll have to follow suit, or when they compare our exes they'll rumble us.'

'My exes are always a pale shadow of you boys', anyhow.'

'Under normal circs that doesn't matter. But Joe and I are going to lay it on with a trowel, and we need your support.'

'You won't get it,' said Maggie shortly. Cameramen's expenses were an old sore spot. She was well known for not padding hers at all. While this didn't exactly endear her to the crews, normally they just laughed about it. But for some reason, perhaps because it was late and they were all fed up, tonight was different.

'Listen, it's time someone told you,' said Mike with an edge to his voice, 'we're all getting sick and tired of your idiotic puritan ethics. It's all very well for you, you're a single woman. We married men have to pretty well live on our exes, and you're just queering our pitch.'

'Pad your exes as much as you like,' said Maggie wearily. 'Just don't expect the rest of us to be dishonest to keep you in countenance.'

She realised at once she'd gone too far. The men turned to each other with a look of incredulity.

'*Dishonest!*' they both shouted.

'You little *prig!*' added Mike

'Who are you calling a prig?' shouted Maggie in sudden fury. 'Anyway, I'm not a single woman. I've got a child to support –'

'Just look at her, Joe! Sitting there on her little pedestal of purity, putting down tuppenny bus-fares instead of taxis and sandwiches instead of proper meals and pretending she keeps her kid in a boarding-school on her salary –'

'So I do –'

'Well, we're not all prepared to live like paupers while all the

327

advertisers' lolly goes into the pockets of Lew bloody Grade and his cronies! We're the ones who do the work, and incidentally we are *your colleagues* to whom you owe loyalty, but *of course* you consider yourself too good for the likes of us and you always have and every one of us knows it!'

Maggie, in her already weakened state, felt absolutely winded by this unlooked-for attack. 'I wish you'd leave me alone,' she muttered. And then, looking from one to the other and believing, just for that moment, that every camera crew in ITN hated her, she lost her temper.

Raking in her bag she pulled out an expenses pad, scrawled her signature at the bottom, tore off the page and threw it at Mike. 'Here – make it out yourself! Say we had to buy the stars dinner at the Ritz, say we hired a Rolls to get us there. Say we spent the night! Say any bloody thing you like, just get off my back because I'm not in the mood!'

In the end the plane was diverted to Gatwick and the story was scrubbed. Maggie got home at midnight, tired, nerve-wracked, and convinced that on top of everything else, her years at ITN had been invalidated at a stroke.

As she opened the front door, she saw a letter in the basket. No – there were two. Maybe one was from Matt? She switched on the hall light. One of the letters was addressed simply 'Maggie' and had been hand-delivered. It was from Tanya.

She ripped it open and read it then and there. It was very brief.

'Had to let you know – I've met him! Just hung around near the U. till I bumped into him – *unbelievable* to see him again – sheer magic, as if we had never parted! Thanks God I had courage to be brazen ... I'm so excited, so happy, I can hardly think straight. Just *had* to tell you. It's all through you. T.'

The shock shouldn't have been so violent – she should have been expecting it. But she felt as if she'd been punched in the stomach. She found herself sitting on the stairs, dry-eyed but stunned. She sat there, clutching the letter, until she heard some other flat-dweller's key in the front door The prospect

328

of having to confront a semi-stranger sent her fleeing up the stairs to the sanctuary of her own flat.

There she switched on all the lights and read the letter again. She kept on reading it, perversely prodding the wound, making it larger and more painful. Her jealousy was patent, tangible. She felt very violent toward Tanya, physically violent – she wanted to hit her and scream at her. She wanted to do worse – to notify Oliver. She considered phoning him this moment. Instead she sat down at her desk and pulled a notepad toward her to begin writing him a letter. She formed the words in her head, got as far as 'Dear Oliver,' tore the page up and stifled a cry of bewilderment and grief.

She went to her kitchenette and poured herself a brandy. She drank it down, and then stood quite still for a few minutes, waiting for it to calm her, but it didn't, it just made her feel light-headed and more than ever inclined to do something crazy.

I must walk about outside, she thought. *Walk the devil out of myself. I'm behaving as if I owned him. I didn't feel like this when Bruce ran away with another woman after years of marriage . . . I collapsed, but it was different. I ran away from it into something like a nervous breakdown. There's no such escape-route this time. I must just bear it, come to terms with it. But why? For what? Then I had Matt, I came to terms with my loss for Matt's sake. And Tolly helped me, and Joan. Who will help me now? Nobody. I don't know one soul I can even confide in. Who the hell would understand how much it's hurting, let alone why? I don't understand it myself.*

But she did, all too well. It hurt because Tanya was going to lay hands on Joel again when Maggie felt deep in her guts that he belonged to her, that he was her salvation.

She changed her shoes and put her keys in her pocket and walked down the stairs again. On the bottom one she saw a white square, and only then remembered there had been two letters. She must have dropped the other. She picked it up. The handwriting was strange. She opened it, glad to find she could still feel a mild and natural curiosity.

The letter-heading jumped out at her: 'University of London'.

She felt faint.

She couldn't face the stairs again. Clutching the letter as if

329

it might fly away, she went outside and sat in her car. By the dim inside light, she read the letter, also very short:

'Dear Maggie,
I, too, feel there is unfinished business between us, and it isn't entirely what you may be thinking. What about meeting? I suggest the coffee-shop in Dillon's in Bloomsbury on Saturday at 5.30. If you can't make it, give me a ring at the University and we'll rearrange.
Yours,
Joel Langham.'

'I, *too*, feel – ' Nothing had been said. It was a shared, unspoken feeling. The beginning.

It was half-an-hour, spent just sitting, immobile with joy, before she thought of looking at the date. It was yesterday's, of course. And Tanya's letter had been written today.

She got out of the car, slammed the door and ran back into the flat. She searched her desk frantically for his private telephone number which she had scribbled down six days ago and which she hadn't dared look for since in case she used it. In the end she had to look it up in the directory. Not giving herself time to think, she did the only thing that seemed possible.

'Hallo, Langham here.'

'Joel, it's Maggie.'

She was dry-mouthed with terror. She would know, now, the instant he spoke, what today's meeting had done.

'Ah! Hallo!'

She shut her eyes. There was no doubt at all about it. Nothing had changed. The impulse – or whatever it was – which had led him to write to her was not one he regretted, twenty-four hours and a meeting with Tanya later. He sounded as glad to hear her voice as she was to hear him.

'I've just got your letter.'

'Well, can you come?'

'By good luck you've picked my day off. Normally 5.30 is hopeless.'

'I can see we may have trouble synchronising our free time,' he said drily. 'See you tomorrow.'

330

Chapter Thirty-Three

Things were happening to Maggie with quite numbing speed and force. The momentum accelerated sharply over that weekend.

On the Saturday, she met Joel as arranged in the coffee-shop of Dillon's Bookshop in Bloomsbury. They sat talking together over coffee for two and a half hours and then rambled off for dinner in Hampstead, where they talked for two hours more. If their 'unfinished business' had been capable of expeditious completion, it would, presumably, have been tidied up quite neatly by the end of that evening, but it was perfectly clear to both of them as he dropped her off at her flat that it was nowhere near finished.

He did not offer to kiss her, but she was perfectly well aware that he wanted her quite as much as she him, and she rejoiced that he made no move so early in the game. Any move he had made would inevitably have invited associations with Bruce and several subsequent alleged lovers, who had not been 'green' enough to restrain themselves but had impatiently and redly pounced.

Later she lay in bed, very much happier than she had been after many a sexual encounter. One powerful element in this happiness was the discovery she had made, quite early on, that meeting Tanya again after so many years – 'quite by chance, incredible coincidence, just bumped into her outside the University' (how could an intelligent man be so naïve?) – had been 'a very interesting experience' for Joel. Her name had not recurred in the conversation. And it did not occur either in the lengthy one they had on the phone the following morning. The 'risk' had proved, from Joel's point of view, no risk at all.

Maggie had just a few hours to enjoy untrammelled bliss before the doorbell of her flat rang (this was at lunchtime on the

331

Sunday). To her shocked surprise it was Tanya, encumbered by Imogen and several bulky holdalls. Maggie's heart almost failed her, for she read the signs. She shut Ginny out of earshot in the little bedroom with some of Matt's old picture books and led Tanya on to the balcony. She came straight out with it.

'I'm leaving Oliver.'

Into a silence whose frozen quality she seemed unaware of, she explained that she had found out that she couldn't deceive Oliver 'properly' while living under his roof. That deceiving him 'properly' meant with someone she really loved, to wit Joel, went without saying between close friends. So could she move in with Maggie for a few days?

'You're not planning to – to deceive Oliver – here, are you?'

'Darling, would you mind?'

Maggie turned away, her worlds colliding like thunderclouds, creating an equivalent turbulence.

'In that case, of course I won't. There's no particular hurry now. I'll find myself a little flat, until I can simply move in with Joel – didn't you say his flat was quite big?'

Maggie nodded dumbly. She forced her mind into blankness, but a little pointed face intruded.

'What about Ginny?'

'Where I go, she goes,' said Tanya firmly. She seemed very much in command of herself and the whole situation.

So now it was Tanya's turn to occupy, with her child, the spare room, Maggie's to clear it for them and make up the two little pine beds and put out soap and towels, just as Tanya had for her and Matt, years ago. It was some measure of Maggie's emotional condition that she was able to float, as it were, safely above Tanya and her potentially ruinous illusions. She felt dimly, like Viola in *Twelfth Night* (which she associated with Tanya – they had played in it together at RADA) that time, not she, must untangle this. She did not want to talk to Tanya, though, so she went out that evening, pretending she had to work. She learnt on her late return that Tanya having phoned Joel about twenty times was frustrated at finding him out. This was no surprise to Maggie, who had been to a film with him. Maggie said little and went to bed. She felt something very strong which kept her awake for hours; she couldn't decide if it was fear, or guilt, or love, or what.

Next morning early, the phone rang. Maggie answered it in

332

bed. It was Joel. They talked and made jokes and laughed for some twenty minutes until Maggie heard Tanya moving about in the big room and, feeling suddenly light-headed with furtive happiness, ended the conversation. She and Tanya had breakfast together with Imogen. Imogen was subdued to the point of complete speechlessness – most unlike her. Tanya, to Maggie's embarrassment (as much for Ginny's sake as her own) kept talking on and on about Joel, how little he had changed, what they had talked about, how she was longing to see him again.

By 11 a.m. Maggie was at ITN as usual. Having recovered her normal spirits she was prepared to put her back into her day's work; she didn't notice Mac's expression, nor his unwonted silence, and when the editor's secretary found Maggie at her desk and said the editor wanted to see her, not a moment's apprehension crossed her mind. She supposed he wanted to congratulate her on that rather good little story she'd done on Friday.

What he actually wanted to tell her was that she was sacked.

Powerful as her happiness was, the shock of this news stripped it at once to the bone, like the stroke of a grizzly's claws. She sat there, aware of the soft carpeting under her shoes and yet feeling as if the ground had fallen away beneath her. The editor, a kindly man, was explaining that for his part he wouldn't have taken the matter so seriously but that evidently there were other forces at work. When Maggie, with dry lips, asked what there was to take seriously, he pushed across his desk at her a piece of paper torn off an expenses pad with her signature across the bottom. Higher up, in a very good imitation of her scrawl, was the most inventive list of fiddles that even Mike and Joe had ever devised.

She burst into a strained laugh. 'But this is nonsense! I didn't write this – it's a cameraman's idea of a joke. I can sort it out in five minutes!'

The editor went on looking at her out of sad, shrewd eyes.

'Maggie, I wouldn't stir up a hornet's nest about it. All you might do is get one of our best crews into trouble, which frankly wouldn't please anybody. I'm afraid this is only an excuse. Somebody up there has had a down on you for a long time. They want a new face.'

Maggie couldn't take this in at first. 'But – but I've never fiddled my exes in my life –'

333

'I know that. It's bloody unfair. Look. How would it be if we just took you off the road? You might like to scriptwrite for a bit, while you look round –'

'Scriptwrite!' Maggie exclaimed violently, in an unconscious echo of Tanya. 'After reporting! No thank you!' What, sit at the scriptwriters' table in its backwoods corner, with everyone knowing she was in some kind of disgrace? Despair made her reckless. 'How can you let this happen? You're the editor! Why didn't you fight for me?'

He looked down at his folded fingers.

'I did. But to be brutally frank, Maggie, I haven't been too satisfied with your work lately myself. I think you may be getting a bit stale. Mac agrees, though reluctantly, because like all of us he's very fond of you. I think you're right about scriptwriting. Make a clean break. I promise you, nobody who doesn't have to, will know what's happened. Put a good face on it in the newsroom and no one'll know you're not just off in search of fresh fields. After all, you weren't an actress for nothing.'

Mac, shifty-eyed with embarrassment and unexpressible sympathy ('I've had the push so often myself I know what it feels like. You just have to say fuck 'em and go on to the next thing') gave her the rest of the day off. She marched out with head high but a dangerous hot lump in her throat and shaking knees. Going home on the bus and then toiling up Regent's Park Road through the rain, battling with her shock, she laid this blow against Joel's name for comfort, but it gave her none. The relationship was too new. She felt she couldn't, at this delicate stage, bring him a desperate need, an insoluble dilemma. She didn't see how, in the near future, she could offer him herself at all, for now she would be jobless. She shuddered as she thought of it, for, as she only too well remembered, without a routine, a sense of worth and purpose to hold her together, she became hollow, insecure, terrified. The very person who had attracted him initially would turn to mush and rubble when the armour of her work had been broken off her. One needed stamina and confidence to conduct a love affair.

No. The most comforting name she could think of now was Tanya's. She had seen Tanya through the initial stages of *her* professional disaster; now Tan would surely do the same for her. And she was not far to seek.

Maggie entered her flat in a rush, hungry for the sanctuary

334

and succour of home. At first she thought the place was empty, and paused, horribly disappointed not to find Tan waiting.

'Tanya? Are you here?'

She heard a movement out on the balcony and saw a shadow. She started in that direction, and was startled to come face to face with Oliver. He held Imogen by the hand. His narrow, goatish face looked statuesque with outrage.

'Hallo, Maggie,' he said grimly.

'Oliver! What are you doing here?'

'An odd question, under the circumstances ... Did you suppose I'd just sit back while my wife and daughter walked out on me? I've come to take them home.'

'Oh ...' Maggie slowly took off her wet coat and hung it up. 'Well! Where is she?'

'In the bedroom. Re-packing.'

Maggie looked from Oliver to Imogen. She was wearing dungarees and so looked less than usual like one of those precocious and un-child-like Victorian children, but her elfin face was huge-eyed and stricken, her mouth pinched. Maggie felt an uprush of love and sympathy for her, as another like herself whose world was abruptly tottering, and crouched to face her.

'Hallo, Gin-gin,' she said tenderly.

The child didn't answer. Tension was crackling through the air; she seemed frozen by it. The realisation of the likely effect of all this on Ginny ejected Maggie, for the moment, from the plummeting cockpit of her own crisis.

'Would either of you like anything?' she asked briskly.

'Thanks, no,' said Oliver austerely. 'We're leaving at once.'

'Well, I want to talk to Tanya first.'

Oliver opened his mouth as if to object, then shrugged. 'Your privilege,' he said shortly.

Maggie went into the spare bedroom. Tanya was indeed packing. She was also crying.

'Tan, what's going on?'

Tanya threw herself into Maggie's arms.

'Oh God! It was so horrible – stamping in here, behaving as if he owned us –'

Maggie gripped her sharply. 'Shh! Keep your voice down, you don't want Ginny to hear.'

Tanya stared at her wildly.

335

'Ginny knows all about it!'

'You've told Ginny?' Tanya nodded fiercely. 'What have you told her?'

'Everything. That I'm leaving Oliver. That I've got a lover.'

Despite all she knew of Tanya, despite all that had happened, this shocked Maggie.

'Tanya, darling, she's only six!'

'She's a human being, she's my daughter, she's shared everything with me so far, why shouldn't she share this?'

Maggie looked into her friend's eyes, saw argument was useless, and turned away.

'All right. So what's happening now? Are you going back with him?'

'Ginny is. It'll be better. I'll be freer. I was wrong to bring her, only I love her so much, it's such agony not to have her with me. I'm just putting her things into a bag and then Oliver can take her –'

'He's under the impression you're going home with him too.'

'He can't drag me! I don't want him, I can't bear to be with him. I want Joel, and I'm going to him. This time there's nothing in the way.'

Maggie sat down on one of the pine beds. Tanya turned from her and went on frenetically throwing things into the hold-all, sniffing deeply every few seconds as the tears kept coming. Maggie's life seemed to flash before her, or at least, her life as it had involved Tanya. Had it all led up to this, that she must crush her utterly or else give up her own hopes?

'Tan, how can you say there's nothing in the way?'

'What do you mean?'

'What about Ginny?'

'What about her?'

'If you leave her father, what effect will that have on your relationship with her?'

'Nothing I do can affect Ginny and me. That's inviolable. We're a unit, forever.'

'Don't, Tan!' Maggie said sharply.

'Don't what?' Tanya asked.

'Make the same idiot mistake I did! You leave her now to run after Joel and you'll lose her as surely as I've lost Matt.'

A shadow of fear crossed Tanya's face, ousting, for the moment, the ruthless defiance and determination.

336

'What are you talking about? You haven't lost Matt!'

'Yes. I have.'

Tanya shifted the bag and sat beside her.

'You've never said that before.'

'But it's true. Effectively, I have no son. And if you do this, you'll have no daughter. She'll belong to Oliver or whoever replaces you in her life. And there's a difference between us. I've got time to replace Matt, to have another baby. But you're that much older than me. By the time you make the fatal discovery I've made – by the time you realise that you've forfeited Ginny by putting your own needs before hers – it'll be too late for you.'

Tanya was now looking at her piercingly, listening to and weighing every word.

'Replace Matt . . .' she repeated slowly. 'Maggie. Have you finally found someone?'

Maggie stood up and went to the window. Here it came.

'You have,' said Tanya's astonished voice from behind her. 'Who is it?'

'How can you care at a moment like this?'

'I do care, Maggie! You're my dearest friend. I've waited years for this, I've longed for it for you.'

Oh my God, thought Maggie. Now the knot must be untied, not by time but by me.

She turned, and in that second had proof of her closeness to Tanya, because Tanya took one look at her and knew. Her face contracted.

'It's not Joel,' she whispered. 'Please, Maggie. Say it isn't.'

'It is,' said Maggie.

'Oh, you *poor* – ' Tanya began, starting towards her in a movement of pity.

'Tanya, don't be sorry for me! It's not hopeless as you obviously imagine. It's only just starting, but I know this much – he doesn't love *you*.'

The tender, pitying look dropped off Tanya's face like a mask, leaving it bone-white. She clenched her teeth, and showed them bared to the gums. It might have been a look of menace, but Maggie thought it was simple shock.

'What are you saying?' Tanya asked under her breath.

Maggie sat down by her and tried to touch her but it was like touching a block.

337

'Just that we met again, at his invitation, we've spent two evenings together, and I know, quite certainly, that there is something between us.'

'How could you?' said the death's-head version of Tanya which was staring at her.

'How could I know? – Because –'

'*I don't mean that*! How could you – see him? When? It must have been after you'd had my letter!'

'Yes. His letter, asking for a meeting, came at the same time.' Tanya sat rigid.

'You read my letter and then you read his letter and you decided quite coldly –'

'Coldly! – No –'

' – to meet him, when you knew how I felt?'

'Tanya, you have got to face it. I'm afraid what matters now is what *he* feels. And whatever you imagined he felt, when you met him again, wasn't true, because he told me –'

She stopped. She thought Tanya was going to hit her.

After a long, long silence, Tanya dropped her head, shook it violently, swallowed noisily, and then stood up with a jolt.

'Enough,' she said. 'We're going to settle this here and now.'

'How?' asked Maggie in bewilderment.

'How? By phoning him. *By asking him.*'

Maggie jumped up. 'Tanya, stop! You can't! You *are* crazy!'

Tanya spun round and faced her. Her face was frenzied. 'I know!' she shouted. 'For years I've been crazy! I went crazy in the war. I went crazier after it. I sublimated it into my acting and that was fine until I met Joel. Then all my craziness, or let's call it by its proper name, my psychosis, my *insanity*, came out, and luckily it took the form of a passionate devotion which he accepted from me as long as it didn't go too far. But love is one thing and insane love is another and in the end he ... he "put me away". There's an irony! He put me away from him and I put myself away, into my career. And that was fine too, in its traumatic way, till the theatre blew up in my face like the minefield it is, and spewed me out again ... Well, you were here and you saw me at the time, you saw how I was, you shouldn't look so surprised to discover I'm mad. Then I took refuge with Oliver, that's all it was – ' And here, to Maggie's horror, she threw open the bedroom door and shouted the words out – 'I didn't deceive anyone about it, I told him that's

338

what I needed and what he was to me. Didn't I tell you that, Oliver? Did I ever, ever pretend that I loved –'

Maggie broke from her horrified stupor and sprang at the door, slamming it sharply. She caught Tanya by the arm to drag her further from it, but Tanya, with the strength of fury, broke free.

'Don't touch me. Don't interrupt me. I'm telling you. All right. I'll keep my voice down. But there were no lies. Next, I channelled my madness into having a baby. As a matter of fact that turned out to be the sanest thing I ever did. But when it was done, it proved not to be enough to use up all this – this – furious, mad, irrational energy I have. So, I let it rip. I used it. I used it to get my career back. To make sure my daughter would be a *mensch* with some understanding of life so she would never be shocked into lunacy like I was. But most of all – at the bottom – I fought to be sane, to be normal. To be like other women who simply do not go on yearning for some man they haven't seen for years and years, but forget him at last and all the other damaging things as well, who can shake off their scars and come up clean and whole.'

Suddenly she sat down on the floor. She did not put her face in her hands. She sat there between the beds, crumpled, panting. The choleric colour faded from her face. Maggie went down beside her, speechless. After a while, Tanya went on in a tired voice, as if she had to finish but was almost spent:

'And through a lot of it, I had you, Maggie. My good friend that I loved. I didn't tell you everything. Of course not. One can't tell anybody everything. There's so much one doesn't know oneself.' She looked at Maggie piteously. 'Do you think I knew, when I gave you his name and address? Do you think I was aware that all that suppressed feeling was still alive and kicking down there in my guts? I thought it was dead, I did, Maggie. It wasn't a trick on you. It was a trick on me. And now look how it's turned out. I'm going to lose him again. It will be so different from before. Before, I knew he belonged to his wife, that I was on the wrong side of the blanket. I deserved to lose him. But now – he's free – he's free – and he doesn't want me. The only thing that could be worse for me than that is if he is now going to fall in love with you. Because I'm mad, such a thing would make me hate both of you to the point of wanting to kill somebody.'

Maggie sat silent on the floor.

Suddenly both women became aware that someone had come in to the room, and looked simultaneously over their shoulders as they sat half-hidden by the beds. It was Ginny. She stood there in her red dungarees looking down on them with that expression of what Tanya – in RADA days – had used to call 'appalment', which children naturally adopt when adults are frightening them out of their wits with unadult behaviour.

The sight of Ginny galvanised Tanya as the sight of Matt, with the same expression, had once galvanised Maggie. She leapt to her feet and, wiping her eyes hastily with the heels of her hands, picked up the little girl in her arms.

'What's the matter, Mummy?' Ginny asked shrilly.

'Nothing now, darling. You know me. I have to burst sometimes, and shout and cry a bit, but then I'm better.'

'Are you better now?'

'Yes,' said Tanya with commendable conviction. Maggie was also on her feet by now, straightening the beds inanely and closing up the holdall with Ginny's things in it.

'Daddy's out there. He said to tell you it's time to go home.'

Tanya put her gently down. She glanced at Maggie and for a moment the vital energy left her and she seemed to sag. But then she took a deep breath. It was the kind of deep breath actresses often take just before they go on stage, a therapeutic sigh which at once relaxes tension and tanks up on oxygen.

'Okay, darling. Go and tell Daddy I'm nearly ready.'

Ginny ran from the room leaving the door open. Maggie closed it. Tanya said, 'No more, Maggie. No more, ever. Will you go now, and leave me to pack? Go – right away, please. I don't want to see you any more. I'll be gone in half an hour.'

Maggie didn't take in the 'any more', or if she did she didn't take it to mean anything but 'any more today'. She started out of the bedroom. Tanya's voice caught her for a moment at the door.

'Maggie.'

She turned. Tanya was standing straight, looking at her. She was never to forget that look, although she didn't then grasp its valedictory quality. It was the look of the friend in the sea at the friend in the lifeboat. Although not a forgiving look, it was at least hate-free.

'I can't help it,' Tanya said.

340

Maggie half opened her hands in a gesture of mutuality. Then she went out of the room.

Oliver was not visible in the living-room so she didn't have to speak to him. She just took her coat and went out. She felt profoundly shaken. The scene with Tanya, and Tanya's sudden uprush of courage in recovering, had knocked the edge off Maggie's shock at the loss of her job. She walked to the top of Primrose Hill with her head down, reliving the two scenes of the morning – her own in the editor's office, and Tanya's in the bedroom. She wasn't consciously comparing them but she was aware in her depths that Tanya's sorrow outweighed hers. It didn't make hers unimportant but it put it back into proportion.

At the top of the hill she sat down on the bench where, years ago, Matt had carved his initial. She looked for it and found it among all the others. She wondered if they ever replaced those benches, and was glad that they hadn't replaced this one so far. She traced the M with her forefinger and then cleaned the dirt out of the full stop with her little fingernail. Then she laid her hand gently over the M and leaned on it, feeling the cool wet autumn air on her hot eyes and face. After a while a stiff wind got up. The sunlight came and went through some lumbering clouds, and Maggie watched the leaves being blown off the trees below her.

She must face facts, just as she had watched Tanya face them. She needed time to settle her soul into this new situation. There was no way to evade the horrors of tomorrow and the next day and the next, for a whole month, going in to the office and 'putting a brave face on it'. She must pass through that particular fire and try to make sure it tempered and did not scar her. If she could cope bravely and efficiently with this situation, she would have earned the right to claim Joel's support afterwards.

Fine, noble thoughts.

She even reflected that it would be a sort of double betrayal, to rush now straight from Tanya's despair to the cause of it. With the empathy that had grown so strong between them, she could feel Tanya's pain, and for a while it crushed down the volcanic eruption of love and joy in love – the sensation of being 'in the pit', which to Maggie felt like a crater, long regarded as extinct but now abruptly hot and heaving premonitorily. But when a little more time had passed, enough so that she could

341

contemplate going back down the hill to her empty flat to face what had to be faced, Maggie's good intentions began to crumble.

She lifted her hand and stared at the worn initial.

Of course it was all nonsense, what she had said to Tan about another baby. Looking at the M that Matt, in his moment of isolation, had carved so savagely, she saw only the full stop. She felt she would rather die than go through all that again, than risk hurting and failing another child and bearing a new set of scars herself.

If she and Joel were to become lovers – and unless she stuck to her wavering resolve to stay away from him for a season, it could well happen this very night – they would have to focus solely on each other. They would have to seek and find in themselves the resources to be each other's prime satisfaction.

Maggie suddenly felt certain that if she drew back, gave herself even a week in which to consider at any depth whether she was fit for the undertaking of making a man like Joel happy, she would inevitably decide that she wasn't. Every day that passed – especially such as lay immediately ahead – would diminish her short supply of confidence. Before she knew it she would have shrunk back into her cold, safe, desexed hermit shell, there to cower unloved and unloving, probably for ever.

She sensed Margaret, ever-ready with her trenchant, cruel honesty and its attendant guilt. What do you add up to? she asked scathingly. What have you to offer after thirty-five years of living, what have you to display on your banner? You who stole from your father, neglected your benefactress, welched on your career, married out of cowardice and made a rotten wife? You who misjudged your brothers, disappointed your mother and, worst of all, jettisoned your son out of pure funk and selfishness? Now you've lost your job and brought your best friend to the edge of desperation. Well done. And you think at this point you merit a great come-lately love? Don't make me laugh.

Maggie jumped up furiously from the bench, as if confronting an actual accuser. Then she thrust her hands into her coat pockets and stared defiantly over the zoo. The wind blew in her face, bringing her the faint sound of lions roaring ... It must be feeding time. She wished with all the ferocity in her nature that she could tear Margaret out of her and throw her

342

to the lions so that they could devour her and silence her accursed nagging voice for ever.

But all she really wanted was to obliterate her past mistakes, to have a new, unmarked person to offer to Joel. That was only what every woman wanted when she fell in love. Even Portia – rich, beautiful, intelligent – was filled with a sort of hysteria of humility when it happened to her, craving to be trebled twenty times herself so as to be worthy. And Portia was young. She'd never harmed anybody. More pertinent still, she had never faced the dreadful possibility that she was incapable of love. She'd seen the gates opening on the magic landscape but she didn't have to weigh her own merit and the cost to a friend against the incredible relief of that hot trembling in the loins and the heart, proclaiming the possibility of a fulfilled and happy normality when she had secretly abandoned all hope of it.

Standing there in the wind, Maggie conjured up her injured flock.

She begged pardon of her father as sincerely as she could, and he shrugged and vanished, leaving her unshriven. She faced Fiona Dalzell and couldn't utter a word, but her old teacher patted her shoulder and said robustly, 'Nonsense, it wasn't you at all! Don't you dare burden your conscience with me, my girl!' Next, with deep reluctance, she produced Bruce, but when he appeared he was a stranger – long-haired and weird (she'd heard that he was living in a mid-west commune and this must be her subconscious image of him). He looked at her, as she at him, incredulously, and said, 'Do we know each other?' Her mother swam in front of him and blotted him out with a hug, saying, 'Darling, don't be so silly, you gave me my life's greatest treasure. Don't repine!' and swam away.

Ian rose before her in his open-necked Sunday shirt, also with hands in pockets, and they gazed at each other with the still strange, unwonted absence of antipathy that had developed between them, since his transformation-by-Matthew. Finally he said gruffly, 'I suggest we forget it, Maggie. Matthew's going to be all right – he'll probably turn out better than Anthea. I'm no great shakes as a father. Maybe you should have taken her on in exchange, you'd have been better with a girl.' And Stip appeared dressed like a harlequin and whirled her round briefly in a dance, after which he said, before vanishing in a grand balletic leap: 'I'm going to be the family success, after all, but

343

I know I'm a disgrace to the clan. Don't hate me.' So she knew they each had their own guilts to contend with.

And at last came Matt, sturdy in his tracksuit, pounding up the hill from the corner gate toward her, his eyes and mouth grinning, not so much with pleasure at seeing her as with the sheer joy of being alive and able to run up a hill without strain. When he reached her he stopped. He was puffing slightly and his face was flushed – how bonny he looked! At least for his handsome young body she could take some credit, for she had bred it and fed it, though the splendid red hair and broad shoulders were Bruce's legacy. 'Hi Mum,' he said, and she at once asked, as one only can in day-dreams, 'Have I been a rotten mother? You can tell me the truth.' And the transparent Matt of her conscience replied, 'I suppose a bit, I mean when I think about it, but at least you were never there to nag me or screw me up like a lot of chaps' mothers I know. Anyway I'm okay, so you don't have to worry.' And he gave her a brief wave and gave himself up to the delights of skimming down the hill without touching, having forgotten to give her a kiss.

She did not dare summon Tanya to exonerate her because she knew she wouldn't. She would have to trust her, or rather her basic attachment to life, not to poison everything with some fatal dénouement ... And now, irresistibly, Maggie veered toward Joel. Now she could 'warm her thoughts against his name' because he too had done terrible things in his life, and left pain behind him. When (tonight – tonight!) he had finished making love to her, when he had filled her body's empty places with himself and released the pent-up molten flow of her sexuality, they would lie in his bed and talk. He could not shrive her (no-one really could) but he could partner her with his attention, and while he listened Margaret would have to keep quiet. Because if Maggie had deserved Joel, she could not be all bad.

She wiped her face and gave a deep sigh. The lions were quiet now. They must be momentarily content in their cages, obliviously gnawing their carrion ... Maggie found she, too, was hungry.

She left the old bench with the M on it and walked slowly down the hill through the blustery wind. Half-way down she realised that she knew Joel's number by heart. She began to run.

344

A selection of Penguin Books by Lynne Reid Banks

THE L-SHAPED ROOM

Unmarried and pregnant, Jane Graham is cast out of her suburban home. Lighting dejectedly on a bug-ridden room in a squalid house in Fulham, she gradually comes to find a new and positive faith in life.

THE BACKWARD SHADOW

After the birth of her son, Jane exchanges the L-shaped room for a remote country cottage. She is joined by Dottie, and together they embark upon an enterprise that is to change both their lives.

TWO IS LONELY

Now living with her son in the country, Jane is a long way from the L-shaped room ... 'A tender and delightful final volume ... Lynne Reid Banks has that rare gift of evoking a scene or a situation in little more than a line' – *The Times*

CHILDREN AT THE GATE

Gerda is a Jewish-Canadian divorcee alone in a miserable room in the Arab quarter of Acre. It is the only home she has left. Her sole comforts are drink and a mysterious Arab friend, Kofi ...

AN END TO RUNNING

Seeking refuge from the domination of his sister and from his own Jewishness, Aaron Franks turns to Martha, his secretary. Together they travel to Israel and a kibbutz – Martha with strong misgivings, Aaron full of anticipation.

DEFY THE WILDERNESS

After fourteen years of self-imposed absence, writer Ann Randall returns to her beloved Israel. In Jerusalem, she attempts to interview veterans of the first Arab–Israeli war. 'A powerful and professional novel' – *The Times Literary Supplement*

DARK QUARTET

The story of the Brontës. 'A novel which will open many eyes afresh to the lives of the remarkable and gifted Brontës' – *Yorkshire Post*